# D'ARC

Also by Robert Repino

*Mort(e)*
*Culdesac*

# D'ARC

## A NOVEL FROM THE WAR WITH NO NAME

## ROBERT REPINO

Published by
Soho Press, Inc.
853 Broadway
New York, NY 10003

Library of Congress Cataloging-in-Publication Data

Repino, Robert.
D'arc : a novel from the war with no name / Robert Repino.
War with no name ; 2

ISBN 978-1-61695-686-8
eISBN 978-1-61695-687-5

1. Imaginary wars and battles—Fiction. I. Title
PS3618.E76 D37 2017 813'.6—dc23 2016054535

Interior illustrations by Sam Chung@A-men Project and Kapo Ng

Interior design by Janine Agro, Soho Press, Inc.

Printed in the United States of America

10 9 8 7 6 5 4 3 2 1

*For my family*

*All armed prophets have conquered, and the unarmed ones have been destroyed.*

—Niccolò Machiavelli, *The Prince*

*If any being felt emotions of benevolence towards me, I should return them an hundred and an hundred fold; for that one creature's sake, I would make peace with the whole kind!*          —Mary Shelley, *Frankenstein*

*If those whom we begin to love could know us as we were before meeting them ... They could perceive what they have made of us.*          —Albert Camus

# D'ARC

# INTRODUCTION

OR CENTURIES, THE Queen of the ants plotted the downfall of humanity from her lair, deep within the Colony. She had witnessed the humans' capacity for evil. To defeat them, she would have to match their cruelty. There could be no armistice in the war with no name. No negotiations. No peace until every last human was dead.

With her enemy distracted, the Queen ordered her Alpha soldiers to attack. Giant insects, answering only to the Colony, the Alphas overran entire countries, dismantling the human age in a matter of weeks. But this would not be enough. The Queen needed allies. And rather than recruit them, she would create them.

Using a strange technology, the Colony lifted the surface animals from bondage. Overnight, the animals' bodies grew, their paws became hands, their legs allowed them to walk upright—a terrifying mirror image of humans. The animals could think, and speak, and learn. And love. And hate. Owing their allegiance to the Queen, they formed into armies that would bring about the final extinction of humanity.

On the brink of annihilation, the humans launched a desperate countermeasure: the bioweapon known as EMSAH, a virus that threatened to undo the Queen's grand experiment. Long after the last humans were driven into hiding, the EMSAH syndrome loomed over the new society that the animals hoped to create. In the fragile peacetime that followed, the Colony watched over the fledgling animal settlements, rebuilt over the remains of human civilization. Those towns that remained loyal to the Queen were rewarded. Those that rebelled, or fell to the EMSAH virus, disappeared from the map, without a trace left behind. There was no other way to maintain order, not with the humans still lurking, waiting for a chance to strike.

Those who survived the war were nevertheless haunted by their previous lives, and by the things they had to do to stay alive. The unit known as the Red Sphinx found it the most difficult to adjust to the new order, having spent the war as ruthless assassins operating behind enemy lines. Their leader, a bobcat named Culdesac, recalled his days in the wild, hunting prey as his people went extinct. A pit bull named Wawa remembered her training as a warrior in an underground dogfighting ring. And a simple house cat named Mort(e) longed to find his friend, a dog named Sheba. Unbeknownst to him, the humans came to believe that he held the key to defeating the Queen.

Retired from the Red Sphinx, and plagued with memories of his friend, Mort(e) one day received a simple but mysterious message: "Sheba is alive." And so began his journey to the last human stronghold, where he discovered his role in a prophecy foretold by a child from his past, a boy who escaped from the Queen's lair with a message of salvation. Everything was linked—Mort(e), Sheba, EMSAH, the Colony, all of it. And the future of all life on Earth depended on whether he found Sheba, and destroyed the Queen.

Which is exactly what he did—though not without terrible sacrifice and bloodshed. And not without discovering the truth:

that the prophecies were false, the animals were doomed to make the same mistakes the humans did, and the war with no name would never really end, not even with the Queen dead and the Colony scattered.

So rather than join the new alliance with the humans, Mort(e) ran away, with Sheba at his side. To him, the only new order worth dying for consisted of two people, no more.

But the echo of the Queen remained, drifting in the wind, carried in the ocean currents, waiting for someone to listen once more. Waiting for someone to shout back so that everyone would hear, no matter where they were hiding.

## PART I

# PEACE

# CHAPTER 1

## THE STORY OF TAALIK

HEN THE DARKNESS passed over the water, Taalik dreamt of the temple again. A temple far beyond the seas, ruled by an ancient queen who went to war with a race of monsters. In the dream, Taalik washed ashore on a beach at nighttime. A mere fish, unable to breathe, he slapped his tail on the sharp rocks until he felt the scales cracking. His fins strained as he tried to return to the water. His lidless eye froze stiff in its socket. And then, he rose from the sand on newly formed limbs, like a crab. The claws sprouted underneath him. He opened his mouth and splayed out his gills, and the air passed through. He did not fear the light and the wind. He did not scramble back to the lapping waves, to the muted blue haze where he was born. Instead, he stood upright, no longer weightless but still strong, defying the gravity that pulled his body to the earth. He marched toward the temple—a giant mound of dirt crawling with strange creatures, each with six legs, heavily armored bodies, mouths like the claws of a lobster. Soldiers bred for killing. They worked in unison, moving as Taalik's people did, many individuals forming a whole. The creatures stood in rows on each side of him. Their antennae grazed him as he walked by, inspecting his scales, his fins. His body continued to change with each step he took. The soldiers admired his new shape, with his segmented legs, and a flexible shell that protected his spine, and tentacles that reached out from underneath, four new arms that could grasp or crush. Here, he was no mere animal, but something more, something his people would worship, something his enemies would learn to fear.

Inside the temple, he found the Queen surrounded by her children. He waited for her to speak, and soon realized that she did not have to. He had understood the message ever since that first dream, and for every dream that followed. Taalik would rule, as the Queen did. There would be a new era of peace to wash away the millennia of bloodshed. No longer would his people slip into the depths of Cold Trench while watching out for predators. No longer would they see their children snatched away. They would learn, and adapt. And one day, his people would rise from the water and find new worlds to conquer.

Or, they would die. The Queen made him understand the starkness of it. There would be no circles of life anymore. Instead, there would be one current through the dark water, leading to conquest or extinction. Life or death. And to secure life, they would not run. They would have to kill.

TAALIK KEPT HIS eyes closed as he listened for the Queen's voice rumbling through the water. Orak, his Prime, floated next to him. Ever since the first revelation, she knew to leave him alone at times like this. The Queen spoke to him only when she wanted to. Even after he opened his eyes and drifted there, Orak waited. The others hovered behind her. They followed her lead. She was the first to convert, the first to mate with Taalik, the first to follow the current with him. Orak kept the others in line, reminding them of their place, but attending to their needs as well, helping to protect the eggs and rear the hatchlings. As Prime, she enforced Taalik's orders, even when they went against her counsel. She owed her life to Taalik. All the Sarcops did. But he owed his life to her.

Taalik and his people waited under the Lip, the vein of rock that jutted out into Cold Trench, offering shelter from the predators who swam above. This refuge would not hold forever. Their enemies searched for them, driven mad with fear of this new species. Taalik tried to make peace, even ceding territory to those who claimed it as their own. But some creatures, the sharks and other carnivores, would not relent. They would never hear the Queen's song. They would never accept that the world began, rather than ended, at the surface.

*Does she speak to you today, my Egg?* Orak asked.

He left her waiting too long. Even Orak's enormous patience had limits, especially with the family huddled under the Lip, the food running out. A fight had broken out the day before. Orak punished the unruly ones by ordering the soldiers to feed on their eggs. They had already uprooted the nurseries and hauled them to this desolate place. Feeding on the unborn would lighten the load, and strengthen the ones bred for war.

*The Queen is silent this day, my Prime,* Taalik said.

A shudder in the water. Taalik gazed into the slit above, where the Lip extended across this narrow stretch of Cold Trench. In the sliver of light he saw them, the fleet of sharks, white bellied, tails waving in unison. At the lead, fatter than the others, was the one Taalik called Graydeath. He recognized the freshly healed gash on the shark's belly, courtesy of Taalik's claw. Graydeath managed to bite it off in their last encounter. The darkness passed over the water forty times before the limb fully regenerated. The other Sarcops watched the healing in amazement, and declared that no one, not even the ocean's greatest shark, could kill the Queen's chosen one.

*They smell us,* Orak said.

*We smell them,* Taalik replied.

No enemy had ever penetrated this far into their territory, least of all an army of sharks on patrol. An act of war. It meant that the scouts Taalik dispatched had most likely been killed. He had ordered them to map the shoreline, and to find all of the shallows where his people would have the advantage. But the scouts also served as bait, drawing attention away from the Sarcops as they moved their young ones under the Lip. *They die for us, my Egg*, Orak told him later. *Now we live for them.*

Taalik watched the fleet passing overhead. He waited for the procession to end. It did not. It *would* not. Sharks of every breed crossed his line of sight, as thick as a bed of eels in some places. Mouths began where rear fins ended. In their rage, these solitary creatures banded together to fight a common enemy. The sharks baited him. They wanted the Sarcops to emerge and attack from the rear so that they could swoop around, encircle the strongest ones, and then descend upon the nest to destroy the eggs. Taalik saw it unfold in a vision planted by the Queen herself: Cold Trench clouded with blood. The torn membranes of eggs carried away by the current. Graydeath devouring the younglings while his followers waited for him to finish, not daring to interrupt his victory meal lest they become part of it.

*Summon the Juggernauts*, Taalik said.

Orak emitted a clicking sound, followed by three chirps—the signal that alerted the soldier caste. The Juggernauts formed their phalanx, with Orak as the tip of the spear.

Every year, when they hibernated, the Sarcops dreamt of the Queen and her empire. And when they awoke, the Queen bestowed upon them new gifts. A language. A philosophy. Until then, their entire existence revolved around fear. Fear of others, of both darkness and light, of the unknown. After the Queen's revelation, and the miracles that followed, a calm determination set in. The Sarcops would not merely react to the environment. They would reshape it as they pleased. Soon their bodies changed along with their minds, as they had in Taalik's dream. First, they sprouted limbs. Then their armored plating, making them resemble the Queen's ferocious daughters. Their mouths and throats changed. Before long, they could make sounds to match all the images and words in their rapidly evolving brains. And then, slithering from their backs, a row of tentacles that allowed them to manipulate the world around them. Only the most loyal Sarcops advanced far enough to earn the distinction of Juggernaut alongside Taalik. The rest changed in other ways. Their senses improved, their teeth sharpened, their fins became weapons. The agile Shoots could swarm their prey. The slender Redmouths could bite into their opponent and twist their bodies, pulling away flesh and bone in a whirlpool of blood. The crablike Spikes could mimic the ocean floor, setting a trap for enemies who strayed too close. Though the Juggernauts formed the vanguard, all the Sarcops knew how to fight. All would have the chance to prove themselves worthy.

Taalik told his troops that they would follow him under the Lip at full speed. They would overtake the fleet at the northern end of the crevasse, near the water's edge. There, Taalik would kill Graydeath in front of everyone. No more hiding. Today their enemies would learn what the Sarcops could do.

Taalik called for Zirsk and Asha, his third and seventh mates, who carried eggs in their pouches. When he confronted Graydeath, these two would release their eggs. Doing so would distract the sharks, who saw only the food in front of their faces. Orak watched them closely as they listened, ready to pounce on any sign of disapproval. As a consolation for their pending sac-rifice, Taalik assured them that they would recover some of the young. *We will cut them from the bellies of dead sharks*, he said. *The young ones will have a story to tell.*

He turned away from his soldiers and headed north, using the rocky Lip for cover while keeping an eye on the movement above. He felt Orak's presence, slightly behind him. She could lead if he died. But he would live. The Queen still had so much to show him.

Cold Trench grew shallower. The cover of the Lip gave way to open water, where the sharks blotted out the light piercing the surface. Taalik ascended, faster than the others, homing in on Graydeath. He felt so tiny in the expanse. The ground rising behind him blocked any hope of escape.

The water shivered as the sharks detected movement. Graydeath aimed his snout at the intruder. His mouth split in half, a red pit of jagged teeth. Scars from numerous battles left deep divots in his skin. A severed claw still punctured his dorsal fin, a permanent reminder of some creature that died trying to fight the sharks.

Taalik charged at him, claws unsheathed, tentacles reaching out. They collided, a sound like boulders toppling into the trench. Tumbling and twisting, Graydeath pulled free from Taalik's grip and clamped his teeth at the root of one of his tentacles. Taalik struggled to keep the mouth open, to stop the shark from shearing off the limb at the base. Blood leaked from the puncture wounds, driving Graydeath into a new realm of delirium. Taalik tried to pluck out the eye, but Graydeath squirmed his face out of reach, using his mouth as a shield. The shark's momentum dragged Taalik away from the battle, away from Cold Trench, and toward the shallows, where Taalik would not be able to escape.

Taalik let him do it. Sensing victory, Graydeath thrashed again, letting go of the wounded tentacle and twisting his snout toward Taalik's head. With his claws, Taalik held the jaw open, gripping so tightly that some of the teeth broke off like brittle seashells. He pulled the shark toward land, toward the edge of the known world. They crashed onto a bed of rocks, kicking up dust and debris. A primitive creature, Graydeath nevertheless sensed the violation of the natural order that awaited him at the surface.

Desperate, he tried to buck free of his opponent. A wave caught them, slamming them onto the earth. From here, Taalik could stand. And when he did, he broke free of the water. And even with the monster still trying to tear his head off, Taalik gazed at the new world, the land of the Queen—a golden patch of fine sand stretching from one end to the other, anchoring a blue dome.

Holding his breath, he dragged the shark out of the foamy waves. Taalik's body grew heavy, as if a giant claw pressed him under the water where he belonged. The shark's eyes shimmered under the piercing light, stunned at the impossibility of it all. The Queen called everyone to this place, though only a few would prove worthy. Graydeath, a king of the deep, writhed in agony. No water would rush through his gills ever again. His enormous eye caked in sand, the shark trembled as his life bled away at last.

Taalik felt as though he would burst. Unable to resist any longer, he opened his mouth, allowing the gills to flare out. Water sprayed from the two openings. The strange, weightless fluid of this place flowed through him, expanding his chest and rounding his segmented back. He released it with a choking cough. Inhaling again, deeper this time, he felt the power of it. And then he let out a roar that rattled his entire body. His voice sounded so different here, higher pitched and free to skitter away in the wind. There were no waves to muffle him. He screamed his name to announce his arrival, to shake the earth so that even the Queen, in her fortress, would hear.

This shark that lay at his feet did not have a name, save the one Taalik gave to it. Graydeath did not even understand the concept of a word, how it could rumble from the throat, and swim through the water, or float in the air, before finding purchase in someone else's mind. The Queen showed Taalik how to do this, first in his dreams, and now while he was awake.

Taalik gripped the bulging eyeball of the shark and wrenched it free of its socket. He held it aloft and said his name again and again until the blood dripped down his claw.

TAALIK TOWED GRAYDEATH to the site of the battle, where the Juggernauts overwhelmed the few sharks who remained. As Taalik expected, most of them fled when their leader disappeared. Warriors on both sides halted when they saw Graydeath with his jaw gaping, the lifeless fins flapping in the current. Detecting the scent of blood and defeat, the sharks retreated, leaving behind wounded comrades and severed body parts. Taalik immersed himself in the smell of it, the taste of it. The Juggernauts swam in great loops around him as he placed Graydeath's corpse on the ocean floor.

Orak rushed to Taalik and immediately went about inspecting his wounds. She nudged him, forcing him to rest on the ground while she licked the gashes at the base of his tentacle, keeping them free of pathogens so they could heal. Taalik knew not to argue with her. His fourth mate, Nong-wa, attended to Orak's injury, a bite mark near her left pectoral fin. The three of them watched as the others killed the stragglers from the fleet. Zirsk and Asha ordered the Juggernauts to slice open their bellies. As Taalik promised, some of them released the eggs they had swallowed. After inspecting them, Zirsk and Asha claimed the eggs they knew to be theirs. The others cheered them on, clicking and chirping each time they ripped open one of their captives. Sometimes, the sharks would try to swallow the eggs again as the Sarcops extracted them, unaware that they died in the process.

*Nong-wa, help with the eggs,* Orak said.

Nong-wa got in a few more licks before swimming over to the others.

*Taalik, the First of Us,* Orak said. *I was afraid you would not return.*

*I was afraid I would not find you when I did.*

*These fish cannot kill me.*

*No,* Taalik said.

Another shark split open, but yielded no stolen eggs, only a small, undigested fish. The Shoots devoured both.

*I must tell you something,* Taalik said. *I fear the others are not ready to hear.*

*What is it, my Egg?*

*I pulled that shark above the waves. The place we cannot go, from which none return.*

Orak stopped licking for a second. *And yet you returned.*

*Yes. The shark died. I lived.*

Taalik described the enormous weight pinning him down, the thin, tasteless air that he nevertheless could breathe. He talked about the color, the brightness of it. *The Queen chose me to break this barrier,* he said. *The place above the sea holds our destiny.*

*Lead us there.*

*We are not ready. Too many would have to be left behind.*

*That has not stopped us before.* He knew she meant the gambit with the eggs.

*There is something else,* he said. He extended his claw and held out a shiny object. She reached for it with her tentacle.

*What is it?* she asked.

*I do not know. I pulled it from the shark's fin.*

She rubbed her tentacle along the curve of the object, and then gently tapped the sharp end. *A tooth? A claw, perhaps?*

*No. It is some kind of weapon, forged from the earth somehow. From the rock.*

*Who made it?*

*The monsters from my dream. Enemies of the Queen. They live above the surface. They tortured the shark, and his people. I saw the scars on his hide. I felt his fear. When I pulled him from the water, he thought I was one of them.*

*The monsters are at war with the sharks, just like us.*

*They are at war with everyone,* Taalik said. *They are more dangerous than the sharks. When the darkness passes over, I see millions of us, piled on the dirt, drying out under the sun. These monsters have hunted us for years. Destroyed our home-lands. They hate us as much as they hate the Queen. Many of us will die if we proceed.*

Orak returned the object to Taalik. *Then we die,* she said.

She swam around to face him. Behind her, the Juggernauts held another shark while Zirsk ripped him from his gills to his rear fin. *You are the First of Us,* Orak said. *You gave us meaning and hope. But you cannot take it away. You cannot tell us what to do with it now. You gave us a choice, and we have chosen to follow you.*

She continued licking his wounds, ignoring her own injury, as was her way. He wrapped a tentacle around hers, twisting several times until the suckers latched onto one another.

They would have to abandon Cold Trench, he told her. They would not survive another hibernation period, when their enemies were sure to strike. The Sarcops would move north, fol-lowing the magnetic beacon at the pole. With luck, they would find a safe haven in the ice.

Before him, Zirsk and Asha nursed their eggs. Shoots and Red-mouths tugged on the corpses of their prisoners until some of the sharks split in two. Taalik observed in silence. Tomorrow, he would point them toward their future.

# CHAPTER 2

## RONIN

ORT(E) STEERED THE boat into the mouth of the river, aiming it upstream, into the valley where he and Sheba would find peace and safety. Where things would begin again.

Sheba spent most of their two-day voyage sleeping below deck, leaving Mort(e) to stare at the interior of the cabin. Before long, he memorized all of the junk left by the humans who let him take the boat. A troll doll, with crazy orange hair. An angry kabuki mask hanging on a nail. A flag with a red sun in a white field. A *Seven Samurai* poster. A calendar from before the war, with a red X on December 23 and a brief note: "Christmas party—Pat's."

As soon as Mort(e) revved the engine to fight the current, Sheba screamed like a human child. The ragged sound of it made him wince.

Mort(e) cut the engine. The boat tilted to the port side as the river returned it to the ocean. He called her name. She answered with another shout, accusing him of doing this to her.

He couldn't afford to let the boat drift. They had used the last canister of fuel, and he still needed to get many miles north, past the dead towns on the riverbank. He restarted the engine. Searching the shoreline, Mort(e) spotted a rickety dock poking into the river, the only structure left on a piece of land where a mansion once stood. The house lay in ruin, destroyed by a fire. With Sheba screeching behind him, Mort(e) white-knuckled it all the way to the dock. When he was close enough, he switched off the power, exited the cabin, and tossed a line around one of the posts. Bracing his foot on the gunwale, he tightened the slack and tied the rope to a cleat. Sheba's howling stopped long enough for her to take a breath. Then she began again.

"Hold on," Mort(e) grunted.

With the boat secure, Mort(e) raced to the stern, where Sheba lay on a pile of blankets, writhing, her snout buried under a fold in the fabric. Her tail stiffened like a third leg. Her muscles tensed, locking in some unspeakable pain that could not be released. Mort(e) placed his knobby hand on her side and stroked the fur. She did not seem to notice. Above them, the overcast sky offered no solace, the clouds so dense that Mort(e) could not locate the sun.

The Queen had given him the pill that would make Sheba into a creature like him. It would uplift her from a mere animal into something more. But the transformations were never like this. Typically, the Change took place while the animals slept, making their former lives feel like a dream. And now, with his only friend twisted in agony, Mort(e) considered the awful possibility that the Queen tricked him. That the pill would kill Sheba, and he would be doomed to watch it unfold. Maybe it was the Colony's final revenge on those who resisted.

And why did he give Sheba the pill in the first place? All the selfish reasons cycled through his head. He had endured this change, and all these years without Sheba, and now she would become like him. That would set things right somehow. It all seemed insane at this moment, as the boat bobbed in the current, and his ears flicked at the sound of Sheba's broken voice. She did not ask to change. She was one of the lucky ones, someone who wouldn't have to remember the uprising or the war or the aftermath.

Mort(e) bent over her body, placing his ear on her ribs. His whiskers mingled with her fur. "I'm sorry," he said. She continued to tremble and sob, the echoless sound going dead over the water. Mort(e) held her, the way he had when they were both still pets, when the world was nothing more than a single house. He whispered to her the things he couldn't say when he was still an animal. "Don't worry. Don't be sad. I am strong. I will not leave you."

Soon, the crying abated. Sheba's voice descended to a low grumble, while the water sloshed against the hull.

He heard a sound within her, like knuckles cracking. Mort(e) clenched his eyes shut and immediately hated himself for his cowardice. Beside him, Sheba twisted and contorted. Mort(e) felt her vertebrae rubbing against his stomach as her spine extended. Her howling began again, and then dissolved into a gasping sound.

She went quiet. Mort(e) placed his ear on her rib cage, trying to find her heartbeat. And then a hand came to rest on his, wrapping around the gnarled nubs where his masters had declawed him. Mort(e) opened his eyes to see Sheba transformed, sitting up and gazing over her shoulder like a human woman rising from a bed. Her face had grown longer, though the brown eyes remained the same, glistening and pleading. Pink hands extended from her furry wrists. Her tail flopped on Mort(e)'s legs.

She rolled over and faced him. Mort(e) gave her space, unsure if she viewed him as a threat. They faced each other on all fours, as they had years earlier at the home of his masters. She leaned in, sniffed him. Licked him once. She opened and closed her mouth as she tried to form the words. Like every other animal who endured the Change, she seemed most surprised by her altered vocal cords, an alien technology implanted while she slept.

"I," she said.

Mort(e) nodded.

"I know you," she said.

Mort(e) collapsed. He rested his face in his palms as he tried to keep himself from breaking down in front of her. Gathering himself, he stood up. He reached out his hand to her. She took it and unsteadily rose beside him.

"I know *you*," Mort(e) said.

FOR THE NEXT few hours, they made their way along the river. Sheba crouched in the fisherman's perch, staring at the water as it flowed underneath. She ran her fingers over the name of the boat, stenciled on both sides of the hull: *Ronin*. A word she could pronounce, but not yet understand. The human who let him take this boat told Mort(e) that the word referred to a warrior without a master. "Like you," the man said, jabbing his finger.

The shoreline provided Sheba with some distraction. They passed the abandoned city of Philadelphia, the wasteland where Mort(e) had searched for Sheba years earlier. In the haze, the city resembled a forest in wintertime, the buildings stripped bare, no signs of life. The tops of two skyscrapers had been blown off, the metal beams poking out like broken bones. A breeze whistled through the streets. The arterial highways remained choked with stalled cars and trucks, their windshields caked in nearly a decade's worth of dust. A few boats rested half-submerged in the harbor, including a cruise ship and a Navy destroyer. Many of the buildings had crumbled into ruin from the street fighting that took place during the war. Alpha soldiers and humans fought to the death among the shopping malls and restaurants. There were no corpses visible from either side—the Colony made sure that not a single scrap of flesh went to waste.

Sheba craned her neck as she tried to sniff, but the dried-out city yielded nothing. Mort(e) wondered how much of this she knew about, how much she remembered. How much the Queen may have tried to teach her. Sheba may have been the luckiest person in the world to have missed all this. And from all available evidence, she had not aged in the Queen's captivity. Perhaps the Colony gave her the same chemicals that kept the Queen alive, so that Sheba would be there when Mort(e) fulfilled the prophecy by coming to her rescue.

More towns and villages rolled by. The entire area had succumbed to the Colony's most recent quarantine, and what had not been destroyed was discarded. Part of Mort(e) wanted to find someone alive here. But part of him was grateful for the silence. He wanted this time alone with Sheba, to introduce her to the surface world without interference.

Two hours later, with the gas tank nearly empty, Mort(e) decided to ditch the boat. From there, he hoped to dock on the Pennsylvania side of the river and then hike into the mountains. They would search for a house or cabin left behind in the evacuations. It would not provide safety forever, but it would work for now. Besides, the areas to the north and south were suspect, with both New York and Washington destroyed, and countless animal settlements quarantined by the ants during the Colonial occupation. The forest provided the only refuge.

Mort(e) docked the boat on a concrete jetty, parking it next to a yacht named *Karen's Way*, written in powder-blue cursive lettering. He estimated that they had landed somewhere south of the Delaware Water Gap, in an area sparsely populated even before the war. Only a few cabins, outhouses, and fishing piers remained.

He gathered as many things as he could—bottles of water, some beef jerky, a new backpack for Sheba. When he handed it to her, she took it without question, still dazed from her transformation. She let him load a first aid kit, flashlights, and other supplies into the bag before pulling the straps onto her shoulders. He stopped and looked at her. She stood taller than he, as expected. Her muscles were taut and veined, with a jaw capable of tearing off someone's limbs. With her powerful hands, she tightened the straps on the bag. Like Mort(e), she must have wondered how she had gotten by without these extraordinary digits, both strong and nimble.

Mort(e) went through the rest of the cabin. He emptied several crates stowed in the corner, finding only ropes and life vests. By the time he returned to the deck, Sheba had lifted the seat cushions to expose the hidden compartments, all empty. She held an object in her hand—a long leather-encased cylinder. When he reached for it, she shielded it with her body.

"What is that?" Mort(e) asked.

He held out his hand. It took her a moment to accept that he did not plan to take the object from her, that he only wanted to see. She let him grip the handle. As he pulled on it, the handle came loose, revealing a metal blade within a scabbard. A sword. A goddamn samurai sword, hidden for no discernible reason on this boat. It even had an engraving on the blade, though Mort(e) could not read it. For the first time, Sheba grinned, as he imagined she would in all the years of searching for her.

"You want to keep it?" he asked.

"Yes."

He still needed to show her how to fire a rifle. He did not feel qualified to teach her swordplay. But how hard could it be? Hit someone with the sharp side of the blade, and they'll either die, quit, or run away.

They hiked for two days into the mountains. The landscape, with its bright greens and deep browns, provided a welcome respite from the searing monochrome of the river. The pine needles tickled his feet, and the soft dirt paths reminded him of long marches with his comrades during the war. Along the way, Mort(e) told her everything. He barely stopped, except for when they took a break to eat. The constant talking provided a refuge from her eerie silence. He could not help thinking that she judged him this whole time, that she blamed him for changing her, for making that decision without asking. Someday, he would have to explain to her that he did it simply because he wanted her to be his friend again. He told himself that that was reason enough, that he had earned it, that she would understand and, if need be, forgive him.

So he talked and talked as they made their way along the highways and rocky trails. He told her about the days they spent together as pets, spooning in the basement of the Martinis' house. During this time, she asked only one question.

"What is your name?"

It made him stop dead. Sheba knew the sound of his voice and the smell of his fur, but did not even know his real name. "My masters called me Sebastian," he said. She did not seem to recognize it. "But I call myself Mort(e) now."

He continued, explaining how they lived next door to one another, and how their masters left them alone while they went off and did their human things. Mort(e) watched her reactions, but could decipher very little. She seemed not to notice that he was talking about her.

Mort(e) decided to leave out the part about her children. If she remembered what had happened to them, she did not need to be reminded. If she didn't know, she did not need to learn. Not yet. Things were too fragile.

He told her about the war that separated them. The war between the Colony and the humans, in which the Queen recruited the animals to kill their oppressors. After Mort(e) murdered his owner, he joined the army, fighting for the Queen. He became good at it.

"I guess I should be glad you weren't there," Mort(e) said. "But I still missed you."

Sheba did not respond.

He told her how, years later, he received a message telling him she was still alive, which put him on a journey to find her. He related all the events while they prepared a campsite in a clear-ing. As Sheba tested her new hands by trying to open a can of beans, Mort(e) described rescuing her from the Queen's chamber. He told her about tossing a grenade at a swarm of giant ants, and how she chased the bomb into a tunnel, thinking they were play-ing fetch.

"I don't remember," she said.

He would have to save the rest for later. After they ate, they stretched out under the trees that muffled the light from the stars. In the dampness, Mort(e) shifted his body toward Sheba, hop-ing to catch some of her warmth without waking her. She rolled away from him. He curled himself into a ball and shivered.

THE NEXT MORNING, shortly after setting out, they emerged from the forest onto another dead highway. A sun-scorched road sign indi-cated that they were on Route 476, leading north into the Pocono Mountains. They were on track, and had been lucky to avoid any stragglers from the quarantine.

She would come around, he thought. Unless she didn't. And then he'd be alone in this wilderness again. Someday, he would have to ask her to tell him how she got through those years. He needed to know if she thought of him, even if she remembered only his smell and not his name. Did she even realize how much it hurt him to wait for her to say these things? Was she so far gone that even the pill could not change her?

For a long time, Mort(e) kept his head down and watched his feet landing on the cracked asphalt. The monotony of it became soothing after a while.

Then he heard the blade slide from its scabbard. *Shhhhinnng.*

Sheba's eyes, deadened until now, opened so wide that they seemed to take up her entire face. She sniffed the air, her nostrils puffing outward and gulping in the scent. For a second—a very long second—Mort(e) thought that she planned to use the sword on him. But her head swiveled like a mounted machine gun, stopping and then darting in a new direction.

"What is it?" he asked.

She sprinted toward the forest, vaulting the concrete divider.

"No," Mort(e) said. "No, no, no, no, no."

He went after her. The pine trees masked whatever scent she was tracking. Mort(e) could see Sheba only in flashes among the foliage, many paces ahead. He released the safety on the machine gun strapped to his shoulder.

Then he smelled it, and his heart sank. An Alpha soldier had passed through, flattening the grass, leaving tracks in the mud, deep gashes in the bark. There was no telling what these giants were capable of doing now that the Queen was dead. They received no instructions, an army disbanded but prepared to kill.

At a clearing in the forest, the beast had trampled the weeds flat. The tracks ended at a pond. Sheba stood beside the water, gripping the sword in both hands. Mort(e) wanted to tell her to leave it alone. But he also wanted to see what she would do.

Before he could decide, the surface of the pond exploded. The Alpha leapt to her hind legs, four claws extended, her jaw split open. Sheba sidestepped as the creature landed in the dirt. As the Alpha lifted her head, Sheba swung the sword and connected, severing an antenna. Mort(e) charged, trying to aim, but Sheba stood in the way.

The earth shook. Mort(e) turned to see dozens of Alphas stampeding through the clearing like a herd of buffalo. Their claws hit the ground in irregular hoofbeats, each foot ripping out a mound of dirt. They did not seem to notice him. Their antennae pointed to some far-off destination. Mort(e) considered firing, but was too panicked to even swing his gun in their direction. Instead, he ran and tackled Sheba as she prepared to strike again. They splashed into the pond as the horde of ants stormed through the forest.

Under the water, she held still while an Alpha dove in and swam past them, scraping Mort(e)'s leg.

Mort(e) and Sheba surfaced. The stampede had passed, all dust and bobbing abdomens. Sheba waded to the edge of the pond and broke into a run.

"Oh, come on," Mort(e) said.

She caught one of the slower ants, the one with the missing antenna. A quick swing of Sheba's blade lopped off one of the ant's legs, causing the beast to topple to her side, dragging herself along. Sprinting, Sheba jumped onto the abdomen and plunged the blade into the flesh, down to the hilt. The Alpha skidded to a halt. When the ant tried to twist her body around to snap at Sheba, the dog pulled the sword out and stabbed the Alpha at the base of her neck. The ant shuddered.

Another Alpha approached, its antennae probing. Mort(e) aimed his gun. But he did not need to shoot. Sheba kept her eye on the other ant while she twisted the blade, silencing her prey. The curious Alpha scurried away.

Sheba yanked the sword out, taking with it a stream of black gore. She slashed at the dead ant. Another leg fell to the ground. Then a chunk of armor. Then, with one big swing, Sheba took off the head. It thunked onto the dirt. She stood on the thorax panting while blood emptied from the wound.

"Do you feel better?" Mort(e) asked.

"Yes."

The rumbling of the herd died out. Sheba wiped the blade on the carcass and slid the sword into its scabbard.

THEY SPENT THE rest of the day dismantling the Alpha. Mort(e) learned how to do it years earlier, when an Alpha fell in combat and needed to be euthanized. Tiberius, the company medic, showed Mort(e) how to dress the animal for cooking, how to store the meat. The trick was getting to the body quickly enough.

Waiting too long meant that the meat would stick to the exoskeleton instead of sloughing right off. If the Alpha had a stinger, the bulb needed to be removed intact with a sharp knife—otherwise, all the good parts below the thorax could be ruined. Culdesac, the commanding officer, preferred to roast the legs over a fire and then suck out the soft insides. Land lobster, he called it.

Mort(e) taught Sheba the entire process, as much as he could remember. She couldn't help sniffing the guts and muscles. She had been their prisoner for so long, tricked into believing that her quiet life as a pet had never ended. Now Mort(e) could give her the gift of tearing apart one of these creatures with the very hands that they gave to her. Passing along Tiberius's knowledge, and seeing Sheba laugh for the first time, pleased Mort(e) in a way that he would have to keep to himself. He didn't want to let on that he viewed these past few days as some kind of audition.

Over a campfire, they ate roasted land lobster one leg at a time. The severed claws rested in the coals until they were piping hot. Sheba enjoyed the food so much she hummed while she chewed. Neither of them had eaten this much meat in years. They held a competition to see who could extract the largest piece of flesh without breaking it off. Mort(e) won the first time. He let Sheba win the second. "But really we're both winners," he said. He waved at her with the claw. She giggled. Then she doubled over with laughter when he used it as a backscratcher. Apparently, the act of killing brought out her sense of humor.

"You know," Mort(e) said, "I've been wondering what we would do for food. I'm not much of a farmer."

He dropped the hollow leg into the fire.

"Those ants are wandering around with no orders," he continued. "Alphas are usually covered in smaller ants, but these ones got separated somehow. They don't know what to do. If we could track the herd, round 'em up, we could start a little ant farm."

"No," Sheba said. "A *big* ant farm. Big ants."

Mort(e) laughed and reached for another leg. Sweet steam rose from the broken joint.

"Not sure how long they live," Mort(e) said. "But Tiberius taught me how to smoke the meat. This one alone could get us through the next couple of weeks. Just have to find a space large enough to hold the rest of them."

They would find the biggest house, he told her. Deep in the woods. A decadent human dwelling with a fireplace and a rug with a patch of sunlight on it.

"They won't find us for a while," he said. "The warmongers and the prophecy peddlers." And if they did, Mort(e) and Sheba could continue west and hope they would find more trees and water instead of decay and death. They couldn't trust anyone, even those who fought in the war. The forest would be their home, he told her, as it had been for their ancestors, long before the humans ruined everything.

The time had come for him to say what he wanted to say for days now. For years.

"I didn't go looking for you so you could be my pet," he said.

Sheba stopped fiddling with a leg and placed it in the fire.

"You're free now," he said. "I can't be your mate. I won't be your master. I'm your friend. I don't know how many lives I have left, but they're yours, if you need them."

He told her the saying that Culdesac taught him: *You are the master over someone who has told you his story.* But the old bobcat applied it only to enemies, not friends. Mort(e) and Sheba knew each other's stories, and they needed to be gentle with that knowledge. They could use it only for the good of the other.

When she did not respond, Mort(e) took her hand. "There is a whole world out there, but I'm going deeper into the forest tomorrow. Do you want to go with me?"

Sheba gazed beyond the flames, out to the mountains rising like black monoliths.

She let go of his hand. "Tell me what happened to my children," she said.

It was her longest sentence so far. But Mort(e) felt relieved. He knew what she meant. She would go with him if he told her everything, even if it made her sad. It broke his heart to think of how many moments they had shared as animals, unable to speak. In these woods, he would learn about her all over again. A war destroyed everything, and yet they survived. They would take what this world left them. They were alive and together—they had that right.

Mort(e) walked over to the pile of firewood. He dug out the largest piece, a trunk thicker than his waist. The embers danced as he heaved the log into the fire.

Sheba waited for him to begin.

# CHAPTER 3

## THE STORY OF FALKIRK

ALKIRK ARRIVED AT the refugee camp late in the afternoon. Another winter had ended, though the forests held on to the chill, with fog tumbling over the melting snow. The muddy ground, soaked with drainage from the mountains, squished under his feet. He didn't wear shoes like some of the other agents, and the humans he worked with would often tease him for it. When they asked him why he still went barefoot, he'd respond, "Because we won the war."

The camp consisted of a few dozen lodges, hastily constructed from sticks, tarps, and mud. As far as he could tell, everyone in the camp was a beaver, probably all related. Falkirk could smell them on the way in, thanks to the fetid scent mounds built out of mud and cemented with urine—an odd territorial habit left over from before the Change. At least the beavers had the good sense to put their latrine somewhere else—otherwise, Falkirk would have been tempted to tell his superiors in Hosanna that he hadn't been able to find these people.

An altar stood in an open square, with a stone top and legs made of tree trunks. A priestess with a white stole held aloft a jar of burning incense. Two underlings stood behind her, their leathery hands folded. While she sang a prayer, they hummed the background tune. Beavers always sang like this. It mimicked the sound of the water flowing, a vibration that drove them to build their elaborate dams. The priestess sneaked in a few lyrics praising the three goddesses that represented the water, the earth, and the forest. Under normal circumstances, Falkirk would have reported this blasphemy to the elders in Hosanna. This time, it would have to wait. Besides, this community sat at the edge of Sanctuary Union territory, surrounded by the wolf clans. They had enough problems without Falkirk tattling on them.

Like some medieval outpost, two beavers guarded the entrance to the camp, both holding spears. Falkirk expected them to cross the weapons like an X if he tried to pass. As he got closer, the sentries mumbled to each other, no doubt wondering what a dog was doing here. Falkirk pulled out the Sanctuary Union ID badge from his satchel. He did not expect them to understand the lingo about his rank and status. He only wanted them to see the eyeball symbol in the upper right corner, announcing him as a bona fide agent of the Department of Tranquility, Special Operations.

"Come with us," one of the guards said. "We'll take you to Castor."

"No," Falkirk said. "Go get him. Bring him here. We have work to do."

As the guard went into the camp, Falkirk could hear the refugees debating over where he came from. Minutes later, he saw the guard approaching with Castor, a beaver who wore goggles perched on his forehead. His species tended to have terrible eyesight, and the lucky ones constructed lenses that helped them to see. Near the entrance of a lodge, an elderly beaver stopped Castor as he walked by. Falkirk knew from the reports that this was Nikaya, Castor's mother, the founder of Lodge City. Castor had taken over as leader now that she had gone nearly blind, possibly senile. She said a few words to him. Castor nodded and kept walking.

A young kit trotted behind him, perhaps only a few years old. A tuft of orange hair stuck out from the top of his head, like a permanent flame. The child held a toy zeppelin carved from wood, with the word *Vesuvius* stenciled into the side. All the children in the Union loved the *Vesuvius*. While Castor introduced himself, Falkirk thought of his own son, who once owned a similar model salvaged from an abandoned toy store.

"Thank you for coming," Castor said. "Do you need anything before we go?"

"No."

"Are you a wolf?" the kit asked.

"Booker!" Castor said. One of the guards snorted. Castor apologized to Falkirk, who waved it off.

"I'm a husky," Falkirk said. He saw a mixture of relief and disappointment in the kit's face.

"Forgive my son," Castor said. "He's very curious."

Falkirk nodded. He told Castor to lead the way.

THEY ARRIVED AT a freshly carved path, where the beavers had felled several trees. Covered in teeth marks, the stumps had been whittled into cones. Falkirk placed his hand on them to gauge their smoothness.

Castor asked many questions. Falkirk answered the ones he could, and deflected the ones that trespassed into classified information. Special Operations existed for a variety of reasons. Chief among them was tracking anomalies related to the Change. As expected, the beaver inquired about the kinds of rumors that only people living in the sticks would take seriously. Falkirk patiently explained that there had been no confirmed cases of wolves cannibalizing their own out west, or of trees uprooting themselves and walking around, or of the Queen's hormone causing long-term illnesses or birth defects. Castor also asked about the reports of murders in the capital. Some of the traveling merchants claimed that it was a serial killer, like something out of an old human horror movie. Hosanna was a big city with many different species, Falkirk told him. It was impossible to keep an eye on everyone.

Eventually, Castor moved on to the stories involving mutated fish. The fish-heads, they were calling them. Here, Falkirk had no trouble saying that the SO had investigated the rumors, which thus far yielded nothing. "If these fish-heads don't want to be found, that's probably a good thing."

The steep hill they climbed left Castor too out of breath to ask more questions.

"Have you ever been in a zeppelin?" Booker asked.

"I have," Falkirk said.

"I've seen them flying over Lodge City."

"When?"

"Last spring."

"Did it hover over the city for a while?"

"Yes."

"And then turn southwest, to Hosanna, after the sun went down?"

"Yes! It turned on the spotlight and lit up the city! How did you know?"

"That was me."

"What do you mean that was you?" Castor said, panting.

"I used to be the commander of a ship."

"The *Vesuvius*?" Booker asked. His father laughed.

"Yes."

Castor stopped laughing. "Really?"

"Really."

"What happened? What are you doing out *here*?"

"Things change. Isn't that what all of us are doing out here?"

As they crested one final hill, with the sun going down, they crawled on their bellies so they could peer over the ridge without being seen. Booker followed, though he stopped short of the top. Castor pulled the goggles over his beady eyes.

From the hillside, Lodge City sprawled out before them in the failing light. Several buildings from the human era survived, all built from stone—a post office, a high school, a fire station. Around these decaying structures stood massive mounds of earth and tree branches, the lodges that the beavers preferred. A waterwheel stood frozen in the river. Downstream, a partial dam channeled water through sunken canals, perfect for ferrying objects or for swimming. A new church made from logs rose in the center of the town. The beavers had a saying: *the water flows*. It meant that they always had work to do, always a river to bend, always more lodges to construct. For them, this triumph of animal architecture proved how enlightened their species had become. A sort of middle finger extended from their newly formed hands.

From his perch on the hillside, the town seemed out of focus to Falkirk, as if some gel had been smeared over his eyes. He pulled the binoculars from his satchel. Through the magnified lenses, he stared at the town for a long time before he could accept what he saw. "Why didn't you come to us sooner?" he asked.

"Why did Tranquility send only one agent?" Castor replied. "We need an army."

Unable to answer, Falkirk looked again, panning more slowly this time. He could make out the contours of it: a spiderweb, consisting of millions of strands, draped over the town like a snowfall suspended in midair. The streetlamps, along with a few lights still burning in the houses, made the veneer glow like melted gold. Coiled ropes of silk stretched from the rooftops, pillars, and telephone poles, creating a network of pathways above the entire town. The white fibers reached from the base of the watermill across the river, forming a bridge to the other side.

"Have you seen an arachnid before?" Castor asked.

"Only in a vat of formaldehyde. They caught it down south somewhere."

"Over by the soccer stadium," Castor said. "North end of town. You'll see her. We call her Gulaga."

"What does that mean?"

"Mistress of the Gulag, I guess. My mother came up with it."

Before the war, the stadium must have been a nice place to watch a game on a crisp fall evening. But now, the web was pulled taut across the field, from one set of bleachers to the other, forming a giant hammock. Something stirred on the fringes of the web. Falkirk blinked a few times, and everything became still again. Cylindrical objects, wrapped in the silky filament, clung to the edges.

Movement again. He focused in on it. One of the cylinders had burst open. Something squirmed from the inside. An appendage. An arm. The cylinder held one of the citizens of Lodge City. A beaver, trying to claw his way free. He could move only one limb. The other arm had been injured, apparently.

*No.* No, the other arm was bitten off at the shoulder. That's what these arachnids did. They amputated the pieces they wanted, numbed and cauterized the wound, saved the rest for later.

"No," Falkirk whispered. "No, stay still. Stay still."

More movement. This time, the strands of silk came to life, making the entire hammock vibrate. The arachnid emerged from the bull's-eye of the web, camouflaged with the same milky color. Its segmented legs lifted its body and propelled it across the structure, mocking the prey who could barely move. The spider had no face, only a mouth that cleaved open. The monster's fangs clamped shut on the beaver. Then its hind legs curled under its abdomen and spun the beaver round and round, wrapping it in fresh silk that reflected the last drops of sunlight.

Castor began to hum, the deep sound warbling in his throat. Booker sang a prayer of mourning, as was their way.

> *We commend you to the earth,*
> *To the lodges that rise to the sky.*
> *May you find the warmth of your clan,*
> *Where our song can never die.*

They wouldn't shut up. Falkirk lowered the binoculars and gazed away from the town, away from Castor and Booker. *Oh, God, why do you send these monsters? When will you forgive us for what we did?*

Falkirk's empty stomach twisted inside of him. Castor said something about the spider, but Falkirk couldn't hear. Lodge City had blurred into an image of his old house on the day of the quarantine. The day the Alphas ransacked it, making no distinction between inanimate objects and living things. Falkirk watched it all from the safety of a hilltop, having returned from a patrol in the woods. The giant insects scuttled across the roof, in one window and out the other, through the front door. Falkirk wanted to believe that his mate Sierra had taken the children to a safe place, into a closet or under the floorboards. But the house had no safe spaces. And when the ants climbed out of the windows, their jaws glistened with blood, like clown masks. Or like war paint to mock a defeated enemy. Falkirk wanted to keep walking toward them, to let the ants devour him. He turned and ran instead. God was not through punishing him for that.

"Are you listening, Mr. Falkirk?" Castor said.

"He's gonna pass out," Booker said. "Like Ryder did when he saw it."

"Where did it come from?" Falkirk asked.

"The river," Castor said. "See how the web dips into the ponds we built? Gulaga needs to keep her gills wet so she can breathe.

And she has those two claws in front. She's more like a crab than a spider if you ask me."

Castor gave him the short version of what happened. Gulaga appeared somewhere downstream, building a small nest but staying out of sight. But then, one night, the spider snatched several people and locked them in a cocoon of silk. This, however, was merely a trap. The web covered a wide perimeter, and any attempt to infiltrate the area sent alarm signals all the way to her lair. When rescuers arrived, Gulaga seized them as well, and then tried to barricade the entire city. Twice more, Castor and the others tried to attack. Twice, Gulaga ate one of the hostages on the spot. "Maybe we were doing them a favor," he said.

"Is she intelligent?" Falkirk asked.

"She's not dumb."

"But has she tried to communicate with you?"

Castor chuckled. "*This* is how she speaks."

Falkirk kept staring at the city until it fully replaced the image of his old house. He was not the best at his job—that was why Tranquility dumped him in the wilderness—but focusing on the task at hand had been his salvation for years now. It kept away the awful silence of the quarantine.

"We'll need help," Falkirk said.

"It won't arrive in time," Castor said. "Besides, you're here to take notes, aren't you? Observe and report. You're not here to help. The water flows, and you'll just sit and listen."

The beaver was right. "Take me back to the camp," Falkirk said.

They walked in silence. Along the way, Booker held his zeppelin aloft, pretending it could fly, sometimes whispering orders from the ship's imaginary captain. "Set a course for Lodge City!" he said. "Aye, captain!"

THEY RETURNED LONG after nightfall. The camp bustled with people cooking, sitting in small groups and talking, children running around the lodges. Castor led Falkirk to a hovel made of branches and leaves where he would spend the night. As a courtesy, an oil lamp flickered in the corner, and a tarp covered the muddy floor. A pot of bean-and-insect stew waited for him. As he sat cross-legged, eating with a hand-carved spoon, another song broke out, an even sadder one this time. The beavers couldn't help themselves. Falkirk covered his ears, but it made no difference. The low bass sounded like a set of bagpipes, stirring the dirt into a minor earthquake.

*We watch you disappear downstream*
*We await your return with the wind.*

The beavers repeated it, with different families taking turns. Falkirk imagined how his mother would have reacted to a song in her honor. A one-eyed husky named Durga, she would have asked, in her stilted way of speaking, "You learn talking, and you sing this noisy shit?"

Falkirk imagined Durga tangled in the web, growling, her one blue eye bulging as she tried to bite her way through a cord of silk. If the spider got close, Durga would die with her fangs wrapped around one of the monster's legs. From then on, Gulaga would live with a set of teeth marks etched in her armor, a reminder of the most stubborn husky who ever lived.

Durga was raised in a shelter that doubled as a dogsledding tourist trap. Though Falkirk never knew his father, his mother kept him and his brothers safe, mostly by currying favor with the masters, a married couple named Paul and Judy Weyrich. They called him Arjuna in those days. Both humans were tall and strong, though Judy eventually needed a wheelchair to get around. She did the paperwork for the shelter, while Paul took vacationers out on sledding trips, often with Durga leading the way. That is, until she lost her eye protecting the pack from a mountain cat. A *mountain* cat! From then on, Durga would wait at home for Falkirk and his brothers to return. The family would reunite under the soft lamps of the pen, and eventually fall asleep in a pile of fur and tails.

The Change crept into the shelter slowly. Falkirk's youngest brother Koda transformed in his sleep one night. The other dogs barked at him until Paul arrived with a shotgun. Terrified, standing on both legs, Koda leapt out the rear door to escape. The snow swirled where he once stood. The dogs shouted into the void, ignoring Paul when he told them to be quiet. Falkirk believed that his brother disappeared into the night and somehow *became* the snow.

The next night, more of them changed. Falkirk hid in a corner as the dogs doddered about on two legs. He whimpered despite his mother's growls to keep quiet. On the day he finally stood upright, Falkirk saw something he wished he would never see: Durga, trembling in a corner, terrified of her own son. His mother—the ruler of this pack—shivered on the ground, a mere animal afraid of a predator. When she transformed later that evening, her first words to him were, "Find food." She thought she could still boss him around, along with everyone else. But the damage had been done.

The elders discussed what to do. They possessed that power now. They could negotiate and compromise, without repetitive barks or pointless wrestling matches. Once the snowstorm passed, they considered searching for Koda. Durga instead talked them into checking on Paul and Judy. A few grumbled at this, having chafed at the work Paul forced them to do. One of them, a dog from another kennel named Pandu, said that he hailed from a shelter where his brothers and sisters had been culled. Falkirk asked him what that meant. Pandu said that some kennels slit the throats of excess dogs and then burned them so their ash became part of the clouds—that was where the snow came from. Durga did not believe him. And besides, the Weyriches saved Pandu by adopting him. When Pandu asked how they could be sure that Paul and Judy wouldn't try the same thing, Durga cut him off.

"Watch," she said. "Watch in every direction, all directions. All white. White and nothing else. Food here. Out there, nothing. The humans give, the white takes."

Falkirk would never hear Durga master the language. But in those early days, she spoke well enough to convince the others to stay.

They stopped arguing when the smell of roasted meat entered the room, still raw enough to release the fragrance of blood. It came from the house. There, Paul stood on his porch, raising a white flag cut from a bedsheet. The dogs gathered and watched the sweet smoke rise from the chimney, saliva drooling from their lips.

That night, the canines sat around Paul and Judy's dining room table. Judy carried platters of seared steak on the armrests of her wheelchair. None of the dogs had been inside the house before. Animal and human ate together, chatting about the extraordinary events of the last few days. Paul said that the animals had changed all over the world. He told each of them their names, and promised they were welcome to stay. There was no reason to be enemies.

"Why would we be enemies?" Durga asked.

Falkirk's mother took special pride in knowing she had been right to remain at the shelter. Until one morning, three days later, when an Alpha on patrol wandered onto the property. Durga rounded up the dogs, told them that they needed to defend Paul and Judy. They retrieved tools from the shed and surrounded the beast. It took them two hours of hacking at the insect to bring it down. By the time the monster finally collapsed, the dogs were so exhausted they could hardly stand.

From then on, Durga ordered them to form a perimeter to defend the house. And she wanted a special bark if any intruders arrived, along with guards in the humans' quarters. *And* she wanted to chop down the nearby trees and make pikes. She became unhinged. Her one eye, oscillating in its socket, became like the lens of a periscope peering from the depths of her mind. When Falkirk suggested moving somewhere else, Durga refused. "This home is home," she said.

The next day, Falkirk's brother returned with more dogs. They demanded to know where the humans were hiding. Addressing him by the name Koda, Durga asked what they meant.

"I'm Wendigo," he said. "I don't have a slave name."

Wendigo asked if they knew what was happening beyond the white hills. When no one answered, he told them to turn on the television. They didn't know what a television was, so he told them to let him inside so he could show them. For once, Durga was outvoted. With Paul and Judy hiding upstairs, the dogs gathered around a panel that hung from the wall. Wendigo touched a button on the side. Two-dimensional images moved across the screen, showing buildings burning, with more of the giant ants crawling over the rubble. Whenever Wendigo tapped another button, the image would change. One channel showed men in green uniforms and helmets, standing over a pit with hundreds of dead dogs in it. Another channel showed a troop of wolves carrying rifles, walking in formation with the giant ants.

"Do you see what the humans have been hiding from you?" Wendigo said. "The ants are coming to purge the land. We have to leave."

"No," Durga said. "We stop them."

"Stop them from what?"

"From attacking the house!"

In the tense quiet that followed, Wendigo eyed each of them. "She didn't tell you, did she?" he asked. "You might as well still be animals. This gift is wasted on you."

"I decide what we do," Durga said.

"These humans have been using us. They cast us aside when we're too old or weak."

"Shut your mouth."

"Tell them what the humans did to our father."

She slapped him. He let her do it. He didn't even bare his teeth.

"We don't have to be slaves," Wendigo said. "The Queen has set us free."

Durga told them it was a lie, that Wendigo had betrayed them. Despite her protests, the dogs from the other kennel walked over to Wendigo's side. It left Durga and her three remaining sons. She spat and said she didn't need cowards to defend the house.

"Does he speak true about father?" Falkirk asked.

All she had to do was tell him the truth. But she merely repeated the same lines: "Food here. Nothing out there."

And so he joined with Wendigo. And even then, he knew he would spend the rest of his life trying to explain why. As he walked out, the answer was already changing in his mind. First anger made him do it. Then fear. Then shame. He hated himself, he hated her, he hated this place, he hated the way these new words could mean whatever the speaker wanted them to mean. The rebel faction left Durga standing on the porch screaming at them. "The white takes you! The white takes you now!" Even after climbing a hill, he could still hear her voice.

Sitting on the floor of the beaver lodge, Falkirk felt the same wave of nausea from that cold night. He tried to swallow another spoonful of the stew, but his gag reflex wouldn't allow it. He spit it out into the bucket they'd left for his waste.

Though Falkirk did not need company, he didn't mind it when Booker and three of his friends paid him a visit. They asked questions, often giggling or covering their eyes in embarrassment. They wanted to know what Falkirk saw in the web. One of them cowered when Falkirk described the arachnid, prompting his friends to make fun of him for being scared. These children, he realized, were about the same age as his own son and daughter, had they lived.

They asked him about the humans in Hosanna. Were they mean? Did they still eat baby animals? No, Falkirk said, the humans weren't like that. The Department of Tranquility was the most diverse organization in the world, with representatives from every species. Old animals spread rumors about the humans to frighten the children.

Booker raised his hand. "Is it true that when humans fart, they think no one can hear it or smell it?" His friends broke out in hysterical laughter that only grew louder when Falkirk answered yes.

An adult beaver arrived to shoo the children away, telling them that their visitor needed time alone. After finishing his meal, Falkirk considered his next move. The bird patrols would not pass through here for a few more days, meaning that he would not be able to send word to Hosanna until then. It would take at least three days to reach the nearest transmitting station. And what would happen when his message finally made it? His superiors would most likely tell him to abandon the town, leave it for the scientists to study later. Besides, the prospect of human soldiers infiltrating Lodge City—no matter what the reason—would provoke the wolves, which would then anger the remote villages still considering joining the Union.

While recording the day's activities in his logbook, Falkirk sensed someone near the entrance. There, he saw Castor, with his mother Nikaya leaning on him for support.

"My mother wishes to speak with you," Castor said.

"Take my hand, pup," she said. She shambled closer to him and sniffed his neck. "You *are* a husky."

"Mother!"

"Go on, I'm fine," she said. "The dog will watch after me."

"I'll walk her back," Falkirk said. "It's okay."

With great pain, the old rodent took a seat on the tarp, shifting her sagging rump into a more comfortable position. Falkirk sat before her, still holding her hand.

"Thank you for coming," she said.

"Please don't. You've probably heard by now that I'm just an observer."

"And yet the Three Goddesses led you here anyway."

"I doubt that."

"Ah, but our Goddesses are real," she said. "The river, the earth, and the trees are right in front of you. You need to keep what's real alongside what you hope for. It makes you honest."

Falkirk agreed.

"Will you say nice things about us to your friends in the city?" she asked.

"I will."

"Good. Because I know what you've heard about us. I know we're not perfect, that we've bent the rules here and there. I've stood in front of that shrine and asked forgiveness for the mistakes I've made."

Falkirk knew what she meant. Lodge City had been more inclusive once, allowing in other species from the forest, including a cloud of bats who made their home in the rafters of a gymnasium. "I'm not here to investigate what happened with the bats," he said.

"They betrayed us," Nikaya said. "Personally, I think they're behind all this."

Unlikely, Falkirk thought. But the bats certainly had a motive. In one of her last acts as leader, Nikaya ordered the gymnasium demolished, the bats exiled for heresy and intrigue. Despite her grandmotherly demeanor, she had orchestrated a power grab like some medieval human courtier. As a result, her bloodline would continue to run the city, for better or worse.

"No one tried to help those poor creatures more than I did," she added. "But they were going to sabotage everything we built. I couldn't let that happen."

In the awkward pause that followed, Falkirk scratched an itch behind his ear.

"You're not going to believe this," Nikaya said, "but I came up with the idea for Lodge City before the Change."

Falkirk grinned.

"I know, I know," she said. "Everybody claims they were really smart before they changed. But I'm serious. I dreamt about the city. A place where everyone would be safe, where no one would starve, no one would kill."

She gripped his hand tighter, so he could feel the thin bones pressing into his palm.

"The water flows, Mr. Falkirk. There might be a way to fix all of this, but I can't ask it of the others. Not even my own son."

"What is it?"

"It involves breaking a promise. I know someone who can help. Two people, actually. A dog and a cat."

"From Hosanna?"

"No. They're out on their own. I promised not to tell anyone about them. But people will die if I don't."

"Who are they?"

"A couple of ant farmers. Veterans of the war."

"Ant farmers," Falkirk said. "Did they give you the ants for my stew?"

She laughed so loud that one of the beavers rushed over to the cave to see what was going on. "They're *Alpha* ranchers. They've been raising soldier ants for years now."

She let that sink in.

"Holy shit," Falkirk whispered.

"They have experience with taking down big insects," Nikaya said. "It'll take some convincing. But they might be willing to help."

"Okay, okay," Falkirk said, still trying to figure out if she was joking, or hallucinating. "But who are they?"

"You know who they are. A warrior. And a mother."

She didn't need to let that sink in.

# CHAPTER 4

## HOME

**T**HE HERD MOVED as a single unit across the grass, antennae and abdomens bobbing in unison. Even in old age, without orders from their queen, the Alphas marched in formation, their feet landing in the same tracks. At first light, the sun baked their hides, making them hot to the touch whenever Sheba gently redirected them around a boulder or a stream.

These long walks had become Sheba's favorite part of the day. She would begin by mounting one of the stronger Alphas—usually Juke or Gai Den, who barely noticed her weight. Sheba did not have to be bigger than the ants to make them follow her. She needed only to be taller. She and Mort(e) once tried moving the herd on foot, and later with a bicycle they found. But putting a saddle on an ant allowed them to move like the Alphas, to blend in. The former soldiers became so docile in their old age, yet still needed their morning exercise to burn off energy and keep from going insane. Sheba and Mort(e) learned the hard way what happened if they failed to keep the ants occupied. In a scuffle the year before, one Alpha died, and the other was so mangled that her sisters began to pick at her open wounds.

Once every few months, an ant would either become ill or sustain an injury, and putting her down became an act of mercy.

Though Sheba killed an Alpha in a rage years earlier, euthanizing the animals had become a solemn ritual for her, full of regret and quiet longing for some life she barely recalled. Thus, the ranch became a melancholy place, a living graveyard for a species that would soon go extinct. It didn't help that Mort(e) branded the Alphas with the names of soldiers with whom he had served during the war, every single one of them now dead. But it was beautiful in a way. Here, the love that the war took away from Sheba could spring again. Caring for these animals, having them depend on her, gave her a purpose. It made it easier whenever she stared at the mountains and wondered what else was out there.

On this particular day, Gai Den bucked a few times as the herd crested the hill overlooking the valley. To calm her, Sheba stroked her antennae. She led the ants toward the brook, one of their favorite parts of the walk. They examined the stream, sometimes conferring with one another like scouts on patrol. She pulled on Gai Den's reins so the herd could pass. When the last few stragglers took too long, she gave a nudge to get them going.

Sheba drifted to the rear again when the herd climbed the hill, this time to keep an eye on the older ones. Anansi's legs had become so weak that they shook when she walked. She had one more season in her, at best. Though Sheba had grown to love these creatures, she hated that they showed no emotion whenever one of their own disappeared. With each death, the herd tightened its formation, as though the recently deceased had never existed.

Sheba took so long with the hike that Mort(e) stood waiting for her on the roof of the house, where he had spent the previous day fixing broken shingles. He promised to work on it only in the mornings and evenings, to avoid the sun, so he must have been out there simply waiting for her return. She liked this about him. He once told her that he behaved like a loyal dog because of all the time he'd spent with her.

Mort(e) tipped his straw hat before continuing with his work. Sheba locked the gate to the pen behind her. The ants went about their insect things, cleaning each other's antennae and walking in circles to scout the area. She watched them for a while before heading to the house.

"When are you going to be finished with that, Old Man?" she asked. "No one can take a nap around here."

"Thought it would be today," he said. "The winter really did a number on this thing." He tossed a rotten shingle. It landed in the grass by her feet.

He asked how the herd did this morning. She said they were fine, though a few of them definitely showed their age. Mort(e) said they would hold off on euthanizing any of them; they had stored enough dried meat in the smoker for now. "Unless you think one of them is really hurting," he said.

"No. They're still stubborn."

"Good."

He kept hammering away, his tail stiff. Sheba went inside to fetch a drink. While the hammer continued whacking overhead, she sipped the water and thought about what would be left of this life once the ants were gone.

SHE STILL HAD nightmares. No matter how much peace she found in this new life, no matter how much she trusted Mort(e), none of it made a difference. She dreamt of the tall man approaching her as she suckled her children. He towers over her. She tries to fight him. He overpowers her. She runs away. And the worst part: She exalts in staying alive, right before realizing that she has left her children behind. She does not go back for them, because she knows they are already dead. She knows she has failed them.

While Mort(e) suffered during the war, Sheba lived out her days as a pet, with no recollection of the years passing, only images of a soft rug, bowls of food, the warm radiator on her side, the reassuring sound of the kettle boiling. She lacked nothing under the Queen's watch. Life became so comfortable that she barely remembered her doting master, or the sweet little cat who cuddled with her. Even to this day, she caught herself thinking of her life as a pet more than her own children. Their voices came to her now and then, but only in echoes that soon died out. She had no history to call her own. Only fragments of someone else's past.

In recent months, she dreamt of the first few days on board the boat where she had transformed. She recalled the smell of salt, and the strange motion of the water. And the dream often ended in the same way, with her commandeering the wheel, spinning it hard to starboard, and heading out to sea. And whenever she did this, the Old Man vanished, leaving her alone in the great expanse, under a sky the color of fogged glass. Sometimes she would see Mort(e) staring at her from a rocky beach until the mist covered him over.

She asked him if their arrangement—a eunuch cat and a fertile dog—was normal in the former world. He told her that normal had become a rather nebulous term these days. She could tell that he had dreaded this question for a long time. By answering it, he admitted that he could not give her everything she may have wanted. He could not do for her what the father of her children had done, back when they were still animals. "If you leave . . . let me know," he said one night before falling asleep. "Take extra water and some weapons." No bitterness or resentment. He always told her that things change. They are taken away, or they leave, or they die.

ONE MORNING, SHEBA noticed Anansi limping by the edge of the pen, favoring her right hind leg. In great agony, the ant pitched forward and dug her mandible into the dirt. Her antennae smacked the ground, reaching for anything but feeling nothing. Sheba stared at her for a while, the awfulness of it freezing her in place. She barely noticed Mort(e) standing beside her.

"I think it's time for Anansi," Mort(e) said. "Are you okay?"

Sheba said she was fine. Mort(e) pointed at the shed, where they kept the spade shovel. He offered to take care of it.

"No," Sheba said. "It's my turn."

"I can do it, if you—"

"I'm fine. I'll do it."

Anansi had once been the most active of the herd. Less than a year earlier, she slipped out of the formation and wandered off on her own. Sheba tracked her for two days. By the time she caught up with the Alpha, the poor creature was starving, unable to follow instructions. Left with no alternative, Sheba constructed a trap to catch her. She dug a hole in the ground, covered it with leaves and branches, and then lured the ant with the pheromone extracted from the others. Anansi came charging at her. Sheba led her to the hole and jumped over it, while Anansi fell through. When the ant attempted to climb out, Sheba threw her some food. The Alpha ate ravenously, then lifted her head to beg for more. Once she was calm enough, the ant staggered out and let Sheba tie a leash around her neck. Sheba walked her to the ranch without incident, though it would not be the last time she had to retrieve a wayward Alpha.

Euthanizing an ant was a two-person job. Mort(e) retrieved the spade. They used a rope to pull Anansi a little closer to the fence. The Alpha allowed them to lead her to a thick tree stump that Mort(e) had sunk into the ground. Oblivious, Anansi examined the rope with her antennae. Sheba climbed to the top bar of the fence, spade raised, while Mort(e) whispered soothing words to the ant. Then he pulled the rope hard, pinning Anansi to the flat surface of the stump. Before the ant could react, Sheba jammed the spade into the root of the beast's neck. The movement, which they had rehearsed so many times, took less than a second. Anansi collapsed.

As always, Sheba wrapped her furry arms around the Alpha's

neck and rested her face on the skull. A few of the other ants meandered over, inspected the body, and ambled away. Tomorrow, they would tighten the herd once more.

A FEW DAYS later, Sheba and Mort(e) hiked to the fork in the river, where they would meet with a representative of Lodge City to trade in ant hides. They carried the hollowed-out shell on a canvas stretcher with handles fashioned from canoe paddles. Whenever an ant died, Sheba lit a fire on the hilltop, signaling to the beavers that they would bring the pelt the following day. The rodents used the material for all sorts of items, from cookware to armor to roof shingles.

Mort(e) had worked out this relationship with Lodge City a little over a year earlier, not long after they first noticed a glow coming from the riverside at night. Sheba asked him what it was. "Just the beginning," Mort(e) said gravely. Though relieved that there were no humans in Lodge City, Mort(e) said they'd have to move the herd west. Sheba recommended reaching out to the new settlement. She had met only a handful of people while living on the ranch—drifters and traders, mostly. She wanted to see more. Mort(e) told her, once again, that he didn't trust outsiders, having already seen enough experiments with utopias. His utopia for two was the closest anyone would get.

Sheba wouldn't let it go. She mentioned all the things they could buy from the beavers that would make life easier on the farm. Flashlights. Solar panels. A real plow. First aid kits. "You said beavers made good hoarders," she said.

"I said moles."

"You said beavers."

One morning, she mentioned it again over breakfast. "You're going there anyway, aren't you?" he sputtered. "After all I said. Like I don't know what I'm talking about."

"Yes."

"All *right*," he grumbled. So the next day, they went to the city. Upon meeting the beavers, Sheba removed a severed ant claw from her backpack and said they would like to establish a trade. That afternoon, Sheba and Mort(e) enjoyed a feast of insect stew with Nikaya, the matriarch of the beavers, who agreed to barter with them. Using false names, Mort(e) insisted that the beavers keep their working relationship a secret. Sheba told him later that the old rodent may have figured out who they were. "Good," Mort(e) said. "Then she knows that if she talks, I'll kill her."

On their way to the fork in the river, Sheba and Mort(e) encountered a few obstacles in the trail left over from a recent storm. They waded through a calf-deep stream, swollen by the rain. A dead tree blocked their path. They carefully lifted the remains of Anansi over the trunk. Mort(e) almost slipped in the process, but they managed to keep the carcass from falling.

At the river, they noticed the odor of the beavers' scent mounds—piles of mud laced with their piss, marking their territory. This angered Mort(e). The columns indicated another expansion of Lodge City. The stink became so overpowering that Mort(e) asked to stop so he could try to locate the source. He spotted the mound about thirty yards ahead. The pile of dirt came up to his waist. Looking around first, Mort(e) kicked the mound, knocking it over. He recoiled when this released an even stronger scent. Sheba asked if he felt better. "Yes," he said. "Too bad about that mound, though. Must have been a pretty bad storm."

A beaver named Chingachgook had been their contact for over a year now. He usually brought a wheelbarrow full of items to trade. The beaver knew them only by their aliases, Arthur and Madre. But when they reached the meeting spot, they found no one there. Sheba and Mort(e) set their haul on the ground. She sniffed the area and concluded that Chingachgook had yet to arrive.

So they waited. Small talk about what to eat for dinner that night eventually turned into a two-hour-long reminiscence about the days before the war. Mort(e) said that he liked the sound of rivers—they reminded him of the rushing water in the metal pipes of his masters' house. As a house cat, Mort(e) found this noise fascinating, along with the leaky radiators and the droning electric can opener. He asked her if she recalled any rivers from before the Change. She said she remembered her master taking her to some body of water, though it may have been a pond.

With no sign of Chingachgook, Sheba suggested that they retire to the ranch. She wondered if something had happened to the beavers. There had been no problems with their bartering before. In their last meeting, Chingachgook even suggested euthanizing one of the ants sooner, as his wait list now included over a dozen people.

"He must have found a better way to make a living," Mort(e) said, grunting out the last words as he lifted the pallet. "Or the matriarch's dead, and our little arrangement is over."

"Would you like that?" Sheba asked. "Would you want things to go back to the way they were?"

Mort(e) paused. "No. You were right. Trading with these people wasn't so bad."

A good enough answer, she decided. They headed for the ranch, lifting the pallet over the trampled mound.

UPON RETURNING THEY went about their chores for the day. While Sheba fed the herd, Mort(e) repaired more shingles, leaving the damaged ones in a pile on the front lawn. The familiar noises of the ranch made her feel safe. Despite the cold, leaves grew on the branches again. They had defied another winter here.

For dinner, Mort(e) barbecued some leftover ant meat with fresh onions. Sheba found the aroma overwhelming. Mort(e) admitted that his sense of smell might be going, and he needed to give it some shock treatment every once in a while.

It was Fifth Night, the night before their day of rest. Fifth Nights always included a nice meal, a fire if the weather called for it, and quiet conversation in the den. For the first year or so, they typically devoted the time to watching movies. The previous occupants of the house left behind an old VCR that drained all the juice in the solar panels. Mort(e) thought that the actors in the films were insufferable, talking in a way that would never work in real life. Sheba, on the other hand, found the movies fascinating. They watched *The Wizard of Oz* so many times that the Old Man asked for a moratorium. He didn't understand why people would simply burst into song, especially when hunted by flying monkeys, and he bristled when Sheba suggested that he resembled the Cowardly Lion. When the VCR mercifully died, they moved on to books. In the previous winter, they'd recovered a stash of paperbacks in an abandoned cabin. Mort(e) had started and stopped three books in the last month, the most recent being *Paradise Lost*. He took it personally when he didn't like a book, though that seemed to be his way of enjoying it. Sheba meanwhile told him about a volume on naval destroyers of the Civil War, her fourth book about the sea in the last six weeks. Mort(e) asked why she stopped reading the other stories she liked, tales about warriors, both animal and human—Joan of Arc, the Greek myths, all that. When she said she wanted to see the ocean, Mort(e) suggested that they find a canoe and take it upriver, so she could get a taste of the seafaring life. It sounded like a good idea, but she wondered if he merely meant to placate her. A canoe ride was a long way from sailing the Atlantic.

When the conversation died down, Sheba finally told him that she was worried about the beavers. "Did they have another fight with the bats?"

"Probably," Mort(e) said. He reminded her that beavers can dig in the ground, and bats can fly away. They'd both be fine.

"Are you thinking about moving the herd again?" she asked.

"I've been thinking about it for a while."

They had maybe one more summer here. Whether people interfered with their way of life, or the herd dwindled to a few sickly Alphas, they couldn't stay forever.

"And besides," he said.

"Besides what?"

Mort(e) took his time, popping a hunk of meat into his mouth and chewing. "You want to see what's out there."

Mort(e) carried the plates to the kitchen. Sheba remained on the couch. She used the poker to flip the smoldering log onto its side. Mort(e) said he would go to bed early. Sheba told him she'd join him soon enough, that she was in the middle of a chapter on a big naval battle. Once she heard Mort(e)'s body settle into the bed, she watched the fire until it died out. Then she quietly entered the bedroom and curled next to Mort(e) and fell asleep.

SHEBA WOKE IN a panic. Early morning light penetrated the blinds. Mort(e) sat propped on his elbows, his ears stiff on his head, whiskers fluttering. He smelled it, too. Some intruder—an animal. Maybe more than one. Not Chingachgook. Not a beaver at all, or a bat. Something she did not recognize. She reached for the rifle under her side of the bed. Mort(e) retrieved his. They rose silently from the mattress.

They had rehearsed this scenario many times, so much in fact that Sheba began to resent Mort(e)'s constant need for preparation and planning. And yet, as her heart raced, she watched herself do the things Mort(e) taught her. She belly-crawled past the bedroom window to the hallway. Then she took her sword from a hook and strapped it over her shoulder. Rifles raised, she and Mort(e) headed for the kitchen. No one had been inside. Everything remained in place. The plates from the night before sat in the sink. She gave Mort(e) a thumbs up, and they moved to the den. They checked the peepholes drilled in the wall. She saw nothing, though the odor of beavers now mingled with the mysterious animal scent. Mort(e) knelt by the door, cracked it open. She stood behind him, her finger on her trigger. With the interior secure, they would scan the perimeter.

Outside, a spiral staircase led to a crow's nest on the rooftop. Mort(e) went up first. Sheba took cover behind the steps. The sun rose behind them, spreading a shadow from the cabin to the edge of the woods. To her left, the Alphas milled about the pen.

The plan for dealing with intruders called for her to wait at the bottom of the staircase until Mort(e) gave the signal. But then the strange scent drifted by once again, a thick smell. Definitely a meat-eater, a predator. The dread she felt leaked into her legs, making them go weak. In a panic, but still drawn to the scent, she climbed the steps and joined Mort(e) in the crow's nest. He glared at her.

"What's that smell?" she whispered.

Mort(e) kept his rifle on the wooden railing.

"Mort(e)."

"It's another dog," he said, still aiming at an invisible target in the forest.

It hurt him to say it. It was another way he had failed her, another compromise he made to keep them safe. They were so sheltered here, so isolated, that Sheba had never seen another dog before.

"Are you sure it's not a wolf?" she asked.

"No. I'm not."

The herd broke its formation, with half the ants running away from the house in a stampede, spooked by some movement near the tree line. Mort(e) aimed in that direction. Sheba propped her rifle beside his. She spotted someone slinking along the far side of the fence, trying to hide behind the grazing Alphas. Sheba pointed at the dark shape. Mort(e) nodded.

They lifted their rifles from the railing, hopped onto the roof, and ran across it toward the pen. At the edge, they jumped, landing hard enough to scare the intruder. The creature ran, a little bouncing ball of fur. Had to be a beaver. Mort(e) and Sheba turned the corner of the fence to find the rodent waddling away as fast as he could. Sheba trained her sights on him.

"Stop!" someone shouted. "Don't shoot! We surrender!"

The beaver froze. Meanwhile, a dog popped out from behind the trees. White belly and face, with black hair on his shoulders, spine, and tail. Sheba recognized the breed from one of her nature books—a husky. The dog shrugged off a backpack and tossed it to the side. He dropped to his knees and put his hands behind his head.

"If you're going to shoot someone, shoot me," the dog said. "This was my idea."

The beaver cowered. Sheba recognized him. The matriarch's son, Castor. The one who would lead Lodge City into a golden age. If she didn't kill him.

Mort(e) signaled to Sheba to keep an eye on the beaver. As she got closer, Castor curled into the fetal position, shaking. "I'm sorry," he whimpered. He posed no threat. Sheba stayed fixated on this strange wolf-dog with the light blue eyes.

"We'll shoot whomever we want," Mort(e) said.

"Would you like to know what we're doing here?" the husky asked.

"It doesn't matter."

"We need your help," the husky said. "And we want to help you."

"We don't need your help."

"Just give me a chance to explain."

"You're still alive, and you're asking for *another* favor?"

"Old Man," Sheba said. "I want to hear what this dog has to say for himself."

Husky and beaver exhaled. "If we don't like what he has to tell us, we'll feed him to the ants," she said, unsheathing her sword. "Piece by piece. The beaver, too."

Mort(e) grinned.

Sheba turned to the dog, her anger tempered by sheer fascination.

"This had better be good," she said.

# CHAPTER 5

## HOSANNA

THE MORGUE SMELLED as bad as Wawa remembered. The rubbing alcohol and antiseptic spray could not mask the putrid gasses swelling the abdomens of the dead. Several people told her that she would get used to it eventually, but they were all humans, with a sense of smell so weak it was a wonder why they had snouts at all. As soon as she entered, Wawa could feel the stink latching onto her fur, becoming encrusted in it, as if the deceased needed this last reminder of their presence on Earth. The odor contrasted sharply with the immaculate linoleum floors, aqua-colored wall tiles, fresh sheets on the stretchers, and gleaming, polished steel cabinets. They could hose this place with bleach and it would still reek for a thousand years.

The pathologist on hand when she arrived—a human named Marquez with salt-and-pepper hair—greeted her in his lab coat and tennis shoes. "Good morning, Chief," he said, emphasizing the word *morning*. It was 5:00 A.M., and only the Chief of Tranquility had the authority to get him out of bed for an unscheduled visit.

Marquez spoke with an accent different from most of the humans here. He came from Venezuela, one of the countries overrun by the Colony in the early days of the war. *He's seen some things*, the humans often said. He once witnessed a horde of Alphas attacking an oil refinery. The ants tore open the wells, incinerating themselves in great geysers of flame. Marquez knew then that he couldn't fight them. He could only run.

Wawa stood in the corner while Marquez opened one of the cabinets. A slab glided out. The body of a dog lay under a white tarp. The head leaned to the side, allowing the fabric to mold around the face, the matted black fur visible through the covering. Marquez yanked the tarp away. The dog's brown eyes were sunken into the skull. The mouth had petrified into a grin of blackish-gray gums and yellow teeth. A line of stitches crisscrossed the belly. And above the dog's eye, a hole crusted over with dried blood, the obvious cause of death now resembling a minor scrape.

"You wait here," Marquez said. He went to the cold storage locker to retrieve the other body that Wawa had requested.

Wawa placed her hand on the dog's snout and rolled the head in the opposite direction, taking note of the surprising weight of it. The desiccated eyeball watched her with a dilated pupil. Whatever pierced the skull failed to leave an exit wound on the other side. Yet the autopsy could find no projectile, nor any fragments. The wound did not match the weapons typically used for stabbing. Even after Marquez assured her that they found nothing, Wawa ordered multiple X-rays. None yielded the magic bullet. Marquez cursed in Spanish each time.

Wawa saw plenty of dead dogs in the war. Too many to cry over. In this windowless room, however, the corpse reminded her of the cages in which she was raised. In those days, her master brought in smaller pups for her to kill, so that she could build her strength for the arena. She left them in a similar state to this murder victim, with a face frozen in death. In Wawa's dreams, her master put her in the arena to fight Cyrus, her only friend, long gone. Some nights, Wawa would crawl to a corner and wait for Cyrus to maul her to death. Other nights, she would attack, and would watch him die all over again. No matter what she chose, Cyrus never seemed to recognize her.

In the hallway, a pair of boots stamped on the linoleum. Marquez wore sneakers, so someone else must have entered the building. When Wawa caught a whiff of hazelnut coffee, she knew that Strator Grace Braga had arrived. Unannounced, of course.

Grace entered the room with one hand gripping an open thermos. She took a sip, screwed on the cap, and set it on the counter. The strator had an olive complexion with a pockmarked face. Probably an ugly child who grew into something more fierce than beautiful—a bird of prey rather than a swan. Grace wore a khaki vest over a black T-shirt, with camouflage pants and tan boots. A handgun hung from her hip, alongside extra magazines on her belt. Thus, she resembled many of the human soldiers in Hosanna—except for the rings. Grace belonged to an all-human unit known as the Sons of Adam. They protected the Prophet Michael, and every strator wore circular tattoos symbolizing their devotion and obedience. The ring around her neck represented the yoke she took on. The one on her finger meant that she would never marry. The one on her wrist had something to do with her pulse, to show that she offered her very blood to the cause. Yet another ring circled Grace's heel. As with the legendary Achilles, this one reminded the strators that they were human, plagued with weaknesses that their enemies could exploit. It must have been the most painful one, given that it went around the sole of the foot. No wonder Grace was rarely in a good mood.

While male strators wore a tattoo on their side, a reference to the story of God fashioning Eve from Adam's rib, Grace wore a tattoo around her left breast to show that she would not have children, that her milk would stay in her body. Grace, however, already had a daughter, a girl named Maddie born shortly after the war began. Wawa could imagine Grace stealing food for her daughter, telling those around her that they would keep her alive no matter what. It was a testament to Grace's reputation that the Sons of Adam let her join, and chose her to lead, despite her status as a mother. But Grace earned it, having once killed a canine soldier with her bare hands. At least, that's what the strators said. And besides, Maddie would one day fight alongside her.

"Are you going to explain what you're doing here, Chief?" Grace said.

"Good morning, Strator. I'm just following up on a hunch."

"You know that the Sons of Adam need to be informed of your investigation."

"I planned to give you a report in the morning."

"You *planned* to do this without me. But here I am, bright and early."

The rusty wheels of a stretcher squeaked in the hallway. The body entered first, covered with a sheet, with the doctor pushing from behind. The presence of the strator startled Marquez, but he quickly composed himself and wished her a good morning.

The corpse barely fit on the stretcher. Unnatural bumps poked the sheet, making the body resemble a pile of meat rather than a creature that had once walked and breathed. A powerful stench of ammonia and rotten fish leaked from under the covering.

"Bring it closer to the dog," Wawa said. She took a pair of rubber gloves from a cardboard box and snapped them on.

Marquez lifted the sheet to reveal the monster underneath. Part fish, part crab, part cephalopod. A bulbous head. Black eyes. Segmented armor on the spine, with four tentacles unfurling from within. Two jointed claws extending from the shoulders, with longer ones at the pelvis that could be used for walking. A long tail with spikes on the end of it. Wawa had seen it only once, a day or two after it had been found dead in the river, near the new dam. A bullet had struck it in the neck, probably fired from a fishing boat. Already weakened by illness and starvation, the beast apparently bled to death and drifted to the riverbank. Wawa noticed Grace's reluctance to get closer. This abomination scared even the Sons of Adam.

Wawa gripped one of the tentacles and lifted it to her face to examine the barbed suckers. Her palms went numb from the coldness of the flesh. A clear, icy slime collected on her glove as she slid her hand along the appendage to the tip. A bony spike protruded from the end. Wawa extended it to the hole in the dog's head.

"What do you think you're doing, Chief?" Grace asked.

"Trying to find a murder weapon."

She could tell right away that the spike was too thick to match the wound. Grace leaned in to watch as Wawa tried the other tentacles, along with the tips of the claws. Nothing fit.

"Hmm," Grace said. She took a sip of her coffee. "You do realize that Mr. Fish here died long before the dog was killed."

"I do. And it's Miss Fish to you. My guess is that she's laid eggs before."

"Either way, she couldn't have done it."

"No. But there are others out there. I don't think all those reported sightings are wrong."

"Surely you must have some suspected motive in mind if you're here this early."

"To be honest, I thought that if we could link the murders to the fish-heads, the motive would become apparent." Wawa let the tentacle drop, annoyed with herself for even trying to explain. Regardless of the strator's authority, Wawa was the Chief of Tranquility, and she would investigate as she saw fit.

"Marquez, I'd like to see the records on all the murder victims," Wawa said.

"Chief."

"—I want to know the measurements on the wounds—"

"Chief," Grace repeated. "That won't be necessary."

"Why not?"

"We've already done all of that."

"Who's done what?"

"The Sons of Adam looked into this a week ago. There is no reason to suspect that these creatures are behind the murders." She took another slurp of coffee.

It took a moment for the smug tone to settle in, and another for the words to make sense. The Sons of Adam had gone behind Wawa's back again, acting as if they ran everything and reported to no one. They spoke for Michael now, and claimed that the Prophet could intercede on their behalf. Each of them told their own wild tales of miraculous healings, visions, speaking in tongues, communing with the dead. Grace's daughter suffered from epileptic seizures, sometimes so bad that they required Grace to hold the child down and let her bite on the fleshy part of her hand. Michael supposedly pleaded to God on Maddie's behalf, and the girl had not experienced an episode in years. The Prophet favored these warriors, and thus they could get away with whatever they wanted.

With her feet growing cold on the morgue floor, Wawa had a sudden desire to take the day off, go home, and sleep under a comforter. "Marquez, put all of this away," she said. She refused to acknowledge Grace on her way out.

Outside, the sky turned pink. The morgue was located at the southern end of the city, in a concrete government building close to the old navy yard. Still grumbling, Wawa trudged across the cracked asphalt, heading for the open space on the waterfront where she could gather her thoughts. To the north, the broken skyscrapers stood watch. The giant airship *Vesuvius* was tethered to a temporary platform on the thirty-third floor of the Liberty One building. Her sister ship, the *Upheaval*, formed a tiny dot on the horizon as it hovered on patrol. One day, Wawa thought, the strators might get tired of this place and hop in their ships and fly away. Two lifeboats to take them to safety, so they could start over. With a new god, if need be.

Northeast of the navy yard, a suspension bridge once known as the Walt Whitman had been sheared in the middle, creating a gap between its two towers. The steel cables hung like untied shoelaces. Beyond that, the new dam formed a monolith that connected both sides of the river. On the other side, the Camden waterfront moldered, a ruin of burned-out husks. The battleship USS *New Jersey* rested partially submerged, its cannons rusting and its name peeling off.

Wawa parked herself on a bench by the river. A full day still awaited her. Her subordinates owed her a report on the latest crop of refugees requesting asylum. Apparently, some cats were demanding a feline-only housing unit, a form of species segregation explicitly banned in Hosanna. Elsewhere, a group of rodents balked at helping with the cleanup of the quarantined neighborhoods, which was understood as the price of admission to the city. After dealing with all that, Wawa would have to speak at an initiation ceremony for a new class of cadets, where she would shake their hands and tell them that they would make a difference.

"Chief," Grace said, somewhere behind her. The strator was a little out of breath after running, thermos in hand.

"What can I do for you, Strator?"

"We're not done catching up."

Grace removed the cap from the thermos and poured some of the coffee into it. "Would you care for some?"

"No." Grace knew damn well that Wawa preferred tea, and drank it so often that her subordinates sometimes played jokes by hanging tea bags on her office doorknob.

"I tried to quit this stuff years ago," Grace said. "Three days later, the Alphas took Boston. I never stopped drinking it since.

Bad things happen without it." A pause followed. "You needed to see that creature again, didn't you?" Grace said.

"Yes."

"Ugly little bitch, isn't she? Those eyes, my God."

"I think she's beautiful. Marquez tells me she's adapted in extraordinary ways."

"They're abominations, same as the Alphas. And once people realize that, we're going to have a panic on our hands far worse than any quarantine."

"I've survived a quarantine," Wawa said.

"I know."

The sun burst over the rubble of Camden, forcing Wawa to squint.

"I'm putting in a request with the Archon," Grace said. "The Sons of Adam will be handling the investigation from here on. I wanted to tell you to your face."

Wawa knew it was coming. Grace had already demanded resources from Tranquility, invoking the name of the Prophet. She even had the gall to suggest that all Special Operations agents in the field be summoned to Hosanna.

"You don't have the authority to do that," Wawa said.

"Not yet. But we will. Don't fight me on this, Chief. You'll lose."

"Are you threatening me, Strator?" Her fangs protruded when she said it.

"If that's what it takes to get you to listen, then yes."

If Culdesac were here, he would have chided Wawa for letting this human live so long.

"I was at Golgotha," Wawa said. "I shed blood right next to the humans."

"I don't care about the past. Ask the Archon for a medal if you need one."

Wawa stood. "Do you know who you're talking to?"

"Save your Red Sphinx routine for the cadets," Grace said. "You know why the strators need to handle this. We can't have any more fuckups from Tranquility, like last time."

Wawa knew what she meant. Tranquility took the blame for anything that went wrong. Only a few months earlier, Special Operations tried to establish contact with the Rama satellite, a device designed to harness sunlight and reflect it onto the earth. Paired with the new solar farms, the Rama would provide an additional source of energy. But the agents failed. And so, the device—a decade-long effort costing billions of dollars—orbited the earth silently, uselessly. From then on, the humans referred to it as the "ramen" satellite, which, Wawa was told, meant that it was cheap and worthless. And, to add salt to the wound, one of the strators—a short, stocky man named Harold Pham—suggested that the animals as a whole were to blame. "The people who knew how to work that satellite were killed in the war," he said. "*Murdered*. Everything they knew died with them."

"No need to dwell on the past," Grace said. "All I care about is protecting the Prophet. Now, we've both reached the same conclusion about these murders, haven't we? This latest victim has the same . . . background . . . as the others. Correct?"

"Yes. We tracked down his records last night."

"Then the Prophet is in danger. I can't leave this in anyone else's hands. I just can't."

"Right," Wawa said. "We can't have animals running things, can we?"

"Don't forget that every strator lost someone in the war," Grace said. "All because some animal that they fed and cared for just turned on them one day."

The humans were not supposed to talk like this. But the rules did not apply to strators. "I remember the last time I spoke with my family," Grace said. She told Wawa about being stationed at Fort Hood, before the war. She received a call on her cell from her grandmother in Florida. Apparently, the old woman accidentally dialed the number. At first, Grace shouted, hoping someone would hear. "I said, 'Mima, Mima!' Nothing." But then she settled in and listened as the family gathered around the dinner table and exchanged stories, the voices going from English to Spanish and back again. She heard the utensils scraping on the plates. She heard her Mima scold the younger ones who would not sit still. The call ended suddenly. Grace would not let herself cry. Until, that is, a few days later, when the ants overran four American cities, and blacked out most of Europe. She never got the chance to tell her Mima about it.

"I know you lost people, too," Grace said. "But not like we did."

"Of course not," Wawa said.

Grace made it a point to lean in so that her coffee breath brushed the fur on Wawa's face. "If anyone threatens the peace—even those people who don't even realize what they're doing—I swear I will make them regret it. Tell everyone in Tranquility if you have to."

"Happy to share it, Grace."

Grace placed her index and forefinger on her temple, tapped them on her chest, and extended her palm—a Blessing of Michael meant as a sign of respect to the Prophet. Then she twisted the cap on the thermos and walked away. Wawa sat on the bench and savored the last few minutes before she would have to go to work. She would waste part of her day thinking of what she could have said to Grace, and would probably end up in the morgue again to gawk at another body.

# CHAPTER 6

## ARMOR

**HE DOG AND** the beaver waited, kneeling in the dewy grass, hands behind their heads. Castor whimpered. The husky remained calm, even with Sheba's sword hovering under his chin. He placed his ID card on the ground and invited Mort(e) to inspect it. The card had the seal of the Sanctuary Union government, along with an illegible signature from the Chief of Tranquility. If not official, then at least an impressive forgery. Mort(e) would have preferred a wolf to someone from Hosanna, the human-run theocracy. He returned the card, and cursed his decision to build the ranch here rather than deeper in the woods.

The beaver blurted out a string of nonsense about some monster attacking Lodge City. "We had nowhere else to go, I swear."

"Darling, we haven't fed the ants any real meat lately," Mort(e) said.

"No, we haven't."

One of the Alphas butted her head against the fence. Castor jumped.

"Please let me tell you why we're here," the husky said.

"Let me tell *you* a story first," Mort(e) said. "Two people—a dog and a cat—survived the war, came out here to start a new life. And they promised that if anyone bothered them, they'd put the bastard's head on a pike, human style. Our beaver friend here didn't get the message, so we'll have to be a little more forward."

"If you give us a chance, I swear," Castor said.

"No," Mort(e) said. "No, I'm done." He turned to Sheba. "Should we shoot them first, and then feed them to the ants?"

"Old Man…"

"You're right. Alive then. The ants like to hunt."

Sheba lowered the sword and gestured to the house, signalling that she wanted to take them inside. This had gone far enough for her taste. He pinned his ears to his skull, as if to ask, *Really?* She scrunched her snout. *Yes, really*.

"You, husky," he said. "Tell her thank you for saving your life. Say it like you mean it."

"Thank you," the dog said with a bow.

"Now you," Mort(e) said to Castor.

"Oh, yes, thank you. Thank you."

Mort(e) gave Sheba another look. *Happy now?* She nodded yes.

THEY GATHERED AROUND the kitchen table sipping a sugary drink that Mort(e) brewed from his honey farm. Falkirk the husky laid out the story of what happened to Lodge City. A new mutation, the kind that had been rumored for years, had seized control of the town. An amphibious spider nicknamed Gulaga, almost as big as the Queen but more mobile. Castor filled in the rest, giving names of people killed. Sheba asked about Chingachgook, and Castor said that he had gone missing, presumably trapped in the web.

When Falkirk admitted that Nikaya had revealed their secret, Mort(e) pounded his fist on the table. "I told you," he said to Sheba. "Didn't I tell you they'd sell us out?"

"You told me."

Mort(e) asked about sending for help, perhaps by dispatching a bird patrol to the nearest outpost. Falkirk waved him off. "No time for that. We're on our own."

"What makes you think *we* can help?" Mort(e) asked. "You'd need an army for this. And don't tell me you believe all those legends about us."

"You mean the one where you're ten feet tall, or the one where you walk on water?"

Sheba laughed. "Or the one where I'm the most beautiful dog in the whole world."

Falkirk snorted, tilting his head in thought. This brief exchange between the two dogs triggered a gnawing sensation in Mort(e)'s gut, like a hand clawing its way out. His tail stiffened. In a quick flash, like images in a flip-book, he imagined this husky in his bed with Sheba, coiled around her, as his human masters had done years earlier.

"What did you expect to find here?" Mort(e) asked.

"Guns, mainly," Falkirk said.

"It doesn't sound like they'll do much good."

"They might. We have a plan."

With that, Castor pulled a map from his satchel and unrolled it on the table. Falkirk pointed out the stadium, the heart of the web.

"What are those red dots?" Sheba asked. Mort(e) counted eight of them.

"Eggs," the beaver said.

"Eggs," Mort(e) repeated, dragging out the word.

"I would have expected the spider to keep them close," Falkirk added. "But they're spread out. Maybe as a defense system. Or maybe because if they hatch all at once, the young ones will eat the mother."

"This keeps getting better," Mort(e) said.

Tracing the images on the map, Falkirk indicated the access points to the town—the river and an old highway exit—both of which might allow a person to sneak in. Mort(e) glanced at Sheba, who watched the husky as he spoke. She did not respond right away, so Mort(e) shifted in his seat to get her attention. When their eyes met, Mort(e) sarcastically stroked his chin.

"Are you listening?" Falkirk asked.

"Your plan is going to get someone killed." Mort(e) slapped his palms on the map and spun it toward him. He pointed at the river. "You call this an entrance here? Let's be honest. The only way you can get a clean shot at this spider is by using someone as bait. Say I get stuck in the web. Are *you* going to save me?"

Falkirk lowered his eyes.

"How about you, Bucktooth?" Mort(e) asked Castor. "If you have a chance to free your friends or me, who you gonna choose?"

Sheba let out a loud sigh.

"The way I see it," Mort(e) said, "that town shouldn't even be there. Maybe it upset the balance of things. For all we know, that spider is simply reclaiming her territory."

"That's not fair," Castor said. "We were careful to make this a self-sufficient city."

"Oh, really? So sufficient you had to kick the bats out, right?"

Castor and Falkirk turned to Sheba for help. She chuckled. "You got him started," she said.

Castor tried to make another point. Falkirk held out his palm to silence him.

"You're right," Falkirk said. "My plan is terrible. I've never done this before."

"No one has," Sheba said.

"But there is another reason I needed to find you."

"If the job of messiah is still open, I'm not interested," Mort(e) said.

"It's not that. It's the murders that have been taking place in the city. You've heard about it from the merchants, haven't you?"

Mort(e) looked to Sheba. She was the one who liked to hear gossip from the capital.

"Chingachgook told me about it," she said.

Falkirk folded his hands and rested them under his snout. The table creaked as Sheba leaned in. "The murder victims have one thing in common," he said. "Every single one of them has used a translator."

The translator—the device used to communicate with the ants. It scrambled the brain, crippled the user. But it also provided access to the limitless knowledge of the Queen. The never-ending sorrow of hundreds of years of bloodshed. Mort(e) almost died trying to use one, and was never the same afterward. The over-flowing information faded away, but whispers of it remained. He experienced déjà vu while reading, while listening to music or the noises of the forest at night, as though millions of other lives had been crammed into his mind. He had changed twice, really. The day he became sentient, and the day he became like the Queen. Like a god, only with amnesia.

"Why would someone try to kill people who used the transla-tor?" Sheba asked.

"We don't know. But there are plenty of people out there who view the Queen's experiment as an abomination. Maybe they think they're cleansing the earth of her presence."

"If anyone comes here looking for a translator user, they'll be sorry," Mort(e) said.

"I hope you're right. But whether you help us or not, you can't hide anymore. The world will come looking for you."

Another glance from Sheba, this one saying, *he's right*.

"Your prophet, Michael," Mort(e) said. "He's used the transla-tor more than anyone." His voice trailed off. He pictured the boy the last time he saw him, a skinny child, too small for his age, incoherent and spouting nonsense. An odor of despair hanging over him.

"He's safe," Falkirk said. "An elite unit guards him. Human soldiers."

Mort(e) shifted the map over to Sheba. He had trained her to seek out the weak points, the high ground, the escape routes, the way Culdesac taught him. He watched the disappointment wash over her eyes when she failed to find any of them.

"I'm sorry," Mort(e) said. "You should never attack unless you know you can win. And this gulag as you call it is an unwinnable situation."

Sheba's head dropped as she slid the map toward Castor. "We can give you some rifles."

"Sheba," Mort(e) said.

Her head lifted, and her eyes drilled into Mort(e). "Okay, okay," he said.

Castor rolled the map into a tube and stuffed it into his bag. The two guests stood up, their chairs squeaking awkwardly on the floor.

Sheba stayed seated, her hands folded in her lap. Mort(e) gave her a second to join them. When she remained still, he told the others to wait outside.

"You know I'm right," he said.

"You're always right, Old Man."

Mort(e) led Falkirk and Castor to the garage. Inside, firearms of every kind hung on hooks attached to the walls. It took a few seconds for Mort(e)'s guests to take it all in.

A rack on the floor held six rifles with scopes. Remington 770s with bolt action. Mort(e) let the beaver and the husky each take one, along with two boxes of ammunition.

"Great," Falkirk said. "Maybe I can shoot the hostages before the spider eats them."

"That's a good idea," Mort(e) said. "I should mention as well that we have enough explosives to level the town."

"We're trying to *save* the town," Castor said.

"Let's go," Falkirk said. "Thank you."

They took the pebbled trail leading into the woods. Castor slowed and turned to Mort(e). "I heard stories about you," the beaver said. "I heard that you helped people." Castor told him where to find the refugee camp, in case he changed his mind. "Maybe you'll remember what you were like, and you'll come join us."

"I'm remembering right now," Mort(e) said. "Those stories you heard were meant to manipulate you. To get you to stop facing the real world."

Castor pulled his goggles over his eyes.

"There are spiders everywhere," Mort(e) added. "*That's* the real world."

With that, the two intruders disappeared into the forest.

PERCHED ON THE roof, Mort(e) used the claw of a hammer to pry away more rotted shingles. When the sun rose above the trees, Sheba stomped out of the house and mounted one of the stronger Alphas. They had a ritual when she took the herd out on a walk. He would say, "Be good to my girls," and she would correct him: "Ladies." This time the entire herd marched away from him in silence, all of them following the lead ant with the dog sitting on her thorax.

Mort(e) was ready to talk when Sheba returned a few hours later. But she would not acknowledge him. Instead, she led the ants into their pen, leaning over and patting them on the side to get them moving, all while speaking softly and sometimes even smiling at them.

She went inside. Mort(e) had replaced all of the tiles by then. Instead of joining her in the house, he went to the garage once more, a mausoleum decorated with the tools of his trade. He picked out a rifle at random and cleaned it. Before long, he had taken apart and reassembled a number of weapons, simply to pass the time.

• ∘ •

MORT(E) ENTERED THE house at dusk. Sheba had left him some food from the cupboard. They usually took turns cooking. Tonight, there was a hunk of smoked Alpha jerky on a plate with a bowl of water next to it. The dried meat felt cold in his hands. It took five minutes to make it through two mouthfuls. He dropped the rest of it on the plate and went outside to find Sheba.

As he expected, she was tending to the Alphas. Using a shovel, she tossed piles of slop from the compost bin into the grazing area. Sheba emptied the bin once a month, providing a treat for the ants. As usual, the Alphas gathered in a formation, with the first in line collecting her share of food and moving to the rear to let the others go next.

Sheba must have sensed Mort(e)'s presence, and yet she kept shoveling with her tail to him. One of the weaker ants, named Cromwell, was too hobbled to eat the food off the ground. Her legs shook whenever she lowered her head. Sheba let the ant eat from the shovel. As she chewed the food, Cromwell's antennae came to life, probing Sheba's arms. Sheba let her do it, ignoring an antenna that clumsily bumped her in the snout.

"It's okay, girl," she said as a cloud passed overhead.

When Cromwell finished, Sheba continued tossing the feed over the fence.

"Say what you have to say, Old Man." She wouldn't look at him.

"There's nothing we can do for them."

"I heard that already."

"Those beavers brought this on themselves. They redirected the river. Carved out the forest. Exiled the bats."

"Heard that, too."

"Well, I guess I came out here to see what you had to say."

Sheba threw the last shovelful over the fence and leaned on the handle. "Oh, *now* you want to hear it? Well, I sound like a broken record, just like you."

"You're not happy here."

"Don't start. I never said that. It's just that we've isolated ourselves on this ranch, and you've put that ahead of everything else."

"I've put our safety ahead of everything else."

"Stop it."

She slammed the shovel on the ground and walked past him, toward the house. The oblivious ants continued to feed, some of them licking the scraps off their sisters' hides. Mort(e) watched her getting smaller, the way he had years earlier, when they were both still pets, still slaves. When he was too powerless to protect her. He had never been able to convey to Sheba the helplessness he felt in that moment, a mere house cat who barely understood what lay beyond the walls of his master's house. He never made it clear to her what he was willing to do to avoid feeling that way again. To avoid failing her again.

"Hey," Mort(e) said, running to her. "I'll protect us from myself if I have to. Do you understand? I'm making up for a ton of bad decisions here. Going all the way back. Back to when I first met you."

Sheba stopped. "You don't owe me for what happened to my children, Old Man. You couldn't have saved them. And I don't owe you for bringing me here. Not anymore."

"It's not about owing. It's about putting the people you love first."

"There are *people* in that town!" she said. "Not enemies. Not animals. People."

"I've seen people get killed, Sheba. You think I don't know—"

"Don't give me another speech about the war. Please, not now."

"Well, that's why the husky came to me for help, isn't it? I know about war."

"Yes, and little else."

Mort(e) spun away from her, trying to think of something else to say. Many miles away, Lodge City was silent, its lines of smoke extinguished.

"I'm going to the camp tomorrow," Sheba said. "To see if I can do anything. Don't you dare talk to me unless you want to help."

She left him standing there. When the door shut behind her, the sound echoed from some empty space inside of him.

MORT(E) WISHED THAT this house included a basement, like his first home. A cool, dark cellar with a scratchy rug and a furnace that kicked on at odd hours. This bungalow, with its creaking hardwood floors, offered no such solitude. That night, while Mort(e) slept in the den, he could hear Sheba fidgeting in the bed they normally shared.

Mort(e) and Sheba usually spent the night twisting into various poses, dancing in their sleep. He'd rest his head on her ribs and listen to the air go in and out. She'd face away from him, their spines touching, sending warmth down to their tails. Or they would reverse-spoon, head to tail, the smaller cat forming a circle inside of the dog's outstretched limbs. Their bodies changed, and yet the ritual remained.

Alone on the carpet, however, Mort(e) contorted into unfamiliar positions, each one leaving him chilled. The pillows provided a poor substitute for Sheba. He fell asleep grudgingly, his mouth propped open so that his tongue went dry, his whiskers crumpled awkwardly against his face, his tail squeezed between his hip and the floor. The dreams began with two-dimensional images of his master's house scrolling by. He could not even lift his hand to touch them. *Stop*, he said. *Stop. I know it's a dream. I'm waking up now.*

But he couldn't escape. He inhabited his former body here, standing only a foot off the ground. Though Mort(e) refused to move, the dream shuffled him along anyway. He had grown used to it by now. Ever since using the translator, certain dreams repeated themselves, like Sheba's videos. The Queen's revenge on those who trespassed into her world.

He floated along the carpet, up the stairs, past the room where his masters slept. *Fine*, he thought. *Let's do it again*. He traversed the house like some spirit pushed by the wind. He could smell Sheba. Every room he entered, her scent grew stronger, and yet he could not find her. Passing by the children's room, he heard Michael calling to him. *Help me*, the boy said. *In here. Save me*. Another useless echo of the translator. A misfiring in his brain. He ignored it. The camera-like view peered under the bed, poked into closets and behind the big chair in the living room. He should have seen her by now. That was how the dream worked. She would be reclining in their spot in the basement, or leashed in the driveway, or sitting obediently by the kitchen door.

Instead, he heard water sloshing against the walls. The room tilted. At the window, a new odor greeted him—salt, creeping into his throat. Outside, an ocean extended as far as he could see, disappearing under a fog. Everything he remembered drowned in the waves—the telephone poles, the neighboring houses, the cars. The house became a drifting boat, an ark ferrying them through a flooded world. He could hear the hull groaning.

The house was sinking.

Bluish-green water climbed the steps. Somewhere in the house, he could hear it gushing from a breach in the foundation. The water lapped at the great mirror that hung from the wall. Photo frames and vases slid from the mantelpiece and splashed into the water. Mort(e) retreated to the attic, the place he once took Sheba when they were still pets. She had to be here, hiding under an old coat or in a cardboard box.

The water overwhelmed her scent. It did not care that Sheba had disappeared. It simply flowed into the empty places, following a path of least resistance.

Mort(e) woke to find the sky brightening from black to purple. He sat up. It took a few deep inhales for him to accept that the salt water had not followed him into the real world.

MORT(E) KNEW WHAT to do. His mind narrowed to his training, leaving no room for questions or doubts. He slipped into those days during the war, when he would gear up in freezing temperatures, in the rain, in the middle of a mortar attack with his left ear partially deafened. Then as now, he would prepare himself to die without seeing Sheba again.

In the garage, Mort(e) started with a tactical vest, a lightweight camo with four pockets in the front. In the pouches, he placed salted Alpha meat, a water bottle, and a grenade. He fastened a utility belt around his waist, to which he clipped a small first aid kit and mini-binoculars. Then he turned to the guns. A CZ 550 elephant rifle with a sniper scope, and a bandolier of bullets capable of piercing concrete. The oil smelled stale to him, so he disassembled the rifle, greased it, and put it together again. As much as he hated wearing shoes, he opted for a pair of Army-issue desert boots, specially fitted for him at Camp Delta during the war. Their steel tips could snap a human femur if he kicked hard enough.

He went outside to listen to his clumsy boots on the gravel path. Too loud, he thought, but he would take them anyway. The front door of the house opened and Sheba stepped out. With her eyelids drooping, she took inventory of the weapons that weighed him down.

"I know how we can save the hostages," he said. "I *think* I know."

"You wanna help now?" she said, yawning.

"I can help all of us, actually."

"What does that mean?"

"I'm going to talk to the bats. Maybe we can broker a peace deal."

"The bats hate the beavers."

"I think I can bring them on board. They just need the right incentive."

"Which is?"

"The same thing we want. A home. Safety. Being left alone."

Grimacing, Sheba tightened the straps on his vest, like a human mother fixing a hopelessly disheveled boy. She palmed the grenade, shook her head, and then let it dangle. "You said it would be impossible."

"No. I said unwinnable."

"Whatever. You said it would take an army."

"It will."

"Where do we get one?"

Mort(e) pointed at the pen. The Alphas arranged themselves in rows like an audience entranced by a play.

"They're not lasting through this season," Mort(e) said. "We can either put them down, one by one, or we can let them go out like real ants."

"Okay," Sheba said. She repeated it a few times until her voice trailed off.

"Take them to the refugee camp," Mort(e) said. "I'll go to the bats. I should be able to meet you at the camp tomorrow afternoon at the latest."

He explained his plan to attack the city, starting with bat recon, and ending with an Alpha assault. Before he could start comparing it to some battle he had witnessed, Sheba wrapped her arms around him and squeezed until his ribs popped.

"Thank you, Old Man."

Mort(e) let her hug him for a while before telling her he had to go. And even then, they kept hugging, their eyes closed, until the brightening day reminded them that they had work to do. As soon as they disentangled themselves, Mort(e) walked to the trail in the forest.

# PART II
# FLIGHT

# CHAPTER 7

## THE FLOATING ISLAND

HE SARCOPS MOVED north into the frigid, barren waters. Scouts probed the territory, desperate to find food, while a line of Juggernauts protected the rear of the convoy. Taalik's mates circled him closely. Every morning, Orak gave him a report of the dead. Starvation and exhaustion had long since weeded out the older, weaker ones. These days, most of the casualties were young, the recently hatched. Their tender corpses served as food for the others.

At night, Orak kept watch while Taalik mated with the other females. She no longer participated herself. He asked her to continue—perhaps one day the Queen would restore her ability to bear young. But Orak refused. The Sarcops needed Taalik to mate as often as he could. For her to continue simply because he favored her would only hurt everyone else.

The darkness had passed over the water more than sixty times since they left Cold Trench. They had entered some dead zone, devoid of life, where the trenches plunged into oblivion, and choppy, rough currents troubled the surface. The expanse swallowed up the familiar smells—fish, seaweed, a line of crabs trundling across the seabed.

Worst of all, the Queen would not speak to him. This after

months of visions and dreams of the war. At night, he saw the Queen's enemies from afar, the humans, mere shadows marching upright on the horizon, searching for prey. They could summon death from great distances, with sharp objects or machines that flew through the air. Long after these revelations ceased, Orak continued to ask about them. *The Queen shows you these terrible visions*, she said. *She should use her powers to find us food instead.*

One day, scouts returned from an expedition, breathless, darting about in a panic. *What is it?* Taalik asked them. *What did you see?* They tried to describe it: an enormous object resting on the surface of the water. A boat? No, they said. Too large. After some debate, they settled on a term—a floating island. Taalik hoped that it was a chunk of ice, broken off from one of the northern glaciers, a sign that they were getting close. The scouts could not say for sure.

Taalik would have to see for himself. He ordered the convoy to wait, which meant once again asking Orak to keep an eye on things. *Do not speak*, he told her. *Just do. Do what I say.*

Taalik made the trip at night, with nothing but blackness in every direction. As the morning arrived, he sighted the floating island. He recognized it from the many visions the Queen bestowed upon him. The scouts were wrong—it *was* a boat, one of the largest the humans had ever built. A testament to their power, their recklessness. The humans could carve out a chunk of their land and transform it into a moving country. Under any other circumstances, the convoy would have slipped quietly under this metal beast. But things had become so desperate that Taalik wondered if the ship could somehow help their cause. Maybe it contained something his people could use. Or perhaps the Queen placed it here as some kind of test. Once that idea began to claw at him, he knew he would have to venture above the water to face death yet again.

The sun blinded him when he broke the surface. It took a moment for his eyes to moisten. When the blurriness passed, the impossible structure loomed before him. The gray hull of the ship—rusted and freckled with barnacles—had to be the length of over three hundred Sarcops swimming end-to-end. A tower was mounted in the middle. Taalik recognized the machines on the deck from his night journeys with the Queen. They seemed to be made of the same smooth material as the hull, as if the ship had given birth to them. These devices could travel through the air the way his people could move through the water. They resembled fish, with fins and enormous blank eyes.

Having held his breath this entire time, Taalik flapped his gills, opened his mouth, and sucked in the air. He took deeper breaths, until he imagined himself draining away the endless blue that hung over the water. This time, it did not hurt. The air gave him strength.

When Taalik reached the ship, he tapped the smooth metal with his claw. The shell on his back split open, and the four tentacles wriggled out. The suckers gripped the hull. He began to climb.

Near the top, he felt vibrations in the metal. Something moved on the deck. He poked his head over the edge. The flying fish stood tightly packed, some with their wings protruding off the side of the boat. The tower sat dormant, its windows caked in salt. White cylindrical containers were arranged in a group, each brimming with rainwater. Parts of the deck had been sectioned off into large rectangles, covered in dirt and lined with rows of green plants. In the middle of all this, one of the beasts from the land—a human—straddled a machine with two wheels that rolled around on the deck. The solitary monster pedaled his contraption in a loop, his head swaying. The man had white hair and pink skin and a long, red nose. A strange fabric hung loosely over his skeletal frame.

With no one else around, Taalik pulled himself on board and crawled underneath the flying fish. He unraveled his tentacles, making himself appear larger than he really was. When the man spotted him, the riding machine skidded to a halt.

The human spoke. Taalik did not recognize the language at first. The Queen's visions taught him many tongues. It took a moment to place this one.

"Who are you?" the man said. "Can you speak?"

This time Taalik understood.

"Only a matter of time, I guess," the man said. He let the riding machine fall sideways with a clatter. "They took over the land, now they've taken over the water."

Taalik swallowed to loosen his throat muscles. The air dried him out so quickly. "Where?" he asked. He pointed at the deck. "Where . . . are we? What is this . . . place?"

The man's mouth stretched to either side of his face, scrunching the wrinkles around his eyes. He extended both arms. "This is the United States of America!"

Individually, those words made sense. Strung together like this, they meant nothing. "Who are you?" Taalik asked.

"Nathan Finch, Last Man on Earth, and Captain of the USS *Harry S. Truman*, the only unconquered territory left for the Allies. Until today, I guess. Have you come to kill me?"

The man seemed giddy at the prospect. "No," Taalik said.

Nathan Finch grunted. "I guess I'd be dead already. You're going to leave me out here then? Just as well. I can stay here as long as it takes."

"How long? How long . . . here . . . are you?"

Nathan Finch eyed him. Taalik wondered if the man was trying to *smell* him as well. "How long have I been here? Going on twelve years."

The man kept busy all this time by marking the ship with symbols, large pieces of artwork depicting animals and humans in battle. Underneath Taalik's feet, a pack of wild humans chased animals covered in fur, with large ears and teeth. Near the tower, a man drove a spear through the neck of a giant insect. The chalky remnants of the word HELP still clung to the deck, nearly scrubbed away by the elements. Even when they should have gone extinct, these primates dug their claws into the earth and hung on.

"They used to send bird patrols to mess with my head," Nathan Finch said. "But I took out a few of them with the fifty cal. After that, I figured the Queen stopped caring."

Finch admitted that the crew members were all dead. The last few departed in a lifeboat three years earlier. That was the last time the captain had spoken to a real person.

"Have you been to the Queen's island?" the man asked. "Have you seen her?"

"The Queen is gone."

"You mean dead?"

"She lives. In me."

"Okay. So you're not here to kill me. What do you want then?"

"Food. To eat."

"Food to eat, sure."

"You must bring."

The man squinted. "Come with me."

They walked to the tower. Nathan Finch pointed to the curved dish on the roof. "I've spent years trying to hail someone, on every frequency," he said. "And then a talking fish comes aboard."

While the man rambled on, Taalik examined the ship more closely. Near some of the painted images of battle, Taalik noticed a depiction of a man wearing Nathan Finch's uniform, holding the hand of a smaller person, a female human. Perhaps this man sketched out his life story, and traveled around it on his riding machine so he wouldn't forget. The Queen had reduced her once fearsome enemy to an old man drawing pictures in the middle of nowhere.

"Do you like it?" Nathan Finch said. "There are some more over here."

Taalik approached an image of a boat floating on the water, its cannons ablaze. When his foot came to rest on the ship's bow, a sound like grinding metal screeched behind him. He turned to see one of the flying fish tipping over the side of the boat. Its fin pointed straight into the air as it tumbled off the edge.

"Oh, God," Nathan Finch said.

A cable zipped across the deck, dragging a sharp piece of metal. Taalik sensed danger, tried to move away, but it was too late. The metal pierced his tail and flipped him onto his stomach, scraping his scales on the tarmac. He tried to grab something as the deck slid underneath him. The tether lifted Taalik into the air and slammed him against the wall of the tower. Dazed, hanging upside down, Taalik reached for his wounded tail to find it impaled on a large metal hook. The cable ran through a pulley at the top of the tower—an elaborate trap that used the weight of the flying fish to snare a large animal.

Footsteps approached. "Never thought I'd have to use that," Nathan Finch said.

The thin air made Taalik delirious. He glanced at the human, who stood inverted before him. "Tell me where you come from," Nathan Finch said.

Taalik tried to pull the hook out of his tail. The barbed tip protruding from the flesh would not budge. He remembered this same object, like a severed claw, stuck into the fin of the mighty shark Graydeath. The humans used these tools to trap his people. How many died like this, drying out in the sun, while the monsters watched?

"We can make this quick," Nathan Finch said. "But I need to know who you are."

Taalik had shouted his name when he first landed on the

beach. But this human did not hear it. Taalik would have to shout it louder. He gripped his tail with his claws, right below the hook. The skin began to tear. His tongue hung out of his mouth from the pain.

"You're making it worse," Nathan Finch said.

The pincers cut deep into the muscle and bone, each layer more agonizing than the last.

"Don't make me get the cattle prod."

The tail broke free with a great shredding sound, like sharks pulling their prey apart. Taalik plummeted to the deck, landing hard on his shell. Blood drained from the wound. Rolling onto his legs, Taalik clamped his tail to slow the bleeding. He rose to his feet. Above him, the cable spun with the severed tip still attached.

"I am Taalik of Cold Trench."

Nathan Finch broke into a run. The movement of the human body was so strange to Taalik. These primates shifted their weight forward, almost falling over, only to catch themselves with each step.

Taalik loped after the man, crippled by the gravity weighing on him. Nathan Finch entered a portal at the base of the tower. Taalik lowered his head to get through the opening.

He followed the boot steps down a flight of stairs. On the third level, Taalik stopped dead when he smelled something familiar. It was impossible, in this stale, greasy place, and yet he could detect the oily redolence of his people emanating from an open portal. While the human retreated into the depths of the ship, Taalik inhaled the scent again. Unmistakable. He had to find out.

Taalik followed the odor to a large, open room. Like every other chamber, the walls and floors were fashioned from the same gray metal. A few pillars supported the ceiling. Here, rows of enormous transparent tubes lined the walls, each filled with a yellowish liquid. A shadowy object floated inside of each one. Taalik made out the shape of a fish, floating dead in the cylinder. Not wanting to believe what he saw, he visited the other tubes to discover a different fish inside each one, some long and slender, others bulkier, with large heads and bulging eyes. One of the tubes contained a creature that was practically asymmetrical, with a wide face and mouth, and an enormous fin on the right side. In the next one, he found a thin fish, its jaw locked open in a perpetual scream. It was one of his people, one of his children, a scout he had sent on patrol. Two ragged holes punctured the fish's body, one near the mouth, the other in the ribs. Both wounds must have come from that ghastly hook the humans used.

Trembling, Taalik staggered to the end of the row. In the last tube, he saw a creature from his dreams, a crablike monster—very similar to the Spikes. It could live on land, using strands of silk from its abdomen to catch prey. A distant cousin of his, another worthy soldier in the Queen's army.

Taalik swore he could hear a voice coming from inside. He placed his claw on the glass. He expected the massive eyeball to focus on him, to recognize one of its own kind. And then, Taalik pitched backward, facing the drab ceiling. The ceiling became like the night sky, pocked with stars. The stars became constellations that streaked by as he traveled through space, toward a blue planet. He penetrated the atmosphere of this world, puncturing the clouds, flying over the sea and the sand and the rocks. A herd of beasts with fur and horns stampeded across an open plain. A family of monkeys with flat faces and long arms huddled in a jungle. A six-legged creature perched in the center of her nest, protecting her eggs as they readied to hatch. All life on this planet was connected. It circled around him. And only those deemed worthy could hear his voice, and the voice of the Queen.

A blast ripped through the room. The cylinder burst open, its prisoner spilling out. Taalik broke free of the dream. Another loud bang echoed throughout the chamber. The human was somewhere near, using one of the terrible weapons that his race had perfected. Taalik made it to the stairway when another shot rang out. His armored shoulder went numb, the claw falling limp. Blood gushed from an open hole at the base of his neck. The light from the open doorway spun around and around. He tried to breathe, but the thin air did him no good.

Taalik crawled through the door. His tentacles failed him. He dragged them along, leaving a slimy trail across the deck. Under the withering sun, Taalik pulled himself to the edge and rolled off. When he splashed down, the salt water rushed into the wounds, filling his body with an almost unbearable pain, like pebbles running through his bloodstream. Still, the burning meant that he was alive. All that mattered was staying alive.

Having sensed the blood of the First of Us, the scouts rushed to him. One of them towed him along, while the other licked his wounds, frantically trying to stanch the bleeding. The last thing Taalik remembered before blacking out was the giant eyeball of the Shoot who repaired his injury, virtually identical to the eyes he saw on the ship, the eyes that he swore stared back at him, asking him why some got to live while others had to die.

TAALIK WOKE TO the smell of the entire convoy surrounding him.

*First of Us, you must wake*, one of the scouts said.

Taalik rested on his side. The bleeding from his wounds had stopped, but his claw remained in its crippled position, curled into his stomach. A clump of mud sealed the severed tail, while the sensation of a phantom limb squirmed and wriggled. Above, the floating island cast a shadow over everything.

*First of Us, the mates call to you.*

The scout referred to Orak. The other mates would have let him rest. She would not.

*I will go to my mates*, Taalik said.

He ascended from the pit to find his people, all of them, hovering in rows, arranged by class. Orak asked them to do this whenever she needed a head count. Taalik followed her scent until he spotted her, surrounded by the other mates. When he reached her, the rest of the harem instinctively formed a protective wall around them.

*Why did you bring our people here?* he said.

*I did not. Our enemies drove us here. While you were out exploring.*

Taalik waited. He needed to let her speak. She had been waiting a while to do so.

*They attacked as soon as you left*, she said. *Some of your children were left behind.*

*Gather the strongest*, he told her. *We must sink that floating island.*

Her mouth opened as she considered what to say next.

*Speak if you must*, he said. *But be quick.*

*Our enemy pursues us, my Egg. We do not have time for—*

*That is our enemy*, Taalik said, pointing his claw at the void hovering on the surface.

*If you had only been there when they attacked. If you had only smelled the blood.*

Taalik swam closer to her, until their outstretched tentacles formed a barrier around them. The movement pinched a nerve in his shoulder, sending a stabbing sensation into his wound. *My Prime. You will do this.*

Orak gazed at the ship. *The Queen revealed this to you?*

*No. I saw it for myself.*

*When will all this stop? When will the Queen be done with you?*

*I do not know.*

Orak called out to the soldiers. They circled her, each caste forming a new ring, a vortex made of scales and claws and teeth. She shot upward, soaring toward the ship. The convoy followed in her wake, a massive tower rising toward the hull of the carrier.

Taalik decided to join them, even though he was too weak to help. The hull widened until it blotted out the light. The warriors collided with the metal, rocking the ship, making the waves break in either direction. Taalik was pinned against the hull, his healthy claw and his four tentacles adding to the strength of the warriors. The structure tilted so far that the deck hit the waves in a great burst. The flying metal fishes crashed into the sea, toppling from the runway and corkscrewing to the ocean floor. As the ship descended, a roaring current sucked a few of the Sarcops into its wake, but they managed to swim away. The carrier collided with the seabed, screeching and grinding before coming to rest.

An incessant, shrill clicking sound cut through the noise. It was Orak, calling the Sarcops to follow her to the north. The rage of the past few minutes evaporated as the convoy regrouped. Orak took her place at the front, her tail and tentacles waving behind her.

WHEN DARKNESS FELL, and the Sarcops came to rest in a trench, the mates chose a spot for Taalik to couple with Zeela, his eighth. The act of mating proved painful for him. The movement stretched his unhealed wounds, causing some blood to leak out. Zeela pretended not to notice, and soon their fluids overwhelmed everything else. When they finished, Taalik sank to the ocean floor.

Soon after she left, Taalik got up and swam through the community. He passed the moveable nursery, where the eggs sat fastened to the ground, made indistinguishable from the surrounding stones. He moved through a group of adolescent Redmouths, wrestling and tumbling about. At the perimeter, the Juggernauts patrolled the expanse, ready to sound the alarm if any intruders arrived. Orak swam among them. Though she must have smelled Taalik, she did not turn to face him until he was right behind her. When she did, Taalik swirled his tentacles around her. She waited a second before reciprocating.

*Tell me what happened on the floating island*, she said.

He described the carrier and its captain, the last man on earth. *He spoke in a language I heard in my dreams*, Taalik said. *And I spoke back.*

*Another sign. Another power bestowed upon you.*

She stopped waving her tail when he told her about the torture chamber.

*Everything the Queen told me about the humans is true*, he said.

*Why would the humans keep people captive like that?*

*They believe they are above everything else, not a part of it. Do you see now that these fish chasing us are pawns? The humans drove them mad, hunting them, destroying their waters.*

An icy current passed between them. Orak flapped her tentacles to stay in place.

*The Queen sees all*, he said. *And this time, she allowed me to see through her eyes.*

*A vision?*

She had little tolerance for evasive answers and metaphor. And still he had to try.

*I saw all life. All the lives that have ever been lived. I could see them. I was them. Everything is connected. Through the Queen. And now through me. Through us. Our enemy does not understand this. We are the only ones who can stop them.*

*And the Queen promises victory? And then peace?*

*She promises neither. Only the hope of victory. The possibility of a new world.*

When she did not respond, he touched one of her tentacles with his. The two appendages braided around one another, creating warmth in the icy water.

*What do we do?* she asked.

*We keep going north. We survive. Until the Queen calls on us.*

*When will that be?*

*Very soon.*

Too soon, he thought.

# CHAPTER 8

## THE WATCHERS

T NIGHT, THE refugees of Lodge City gathered around the altar and sang songs of mourning for their dead. A beaver named Hildy served as the priestess, placing one hand on the altar, and lifting the other to the clouds. Fires burned in the four corners of the camp. The beavers swayed to the music. Castor placed his arm around his son, while Nikaya sat on a tree stump beside them, her withered hands resting in her lap. Soon, the smoke overwhelmed the odors of the camp—the scent hills, the barbecue pits, the washing buckets. All of them forgotten for now.

The humming started again. Falkirk could feel it vibrating in his chest. Hildy squeezed her raised hand into a fist as the singers reached the chorus once more.

*We will meet again*
*In the darkness*
*Where you and I*
*Will be the only light.*

*And by our light*
*We call everyone home*

*Where the water flows*
*And the dirt knows your name.*

It went on like that, all about the cozy lodges where the rodents would always find a home. The clerics in Hosanna did not approve of the old songs, but Falkirk would not dare point this out, not when the beavers wept as they sang.

On the long walk from Mort(e)'s house to the camp, Castor volunteered to be the one to tell Nikaya the news. He said little else after that. Falkirk couldn't blame him. Most of Castor's family was trapped in the web, awaiting their fate. His son witnessed some of the horror. Castor tried to distract the child in the hope that this business with the spider would pass, and things would return to normal. It reminded Falkirk of the time his two pups approached him one evening after dinner, while he was building his model airplanes on the front porch. He could tell that the twins wanted to ask him something, but were afraid. The older one, Amelia, went first, with Yeager, the baby, partially hidden behind her.

"What is it, puppy?" Falkirk asked.

"Papa, will you die one day?"

Falkirk told her that everyone dies. "Even you and Mama?" He said yes, though it would not be for a long time. "Even us? Will *we* die?" Falkirk pulled them in close. "Yes," he said. "That's why we need to appreciate each day we have together. Every day is special." That night, when Falkirk and Sierra spooned together in their room, he told her what had happened. When she started to cry, he asked her what was wrong. "Nothing," she said. "You did good."

Falkirk would see his family again, but not before he finished his work here on Earth. Not before God put him through these many trials, burnishing him into a new creation.

The Lodgers reluctantly agreed to try his plan of sneaking into the web through the river valley, even though the last beaver to try it got snatched up. But what choice did they have? Some of the hostages had been trapped in the web for over a week. It was possible that the spider's venom kept the victims alive, nourishing them as they waited for Gulaga to finish the job. Perhaps the victims remained in some dream state the whole time, believing right until the very end that they were relaxing in a warm lodge, smoking a pipe and singing songs with their loved ones.

A horn blew, cutting through the music until the singing stopped. Heads turned toward the echo, which sounded from beyond the treeline. A second horn blast followed. A young beaver wearing a human army helmet stumbled into the camp, out of breath. "Spiders!" she screamed. "Spiders! Spiders! Spiders!"

The crowd rippled away from the lookout beaver, who bent over to catch her breath.

This Gulaga was smart. Rather than risk another attack, she would send her children to wipe out the remaining troublemakers. Perhaps she even sniffed out Falkirk's plan. He pictured the monster looming behind Amelia and Yeager as they tearfully asked him about death. *Will we die? Will Mama die?*

"Watchers!" Castor screamed above the noise. "Watchers, with me!"

The Watchers consisted of a handful of beavers with little to no fighting experience. Their weapons included a few rifles, a pitchfork, an ax, a bow and arrow, and some assorted spears and machetes. Castor ordered them to take a position at the entrance of the camp. With this primitive arsenal, the Watchers would hold off the enemy while the families evacuated.

Hildy told the others to take what they could carry from the lodges. "We're moving now!" she said. "If you have to look for it, *then leave it*!" Falkirk spotted Nikaya in the madness. Two young beavers tried to lead her away, each taking an arm. Some other adult must have already taken Booker to safety. Nikaya probably wanted to say one last thing to her son before departing, but Castor made a show of ignoring her. A leader was not supposed to check with mommy while ordering people to their deaths.

On command, the Watchers stacked tree logs in a crisscross formation. Falkirk joined in. He managed to carry a tree trunk all by himself and then drop it into place. The barrier would buy some time, but accomplish little else. Still, they held the high ground. The spiders would have to pass through here if they wanted to capture the fleeing civilians.

The Watchers took their places around the barricade. Falkirk took stock of the best soldiers that Lodge City could produce. The two guards stood ready with their pikes. An elderly beaver readied a bow and arrow. Several of the shafts were wrapped in cloth, which he dipped into a bucket of tar. Falkirk pulled the pistol from his holster. Beside him, a Watcher who called himself Fram readied his rifle. This beaver was one of the few to actually fight in the war, and so the Watchers let him use one of Mort(e)'s weapons. A few feet away, Castor pulled his glasses over his eyes and peered into the scope of his new Remington.

Everyone smelled it, an unfamiliar scent that carried with it mud, coarse hair, and the metallic smell of an exoskeleton. Giant insects traveling downwind. The beavers alerted one another by slapping their tails on the ground.

The trees shook, some so violently that their newly grown leaves fell off. Rifles aimed into the pitch. Falkirk wanted to tell these beavers to put out the torches so their vision could adjust to the dark, but it was too late. The arachnids were upon them.

Among the trees, here and there, insect feet clawed the dirt. Something scraped against the bark of a tree. Twigs snapped. Gravel shifted. *They're staring us down*, Falkirk thought. *They're smart. They want us to suffer first*. The priests in Hosanna were right—something evil lingered after the war, and it would punish everyone, animal and human alike.

Castor pointed to the bowman, who lit his arrow on fire and launched it into the woods. He sent two more shots, the arrows slicing across the black sky and sticking into a tree trunk in a hail of sparks. Once his vision adjusted, Falkirk saw dozens of eyes, great orbs hovering, reflecting the flames. *They're huge.* But not spiders—something else.

"Praise the Goddesses," someone said.

A flare burst, maybe ten feet off the ground. In the unnatural light, Falkirk saw the hides of Alpha soldiers washed out in the brightness. A dog mounted on one of the ants held the flare, the flame changing from white to red. It was Sheba, dressed in full battle gear, with a submachine gun, bandoliers across her chest, a sword on her back. The dog held the fire at an angle to obscure her face, creating a void where her eyes, snout, and mouth should have been.

"Lower your weapons," she said. "You're making my ladies nervous."

Castor ordered everyone to stand down. To calm his trigger-happy friends, he vaulted the barricade and placed his rifle on the ground. *Good*, Falkirk thought. There might still be some hope for this rodent leader. Sheba's ant bucked a little. She kicked the thorax to keep her still.

Castor spoke softly with Sheba. Falkirk heard her say that she was there to help, and that she needed a place for the Alphas to stay. Falkirk did not catch the rest of it, and instead focused on Sheba's faceless silhouette. When the flare fizzled out, her image remained burned into his retinas, a ghost that haunted him every time he blinked.

SHEBA DISCUSSED THE plan with Castor, Nikaya, and Falkirk over a meal of insect stew and hot cider. Though awed by her presence, the beavers gasped when Sheba told them that Mort(e), at that very moment, was trying to recruit the bats. "We don't need them," Nikaya hissed. "We need real soldiers." Falkirk reminded her that real soldiers used every advantage they could get. And besides, time was running out. Nikaya continued to object until Castor cut her off. "We need the bats," he said. That settled it. When he asked what to do next, Sheba told him to get some rest. In the morning, the beavers would learn how to ride the ants like a cavalry. Castor nearly spit out his cider.

At dawn, the Watchers gathered at the edge of the camp, where the ants stood in formation. Sheba sat on an Alpha, having shed her guns and ammunition in exchange for a utility vest and a wide-brimmed field hat. She explained that they would need only nine or ten mounted Alphas. The rest of them—about twenty or so—would follow the riders. Unencumbered, these ants would scale the spider's defenses and attack in areas where the others could not.

"The best riders will take an Alpha into battle," Sheba told them. "Your ant will have to trust you the same way she trusted the Queen. *You* will be a queen. You'll give orders. But you can't hesitate. A queen never second-guesses herself. A queen never reverses course."

Sheba went over the basics of handling the animals. She started with tying the bridle to the mandible. Several of the beavers did it wrong, accidentally brushing the inside of the jaw. This triggered the muscles to clamp the mouth shut like a bear trap. The first three beavers who tried it failed, and each one jumped higher than the last when the jaw closed. Castor managed to do it correctly, only to have the beast lunge forward and knock him over. Sheba said that it was a sign of affection.

She then showed them how to mount an Alpha. Though the thorax made for a convenient saddle, the portly beavers found it difficult to shimmy onto it. A few of them were able to climb on top, but their large rear ends made it almost impossible to sit straight. Sheba let them carry on like this a few times before intervening. The ants, for their part, knocked off the incompetent passengers with a shiver.

Sheba's patience resulted in a dozen beavers riding their own Alphas. Like astonished children playing with a new toy, they marveled at the size and strength of the ants.

Falkirk could not stop watching her. All the legends and songs described Sheba the Mother as this nurturing, loving, docile canine. And there were hints of that in the way she doted on the ants. But this mother carried a sword, and called one of the beavers a fat ass when she caught him goofing around on his Alpha. In those early days of the Change, when Falkirk ventured into the white, he never could have imagined that the new world would produce someone like this.

Sheba led the cavalry on a march through the forest. The ants walked in such perfect formation that all the riders bobbed in unison with each step. Riding the Alpha named Jomo, Falkirk ended up on Sheba's left, with Castor directly behind him. On the other side, the beaver named Fram fussed with his mount, the ant occasionally bucking but staying on track. Falkirk's Alpha barely seemed to notice his presence, choosing instead to probe the grass with her antennae. When the herd changed course, Sheba showed everyone how to direct the Alphas to the left. "You're in charge," she said. "But be respectful."

Though the beavers joked with one another about who was the best rider, their banter died out as they drew closer to the city. Falkirk could feel the dread building in them, the kind that only a parent who has lost a child could sense. Sheba made it to the precipice first. The morning fog lifted, exposing the city under the stark gray sky.

Most of the beavers had not seen the city since the evacuation. Once they all cleared the trees, they formed a line and lowered their heads. Some of the Alphas did the same. Then the humming started. The song rang out—the same one Castor and Booker performed a few days earlier—full of woe and torment and regret. Sheba removed her hat and held it to her heart.

The march continued. So did the singing. Falkirk pulled closer to Sheba at the front of the pack.

"Chingachgook tried to teach me one of their songs," she said.

"The one about the lodges?" Falkirk joked.

"No, the *other* one about the lodges."

The beavers executed a key change, and then laughed at how well they pulled it off.

"So you changed Mort(e)'s mind," Falkirk said. "What changed yours?"

"I always wanted to help. So did Mort(e), really. He needed some time to come around."

"But why help? Mort(e)'s not completely wrong. The beavers expelled their only allies, expanded their territory too quickly. They may have even provoked that spider."

Sheba put her hat on and turned to the valley, to the dead city and the wilderness beyond. "We can't hide forever," she said.

A strange, evasive answer, Falkirk thought. Before he could add anything else, she leaned over to him. "Tell me about your city. All its wonders."

He told her all he could. The interspecies council, the refugee camps run by the clerical orders, the dam project. Whereas settlements like Lodge City failed to integrate, Hosanna refused no one—all who entered the city became an ally. And the abundance promised in the days to come only attracted more migrants.

"Mort(e) tells me that Hosanna is corrupt," Sheba said. "You have satellites and airships, but you send only one person to save Lodge City?"

"I didn't say it was perfect."

Falkirk was tired of defending Hosanna from the skeptics

who lived in the countryside. He wanted to say that one dog to rescue Lodge City was better than none. One killer on the loose was better than many. Only a few years into peacetime, and Hosanna accomplished more than the Colony had in this part of the world. Humans and animals joined forces there, ending the war for good.

Rather than point these things out, Falkirk decided to tell her the truth.

"As a matter of fact, people are scared," he said.

"Scared of what?"

"Let me put it this way. The case number I'm working on for this spider attack is 0519. That means there are 518 cases before mine."

"Cases. You mean mutations."

"Yes. Most of them are harmless. But we don't have the resources to address the ones that aren't. And it turns out that the world is a big place. We have both a country and an ocean to explore. But we've been out of touch with the other continents for years. That's what the expedition is for."

"What expedition?"

*My God*, he thought. This dog—the Mother—had been isolated for too long. Even the wolves knew about the expedition, though they mocked it as another example of human arrogance.

"The humans have salvaged a boat," he said. "Probably the biggest one that still floats. They're going to use it to explore the countries that went silent since the war."

The ship would sail the coast of South America, cross the Atlantic, then north along West Africa, into the mouth of the Mediterranean, and on to Europe. With each exotic place he named, Sheba became more animated. Her tail flipped from side to side.

"How long will they be gone?" she asked.

"Officially, a year. Unofficially . . . as long as it takes."

Falkirk told her the name of the mission: *al-Rihla*, named for some human vessel from their so-called age of exploration.

"Oh, that was Ibn Battuta's ship!" she said.

"Very good."

She mentioned that she spent her free time studying maritime history. When Falkirk admitted—to her disappointment—that he did not know the *al-Rihla*'s model, she speculated that it must have been a United States naval vessel. For someone with no real piloting skills, she could give intricate details about the ship's design from the manuals and other books she'd found.

"Do they still . . . need people?" Sheba asked.

"I thought you liked it out here."

This embarrassed her. She swore she asked out of mere curiosity, but Falkirk could tell she was backpedaling.

"They say the expedition is all booked up, save for a few spots," Falkirk said. "But I have to tell you something. The city could use more people like you and Mort(e). I hope you understand that I sent word to Tranquility that I found you."

"You want to bring us simple folk to the city?"

"Yes. You'd be treated like royalty."

Sheba laughed. The Alpha altered her stride to accommodate her shaking body. "You are so lucky the Old Man didn't hear you say that."

"Hosanna is trying to recruit people like you," Falkirk said. "We have an exchange program for law enforcement officials out on the frontier. They shadow a Tranquility agent for a few weeks. And then, if they want, they sign up for the academy."

"We're not law enforcement."

"You're close enough. Besides, people would listen to you. Even the humans."

The trail descended again, leading to a stream at the bottom of the valley, narrow enough for someone to jump across.

Sheba told the beavers to keep a firm grip on the reins; otherwise, the ants would instinctively follow the flow of the water. She went first. Falkirk's mount bucked once, but made it across. They waited as the rest of them gave it a try. Though no one fell off, a few nearly did. One Lodger bounced from the saddle and swung completely around. He grasped the ant's neck while hanging upside down. The Alpha patiently waited while the beaver righted himself.

Once everyone regrouped, the caravan moved on. Sheba rode next to Falkirk again. "Have you ever seen the ocean before?" she asked.

"I've seen it from an airship. The water looks all polished."

He winced as soon as he said it. She didn't ask him to brag.

"I dream about it all the time," she said. "But it always looks like paint. Or stone."

A horn blew in the distance. *Brrrrrrrruhhh*. The sound came from the camp. The convoy stopped to listen.

"Another alarm?" Falkirk asked.

"Yes," Castor said. The horn blew again. "Two signals for spiders."

The horn blew a third time. "What does three mean?" Falkirk asked.

"Bats." Castor lowered his head, exhausted with all of this. Surely aware that everyone was waiting for him to respond, he willed himself to pull the reins of his mount. The Alpha's antennae shot straight up. "Watchers, let's go!"

He forced the ant into a gallop. Falkirk and Sheba moved out of his way. The heavy footsteps tore out clumps of mud. Sheba dug her feet into her ant's side and took off after him.

"We're not ready for full speed yet!" she yelled.

"Let's find out!" Castor said over his shoulder.

Falkirk joined the charge. His eyes watered from the wind blowing in his face. He couldn't believe how fast they could go.

The cavalry soon resembled a train, with Castor pulling them along like the engine car.

The beaver led them on a shortcut through the woods. The ants became an avalanche roaring down the hills. The beasts took over, weaving among the trees, planting their feet on the roots and leaping over ditches.

"Bats!" someone screamed.

Through the leaves and branches, Falkirk saw a shadow pass overhead. Definitely a bat. It squeaked several times, like a newborn rodent. When it circled again, Falkirk got a better view through a gap in the trees. Most likely a male, the bat had the wingspan of a hang glider, its brown wings nearly translucent, exposing the long finger bones that stretched from the wrist. The bat carried something in his hind legs—an Army-issue duffel bag. Instinctively, Falkirk barked, something he hadn't done in a long time.

The stampede broke free of the trees, entering a clearing within sight of the camp. The beavers inside readied the barricades, for whatever good they would do against a bombing run.

"There!" someone yelled. "Over there!"

More hypersonic noises bounced from the ground, pricking at Falkirk's ears. The bat flew in a circle around the camp, the bag swinging like a pendulum.

Several beavers ran from the defenses to greet Castor. One of them held out a rifle. Castor, to Falkirk's continued surprise, snatched the weapon while riding at full speed. Sheba took the lead, directing the ants to form a line of defense. For the next few minutes, heads swiveled as they tracked the bat's movement.

Someone suggested taking a shot. "No," Castor said. "This might be their olive branch."

A gust of wind nearly tipped the bat over, but he soon righted himself. In a series of arcs, the flyer descended until he gently rested the bag on the trail leading to the forest. The bat wore a leather aviator hat, with a fur brim and a set of polarized goggles.

His enormous ears, like two sunflowers, protruded from holes cut into the cap.

With the package delivered, the bat flew into the trees. In an effortless somersault, he perched upside down on a branch, wrapping his wings around his torso like a cocoon. His brown fur blended perfectly with the tree trunk. Only the light glinting from his goggles gave him away.

The bag moved.

Sighing, Sheba shook the reins on her Alpha to get her going. "Come on," she said. "It's safe."

Falkirk and Castor followed, ignoring the voices begging them to stay. When he got close enough, Falkirk could smell cat fur. Domesticated. The duffel bag rolled over and then stood vertically, with two boots sticking out of the opening. The person inside lifted the bag from his head. Exposed, Mort(e) squinted in the light, his whiskers seesawing with each sniff he took. As promised, the cat arrived fully armed, with a long rifle, a sidearm on his hip, and a vest festooned with ammunition and explosives.

"I thought you hated to fly, Old Man," Sheba said.

"Still do."

Addressing him as Mort(e) the Warrior, Castor welcomed him to the camp. "Who is your friend?" he asked.

"That is Mr. Gaunt of Thicktree, the proudest family of the Great Cloud and Protectors of the Sacred Forest." Mort(e) turned to the bat. "Did I get that right?"

The bat remained still. He may have been asleep.

"That's a yes," Mort(e) said. "I think that's a yes."

"The bats agreed to help us?" Castor asked.

"One bat."

Castor's mount took a few tentative steps toward the tree. The beaver said hello a few times. Mort(e) told him not to bother. Gaunt would speak when he wanted to, and even then it would be in Chiropteran, the cloud tongue—nothing but squeaks and chirps. "They're funny that way," Mort(e) said.

"We mean them no harm."

"We'll talk diplomacy later. We need to get moving."

"Did you go to the city?" Falkirk asked.

"Yes. Did a few flybys. There are more eggs than we thought. Three of them are cracked. We have to take them out before they hatch."

Falkirk pictured it—spiderlings, each the size of a table, bursting from the pods, blindly hunting for food. They entered the world ready to kill, and died only when they lost the ability to do so.

"That's why the spider kept the hostages alive," Mort(e) said. "The young ones need something to eat when they hatch."

"I got it," Castor said, checking to make sure no one in the camp heard that.

"One more thing. The bats requested Nikaya's presence at the battle."

"The matriarch? What for?"

"She hates the bats. They figured that if she saw them saving the town firsthand, she'd change her mind about them."

"But she's too old to travel."

"She'll be fine. Do you want me to ask her myself?"

Castor shifted in his saddle. "Okay. We'll bring her. But she'll be at a safe distance."

"Of course. Now get your people ready. Right now, I need to talk to Sheba. Alone."

Falkirk and Castor left them. At the entrance to the camp, the rest of the Watchers surrounded Castor, pelting him with questions. He tried to calm them. "This bat took a risk coming here," he said. "Maybe the cloud is serious this time about working out a deal."

As they debated, a young beaver hopped over the wooden

ramparts and ran to them. "Madame Nikaya wishes to speak with you," she said.

"I figured," Castor said. "We're working with the bats. It's final."

"Should I tell her that?"

"I'll tell her."

Falkirk smiled. This beaver was starting to grow on him.

An argument ensued. Castor maintained his calm, knowing that the rest of the villagers might hear. "The water flows," he told them. Lodge City needed help, and the Messiah—the *Messiah!*—had found it. His comrades responded by going through the litany of crimes that the bats had committed. Theft. Vandalism. Desecrating the altar on their way out of Lodge City.

"We don't know it was them," Castor said.

"Who else would it be?"

They began talking over one another. Falkirk lost interest. Instead, he fixated on Mort(e) standing on the trail. Though armed to the teeth, a walking instrument of death and mayhem, the cat gently stroked the head of the Alpha. Mort(e) gazed at Sheba the Mother, who sat tall in her saddle. When she laughed at something he said, tilting her head back so that her hat nearly fell off, Falkirk felt an intense wave of jealousy, like spiders crawling around in his guts. Mort(e) was chosen to become one with Sheba, as Falkirk was chosen for this fate. No use crying about it now. Not with so much work to do, so many hills to climb, so many chances to face death. *The white takes you*, his mother said. The white took everything, even the few fleeting moments with one of his own kind. But he was still here.

THAT AFTERNOON, THE Watchers mounted their Alphas for the last time. With the beavers dressed in their full body armor, the giddiness from the morning evaporated. They strapped wooden shields to their backs. Leather helmets fashioned from ant hides covered their heads. Each helmet came with a Roman-style nose-piece that bisected their faces. A vest with two wooden plates sewed into it protected the ribcage. Etched into the fabric was the Lodge City crest, a blue river pooling against a horizontal green dam. The families gathered at the entrance to the camp, cheering as each Watcher passed through the gate. The riders said goodbye to their mates by touching noses, a gentle little kiss, so out of place in this war machine.

Hildy stood at the entrance, wearing a white robe and leaning on a staff with a beaver's fist carved into the top. She waved the staff over each of the riders while whispering a prayer. When Falkirk passed, she rapped the carved fist on each of his shoulders. "The Three watch over you," she said. "The river flows through your blood." Then she tapped her nose on Falkirk's snout. She repeated the ritual for Sheba and Mort(e). The cat didn't like it—he flicked his whiskers as if someone had dabbed a piece of dung on his face. One of the stronger beavers rode the Alpha named Seljuk, with the matriarch Nikaya wrapping her thin arms around his waist.

Several songs started at once. The humming backgrounds competed with each other until they all coalesced into one. Castor halted and raised his hand for silence. The singing stopped, but the humming continued.

"Look at me," Castor said. "And look into the eyes of your sons and daughters, your mothers and fathers, your mates. The keepers of the Watch. I promise—I swear—we will return tomorrow morning with our people."

The humming made a key change. More people joined in.

"The water flows. We will break this gulag. And we'll bring you that demon's head!"

The humming changed to a roar. The Watchers slapped their tails against their armor. Prompted by the racket, the bat dropped from his tree, spread his wings, and glided above the path in a looping pattern. An army had risen, assembled from numerous parts—some discarded, some found, some built from nothing.

Falkirk had witnessed so much in these last few days. A monster crushing its prey. A rodent leader rising from a catastrophe. The Messiah delivered by a bat. The fabled Mother riding a massive insect. He had dropped into some vortex where none of the rules he knew applied. Every time he had faced a situation like this, he failed, as his mother promised he would. It made him think that perhaps the punishment God had in store for him was merely beginning, and the true crucible still awaited him.

Or maybe, after all these years, he had finally reached the point where something would go right. He imagined Sierra beside him in their bed, whispering, "You did good." But then Sierra became Sheba, lying on her stomach and facing him, half of her snout buried in a pillow, her body covered under a blanket. She colonized his memory. He could not swat her away. In the same tone of voice she used when she said that she dreamed of the ocean, Sheba said to him, "You did good, Falkirk. You did good."

# CHAPTER 9

## THE BATTLE OF LODGE CITY

FROM THE BRIDGE of a ship, Sheba stared at the jade ocean as it slipped beneath the boat. The shimmering sea had no end, no markers to provide a location. No matter how fast the ship traveled, more breakers curled over the horizon. Until, finally, a distant wave froze in place. A new land, green and pure, offering a future for those with no past.

"Are you ready?" Mort(e) asked. Sheba snapped out of her daydream. The Old Man crouched beside her.

"I'm ready."

They hid behind a ridge overlooking Lodge City, along with Falkirk, Castor, and a few other beavers. Behind them, the cavalry stood in formation. Gaunt waited in a nearby tree. Falkirk and Castor each held one end of a map. The light peeked through, turning the husky and the beaver into silhouettes behind the paper.

With dusk approaching, the web that coated the city glowed yellow. If she didn't know better, Sheba would have said it formed some kind of protective shield that preserved the town, sealing it in a perfect state. But she inevitably shifted the binoculars to the stadium, where the hostages waited, wrapped in bundles. She tried to steady her hands so she could make out the spider. The legs and the segmented carapace stuck out briefly, only to vanish again among the strands of silk.

Falkirk rolled the map into a tube. "If you have anything else to say to your people, do it now," he said to Castor. The beaver walked over to his troops. They stopped talking when he approached, some straightening their backs in attention.

"Now you've done it," Mort(e) said. "They're going to sing again."

Right on cue, the humming started.

"Let them sing," Sheba said.

Gaunt dropped from his perch and swooped over the soldiers. Some of the beavers flinched at the sudden movement, but kept singing nevertheless.

The bat landed in the grass. On the ground, he was merely a furry leather ball, with aviator goggles covering his eyes. His mouth hinged open, displaying what looked like hundreds of teeth.

"Are you ready, Gaunt of Thicktree?" Mort(e) asked.

The bat opened his mouth wider and released a loud shriek.

"All right, all right," Mort(e) said. He stood. Sheba and Falkirk rose with him.

"What *did* you promise the bats in return for their help?" Falkirk asked.

"I told you. Peace and security."

Mort(e) clapped his hands. The sharp noise cut through the humming until the beavers stopped and listened. "We're moving," he said. "You know what to do."

Mort(e) checked his sidearm and ammunition. Sheba approached and helped him with a buckle that fastened at his hip. After she felt the clip slide into place, she tugged the vest to make sure it fit tightly.

"Be careful, Old Man."

"If I wanted to be careful, I'd go home."

Sheba placed her hands on Mort(e)'s shoulders. "You know what I mean. If you die . . ."

"If I die."

"If you die . . . I'll kill you."

They embraced each other and laughed. "I see the gift of speech was not wasted on you," Mort(e) said.

"Shut up, Old Man."

"I know you're sick of my war stories. After today, we'll have some new ones to tell. I'll get sick of yours this time. How's that?"

"That sounds good," she said. "I'm sorry I yelled at you the other day."

"I'm sorry I gave you a reason."

Mort(e) cleared his throat, a signal for her to let go. He stared at something over her shoulder. She turned to see Gaunt eavesdropping on their conversation, having crawled over to them. He rested on his elongated palms, his wings propped on his elbows. In a sudden movement, the bat launched from the ground. He flew over their heads, then circled around again.

"Good luck," Mort(e) said to Sheba. "I'll see you down there."

"I'll be watching you."

A gust of wind nearly knocked her over as Gaunt snatched Mort(e) by his shoulders. The wings flapped so hard they flattened the blades of grass. Airborne, the bat and his cargo crested the ridge, dropping out of view for a second before rising again. Sheba imagined the pine trees passing below Mort(e)'s dangling feet. Her stomach sank.

Sheba climbed onto Gai Den for what she thought would be the last time. The cavalry formed a row along the spine of the mountain, like soldiers on horseback from some pointless human war. Everyone watched as Gaunt deposited Mort(e) on top of the waterwheel. The bat hung from a horizontal beam, right below him. From there, Mort(e) would see if he could take a clean shot at the spider with his elephant rifle. Maybe he could end this with one pull of the trigger.

One of the riders, the hulking beaver named Fram, watched the spider through his binoculars alongside Sheba. "No movement," he said. Sheba watched Mort(e) assembling the sniper rifle, clicking the barrel into place. In the shaky tunnel vision of the binoculars, like peering through a keyhole, she almost expected to hear the metal, the jingle of his bullets. The rifle complete, Mort(e) knelt by the edge of the wheel and aimed at the stadium.

Sheba shifted her focus to the center of the web, searching for the spider's narrow face. It took a few seconds for her to find the two rows of unblinking eyes, like drops of rain on a leaf. No irises, no eyelids, no movement—only convex lenses that could make out shapes. Sheba wondered what had brought the spider to this place. All the animals had a story. None were truly brave or innocent. They all believed they had an excuse for the things they did. This arachnid was no different, just another survivor. Survivors were dangerous.

Falkirk sat on his Alpha beside her. "Sheba," he said.

"Yes?"

"If I don't make it through this, you have to promise me you'll at least think about what I said. The Union needs you. And maybe the *al-Rihla* could use an expert on Alphas."

"You'll make it," she said. "And then you can keep guilt-tripping me yourself."

Jomo stirred. Falkirk tugged on the reins to still her again.

"Son of a *whore*fucker!" Fram shouted, startling everyone.

"What is it?" Falkirk asked.

"The bat!"

The Alphas shuffled as the beavers craned their stumpy necks. Through her binoculars, Sheba tracked Gaunt as he flew away from the wheel.

It was too soon. The bat should have airlifted Mort(e) out of there. The Old Man saw something at the base of the waterwheel. He aimed his rifle and fired. A second later, the pop reached the observers on the ridge.

"Look!" Falkirk said.

Four spiderlings, each big enough to wrap its legs around Mort(e), slinked up the wooden spokes of the wheel, as if the beavers had designed the structure for this very purpose. The translucent creatures, freshly hatched, resembled moving crystal chandeliers.

"I told you those bats would betray us!" Fram said.

"We don't know that," Sheba said. "Mort(e) may have told him to fly away."

Castor fumbled with the map. "There's not supposed to be an egg there!"

"Well, it's there," Falkirk said. "They missed it."

"The bat probably put it there!" Fram said.

Another shot splattered a spiderling. A third ripped a chunk from one of the beams, sending one of the creatures tumbling away in a shower of woodchips. The last arachnid made it to Mort(e)'s feet. He jammed the barrel into its face and fired. The crystalline monster burst apart, the legs shooting out in several directions.

"She's moving!" Falkirk said.

At the stadium, Gulaga lumbered from her perch, her exoskeleton a cream color marbled with brown. Her fangs dripped a milky venom. With each step, the strands of the web echoed with metallic noises, a hopelessly out-of-tune instrument.

The binoculars slowly dropped from Sheba's eyes. "We're charging now. Everyone get into your groups. You know where the eggs are."

"Mort(e) said to wait for the explosives," Castor said.

"No. We have to kill this thing without them."

"Come on," Falkirk said to the Watchers. "Do you want to sit here and watch two strangers die for your city?"

"Fine," Castor said, jerking the reins of his mount. "We'll *all* die for this city. But let's take that bitch with us."

And then, in a rumbling stampede, the Alphas swept down the hill. To Sheba's right, Castor bounced in his saddle as he held onto the reins. To her left, Falkirk's blue eyes caught hers for a moment. Then he faced forward, into the heart of the gulag.

Two more shots fired from Mort(e)'s elephant gun. A third round sparked off the arachnid's hide and whistled over their heads.

"He's shooting at us!" one of the beavers said.

"No!" Sheba said. "He's . . ."

She saw it now. The spider's white coloring was no camouflage. She had coated herself with the web, making her exoskeleton impervious to bullets.

Mort(e) fired again. Sheba heard the bullet skim off the spider's armor. Getting closer, Gulaga stepped from one shrouded rooftop to the next.

As the cavalry entered the outskirts of town, the buildings blocked Sheba's view of Mort(e). The group separated. Castor's team broke off from the pack, heading for the closest egg, in the northern corner of town. Fram led five more riders over the bridge, to the farthest egg, hidden among the support beams. Falkirk joined Sheba and two others as they charged to the stadium. By this point, the Old Man had expected to either shoot the spider or plant the explosives. Both had failed. Maybe they could at least rescue the hostages. But even then, someone would have to serve as bait for the spider. For now, it was Mort(e).

The first layer of web sealed off the street, with long cable-like strands sloping from the rooftops to the ground. Sheba offered to go first. Like the spider, the ants balanced themselves on tiny claws, thereby reducing their contact with the web and allowing them to walk over it. At least, that was what Sheba hoped.

Her Alpha hesitated, testing the web with her foot. Impatient, Sheba jammed her knees into the ant's sides to nudge her along. Gai Den placed her front claws onto the web and hoisted herself onto it. The angle was so steep that Sheba nearly tumbled out of her saddle. A moment later, Sheba was floating above the street on the silky canopy, with the other riders following behind her. The web made creaking noises like a rusty suspension bridge. Once she got high enough, she looked for the waterwheel. She couldn't see Mort(e). Maybe he found a hiding place. Or maybe—

Gulaga changed directions. She was headed right for them.

"Move!" Sheba said.

The web dipped and shuddered under their weight as they raced over each street. The cavalry approached the first egg, fastened with silk to the corner of a rooftop. Falkirk and the two beavers leveled their guns at the pod and fired. Bits of the shell sprayed into the air. A clear fluid gushed from the holes, followed by a thicker substance that resembled tar. When the shooting stopped, Sheba plunged her sword into the egg to make sure. As she jimmied the blade out, an explosion thudded, somewhere near the bridge. A fireball ascended over the water. Fram had detonated another pod. Gulaga stopped in place. Then, perhaps realizing that the egg was gone, the spider continued crawling toward Sheba's unit.

"Go get your friends," Sheba said to the beavers. "We'll hold her off."

The beavers continued on to the stadium. Falkirk let go of his reins and aimed the rifle. "I hope they write a good song about us," he said.

Another explosion sent ripples through the web. Castor and his team must have destroyed another egg. A part of the canopy collapsed as one of the anchors gave way.

Gulaga ignored the distraction, focusing instead on the two defiant intruders in her sights. Sheba readied her machine gun. The reins were wrapped around her shooting hand in case she needed to pull Gai Den away from a quick strike. Falkirk fired, but the bullet embedded in the armor. Gulaga shuddered and kept moving. The creature got close enough for Sheba to see her belly, unprotected by the armor.

With her gun in one hand, Sheba waved her sword with the other. A sliver of reflected sunlight brushed across Gulaga's face just as Sheba pulled the trigger. The flashes from the muzzle lit up the creature's belly. The empty shells caught in the web and hung there. A clear liquid dripped from the spider's wounds onto the canopy.

Falkirk, positioned to her right, opened fire. The spider lunged at the husky, toppling his ant into the web. Pinned beneath her, entwined in the silk, the dog kept shooting. Falkirk yelled something that Sheba could not make out. But then she recognized it. Falkirk was *barking* like a guard dog.

The spider snatched Jomo in her jaws, ripping her from where she had fallen and leaving a frayed hole in the web. Falkirk, caught in the silk, was pulled along with her. Propped on her rear legs, Gulaga sprayed web from her abdomen and spun both ant and husky into the silk. A final patch of web sealed Falkirk's gaping mouth. The barking stopped.

Sheba forced Gai Den closer until she stood within reach of Gulaga's leg. She swung her sword at the knobby joint. The blade bit deep into the shell.

The spider swung around, dropping the cocoon that encased Falkirk. While Gulaga's fangs slashed at her, Sheba managed to rip her sword from the leg and swing it across her body. The metal dug into the spider's jaw, leaving a gash. Gulaga lunged again. This time, Sheba yanked the reins and forced Gai Den to rise onto her hind legs. While the spider and the ant locked jaws,

Sheba stabbed Gulaga right at the hinge of her mandible. But she merely hit bone and sinew, nothing vital. As she struggled to slide the blade out, Gulaga lurched forward, overpowering the ant until both Gai Den and Sheba tumbled over. Sheba sank into the web. Gai Den's weight came down on top of her. The ant struggled, her legs flipping madly. The spider's mouth, with the bloody hilt of the sword still protruding, wrapped around Gai Den's thorax. When Sheba reached for her machine gun, she found it suspended in the silk, as if frozen in a cloudy block of ice.

Like some kind of ghoulish machine, Gulaga spun Gai Den in a web, wrapping her tighter until she could no longer wriggle. Each revolution added a new layer until the blackish red of the ant's armor became coated in silk. Sheba freed her left arm and tried to rip the gun free. She wasn't sure what she'd do once she got it loose. Maybe take one last shot, or maybe put the barrel to her temple so she wouldn't be alive when the beast began to feed.

Something streaked across the sky, right over the spider's head. Sheba ignored it. Then another object cut across her peripheral vision, moving in the same direction as the last. Somewhere to the north, an explosion vibrated the web. Then another, closer this time. The spider, finished with Gai Den, leaned toward Sheba. The jaws separated, leaving only a black void in between. Sheba saw a giant bat fly overhead. An object fell from the creature's claws. Sheba closed her eyes believing that it would be the last thing she would ever see.

A final explosion deafened her left ear. The building that anchored this section of the web collapsed, dropping her and the spider to the street below. Sheba landed hard on the concrete and blacked out.

SHE WOKE IN the prickly grass of her master's yard. Clouds tumbled and unfurled in the blue sky. The screen door creaked open. The air was clean. Her mind was clean, too. No memories, no worries of the future, only the things that she could touch and taste and smell. The soft patch of mud under her paws. The taste of salt on her master's ankles when he returned from jogging. The universe opened and kept expanding. Every day provided wonder and awe, the whole of existence tipping over and pouring out its contents.

Somewhere close by, a dog barked.

She wondered if the noise came from the brown dog across the street, the one who had forced her against the flaking paint chips of the garage. She both feared and desired this dog, the father of her children, her only link to them. Her longing for his warmth remained, even as her children faded. She could not stop it, and yet it felt right, this animal instinct boiling in her blood, never appeased, always hunting.

In the house next door, the orange cat sat on his windowsill. His curved spine lifted and fell with each breath, and yet his face remained still, save for the occasional blink of the eyes. When Sheba tried to turn away, she noticed that she was suddenly standing on her hind legs. Her front paws became like human hands.

The dog kept barking.

SHEBA BLINKED A few times. She lay on her stomach. As she tried to push herself up, a patch of web peeled away from her face and remained stuck to the asphalt. She scratched another layer of the silk from her paws and arms. A few feet away, a rusted bicycle from the human era stood in ruin beside her, virtually melted into the earth from years of exposure. She took a few wobbly steps, dragging long strands of the fallen web like a bride's wedding train. The spider was gone. In the empty stadium, several of the pods had burst open. Fires burned throughout the town. Ash and smoke drifted in the wind.

A dog barked nearby—a cry for help. On the sidewalk, the roll of silk containing Falkirk and Jomo squirmed like an egg about to hatch. A spiderling stood on top of it, trying to dig into the web with its fangs. The creature's skin was completely transparent. The organs underneath pulsated, pumping fluid.

"No!" Sheba shouted. The spiderling wriggled its head deeper into the silk.

Pulling her knife from its holster, Sheba charged the spider. She stuck the knife into the base of its neck. The head reached for her, the fangs trying to clamp around her face. Sheba grabbed the fangs with both hands. The eight legs wrapped around her, but they could do no harm. With all her might, Sheba bent the fangs until she felt a crunch. The spiderling sank to the ground. She peeled the legs from her body, one by one. Lying there dead, the spider resembled a broken toy.

The husky continued to scream for help.

"Hold still," she said.

Sheba hooked the blade under the web and sliced it away, unveiling Falkirk's mouth. His eyes still covered, the dog gulped in air. Sheba ran the knife along the rest of the cocoon. It took only a small incision for Jomo to burst through the casing. The ant rolled to her legs. Her antennae poked around to confirm that she was free. She prodded the dead spiderling and then went about inspecting the rubble from the explosion.

Falkirk peeled the webbing from his face and flicked it away. He growled at the dead spider. But then his panting slowed when he saw Sheba, still brandishing her knife. His tail popped out of the webbing and flopped onto the asphalt. The husky reached out and embraced Sheba, licking her behind the ears. The silk strands glued their bodies together. She laughed and pushed him away. The warm sensation of his tongue tingled on her neck.

"Sorry," he said. "You came back for me."

"Dogs do that."

Sheba heard shouting coming from the river. She spotted Gulaga limping over the rooftops toward the waterwheel. The beavers on the ground below fired their rifles at her, but the bullets had no effect.

Mort(e) stood on top of the wheel. The bat orbited him, carrying one of the eggs in his claws. Maybe the last one left. Gingerly, the bat placed the egg beside Mort(e) and flew away, joining the dozen other bats that zipped around the darkening sky. Mort(e) waited. The spider hooked its legs onto the wheel and began to climb.

"That cat really is crazy," Falkirk said.

"You have no idea."

When Gulaga reached three o'clock on the wheel, the bombs planted along the spokes exploded. *Bop bop bop bop bop bop.* Each blast severed a cord in the web that held the wheel in place. The wood groaned as the river forced it to spin once again. The beavers began to cheer. Their greatest engineering feat, the symbol of their city, had not functioned since this nightmare began. Right on cue, the humming started.

The spinning wheel lifted the spider into the air while Mort(e) and the egg descended. When Mort(e) lowered to eight o'clock, he leapt from his perch into the river, vanishing in a white splash. As the spider arrived at the top, another explosion erupted at the base of the wheel. The shock wave blew out the windows of the surrounding houses. The wheel broke from its moorings and toppled into the river. Gulaga flailed as she reached for solid footing. The structure collapsed onto the spider's body in a great splash.

The humming stopped.

Sheba ran to the water, vaulting over collapsed walls and broken concrete blocks. In some places, the canopy still hung overhead, crisscrossing the rooftops. Elsewhere, the buildings smoldered in ruins, and the web lay across the street like a wrinkled bedsheet.

At the dock, she hopped over the metal railing and landed on the muddy slope that descended into the river, now littered with the remnants of the charred waterwheel. Chunks of wood clogged the flow of water, so thick she thought she could walk across. A team of mounted beavers gathered on the waterfront. One of them dragged the battered hulk of a spider egg by a rope, its ejected contents leaving a streak along the ground.

"Do you see him?" she asked the warriors.

One of them pointed to a spot twenty yards downstream. Something splashed ashore in the slippery muck.

"He's over here!" someone shouted.

Mort(e) lifted his head. When he spotted Sheba, his ears swiveled toward her. He smiled. And for a moment, the shouts died out. Sheba fell to one knee. Mort(e), unrecognizable in all the mud, crawled on all fours to her.

"Found this," Mort(e) said. He slid Sheba's sword out from under him. She took the handle, slick with mud, and examined the blade. Overcome, she dropped the sword and embraced Mort(e).

"I saw you get taken up," he said. "You were so far away."

"I saw you, too. You—"

She was supposed to also say that he was so far away. That was what he was getting at. He wanted her to say they would not do this to each other ever again, that this was enough. No more. And having seen battle for the first time, she understood why. Yet she couldn't bring herself to say these comforting things anymore. They were only words. So she held Mort(e) and stared at the river as the river carried off the discarded bones of Lodge City.

# CHAPTER 10

## THE TRIAL

ORT(E)'S EARS HUMMED while Sheba cradled him. He could feel her heart beating, but could not hear it. The mud that painted his fur had a wet odor, like fish and blooming algae. Throughout the town, towers of smoke spiraled into the sky, spreading a light ash that carried the scent of charred wood and metal. Mort(e) and his toys had turned the city into a hellscape, like some volcanic planet spewing molten rock into the atmosphere.

Mort(e) rested his chin on Sheba's shoulder. "Did you hear her?" he asked.

"Hear who?"

"The spider. She . . ." She what? She *spoke*. No, that couldn't be right. But he heard her somehow. Or felt her. The spider told him to stop. She *begged* him to stop, in thousands of voices, hundreds of languages. And amid all the noise, he recognized someone speaking to him—Michael, the child from his past. *Help me*, the boy said. *Save me.*

"Let's get out of here," Mort(e) said.

The beavers had run off to rescue their friends from the web. Only Falkirk remained. When Mort(e) caught the husky staring, the dog dropped his gaze to the ground and joined the others.

*That's right, keep walking*, Mort(e) thought. *Keep walking all the way back to your human city.*

"I want to watch them free the hostages from the web," Sheba said.

"Okay."

The collapsed web resembled day-old confetti from a celebration. As they walked, Mort(e) grabbed a fistful of it and playfully tossed it onto Sheba's head. She grumbled and laughed as she pulled the sticky strings out. Several blocks away, a stone building imploded. A few of the ants scrabbled over the rubble, hunting for baby spiders. The base of the waterwheel sat by the river, its beams twisted and amputated. The canals leading from the dam had ruptured in several places, flooding the streets. The water, however, did not reach the church in time. A mountain of fire engulfed the wooden building before it crumbled into cinders.

Eventually, Mort(e) was able to distinguish the ringing in his ears from the beavers' humming. He followed the music to the heart of the web, the stadium. Falkirk was there, helping to lower one of the encased hostages to the ground. As soon as the pods touched the street, the beavers cut them open, not knowing who would emerge. The surprise prompted shouts and applause as each bewildered hostage tumbled out. The medics on hand tried to give the victims food and water, while the others stroked their fur and continued humming.

In the parking lot of the stadium, a beaver knelt over the bodies of a female and two kits. Barely alive, they were coated in silk, great sticky clumps of it, like tumors. Mort(e) realized it was Castor when he saw the pile of armor in a heap nearby. Weeping and sniffling, the beaver held out a bottle of water, pleading with them to drink. The female lifted her head and took a few gulps. Castor responded by tapping his nose to hers before moving on to the young ones. The children let out a weak humming sound, making Castor laugh and cry at the same time.

Mort(e) slipped his hand into Sheba's palm. Here, things would start over. A new chance at life. It would ruin it to say it out loud.

Gaunt, of all people, had given him advice on what to do when he saw her again. When Mort(e) first went to the bats, Gaunt welcomed him to the cave. Mort(e) spoke with the elders of the cloud through a bat named Plug, who translated his words into Chiropteran. The old ones hung from the cave ceiling, a cluster of living stalactites. Mort(e) gathered from their body language that the older bats, with their white fur and silver beards, did not want him there. One of them showed his disapproval by defecating in the middle of Mort(e)'s story, splattering a fragrant log of guano at his feet. But Gaunt took Mort(e)'s side. Later, after the council voted in favor of helping the beavers, Mort(e) sat on the cave floor with Gaunt hanging above him. They talked about their families, about how they survived the war. Gaunt was no soldier, but he had witnessed far more than he needed to. The bats grew too quickly after the Change, outpacing their food supply. Gaunt lost his mate in the mass extinction that followed. Mort(e) changed the subject by talking about Sheba, their life on the ranch. Gaunt responded with a few squeaks, which Plug translated as, "You build it again." Mort(e) didn't understand. "You put it back together. You put life back together."

"Yes, yes," Mort(e) said.

"We spend all our life putting life back together," Plug translated. "So you can live in that memory. Just her and you and the life you put back together. No human words you need."

With that in mind, Mort(e) kept quiet and squeezed Sheba's hand. She squeezed back.

A commotion began somewhere behind them. Two loyal beavers carried Nikaya on a wooden seat. The matriarch coughed when a breeze pushed some of the smoke in her face. When she got a clearer view of where the waterwheel used to spin, her head sank. She trained her eyes on Mort(e). He couldn't wait to hear what she had to say.

Nikaya's servants placed her seat on the ground. "This was all part of your plan, wasn't it?" she said. "You wanted to destroy the city with these flying devils."

More beavers converged on Mort(e) and Sheba. Fram approached, his finger on the trigger of his rifle. Mort(e) placed his hand on his sidearm—slick with mud but very much operable. Mort(e)'s smile dared the beaver to try something.

"We had to be sure," Mort(e) said. Just then, an Alpha trotted by with a limp spiderling in her mandibles.

"Good girl, Sugar!" Sheba said.

"You see that, Matriarch?" Mort(e) said. "How can be you in such a foul mood when our ants are having so much fun?"

Sheba let go of his hand to point at a few other Alphas crawling across the roof of a house. "Look at them go!"

"Can't you round up these animals?" Nikaya said.

"We're not rounding them up. They're staying. This city is their new colony."

Above them, the bats flew in great circles, making the wind swirl.

"Where are *we* supposed to go?" Nikaya asked.

"You can go upstream. Downstream. Either way, it will be far from here. Far from *us*."

"We spent *years* building this," Nikaya said, trembling with rage. "What would you know about that, you choker? You were a pet. Your masters had a box for you to shit in. They fed you other animals. We had no masters. We were out in the wild. We—"

"Mother, that's enough," Castor said, entering the circle. "These people saved everyone. We didn't lose a single hostage. Or a single Watcher."

"Look at what they did!"

"We'll rebuild. The water flows."

"They brought the bats here! To in*sult* us!"

"They made peace with the bats. *I* couldn't have done that. And *you* didn't even try."

"We haven't made peace quite yet," Mort(e) said. "There is one last order of business."

Mort(e) glanced at Sheba. She nodded, placing one hand on the hilt of her sword, the other on the gun holstered at her side. With that, Mort(e) let out an otherworldly shriek that startled everyone. Gaunt of Thicktree taught him the signal the day before. It triggered a frenzied movement among the bats. All of them, even those still orbiting the perimeter of the town, coalesced into a black tornado. Acting like a single organism, the bats descended on Nikaya, knocking her attendants away and lifting her above the houses. The beavers shouted over the wind. Some raised their rifles. Instinctively, Sheba and Mort(e) pressed against each other, back to back, to become one unit that could see in all directions. If anyone wanted to hold them responsible for what was happening, they would regret it.

Perched on the ledge of the post office, a pair of bats held Nikaya by her ankles. The matriarch looked to Mort(e) for an explanation. But she knew. She had to know.

Castor unstrapped his rifle and aimed it at the bats. "What are you doing?"

"I'm not doing anything," Mort(e) said.

The tornado dispersed as the bats gathered on nearby rooftops. Some hung from the awnings, but most squatted, poking their heads over the ledges. Gaunt dangled from a street lamp and cloaked his thin body with his leathery wings.

"Ask her what she did," Mort(e) said.

"Don't listen to them!" Nikaya said, her voice straining. "They're liars! They're false prophets!"

"I'm not a prophet. I'm a messiah."

Castor stepped closer to the horde of flapping wings. "Mother, what are they talking about?"

"They're working with the bats! Don't you see? They're trying to destroy everything we've built here!"

"That's enough," Mort(e) said. He made a throat-slashing gesture. In response, one of the bats covered her mouth with his wing.

Fram leveled his rifle at Mort(e). "Messiah or not, you've got three seconds to let the matriarch go before I shoot you with your own rifle."

Sheba tensed beside him. "You're not shooting anyone," Mort(e) said. "Your matriarch is the one who started all of this."

The muffled screaming stopped. Nikaya must have known what was coming next.

"The matriarch ordered her closest aides to take one of Gulaga's eggs and plant it near the bat cave," Mort(e) said. "She thought the spider would take care of her enemies. But it backfired."

Mort(e) told them that the spider almost succeeded in wiping out the cloud. When Gulaga discovered the cave, she spun a web across the entrance, forcing Gaunt and his comrades to gnaw their way out. Many died before they breached the silk barrier and burst out like air escaping a balloon. They knew who did it. When Mort(e) asked the bats for help, they agreed on two conditions. Lodge City would be destroyed, and they would take those responsible as prisoners to do with as they wished.

Castor did not bother to ask her why. The reason was obvious. Nikaya did it to protect her bloodline. And that meant keeping Castor in the dark.

"Who else?" Mort(e) asked. Nikaya tried to scream through the thick flesh of the wing, but no one could understand her.

"There's no evidence," Fram said. "We're taking the word of these bats and these . . . strangers."

"Step forward," Mort(e) said louder, "and I'll try to talk these bats into letting you live."

Two beavers elbowed their way through the crowd, a male and a female. The latter stripped her wooden armor and dropped it at her feet. The male looked like some kind of pencil-pusher, smaller than average, leaning on a cane and limping with a shriveled leg.

"We're sorry, sir," the female said.

"Save it for them," Mort(e) said. He pointed to the bats. "Can they live?"

The bats' ears quivered as they squeaked at one another. Falkirk winced at the sound. When they finished, Gaunt answered with three quick screeches followed by a series of clicks. "Something about the caves," Mort(e) translated. The bats didn't really have verbs—only nouns and a random adjective. "They're going to clean the caves? Some kind of hard labor?"

Gaunt clicked once. It meant yes.

"Wait a minute!" Castor said, pointing at Falkirk. "This dog here represents the law. These prisoners are protected by the Hosanna Charter. Even out here."

The attention shifted to Falkirk. The husky must have realized how ridiculous he looked, all covered in silk. He wiped the web from his fur and prepared to speak for Hosanna. "It's true," he said. "The accused can demand a trial in the city."

Mort(e) bit his lip. These goddamn bureaucrats, he thought. Collaborators with the humans. Mort(e) figured he would have to pistol-whip Falkirk in the snout if the dog tried to follow through. Just walk right up to him with a smile and cave in his skull.

"They should have a trial!" someone shouted.

"The right to trial applies only if the accused denies the crime," Falkirk said. "These people have confessed."

Around him, the crowd murmured.

"The matriarch didn't confess!" Fram said.

The people grew silent as they awaited Falkirk's answer. "It sounded like a yes to me."

"Castor, do something!"

His eyes on the bats, Castor stepped in front of the two confessors and aimed his rifle at Gaunt. The other Watchers raised their weapons.

"Castor," Sheba said. "Don't."

"We don't recognize this bat council," Fram said.

Falkirk walked over to Castor. "You're the leader now. If you want to save the town, you have to let them take her. Please."

Castor lowered his rifle. Nikaya let out a muzzled scream.

A gunshot. The window next to Gaunt's head shattered. Fram took aim again, but a bat descended on him. People dove out of the way as the bat gripped the beaver by the fur, flapped her wings, and tossed him like a doll. Fram landed on his side and rolled over several times before coming to rest at the curb. People shouted. Another random shot ricocheted off the cement. The bats dropped from their perches, a waterfall of leather, fur, and teeth. *Thup-thup-thup-thup-thup*. The people on the ground shielded their faces from the swirling debris. The cloud became like a living thing. An appendage made up of several bats reached from the swarm and snatched the female Watcher. Then another unnatural arm, like a striking snake, swiped the male beaver. His cane clattered to the ground. Mort(e) grabbed Sheba's hand and pulled her along. When they reached the end of the block, Mort(e) saw the tornado of wings lifting away from the town. A few of the Watchers took potshots at the bats as they flew away. While the civilians cowered, waiting for the wind to die out, Castor stood still, the loneliest person there. Mort(e) recognized the expression on the beaver's face—the same dull stare that members of the Red Sphinx wore after losing one of their own, all regret and longing and muffled rage.

· ◦ ·

BY THE TIME Mort(e) and Sheba reached the trail leading out of the valley, the beavers had broken into song again, more cheerful than expected. Maybe they had come to their senses, and realized that they gained more than they lost on this day. From here, they would rebuild. *The water flows.*

Mort(e) took the lead on the trail. Sheba tripped several times because she couldn't stop glancing at the city. From this distance, the decimated town reminded him of those moments on the island of Golgotha, when Sheba, still a mere dog, rested her head in his lap while the fires burned on the beach. Though Mort(e) could speak, he could never convey to Sheba how he felt in those moments. This time would be different. They did this together. They would retell the story years later, finishing each other's sentences, bickering over forgotten names and other details. They would have the same dreams.

Before they could proceed into the forest, Mort(e) spotted a lone figure racing along the trail, moving faster than any beaver. The husky. He waved at them.

"Make this quick," Mort(e) said. "We'd like to go home."

"You can't. We need you."

"We did what you asked. We killed a mother and her babies for you."

Falkirk looked to Sheba for help. "You must have told him everything."

"I did."

"So you know what's at stake. There are other creatures out there like this one."

"There's nothing to discuss," Mort(e) said. "Come on, Sheba. I told you these lapdogs don't listen."

Sheba hesitated longer than Mort(e) would have liked. Eyeing the husky, she finally pivoted away from him and followed Mort(e).

"We need people who have seen these anomalies up close," Falkirk said.

Mort(e) heard Sheba stop. He had to stop, too. "Listen, husky," Mort(e) said. "We're not risking our lives for your *human* masters."

"It's not like that."

"That's what all the slaves say."

"Have some respect, soldier. I'm not a slave. I fought in the war, just like you."

"No. Not like me."

He turned to Sheba. He had not seen her this sad in a long time, not since they first began euthanizing the Alphas. Mort(e) didn't want the husky to hear him begging her to come with him. Instead, he looked into her eyes and hoped she would understand.

"A few weeks," Falkirk said. "That's all I'm asking."

Sheba nodded to Mort(e). She would return to the ranch.

"You're asking too much," Mort(e) said, walking away.

The finality of it left the husky standing there on the trail, his eyes reflecting the fading light. Soon, the dog became indistinguishable from the surrounding forest.

DEEP IN THE forest, Mort(e)'s pupils dilated to pull in the faint light of a crescent moon. Behind him, Sheba shuffled along, breaking twigs, grunting as they climbed over boulders and felled logs.

Mort(e) already missed the ants, maybe because he knew Sheba missed them even more. The Alphas would be the only children they would ever raise and send off into the world. Now they were free, like he was. Freedom would always be preferable to order, peace, even love. Those things meant nothing unless you chose them.

If there were more monsters out there, ones that could read his mind, then the only possible direction was west, away from the doomed settlements that fell in line with Hosanna. With or without the ants, Mort(e) and Sheba would one day find humans at their door, flanked by their loyal animal subjects. Useful idiots. There was no telling how Sheba would react to a smooth-talking human, making promises he couldn't keep. So many others, even those who fought in the war with no name, believed that the humans would save them, like angels descending to the earth. They scared Mort(e) more than any mutant spider ever could.

The darkness broke at the perfect time, just as they climbed the last ridge before arriving at the ranch. Through the thick foliage, Mort(e) caught occasional glimpses of the brand new charcoal-colored roof. They were almost home.

Mort(e) noticed that he heard only his own footsteps. He spun in a full circle and saw nothing but trees. Sheba had fallen behind. When he backtracked, he found her on the trail, kneeling, rummaging through her pack.

"What's wrong?" he asked.

She closed the bag.

"Sheba—"

"I'm going back," she said. "I'm going to Hosanna with Falkirk."

Mort(e)'s throat constricted. His legs went numb and heavy, as they often did in a nightmare. The mention of the husky's name cleared the haze in his mind. A rage began to build in his gut, like tar boiling over. He waited for her to blink, to sniffle, to wag a tail—anything to show that she didn't mean what she said.

"Sheba, listen to me. Falkirk might be a good person. But he works for the humans. They know—they *know*—that the only way they can get to us is if they pull us apart."

Sheba weaved her arms through the straps on the backpack and tightened the buckles. "It'll only be for a few weeks."

"That's how it'll start. But they won't let you leave."

"I can't believe this," she said. "I can't believe you're going to make me say it."

"Say what?"

"You lied to me."

"What are you talking about?"

"You told me you were going to hand over Nikaya to the bats. You didn't say you were going to level the entire town. Was that the bats' idea, or yours?"

When he didn't respond right away, she knew the answer.

"Tell me why you kept that from me," she said. When he turned away, she followed his gaze. "Do it."

She had caught him. He couldn't lie. "Because you would have told me not to," he said.

"So that's it. You get to make the decisions for the both of us and I don't even get a say."

"Sheba—"

"I'm not Sheba." She motioned in the direction of Lodge City. "Sheba's down there, caught in the web. I'm taking a new name, like you did. My name is D'Arc."

"*Dark*? *D, A, R, K*?"

"No, *D*, apostrophe, *A, R, C*."

Mort(e)'s mouth hung open.

"Like Jeanne D'Arc," she said. "Joan of Arc. Remember when I read about her? We talked about her once on a Fifth Night."

"The *C* is silent," Mort(e) said. "That's how they pronounce it in French. So it's really *dar*. Technically."

She stared at him. "Do you want that to be the last thing you say to me before I go?"

*Fuck*, he thought.

She embraced him, and let him rub the underside of his jaw on her neck and shoulders. "Keep the light on at the cabin," she said.

They let go. Mort(e)'s stubby fingers ran through her coat. He resisted the urge to latch on. When she stepped out of reach, the pink skin on his palms went cold.

"Wait—"

"No. I'm going. I'm sorry, I have to do this. Right now."

"I love you," he blurted out.

"I love *you*, Old Man. I'll come back."

Mort(e) stood there, stiffly, watching her disappear as the trail curved into the forest. Long after he had lost her in the trees, Mort(e) remained locked in place. For a second, he saw himself as the pet cat in his masters' house, experiencing the world in flickers, wondering if this was all there was and all there would ever be.

# PART III

# DELUGE

# CHAPTER 11

## THE SHALLOWS

HE SCOUTS RETURNED with Nong-wa's corpse in tow, the mangled body spewing blood in a thick stream behind her. Three of her tentacles flapped in the current. The fourth hung severed, its wound seeping fluid. On the ocean floor, surrounded by his mates, Taalik waited to receive the funeral party. They placed the body before him. Taalik patted her head with his claw. The empty eye socket was raw and torn, the veins fluttering. The open wound became like a chasm yawning around him, its blackness spreading, snuffing out the light. The mates made a clicking sound, their song of mourning, like rocks hitting the seabed.

Taalik could smell Orak's presence. Her bitterness over this death tinged the water. It was Orak's idea to send Nong-wa on a mission, a food run into the deep waters. Taalik usually hesitated to send one of his mates. When he prayed to the Queen for guidance, she fell silent. Having no alternative, he reluctantly agreed. And now this.

Hovering over Nong-wa's broken body, the Shoots told the story of what happened. It played out exactly as Taalik expected. The sharks set a trap for them. Nong-wa sacrificed herself so the scouts could escape. She killed one shark and fought off another before sustaining a mortal wound, a weeping gash to her midsection. She even scolded the scouts for dragging her away. Unable to move, she continued to click at them until her gills went stiff.

When the song of mourning faded, Taalik told the scouts to bring Nong-wa to the infirmary—a deep crater where the wounded recuperated after the last encounter with the sharks. *Take her to the sick*, he said. *Let her strength become theirs*.

The scouts towed the body away. Taalik's claw held her face until the last possible moment, when she slipped from his grasp, her blood clouding his vision.

TAALIK LOST COUNT of how many times the darkness had passed over the water since the Sarcops arrived at this place. They settled here long enough for more explorers to go out and never return. Long enough for their numbers to dwindle, for a few egg crops to produce stillborn younglings, and for Orak to tell him more than once that she was afraid. She later retracted that statement, saying that she could not tell the difference between fear and anger. *Maybe for me there is no difference*, she said.

After the encounter with the floating island, Taalik led the convoy to the colder waters, where they weaved through mountains of ice until a glacier blocked the way. They stopped and marveled at it—a bluish white structure, expanding endlessly in every direction, from the surface to the black deep. The ice lived, they said. It fissured and fizzed, releasing air pockets and thundering with cracks.

Taalik chose a direction, and his people followed, staying close to the ice, trying to blend in. After several days, the water shallowed, and the glacier gave way to an inlet, like a giant claw opening, welcoming them in. The water was clear thanks to the runoff from the melting ice, and the shallowness of it allowed the sunlight to reach the ocean floor. Taalik would have to get used to the brightness. Craters puckered the terrain, and as the

Sarcops passed over them, a family of crabs scurried into their holes. A few of the Redmouths tried to dig them out, but Taalik told them to wait. Those crabs would have eggs, he told them. They could harvest the eggs for food. It was not ideal, but it would do for now.

And it did for a time. Many of their kind knew only famine and desperation. Here, they had a home. The Sarcops replenished their numbers, and soon sent expeditions to find new sources of food.

When the sharks found the Sarcops, having tracked them for many leagues, it took three days to fight them off. In that time, Taalik saw the folly of staying in this place. The inlet provided refuge only to fatten them up and serve them to the enemy. If only they could reason with the attackers, and convince them that their true adversary waited above the surface.

Taalik and Orak led a counteroffensive, hoping to surprise the sharks. But when they left the safety of the inlet and entered the open water, Taalik's mouth gaped at the sight—enemy fish, everywhere, forming a virtual glacier of their own. Every living creature with teeth must have followed the Sarcops here to finish them off, to wipe out the Queen's abomination. These fish were not even intelligent. Instinct and fear drove them to band together, to hunt, to murder. Once the Sarcops were all dead, the sharks would most likely disperse as though nothing had happened.

Taalik ordered a retreat. The Sarcops would never again enjoy the element of surprise. They had nowhere to go.

Desperate, Taalik swam to the other end of the inlet. When he reached the edge of the water, he surfaced, hoping to find that the ice surrounding the inlet was merely a wall, perhaps even surmountable. But upon climbing to the top, he discovered that the gray sheet extended all the way to the horizon, with an equally gray sky hanging over it. If they could survive another season, maybe enough of them could adapt and be able to leave the water. But the Queen had not yet bestowed this gift upon them.

When Taalik rejoined the Juggernauts, he issued standard orders to keep watch. As time passed, the scent of the invaders permeated the inlet, reminding the Sarcops of their impending defeat. Aware that a frontal assault would not be necessary, the enemy preferred to pick them off a few at a time. Some nights, the sharks would let the smell of Sarcops blood hang by the entrance, so that anyone who dared to peer into the deep would breathe in a dead comrade. Taalik continued his ritual mating, despite the odor of the savages clinging to everything. Not even the fluids from his coupling could mask it. This cruelty they exhibited, this pleasure in inflicting suffering, was a new adaptation. So many of the sharks—the older ones—bore the scars from human implements, the hooks and spears, nets and propellers. Even in this frozen place at the edge of the world, the evil of humanity poisoned the water.

A few of the Juggernauts talked about making a run for it. With a surprise offensive, they could puncture the blockade and make it into open waters. Many would die, and the First of Us would be placed at great risk, but it was better than waiting to go extinct. It meant leaving behind the weaker ones, as well as the eggs. Taalik stalled them, saying that they still had food, whereas the attackers needed to forage in the outlying areas. Meanwhile, three egg clutches in a row produced new Juggernauts. They had time. How much, he could not say.

ON THE DAY Nong-wa died, Taalik retreated to a crater far from the entrance to the inlet. Right on cue, as the light disappeared in the west, Riyya, his ninth mate, visited him. She smelled of salt and ammonia—a welcome change from the previous night, when Asha arrived with the enemy's blood still venting through her gills. Riyya said nothing, preferring instead to coil around Taalik until he felt ready to join with her. When they finished, he told Riyya to find Orak.

*Orak does not wish to speak with you*, Riyya said.

After she left him, Taalik rested at the bottom of his crater. He closed his eyes and tried to calculate how long the food stores would last. When he opened them, a blinding light forced him to squint. He no longer swam in the shallows. Instead, he stood on his claws, in the dirt, gulping the thin air. The sun burned white in a blue sky. Massive trees sprung from the earth. He knew then that he was dreaming. The Queen spoke to him at last. She heard his call.

The Queen showed him something he did not at first understand. One of his people—one of the crablike ones—nursed her eggs in a nest spun out of silk. In her perch, the creature sensed the web vibrating, shuddering. An intruder approached. Taalik felt the land-crab's fear. She scrambled to protect her young. But there were so many—beasts covered in fur, mounted on insects kidnapped from the Queen's army, enslaved and brainwashed. *Over there*, Taalik shouted. *No, wait, there are more over there!* The land-crab could not hear him. Predators moved in. The nest collapsed. The invaders cracked open the eggs and killed the young ones as they emerged blinded and confused. Taalik smelled their blood.

Everything went black. Taalik shook with rage and fear. These beasts of the earth consumed all in their path, the innocent and the damned.

A weightless sensation buoyed him. A cloudless blue sky came into focus, with the sun hanging over the glacier. Despite the wind, Taalik did not need to blink or squint.

A human boy stood at the edge of the glacier. Scrawny, with sunken eyes and spindly limbs, wearing a thin fabric over his skinny body. Despite the boy's weakness, he stretched out his arms toward the sun, and it obeyed. With his bony hands, the boy commanded the sun to descend. Taalik knew this child. He had known him his whole life. The boy Michael, the human prophet who once spoke with the Queen herself.

At the edge of the glacier, a column of ice trembled and broke free, collapsing into the black water in a mountain of white foam. The sun brightened as more pieces of the glacier crumbled. Taalik reached out his claws and realized that he could see through the boy's eyes. Together, they commanded the ball of fire to collide with the ice. The glacier buckled. Fissures burst, releasing geysers of salt water. A canyon formed, and the inlet spilled into it.

The deed done, Taalik rose higher into the sky until he viewed the events from orbit. A blue line sliced through the white expanse, leading to the sea on the other side. A path to freedom for his people. Instead of cutting their way through their attackers, they would command the morning star to reshape the world.

Taalik saw a long journey, from the northern ice cap into the green forests of the south. And in the midst of the foliage, a gray slab stuck out, an insult to the natural beauty. A city built by humans. Only there could Taalik take control of the sun. To do so, he would have to find the child, the prophet who wielded the Queen's power.

Taalik plummeted. His tentacles flapped in the wind. The sea spread out around him. When he hit the surface, he opened his eyes to find himself in the crater again.

Taalik took in the smells. Though his body was exhausted, his mind felt sharper than ever, as it often did after a revelation from the Queen. Now he needed to act.

He swam past the nursery and through the crab farms. At the mouth of the inlet, a row of Juggernauts kept watch. The water smelled clean—no sign of the enemy. And yet they appeared without warning these days, as if dropped from the sky. Taalik scanned the soldiers until he spotted Orak. She had already seen him. He waved her over.

*She spoke to me*, he said.

Orak glared at him. *Do you wish to know why Nong-wa is dead?*

*What do you mean?*

*I killed her. I ordered her to go with the scouts because she wanted to ram the blockade, against your wishes. Her death will stall any more talk of mutiny. For now.*

Her voice gave off a sharp iciness, as unforgiving as the glacier that surrounded them.

*Do you see what I am prepared to do to protect you?* she asked. *If I have to save you from this Queen who haunts your mind, I will do that as well.*

*The Queen has revealed a way out. But it will be difficult.*

Taalik looked past her to the entrance of the inlet, its towering walls piercing the surface. The Juggernauts were watching him. *All of you*, he said. *The Queen speaks to us once more.*

They clicked in response, singing praises to Hymenoptera Unus.

*Take every boulder you can find, every column of ice. Create a barricade. Seal the inlet.*

*Seal the inlet?* Orak said.

*Do it now.*

Soon the ground shook with their efforts. Each boulder that fell into place echoed with a loud *clack* through the water, like the claws of some giant lobster.

*My Egg*, Orak said, the first time she had addressed him as such in a long time. *Tell me what you are doing.*

*The inlet must be protected while we are gone.*

*Gone?*

*We must journey across the ice*, he said. *To the human stronghold. The answers we seek await us there.*

*You told us that we must flee from the humans.*
*We can no longer hide. So we will attack before they strike.*
*But you are the only one who can leave the water.*
*The Queen calls on all of us. Today, we find out who will*
answer.

As she contemplated this, another boulder fell into place. A
cloud of dust mushroomed from the growing pile of debris. The
infirmary attendants and crab farmers stopped what they were
doing to join in. A few of the nursery workers held the eggs to
keep them from shaking.

As the chaos surrounded them, Taalik reached out his tentacle
and waited for Orak to take it with hers. She did so, but looked
away.

*Do not be afraid*, he said. *We will harness the sun and make
it do our bidding. The Queen has chosen you as well. To see the
sun for yourself.*

THE INLET BECAME a lake. When construction on the wall fell silent,
the Sarcops floated before the new edifice. They were safe, but
trapped. The barrier cut off the noises from the deep, and sealed
out the scent of the enemy. The water seemed darker and colder.
The odors grew stale. The lake became like a hollowed out carcass, waiting for scavengers to clear it away.

The Juggernauts rallied at the northern end of the lake to sur-
vey the cliff they would have to scale. Taalik could see defeat
bleeding into the eyes of even his most trusted soldiers. Only
the First of Us had crossed over into the world of the Queen. He
told them they would follow the ice until the seas opened again.
They could swim the rest of the way. When one of the soldiers
asked how long it would take to find the water, Taalik said he
didn't know.

*The Queen did not lead us here to abandon us*, he said. *We
will adapt, the way she did.*

That was why they had come here. Only this ordeal would transform the Sarcops into the Queen's new army. She sacrificed herself for them. She took on the weight of the world's suffering, reliving every death in order to redeem all life. Their pain was a mere fraction of what she experienced for thousands of years.

Orak, Asha, Riyya, and Zirsk would join the expedition, along with a handful of other Juggernauts. The rest would stay behind. There were enough males from each class to continue breeding. The remaining females would take charge, and only those males who obeyed would be allowed to mate.

Together, the Juggernauts rose to the surface. When they reached the top, only Taalik emerged into the cold air. Snow fell from white clouds, and a wind agitated the water. Taalik hooked his claws onto the glacier and began to climb. When he inhaled, the cold wind burned his throat, like breathing in a cloud of dust from the ocean floor. As the pain subsided, he looked down. The top of Orak's head poked through the surface, her eyes scanning this alien landscape. She paddled closer to the wall, gripped it, and lifted herself out. Taalik watched as she opened her mouth to let the air in. She fought through a coughing fit until she at last regained control.

Soon the entire expedition clung to the wall. In the lead, Taalik heard his comrades' grunting, along with an occasional crack from a bad foothold. Their first taste of gravity would be more difficult than his, but they would manage.

The wind blew stronger at the top, sweeping snow across the ice. A storm tumbled over the glacier. He stared into it to show he was not afraid.

Within minutes, the rest of the expedition joined Taalik at the summit, awaiting his instructions. He did not have to speak. The storm rolling in spoke for him. They would have to walk right through it.

# CHAPTER 12

## UPHEAVAL

STORM ARRIVED ON the first night of their journey. D'Arc's fur became so soaked that she could ring out the tip of her tail. As she shivered under a tree, Falkirk prepared dinner, using his poncho as a tarp. A couple of bottles collected water next to him. Despite the noise from the rain, D'Arc could hear Falkirk whispering to himself. He thanked God for the food, thanked the Prophet for peace, and asked for guidance in the days to come. And then he said, "Sierra, Amelia, Yeager—watch over me." He mumbled something else that D'Arc couldn't make out.

"Food's ready," he said.

She joined him under the warm halo of the tarp. They sat with their knees facing each other. With a day of hiking behind them, the meal seemed almost decadent. A stew boiled in the pot, made of protein rations, seaweed, and beans. The first mouthful dropped into her empty stomach, warming her. She had spoken very little on this first leg of the journey. At least four days of walking remained, five if this rain continued. In nearly every step she took, D'Arc caught herself thinking, *no, we can still go back*. The excitement from the morning evaporated so quickly out here in the unknown. She would find it again, but she needed to fight through this first.

"Who are those people you were talking to?" she asked.

Falkirk paused. "My family. They're gone. But not really."

The dying fire let out one last pop. An ember landed on her fur. She patted it out.

"Maybe we should talk about Hosanna," he said.

She continued her line of questioning from when they had first met. The husky patiently answered everything, down to details about what the humans smelled like, what music the rats listened to, how big the main temple was.

D'Arc devoted the entire next day to interrogating him about the *al-Rihla* expedition. She wondered about the crew—what species were represented, what skills allowed them to qualify. She asked what they expected to find in the Caribbean, in the isthmus of Central America, on the coast of Africa. But her most important question was why. Why would people leave the fragile civilization in Hosanna to explore?

Falkirk put it this way: "We want to meet a panda who speaks Mandarin."

"What do you mean?"

"We want to see who's out there. We want to hear their stories. We want to tell them ours."

She smiled. He gave her the best answer she could have asked for. "What about a lizard speaking Arabic?"

He laughed. "Or a silverback gorilla speaking Swahili?"

This made her giggle. "How about . . . a kangaroo. Speaking . . . Australian!"

Falkirk furrowed his brow. "Australian's not a language." D'Arc laughed. "It's not!" he said.

The next day, while the rain fell so hard she could drink it as it ran down her face, she asked him if he had killed his master. When he didn't answer right away, she apologized for being

so forward. "It's okay," he said. "But be careful with that one."
Though he did not kill his master, he did join the war, along with
his siblings. All of them died in the conflict.

"What do you whisper to your family at night?" she asked.

"I say, 'Forgive me.'"

She wanted to tell him about her own young ones. They did
not have names, only sounds and scents. She wanted forgiveness,
too—but mainly for the crime of barely remembering them.

To change the subject, she asked what Falkirk did in the military. After Golgotha, when the humans incorporated the animals
into their pack, Falkirk applied to the flight school. He always had
an interest in the humans' flying machines. Maybe God opened
this door so he could redeem himself. Out of hundreds of animal
applicants, he was one of only three selected. He rose in the
ranks so quickly that they even let him command a ship.

"So what happened?" she asked.

Falkirk took a split log from the pile and dropped it into the
fire. "The official report says that I was put on medical leave.
The humans wrote it that way so it wouldn't look like they were
discriminating against animals." The truth was that Falkirk had
done exactly what some of the more bigoted humans said he
would do. He panicked, and almost got his entire crew killed.

For over a year of training, Falkirk endured taunts from the
humans who would never trust a dog, as well as condescen-
sion from those who viewed him as a novelty, a token. He
preferred the outright bigots—at least he knew where he stood
with them. The nicer ones said things like, "You remind me
of my dog." Or they constantly harped on his newfound intelligence. "You can't learn how to fly this thing overnight," they
said. "The Queen can't just zap it into your brain like last time."

On his second flight after earning his wings, the *Vesuvius*
became trapped in a lightning storm. Falkirk tried to elevate it
above the system, only to stall one of the engines in the process.

And then his entire body went stiff, something that had never happened before. The officers on the bridge shouted at him. *What are your orders, sir?* His fingers coiled around the metal railing near the captain's chair. As one of the junior officers took command, the guards pried Falkirk's hands from the railing and carted him out. A few weeks later, he was reassigned to Special Operations. "I was chasing ghosts and dead ends until I came across you," he said.

Suddenly, she felt so small. These animals had been so brave. They lived so many lives while she hid in the forest. She had never failed, like he had. And thus she had barely lived.

D'Arc discussed her own military training without mentioning Mort(e). She thought of her friend with every step she took, every furtive glance behind her, often with a smile or a sigh, occasionally with a blank stare into the campfire. In the mornings, after waking from dreams of the ranch, it felt like something had been lost, another threshold entered right before the door slammed behind her. Things changed, people changed. She would change, too, no matter how much it hurt, no matter what was left of her on the other side.

On the fifth day of walking, after the clouds broke, D'Arc spotted an airship through the tree branches. The ship traveled at such a low altitude that she could make out its propellers and gondola. "The *Vesuvius*?" she asked.

"*Upheaval*," Falkirk said. Unlike the double-barreled shape of the *Vesuvius*, the *Upheaval* had only one balloon. The smaller ship was faster, more heavily armed—a destroyer that accompanied the carrier. D'Arc and Falkirk followed the blimp to the edge of the forest and along a river. Twice she tripped because she couldn't take her eyes off it. At dusk, when Falkirk proposed that they set up camp and eat, D'Arc said they should keep following the ship. Falkirk refused. "You'll get used to them," he said.

"Why don't they use one of those airships for the expedition?"

"For the same reason the bats only sent one of their kind. Not worth the risk."

"Seems like a waste to have those amazing ships and never go anywhere."

Falkirk rubbed his hands. "If we're going to work together, I might as well be blunt with you." Ever since the Union's failed attempt to seize part of the wolf territory, the airships served mainly as reconnaissance vehicles, constantly circling the perimeter. The wolves regarded the animals in Hosanna as traitors for working with the humans. Stories circulated about the wolves capturing people, making them eat their comrades. It was a dangerous world, the kind of world that, deep down, many of the animals wanted.

In the morning, D'Arc woke Falkirk and asked if he was ready to get moving again. "We're not going to catch the *Upheaval*," he yawned. In the predawn light, D'Arc dismantled the camp as noisily as she could. She slammed the pots, splashed water onto the dying cinders, broke twigs for no reason. Falkirk glared at her. "All right, Admiral," he said. "You win."

As the morning fog evaporated, D'Arc spotted the ship again, much closer than she expected. They arrived at a bend in the river, where the canopy opened to reveal the entire sky. *Upheaval* came to a halt and spun clockwise, its nose pointing at D'Arc. A warm sensation began in her chest and spread outward, like a blossoming flower. This world was so full of magic. Life was not simply a struggle to survive. There was a future to explore.

"Do you see it?" Falkirk asked.

"Yes!"

"No," he said, pointing at the horizon. "Do you *see* it?"

She had been so fixated on the ship that she did not notice the city right in front of her. Beyond the next cluster of trees, the river swelled against a stone monolith. The great dam. South of that, the city of Hosanna spread into the valley, mostly brick and tan concrete and gray asphalt, glinting with silver from the skyscrapers. Hundreds of windmills spun furiously, some modern and sleek, others made of wood. The airship hovered, preparing to dock on the remains of an office building. And there was movement. Cars and trucks. When they got closer, she would see people. Closer still, she would meet them, all separate worlds unto themselves, each with their own memories and dreams.

"Come on," Falkirk said. "The city is waiting."

HOURS LATER, D'ARC sat on a bench in the lobby of Tranquility headquarters. While Falkirk chatted with the rat who operated the main desk, D'Arc took in the scenery. People came and went through the massive swinging doors. Off to the side, a family of rats pleaded with a feline officer, who licked his paw as he listened. Two canine agents argued over which one of them had logged more hours on some assignment. When they saw D'Arc watching them, they huddled closer and whispered. Beyond the main registration area stood rows of desks, five wide and four deep. There were even some humans sitting at the desks, men and women, like the images from D'Arc's magazines and picture books. This building must have been a warehouse or a factory before, judging from the windows that went from waist-high to the ceiling. The place was so loud, the scents so acrid and fake. Wading through the crowds on the streets to get here had been disconcerting enough, but this room seemed designed to harness the noise and aim it at everyone.

Falkirk led her up a zigzagging staircase to the second level, where sullen Tranquility officers of every species walked in packs of three or four, talking jargon to one another. Falkirk stopped at a door with a nameplate that read CHIEF OF TRANQUIL- ITY. He knocked once and opened it. Inside the corner office, a chocolate pit bull with a handgun strapped to her belt leaned on her desk. A pink scar spliced her face, and a medallion dangled from a chain around her neck. Beside her, hands clasped, stood a cat with fur the color of granite. Cardboard boxes lined the walls, each filled with books, picture frames, and stationery. In the corner, a life-size statue of a human soldier held aloft a dagger, while her free hand clutched her chest.

"Lieutenant," the pit bull said. "I'm glad you're safe."

"What's going on in here?" Falkirk asked, pointing to the boxes.

"Right, sorry for the mess. My predecessor insisted on having a suite up here, away from the action. But I'm moving downstairs."

"You want to be in the middle of all that noise?"

The pit bull smiled. "It will be quiet with me there."

The smile faded as the chief gave D'Arc a long stare. "It *is* you," she said.

"It is."

"She calls herself D'Arc now, Chief," Falkirk added. He spelled it for her. "Not Sheba, and not the Mother."

"D'Arc, of course," the chief said. "I'm Wawa. This is my assistant, Grissom."

The cat nodded.

"Grissom is about to bring us some tea." She pointed to the door, and the cat obeyed.

Wawa approached D'Arc. "We've met before, on Golgotha. Though you might not remember."

"I don't. But I've heard the story many times."

"Mort(e) gave me this St. Jude medal," Wawa said. The medallion featured an image of a human in a long robe, with a ring surrounding his head, like a sun. The Old Man had never mentioned it. Perhaps he didn't want her to know that he once gave a present to another dog.

"How is he?" Wawa asked.

"He's fine. Healthy. Stubborn."

"I'm not surprised he stayed away."

"I told him to."

Wawa glanced at Falkirk.

"I needed to see all this for myself," D'Arc said. "To do this on my own." It was the first time she had used this rehearsed line since leaving the ranch, and she was already sick of it.

"To do this on your own," Wawa said. "That includes sailing the *al-Rihla*, I'm told."

Falkirk didn't tell her that he added the *al-Rihla* to his report. The husky lowered his head, embarrassed. D'Arc's tail dropped between her legs. The *al-Rihla*—this fantasy of exploring the world—suddenly felt like a terrible idea. The chief seemed to enjoy the tension she created.

The door squeaked open. Grissom entered with a tray of cups and a teapot. Wawa asked him to set it on the checkered rug by the windows. "We can talk about the expedition later," she said. "For now, I want to hear about this spider."

The cat left them to it. They sat in a triangle, the light from the window forming a trapezoid on the floor around them. Falkirk went first, talking about his meeting with the beavers. D'Arc sipped the tea, noting how different this filtered water tasted from the stuff she brewed on the ranch. When Falkirk finished, D'Arc told the chief about life on the ant farm, and the request for help from Lodge City. As they each gave their own accounts of the battle with Gulaga, Wawa leaned in closer, holding the cup to her mouth but not taking a sip.

"So you're convinced that this spider was intelligent," Wawa asked.

"Yes," Falkirk said. "But I don't think it could communicate. Not like the fish-heads."

The pit bull forced down a mouthful of her drink.

"So when do we get started?" Falkirk asked.

Wawa placed the saucer near the edge of her desk, causing the spoon to jingle. "Special Operations has been reassigned. I'm sorry."

Falkirk stood up. "Reassigned to what?"

"The murder case."

"Don't we have people working on that already?"

"We do. And we need more."

"Look, I don't like the murders either, but we're talking about a much bigger threat here."

"I've been over all of that with the Archon. I was overruled."

"What happened?"

Wawa glanced at the statue of the human. The woman's neck had a ring carved into it, as did her wrist and ankle. The eyes opened wide at the sight of something terrifying floating above. "New priorities," Wawa said.

Falkirk paced the floor. "I knew it."

"What are you talking about?" D'Arc said.

"The killer is targeting people who have used the translator," Wawa said. "The Prophet could be in danger. Nothing else matters until this situation gets resolved."

D'Arc remembered now—The Sons of Adam, the humans who protected Michael. They claimed that their leader killed a dog during the war with her bare hands.

"The SOA doesn't have jurisdiction over Tranquility," Falkirk said.

"No, but the Archon does."

"Oh, and our fearless leader would never disagree with the Sons of Adam."

"Lieutenant—"

"The Prophet's in a bunker! No one's even seen him for months."

"Lieutenant, when you're done with your tantrum, I'd like to continue."

"Yes, Chief."

"The sooner we can solve this case, the sooner we can get back to the anomalies. And there is some good news."

Wawa opened a drawer in her desk and lifted out a metal box. "Grab that teapot," she said to Falkirk. "I want to show you something."

"Should she—" he said, gesturing to D'Arc. "*Can* she stay for this?"

"She's part of our officer exchange program, isn't she?"

D'Arc smiled. She tried to imagine what Falkirk had told the chief in his message to her—maybe something about how she promised to feed him to the ants when they first met.

The lid squeaked as Wawa opened the box, reached inside, and pulled out a piece of metal—a pistol, unlike any D'Arc had ever seen. The stock and the barrel were the same silvery color. The gun resembled a laser that a spaceman would fire in some old comic book.

Wawa flipped a latch on the pistol, which opened the breach. She told Falkirk to pour the hot water into the opening. He hesitated. "Just do it," she said. With the barrel full, Wawa clicked it shut again. She pressed a button on the handle, and the pistol came to life with a humming noise. A red light blinked on the side.

"Get behind me," she said. D'Arc and Falkirk exchanged glances and then hid behind the chief. The red light on the gun switched to blue. Wawa aimed at the statue and fired. A projectile burst on the strator's face, followed by debris pinging off the walls.

The door flung open, and Grissom cautiously poked his head into the room.

"It's okay," Wawa said. "Wait outside." Grissom closed the door without a word.

Falkirk walked over to the statue and ran his hands over the strator's face. There was no damage. A fragment of the projectile came to rest near D'Arc's foot. She plucked it from the floor. It was a mere piece of ice, the cold burning her fingers.

"All of the murder victims had a bullet wound and no bullet," Wawa said. "I think they were killed with one of these."

Wawa explained that the autopsies had yielded no clues, so she asked her team to investigate all prewar weapons, including those still in development. This device came out of a joint American-Israeli project, based at an R&D facility in Virginia. At close range, the ice bullet could puncture the skull and then melt, leaving no trace.

"So the murderer has to be a human," Falkirk said.

"Or maybe another user. Who knows how that device can scramble a person's brain?"

They would need to interview the remaining users in the city. But that meant finding people who had yet to come forward. Though many former users served as advisors to Tranquility, others neglected to report this experience when applying for asylum. It made sense; many people, animal and human, condemned the Queen's experiments. And with a killer on the loose, the new residents had yet another incentive to keep their mouths shut.

"D'Arc, do you know how to use a computer?" Wawa asked.

D'Arc told the chief about a laptop she had salvaged a year earlier. She got it to work, and managed to type some words and save the files. Then the computer died.

"That puts you ahead of most people in this town," Wawa said.

"I'm only staying a few weeks," D'Arc said, like a reaction she could not control.

"Good," Wawa said. "That's all the time we have. By then, all the users will be dead. I'll be fired. A fish-head might even be in charge of Tranquility."

She told Falkirk to give D'Arc a tour of the place. Then they would have to get to work. Falkirk had more to say, but the chief gave him a look that said the meeting was over. After exchanging goodbyes, D'Arc and Falkirk walked out, stepping around the melted puddles from the ice gun.

SHORTLY AFTER STARTING the tour, somewhere between the cadet training facility and the crime lab, D'Arc acknowledged that Mort(e) was right about one thing: Hosanna was a sprawling mess of a city, many years away from the promise it showed. Entire neighborhoods needed reconstruction. The administrators would have to figure out how to develop the wetlands near the river, and to decontaminate the abandoned factories. Meanwhile, the lights at headquarters occasionally flickered, a garbage fire burned outside one of the windows, and the line of citizens waiting to file a complaint gained more people by the minute. And despite all of that, D'Arc already knew that she would be staying here for longer than a few weeks.

Falkirk took her to the garage. Inside, two rat mechanics worked on a squad car. D'Arc assumed that they were installing an engine that ran on vegetable oil.

"Of course the husky gets a nice female for a partner," one of the rats said.

"Yeah, Skydog over here gets all the perks!" the other one said.

"It's good to be back," Falkirk said with a sigh. "I missed you guys."

"How come we don't get a nice rat princess to train as a mechanic? I want one with a real fancy name. Like Elizabeth. Or Victoria."

"Or Alexandra," the other rat said.

Falkirk put an end to the banter by asking if he could test-drive one of the cars. The rats insisted that he pick any one he wanted. The husky chose a motorcycle—a red one with a tinted windshield. The rats bent over with laughter, calling him a show-off. When Falkirk said that they would be able to see better on a cycle, the rats laughed even harder.

"We can take a car, if you want," Falkirk said to D'Arc.

"The motorcycle is fine. Either one will be a first for me."

Falkirk got on and told her she could grip his belt. Sitting this close to him, D'Arc recalled the first time she had smelled his fur, that morning at the ranch. Though she panicked then, the scent made her feel safe now, like she was part of a pack.

Falkirk revved the engine. The vibration rattled her skeleton.

"It's good to have you back, Lieutenant," the first rat said.

"What would I do without our morning conversations?" Falkirk asked. He put the bike in gear and rolled forward. D'Arc almost fell off.

"Hold on tight, puppy!" the other rat said. "Skydog likes to fly!"

They sped along the waterfront, toward the dam that blocked off the river. Falkirk weaved between a handful of vehicles, mostly dump trucks hauling debris from the construction sites. In the heart of the city stood a tower made of stone, with the feet of a statue fastened to the top. The rest of the statue had been blasted away. That building, the former City Hall, served as the headquarters for the Archon and his council.

"And look at that," Falkirk said, motioning toward the river. A ship swayed in the current. Painted a gleaming white, the vessel was about two hundred feet long, with windmills spinning on the deck. The word AL-RIHLA was stenciled on the side.

"That's a . . . That's a cutter ship!" she said. "Navy. Or Coast Guard, maybe."

Falkirk laughed. "See what I mean? Maybe you *should* apply."

As they got closer to the dam, Falkirk explained that the river swelled at this point, creating a pool and a new nature preserve. The dam itself formed a bridge to the New Jersey side. A military checkpoint forced the vehicles to form a line for inspection.

Falkirk parked the bike on the exit ramp, right beside the pool. He tapped his nails on the handlebar. "I've been thinking about your new name," he said. "I'm not sure if I like it."

"What's wrong with it?"

"We have enough people around here who claim to speak for God. And then you name yourself after a human warrior who got herself killed doing that very thing."

"She was brave. She was a young girl who took command of an army."

"Maybe it was bravery. Maybe it was foolishness. On everyone's part."

"Well, what does *your* name mean?"

"Actually, it comes from the same era as yours, give or take a few years."

Falkirk adopted the name shortly after surviving a skirmish on the Canadian side of Lake Erie. An American armored division abandoned over a thousand soldiers and rolled away in the night. The infantry was left to fight in the dark. A total slaughter. The next morning, Falkirk's brother told him that it resembled a medieval battle he once read about, in which the cavalry left the foot soldiers behind.

"I didn't pick the name to glorify warfare," Falkirk said. "It's a reminder of the folly of war. That's stuck on me forever."

"I'm keeping D'Arc."

"Fine. But remember that there are people who need you for their own ends. They might speak for God, but they rarely listen. And sometimes they hear what they want to hear."

A police car rolled up beside them, lights whirring. The driver, a raccoon, held a microphone to his mouth. "What's your business there?" Falkirk slapped his ID on the windshield. The raccoon leaned forward and read it. "Sorry, Lieutenant," he said.

Falkirk pocketed the ID as the car drove away, leaving a cloud of grease in its wake. He pointed to a building to the south—the cadet barracks. D'Arc would stay there until they could find a place for her. "Though we could put your name into the housing registry."

"I don't need anything," she said. "No special treatment. I can stay at the barracks."

"It gets really cramped there."

"That's fine."

He watched her for a second to detect any hesitation. She would not give it to him. She had dealt with the Old Man enough to know when someone was trying to read her mind.

On the way to the barracks, Falkirk described his own experiences there. After his demotion from the airship crew, he bunked with the new recruits, most of whom had just arrived from the countryside. The building was once a high school. The academy gutted it to make room for the cadets, but it lacked a real kitchen, galley, or decent living quarters. "So stay away from the protein porridge at dinner time," he said. "And use the hot plate in the cafeteria to boil your drinking water."

"What about breakfast?"

"No breakfast. I'm picking you up at dawn. We're getting started right away."

# CHAPTER 13

## DEVOLUTION

HE HOUSE SETTLED, dusty and quiet. The forest stilled. The hours inched along.

Mort(e) spent the first day without her pacing the abandoned Alpha pen, sometimes grinding his foot into the divots left by the herd. Their oily pheromones lingered, and even the soaking rain could not wash away the smell. He wondered how long it would last. All things disperse, he thought. Given time, the wind carries everything away.

He checked the inventory. The salted meat would get him through the warm months, and he would plant some tubers in the next week. The two plastic barrels were full of water. The bees did not notice how things had changed, and continued their work of producing honey. Mort(e) did a weapons check, testing every pistol and rifle, no longer caring if the gunfire alerted people in the forest. All but two of the guns still worked. He had enough supplies for a long trip into the west with Sheba. With D'Arc. But they would anchor him here until she returned.

How many humans lived and died like this during the war? There must have been thousands of them hiding in cabins, caves, and bunkers, convinced that they were the last of their kind. They probably formed relationships with inanimate objects and covered all the mirrors so they wouldn't have to watch themselves age. They wrote letters to dead people and etched homemade tattoos into their skin. They fiddled with the knobs on CB radios for hours, mistaking every squeak and whistle for a voice. They ran out of liquor and then, while dying from an infected cut, they remembered that the alcohol could have sanitized the wound.

A few days later, when the clouds broke and D'Arc had not returned, Mort(e) gave in and finally wept.

He let the tubers go unattended for an extra week before planting them. Though he didn't care for the work, he concluded that starving was not a good way to die. The smell of fresh dirt distracted him from the idea of dropping everything and going to Hosanna. The reasons to stay on the ranch were solid. He could miss D'Arc on the road, or she could get angry with him for following her, and the whole plan would backfire. But neither reason could stop him from thinking about it every waking hour.

In the early mornings, he heard the noises from the spider over and over again. Though the sound came through as clicks and taps, he could translate the message. Gulaga was screaming for him to spare her children, the way Sheba had begged Daniel to spare hers. Sometimes, the arachnid spoke with Michael's voice, weeping for his parents in the dark. With each passing day, Mort(e) found it harder to believe that he had imagined it all.

It did not take long for him to start walking around the house on all fours, sniffing at things, rubbing the side of his face on doorjambs and table legs to mark his territory. The Messiah, the Queenslayer, reduced to his pre-Change form like some late-stage EMSAH patient.

As the weeks dragged on, these devolved states would last for hours, sometimes days. He would not speak, nor even think with words. During those phases, his mind emptied of the things he regretted saying to her. He would stop thinking about all the signs he had missed, the clues that she would choose the husky and his human city over her true home. Crawling around the house, he saw the world in muted colors. Random sounds, like tree branches bumping a window frame, made his ears perk up. For a few nights in a row, he fell asleep inside a cardboard box that smelled like sawdust.

One day, he started licking his paws and wrists, something he had trained himself to stop doing after the Change. Here, with no one watching, he covered every inch of his limbs, tail, and as far down his spine as his new body would allow. The taste of it transported him to the Martinis' basement. The next day, while coughing up clots of hair and saliva, he imagined Culdesac finding him like this, the bobcat grousing about lazy pets who never learned how to survive in the wild.

Mort(e) concluded that he deserved this somehow. He drove her away. All those years spent searching, and he never learned to actually live. Before all this, loving her meant hoping to find her again. Now it meant letting her go. And for the first time, he hated it all. He wanted love to mean something else, though he wasn't sure what exactly, so long as it brought her here again, so she could replenish her scent in the bed sheets. When that ran out for good, Mort(e) would have no reason to keep breathing.

A COLD FRONT descended on the ranch. Mort(e) slept coiled in a circle on the rug. With his ear to the floor, he heard the wood creaking, and the occasional insect burrowing into the soil. All the noises hurt, and yet the pain gave him strength, hardening him into a block of stone that would one day be indistinguishable from the ruins of this house.

Whatever fate awaited him here, he didn't want to be cold anymore, so he decided to build a fire. Using a crowbar, Mort(e) levered each fence post from the dirt, stacking them under the overhang of the roof. With an ax he split the posts into smaller pieces of firewood. The damp air seeped into his fur, sucking out the warmth. No matter how much heat he generated with each swing, the cold would win.

As he lifted the handle over his head, the unmistakable reek of rotten fish entered his nose. No hint of canine in the odor, only scales and oil. The spider's voice echoed in his mind again, faint yet still screaming, cursing him.

They had come for him at last.

"All right," he said with a calmness he could barely recognize. Mort(e) entered the side door and picked up the shotgun leaning on the stove. He stationed the weapons all over the house these days for easy retrieval. On his way through the living room, he grabbed the rifle resting on the coffee table. He kicked the front door open and walked out, double-barreled, ready to meet his fate. Once outside on the porch, he leaned the rifle on the railing, then aimed the shotgun into the trees and fired. No targets, just pumping the forestock and blasting into the trees, the leaves bursting with each shot. The gun empty, Mort(e) dropped it, picked up the rifle, and switched off the safety.

"Leave me alone!" he shouted, the cold barrel pressed to his cheek.

A silence fell, but the scent remained, thick and noxious.

"Hold your fire!" someone yelled from behind a tree.

Mort(e) pulled the trigger again. "No!"

Something flapped over the house. A bat. Had to be. Mort(e) slid along the wall, aiming upward, but unable to see past the awning. He would not take cover inside. Whoever was out there needed to see him brandishing his gun like a crazy person.

"Mort(e), it's Castor!" the voice shouted. "I need to talk to you!"

Maybe both species blamed him for destroying Lodge City. They joined forces to flush him out. But they would not take him alive.

"Mort(e), it's about Sheba!"

As he scanned the forest, the bat flew over the house again, well within range. Mort(e) tracked it through the scope until the creature perched on the edge of the roof. Dangling over the porch railing, Gaunt of Thicktree resembled some demonic wind chime. The bat watched him through his polarized goggles. Mort(e) lowered the rifle. If Gaunt would risk his life by getting this close, then Mort(e) needed to listen. Besides, he had not spoken to a real person in weeks.

"Come on out, beaver," Mort(e) said. He tried to remember how to tell Gaunt that it was good to see him in Chiropteran. But, good bats that they were, they did not have a word for *see*. It took Mort(e) two tries before he managed to squeak out, "I hear you now okay, yes."

Gaunt gave four short squeaks. *Eee-eee-eee-eee*. Mort(e) did not understand. The bat may have been laughing at him.

The beaver came bumbling out of the forest, hands raised, his glasses perched on the crown of his head. Mort(e) leaned the rifle on the railing so Castor would not have to worry.

"You're all friends again?" Mort(e) asked.

"We're partners. Rebuilding Lodge City together."

"It didn't look that way the last time I saw you."

"You were right about Nikaya," Castor said. "Enough of us know that now."

Gaunt chirped in agreement. He added something about Nikaya sweeping out the caves.

"What is that smell?" Mort(e) asked.

Gaunt gave a disapproving screech. It literally meant *bad*, though in this context it may have been closer to *nasty* or *disgusting*.

On the trail, five of the Watchers emerged from the trees. That bigmouth Fram was noticeably absent. The beavers pushed a wheelbarrow covered with a blue tarp. The smell seemed to ooze from underneath the plastic, drawing flies. Castor signaled for one of the beavers to remove the covering.

Underneath was a pile of greenish-brown slime that nevertheless included distinct parts. A head with black eyes, tentacles spilling over the sides, a pair of stout legs. Two bullet holes in the chest leaked a clear fluid, while the mouth hung open like a bear trap. The husky had spoken of creatures like this. D'Arc ran off with him to look for the goddamn things.

"You saw D'Arc?" Mort(e) asked. "I mean Sheba. My friend."

"Don't you want to hear about this?"

"But you saw her? On her way to find the husky?"

The beavers looked at one another. Mort(e) didn't care about the pity in their expressions. "She came for Falkirk and they left together," Castor said. "That's all I know."

"Go on."

The creature was female, Castor said. They named her Lola. They found her crawling near the remnants of Gulaga's web. One of the Watchers panicked and shot her. Though wounded, the creature caught the beaver by the neck and tossed him against a wall, breaking his spine. When she retreated to the water, the Watchers cut off her escape. She tried to run through the stadium, only to get tangled in the strands of silk. It took more shots than Castor had expected, but the creature finally stopped moving.

"We came here to show you this." The beaver grabbed the claw and lifted it away from the creature's body. It had a thick keratin armor, supported by strong muscles under the exoskeleton, yet the tips of the pincers were delicate, almost like human fingers. It could strangle a beaver and then write him an apology letter.

"What about it?" Mort(e) asked.

"You don't recognize it?"

"It's a claw."

"Exactly," Castor said, letting the appendage drop. "It's identical to the spider's claws. Smaller, yes, but the same shape." He ran his finger along the curve of the pincer.

Mort(e) had seen the spider's limbs only from a distance. But he remembered well enough. While flying over the city with Gaunt, Mort(e) could have sworn that he even saw the spider pulling the web tight, like an old woman knitting.

"The husky came here to investigate anomalies, right?" Castor asked. "I'll bet these things were related somehow. Maybe the fish-head was checking on her cousin."

"Did you have to drag the body all the way out here?"

"You took some convincing the last time we visited. Remember?"

"I can't help you on another adventure," Mort(e) said. He stopped himself from telling Castor that he had lost enough.

"You don't have a choice. You need to go to the city and get your friend out of there. Right away. Find the husky and give him the claw." Castor gestured to one of his underlings. The beaver unhooked a cutlass from his belt. With one hand, he extended the claw from the wheelbarrow. With the other, he hacked away at the joint. The keratin proved resilient. Mort(e) could hear the blade biting into it, but it barely left a mark.

"I don't think I'm the best person for this," Mort(e) said.

"You're the Messiah. They'll listen to you."

*That's not necessarily a good thing*, Mort(e) thought.

"The night after we killed the fish-head, we saw something," Castor said.

He described it as a tidal wave on the river, pushing the water aside so that it boomed against the riverbank in great white columns. And inside the churning foam: fins, tentacles, armored plates like great tortoise shells. The Watchers stood guard, guns raised, in case any of the monsters made landfall. But the fleet continued on its way, uninterested in the tiny settlement.

"They're going south," Castor said. "I'll bet they've always—"

A grunt and a snort to their left, like some wild animal stalking them in the woods. Castor went stiff, his jaw fused shut around the last word he spoke. The beaver with the cutlass stepped away from the body. The claw, still attached, hung limply, the pincers touching the ground. *No*, Mort(e) thought. *That did* not *come from the—*

The creature bolted from the wheelbarrow, toppling it over. Impossibly fast. The beavers flinched. Mort(e) raised his hands as the greenish blur collided with him. He tumbled to the grass. Castor dropped next to him with a groan, face first. Rolling onto his belly, Mort(e) saw Lola running toward the house. When Gaunt saw her coming, he released his grip on the awning and flew away. The fish-head disappeared around the side of the building.

"You told me she was dead!" Mort(e) said.

"She *was*!"

Mort(e) got up and pursued the creature around the corner. The stink of ammonia made his eyes water. Through the haze of it, he spotted Lola perched on a boulder. The tentacles slithered like a pack of snakes. The skin changed from green to a dark gray—the same tint as the boulder. Lola turned and looked at him with massive black eyeballs. She blinked. Mort(e) saw the anger. He recognized the intelligence. As the creature leaned closer toward him—perhaps so Mort(e) could get a better look—he saw something else. He *felt* something else, the same thing he felt in his encounter with Gulaga. Though this fish-head was far from home and left for dead, she wasn't afraid. And she wanted Mort(e) to know that.

Lola bounded into the forest.

The beavers arrived. A few aimed their rifles into the woods, only to lower them in frustration. Mort(e)'s stomach twisted, sending another clot of hairballs to the top of his throat.

"They're headed for the dam," Castor said. "They're headed for Hosanna."

# CHAPTER 14

## COMMUNION

FALKIRK CLIMBED THE staircase to apartment 5C. A single fluorescent light illuminated the crumbling linoleum floor and the cracked plaster walls, painted a mustard color. At the door, he gave five knocks before opening. Inside, he found D'Arc where he had left her, kneeling beside a window with the curtain drawn. A sliver of overcast sky provided the only light in the room. Holding a telescope, D'Arc watched the apartment building across the street. The room was empty save for the rifle and sword leaning on the windowsill.

Falkirk dropped the satchel full of food on the floor. The cook at the mess hall gave him some vacuum-sealed simulations of the dog treats that Falkirk ate as a pet. Though vegan, the imitation treats were almost as good as the real thing.

"See anything?" he asked.

"Just the squirrels. When they left for work. Same time as yesterday."

Falkirk told her to take a lunch break. As they switched places, she asked him if he would eat with her. "I already ate three of those treats on the way here," he said.

Before this stakeout began, they spent two weeks interviewing translator users all over the city. The users had nothing in common other than a high rank in the Colonial army. A few admitted to knowing some of the victims. One of them, a cat with a hook for a hand, broke down in tears upon learning that her former commanding officer had been murdered.

The search for anyone with a connection to the ice gun also came up empty. But they caught a break when D'Arc, while combing the endless spreadsheets, noticed a discrepancy in the list of refugees entering the city. The database did not include people with a pending military status—in other words, anyone who might be of use to Tranquility. As a result, the records suffered from an indefinite lag time. Armed with the full list, D'Arc came across a translator user who had served in the Potomac campaign, near the weapons facility in Virginia. And, even better, no one had seen him for over a week.

Falkirk groaned when he saw the species: opossum. An inscrutable race. When the war ended, few opossums felt the need to wait in line for refugee status in Hosanna. They could survive on anything and barely needed shelter. The user D'Arc had found went by the name of Yatsi, an advisor to Tranquility who helped train recruits in infiltration and spying. Yatsi moved to the city three seasons earlier, staying at the residence of his brother, a sanitation worker who called himself Teyu. When D'Arc and Falkirk visited the apartment, no one answered. They interviewed the neighbors, all of whom claimed that neither of the brothers had stayed at the apartment for days.

Yatsi was most likely a target, not a suspect. But the opportunity to run a stakeout with D'Arc proved too good to resist. For at least a little while, Falkirk would have her to himself, away from the idiots who jokingly called him Skydog.

His personal feelings aside, D'Arc lived up to her supernatural reputation. She was bright, inquisitive, precise, able to adapt, eager to learn. She made the most of her time at the barracks, enlisting the help of her young bunkmates to learn about city life.

Given that all the cadets were animals, the layout of the barracks was more conducive to pack behavior. Isolating dorm rooms were removed, replaced with a communal sleeping area. In a matter of days, D'Arc went from never seeing another dog to spooning with dozens of them every night.

As far as the cadets knew, D'Arc was a law enforcement officer out in the frontier, shadowing a Tranquility agent while waiting to hear about her application to join the *al-Rihla*. While the first-year cadets gained experience by handling paperwork for headquarters, D'Arc got to do some actual investigating. Every morning when she met with Falkirk, she shared stories about her new friends, the food they cooked, the habits that the various species kept. One night, a pug named Razz brewed a homemade alcoholic concoction, a kind of moonshine. The next morning, Falkirk needed to pull over to let D'Arc vomit. She kept saying she was sorry. "It's all right," Falkirk said, laughing.

Without mentioning it, D'Arc extended her time in Hosanna, and eventually stopped talking about the ranch. Out of respect, Falkirk stopped asking about it.

Ever since this penance began, Falkirk's life had been wound so tightly around his neck. But now, he felt this burden begin to ease at last. When D'Arc saved him from the web, a future revealed itself, in defiance of the present. The Prophet taught that no one was beyond saving, even people whose own mothers had cursed them. *Do not give up on me, Michael*, he thought. *I know the way back now.*

"There's a communion this week," he said.

D'Arc looked up from her meal. "You mean a prayer gathering?"

He said yes. The Sons of Adam held the communions once a month. The strators and the elders lined the balcony of the Prophet's residence, leading the faithful in song and praise. Sometimes Michael even made an appearance.

"The people who go," D'Arc said. "They're *all* believers?"

"Not all of them. A lot of them want to see the humans."

"But you believe. Don't you?"

"I believe."

"Even though . . ."

"Even though there are reasons not to?"

D'Arc lowered her head and took another bite of her lunch.

"If you go with me this week, some of your questions may be answered," he said.

"Do I have to sing?"

"Yes. And if you mess up the words, the strators will arrest you."

She stopped chewing and stared at him.

"I'm kidding!" he said. It may have been the first joke he had ever told her.

"But wait," she said. "The humans are seriously devoted, aren't they? Razz told me that the strators would all jump off a cliff if the Prophet told them to."

"I don't know about that. Everyone interprets the words of the Prophet differently."

"What about you? Do you hear God's voice?"

He needed to tread carefully. She may not have been ready to listen. "I hear my own voice," he said.

He told her about wandering the countryside after the quarantine, waiting to die. And when the Colony fell, he sought out the alliance of humans and animals. When he saw the mortal enemies joining hands, begging forgiveness of one another, Falkirk knew that God had new plans for him. And they would not be easy. He would be tested.

"The person I was would have to be burned away," he said. "There's no other way to change. Fire and ice. Acid and steel. They do the trick."

"You've convinced me," she said. "I'll go with you."

She returned to her telescope. One day, maybe soon, she would understand what he was talking about. Then he could ask her the question that still nagged him, ever since the gulag: Was she part of his long crucible, or the end of it? Or perhaps *she* was the real test. He would need to prove his worth by protecting her. Even if that meant following her across the sea, far from here, where it was quiet enough to hear God's voice.

THAT NIGHT, FALKIRK dozed on the floor while D'Arc kept watch. A lovely dream washed over him, transforming the cracked ceiling into storm clouds, and the hardwood to a crunchy snow. He walked on all fours. His paws made a sucking sound as he extracted them from the footprints they made. Far off into the white, smoke curled from the chimney of the Weyrich's cabin. Falkirk was so excited that he emptied his bladder. The hot urine hissed in the snow, releasing a burst of steam that tickled his belly. The clouds brightened and the wind blew, carrying the howls of his brothers and sisters. They called him forward. Or they warned him to stay away. Falkirk could not tell anymore. *Tell me*, he said. *Talk to me.* Soon the wind and the howling merged into one screeching noise. A voice emerged from the din. His mother. *The white takes you*, she barked.

"*Fal*kirk!"

He jolted awake. The brief sensation of falling made his legs weak. He rolled to his side, facing D'Arc, who peered out the window through the telescope. "What is it?" he asked.

"One of the opossums just went inside."

"Which one?"

"I don't know. Does it matter?"

It didn't. Rubbing his eyes, Falkirk got to his feet and went to the window. Across the street, the light clicked on in the opossum's apartment. D'Arc stayed at the telescope. Falkirk took the binoculars from the windowsill.

"What was he wearing?"

"Vest. Work boots. Duffel bag on his shoulder."

The shades were open in only one window, and the opossum did not go near it.

"Let's go over there," D'Arc said.

"I'd like to see what he does first."

"Let's talk to him now. Maybe catching him by surprise rattles something loose."

She was already heading for the door.

"I'll wait by the fire escape, and you ring the bell," she said.

"Remember all those procedures we talked about?"

"Of course I do. They got us stuck here."

Minutes later, Falkirk stood at the main entrance. He entered the building and climbed the five flights. A few of the marble steps trembled underfoot, as did the metal railing. At the top floor, Falkirk stopped at the opossum's apartment and caught his breath. He listened for movement, heard nothing, and banged on the door. "Tranquility," he said. "Open up, please."

Footsteps approached. Falkirk held his ID in front of the peephole.

To Falkirk's surprise, the opossum opened the door all the way. The apartment was dark, and the animal's enormous pupils constricted under the hallway lights. Falkirk could tell that this was Teyu from the scar that ran from his eye to his neck, a result of an accident at work, according to the reports. His left hand was missing two digits, lost in the war in some human-made trap. Possibly gnawed off, judging from the uneven pink scar left behind.

"You are fast," the opossum said.

"What do you mean?"

"I called the police. Someone is climbing my fire escape."

Falkirk groaned. "Sir, I'm terribly sorry. That's my partner outside."

To be safe, Falkirk asked Teyu to stand in a corner while he opened the window. Passing the kitchen, Falkirk noticed a plate of unidentifiable scraps on the counter, probably taken from the trash. These people made no apologies for holding on to their old ways. At least the food didn't stink. Yet.

Leaning out the window, Falkirk saw D'Arc making her way to the top. "I thought you said you were going to *wait* by the fire escape."

"Was I that loud?"

"Yes."

Falkirk radioed in to headquarters to alert them about the false alarm. With the tension behind them, he and D'Arc sat on the couch while the opossum fixed himself a glass of water mixed with a spoonful of powdered beetle. Teyu offered some to his guests. Falkirk could not tell if the opossum meant it as a joke.

"Why are you here?" Teyu asked.

"There's a murderer targeting people who have used the translator. And you and your brother have been missing for several days."

"My brother is the translator user. Not me. And he is not missing."

"Where is he?"

"On his way to Fort Pius. He helps to train cadets there."

Fort Pius was located near the edge of Union territory, one of the few bases remaining from the occupation. Yatsi went there every couple of months to help with maneuvers. "My brother takes the soldiers on some campout, walkabout," Teyu added. "I do not know what."

This opossum rarely spoke with others, that much was clear. But he answered calmly, and with confidence. He did not seem threatened.

"Do you know who he works with?" Falkirk asked.

"No. But someone at the academy should. You ask. Someone knows."

"Where have *you* been?" Falkirk asked.

"The hospital. I had an infection. In my mouth." He opened

his jaw wide and pointed at the raw, purplish gumline above his left incisor. "I stayed for a few days. Check their records."

D'Arc nodded to indicate that she would check on it right away.

"Do you know what's been going on here?" Falkirk asked.

"The human told me. At the hospital."

"A human spoke to you?"

"Yes. With the rings." The human had asked him about Yatsi, the translator, everything. The strator was most likely Duncan Huxley, Grace Braga's number one.

Falkirk cut things short when he felt the conversation straying. Yatsi might be dead already, and his brother would not provide anything useful this evening. Besides, the humans had gotten to him. If he needed to lie, he was well prepared.

Falkirk thanked the opossum and got up to leave, ignoring D'Arc as she silently pleaded with him to stay. Outside, as they walked to the safe house, D'Arc asked why they left so soon.

"The place is compromised," Falkirk said. "Our best bet is to keep an eye on it."

Falkirk regretted losing this chance to show D'Arc some exciting detective work. He wanted an excuse to wrestle the opossum to the ground in front of her. And then, with his knee on the suspect's spine, he would order her to call for backup. He soon became so lost in the image that he couldn't hear D'Arc speaking.

". . . when we report this to the chief, right?" D'Arc finished saying.

"Right, right."

"What is it?"

He stopped. They stood on the sidewalk, under a streetlight that cast fuzzy shadows onto the concrete. "I was worried that this wasn't what you expected."

"It's not," she said. "But this is the first time that's ever happened to me. Not knowing what to expect. I think I like it."

The relief he felt was almost embarrassing. He resisted the urge to pant, despite the heat building in his chest and shoulders.

"Let's close up shop," he said. One day—very soon, he realized—his thoughts would not simply hide behind his eyes, bottled up in his mind. They would spill from his mouth. And she would understand.

THE COMMUNION BEGAN after dark, with a horn sounding from the dome of the temple. Fashioned from an old cathedral, the temple had only three walls, made of white stone, with the gargoyles chiseled away. The humans had removed the front of the edifice, exposing the pillars, chandeliers, and wooden pews. From several blocks away, Falkirk and D'Arc could see inside, to the altar where the elders delivered their weekly sermons. Rows of seats continued outward into what had once been the potholed street. The founders of Hosanna tore out the asphalt and planted fresh sod, transforming the church into an open-air plaza that occupied the entire block. The old ways called for a castle. But after the war with no name, the walls came down to invite everyone in, so that friend and foe, master and slave could stand together before God.

"You're awfully quiet tonight," D'Arc said.

"I'm saving my voice for the singing."

Standing on a corner, D'Arc seemed out of place with the hilt of her sword leaning on her shoulder. All around them, animals waited eagerly for the march to begin.

From the foot of the marble altar, the humans streamed out, over a hundred of them, all wearing robes made of simple white cloth cinched at the waist with a rope. With the street lamps out, their candles provided the only light, a symbol of their journey through a time of darkness. With their free hands, they gripped the shoulders of the people in front of them, so that the entire procession became like a dragon's tail unfurling into the streets.

The Queen was wrong about these humans. Though they had evolved to track and kill prey, here the candlelight transformed them into the angels they claimed to be. For all their faults, they uncovered the truth before the others. They fell, but they also repented. It was hard for Falkirk to accept sometimes, especially since his own trial had no end in sight. But if it wasn't true, then nothing was true.

The procession exited the building and veered to the right. The animals waiting on the sidewalk joined the humans in the street. Most brought their own candles. The lucky ones in the front got to touch a human. The dogs were so excited that their tongues hung out. Falkirk saw a bear as well, towering over the human in front of him, his paw nearly swallowing the man's upper body. And yet the human remained serene, a faint smile on his lips. Falkirk noticed the scent of sweat and fur, mud and soap, incense and wax. By the time the singing started, a galaxy of tiny flames rolled along the battered street.

> *Here I am Lord. Is it I Lord?*
> *I have heard you calling in the night.*
> *I will go Lord, if you lead me.*
> *I will hold your people in my heart.*

As the march approached the intersection where Falkirk and D'Arc waited, the light from the candles reflected off the windows of two office buildings, like molten gold. Beside him, the flames danced in D'Arc's eyes. Falkirk wore the same expression at his own first communion. He needed to enjoy this moment. Before things changed again, as they always did.

As the human vanguard passed, Falkirk and D'Arc lit their candles and joined the procession. She held his shoulder, sending instant warmth through his vest and into his fur. He took the shoulder of a cat in front of him. The crowd grew so large that it had to stop and start again, forcing people to jostle one another. D'Arc maintained her grip on Falkirk, even when two people squished her as they rounded another corner.

After a few blocks, he could see their destination—an early-twentieth-century university hospital, three stories tall and nearly as wide as the block, made of red brick, with white stone columns supporting the main entrance. Whereas the temple became a town square, the Prophet's residence functioned more like a castle. Strators stood on the roof. Stair towers on opposite ends of the building acted as turrets, complete with narrowed windows that served as sniper nests. Anyone who wanted to get to Michael would have to pass through several layers of mortar, muscle, and lead. And yet, with the candlelight flickering against the bricks, the building became like a country house, an inviting place where people would gather, sing songs, tell stories. The pilgrims filled the courtyard, while the rest clogged the street. The grass patches were still flattened from the last communion. Two trees on either side of the cement walkway guarded the entrance, and a few cats and squirrels climbed the trunks to get a better view.

The crowd swelled, closing the gaps between the specta-tors. D'Arc became wedged behind Falkirk so that her chin poked over his shoulder. He pictured her once again leaning on the gunwale of the *al-Rihla*, where she belonged, watching the sunrise.

"What happens next?" she asked. Her warm breath smelled like milk.

"We sing. Until the humans come out to talk to us."

"Will we see Michael?"

"I hope so."

He felt a thud in the asphalt, a quake that made his knees wob-ble. Another thud seemed to warp the street. The singing died out as everyone heard it: an avalanche, rumbling, getting closer.

"What is that?" D'Arc asked.

Then, the impossible. A red car slid through an intersection several blocks away, carried by an unseen force, and slammed into a row of parked vehicles. The car resembled a toy, like something Yeager or Amelia would have pushed across the carpet. More vehicles and other debris followed it. They were elevated somehow, lifted higher than the street signs by—

*Water.* A *wall* of water, bubbling white, engulfing the street.

D'Arc gasped in his ear. Falkirk dropped the candle, extinguishing the flame.

# CHAPTER 15

████ ██ ████

## TROJAN HORSES

"**HOW MUCH LONGER** are we going to do this to each other?" Wawa asked.

On the other side of the desk, Strator Grace Braga sat with her legs crossed and cracked her knuckles, one at a time. She wore her usual outfit—black T-shirt, khaki vest, camouflage pants with a holstered pistol. Ropey muscles bulged from underneath her sleeves. Her thermos made a coffee ring on the desktop. Behind Grace, the windows of Wawa's new office put the chaos of Tranquility's headquarters on full display. The officers on the floor argued, laughed at jokes, ferried papers and boxes from one place to the next. A few of them watched from their stations while pretending to write reports. A cat even had the gall to turn in her chair. After a withering glance from Wawa, the cat got back to work.

"I asked you a question, Grace."

Wawa had summoned Grace to headquarters to talk about the SOA's latest power grab. The day before, Grace lobbied the Archon for full access to Tranquility's files, as well as the discretion to deploy Special Operations as she saw fit, bypassing the chief. One of Wawa's own agents told her that he was under orders from the strators not to share anything with Tranquility.

"Do you think we're hiding something?" Wawa asked. "Is that it?"

Having run out of knuckles, Grace folded her hands on her knee. "As a matter of fact, I do. I'm told you recruited an outsider to help with the investigation."

Wawa opened her mouth to answer, then stopped.

"A certain person of interest," Grace said.

"D'Arc?"

"*Sheba*. The Mother."

"She changed her name, like everyone else. She asked that we not broadcast it."

"I don't care what she asked."

"What's your business with D'Arc? You want to recruit her for the Sons of Adam?"

"I want to know what she's doing here. I want to know why she isn't at her rightful place, at the Warrior's side."

"She's her own person, Grace. She can do whatever she wants. Besides, aren't you already monitoring her?"

With her lips closed, the strator ran her tongue across her teeth.

"If you have evidence that D'Arc has done something wrong, let's see it."

"It's not D'Arc I'm worried about. It's Tranquility. You've got the wolf country debacle. The Ramen satellite. The refugees. Now this. You're on a roll."

"I've made my point," Wawa said. "You've made yours. The door is right behind you."

Grace didn't move. "It's amazing," she said. "It's amazing how human you are."

Wawa exhaled loudly through her snout.

"I'm sorry if you take that as an insult," Grace added. "It's just that, you speak like us. You have the same inflections. The same mannerisms. How much of that was learned, and how much was drilled into your mind?"

Wawa knew to keep her cool. She couldn't afford to have Grace storming out of the office in full view of everyone. "Does any of that even matter anymore?"

"It matters. Have you ever wondered what else might be planted in that brain of yours? Some hidden instructions. Equations. A trigger mechanism perhaps. All buried beneath your human façade so you can earn our trust. So you can lecture me from behind that desk like a high school principal."

Her heart pounding, Wawa pretended to grow tired of the conversation. "I'm meeting with the Archon tomorrow. I want him to tell me to my face why he's going along with all this."

"The Archon," Grace said. "The Archon was there when we took a risk and trusted one of your people. Did he ever tell you about that?"

Wawa shook her head no.

About a year into the war, Grace served on a salvaged Coast Guard ship. The humans used it to ferry refugees along the Hudson. One day, they came across a raft with a dog on it. The creature was in wretched condition, bloodied and starving. When they questioned him, the dog swore that the ants had turned on him for helping the other side, and he barely escaped with his life. The crew brought him aboard, hoping that capturing an animal defector was worth the risk.

"The next morning," Grace said, "The dog killed three soldiers."

Grace—then six weeks pregnant with her daughter Maddie—fought hand-to-hand with the dog until she got a grip on the canine's neck and would not let go. She demonstrated the hold for Wawa by forming her hand into a claw. In his final moments, the dog's eyes fluttered and his tongue popped out. "A Trojan horse," Grace said. "But you don't even know what that means. And if you do, there's no telling if it was learned, or programmed."

"Learned."

"Learned. Did you *learn* to feel guilty about the things you did in the war?"

"No. That must have been programmed."

Wawa hoped that Grace would use this as a cue to leave. The strator was late for the communion ceremony on the other end of town.

But then, the first quake hit the building. The thermos wobbled. On the main floor of headquarters, the hanging lights jiggled on their wires. Everyone stopped. Wawa rose from her desk.

"What was that?" Grace asked.

The tremor passed. As Wawa exited her office, a thrum started, distant, as quiet as a breeze. She felt the vibration through the tiles on the floor. This headquarters, she realized, was merely a larger version of the cell in which she had once lived. In the cages, she learned to distinguish the noises, the voices bouncing off the concrete, the *clop-clop* of her master's sneakers. Distant sounds closing in always signaled danger.

"Maybe a truck overturned," Grace said.

Wawa made a note of the humans in the room, where they stood, the fear on their faces. Hogan Brierley, a former Navy SEAL, checked his sidearm, while a drop of sweat rolled along his cheek. Daiyu Fang, who had traveled to this continent on a decrepit Chinese submarine, held out her palms in the universal *I don't know* gesture. Carl Jackson and Nell Becker stood by the window, peeking outside in the hopes of finding an answer. None of them—not a single one—could hear the noise approaching. God had chosen these people despite their flaws, their weaknesses, their blissful ignorance. Maybe that was the source of all their problems. They perceived only a mere sliver of the world, yet assumed they knew all of it.

Ever since the war ended, Wawa swore that she had learned to forgive the humans. And yet a dark part of her, buried deep within, drew some pleasure from watching the horror spill into Grace's eyes as she finally began to hear what was coming.

A roaring avalanche shook the walls. Some of the officers held onto their desks to steady themselves. And then the approaching thunder slammed into the building and continued rushing on, gurgling and sloshing. Wawa knew then that the dam must have burst. Water gushed through the front entrance. It spread throughout the room, clear and cold. Someone actually howled at the sight of it. Wawa tried to think. This first floor of headquarters stood about ten feet above street level. They still had time.

She rushed to the doors and pried them open. The lobby was submerged in shin-deep water. Outside, the streetlamps reflected off a choppy river that flowed over the asphalt. The rooftops of several vehicles poked stubbornly from the water. The electrical grid gave out, several buildings at a time. Hosanna went dark. This city, this pack for which she bled, for which she sacrificed so much. Long ago, she told God, *I'll suffer for all of this, if that's all you'll let me do.* She stayed awake at night imagining the ways she could die in the line of duty, and the things she would say when the moment arrived. She would not share her life with someone. She would hand it over for everyone. Perhaps tonight.

Wawa climbed on top of the nearest desk. The officers gathered around her. To their credit, they held their positions even as the water rose above their ankles. Grace stood conspicuously outside of the circle, checking her pistol.

"Listen up," Wawa said. "This whole city is depending on what we do right now." She searched the faces for someone she knew well. Her gaze settled on a fox whom she had recently promoted to lieutenant. "You, Havoc," she said. "Take four people. Get to the motorboats on the dock. If they haven't been washed away, we'll need them."

"Right," Havoc said. He picked out four people and headed for the door.

"Who did this, Chief?" someone shouted.

"We'll find out later." She pointed at a raccoon named Veren. "You: there's a generator in the storage facility next door. We need it." Doling out tasks made her calm, and brought her out of her master's cage. Within a minute, she sent people to retrieve weapons, first aid kits. She sent Grissom to the dispatch room to see if any of the equipment could be salvaged. "And brew some tea," she said. "You'll be up for a while."

"Chief," Grace said. "What are you going to do about the communion?"

Wawa remembered that Grace's daughter was at the ceremony. "We're sending the boats there first," she said.

Wawa pictured the scene they would find. Survivors would call to them from telephone poles and rooftops. Floating bodies would congregate in alleyways, in hotel lobbies, in restaurant kitchens. Many of the dead would still have their eyes open, so they could stare down the rescuers who arrived too late.

Something slammed into the front doors of the building, loud enough to make everyone flinch. Outside, people shouted. Havoc stumbled in, soaking wet, wide-eyed and panting. Three jagged slashes had torn his vest almost completely from his torso.

"Lock the doors!" he said. "Get those desks over here!"

When no one obeyed, Havoc frantically grabbed a desk and pushed it through the water toward the door. "Help me with this! They're here!"

Wawa knew right away. Alongside Havoc, she put her shoulder into the desk, ignoring the murmurs from the others. "Help him!" Wawa said. "We need to set up a barricade!"

As soon as the desk made contact with the brass handles, the door exploded in a burst of shards and splinters. The force of it knocked Wawa on her tail in a great splash. As she tried to sit up, a creature bounded over the desk, leaping into the crowd of officers. The fish-head had skin the same greenish color as the river. Its claws and tentacles slashed the air, shooting streams of water across the room. The monster made a strange sound as it breathed. *Awwk. Awwk.* A dog and a cat dropped to the ground face first, clouding the water with their blood. Several officers drew their guns. The shots echoed in the stone hall, piercing Wawa's ears. She got to her feet, drew her pistol, and tried to aim. She told the others to move, but no one listened. Beside her, another creature jumped through the door and collapsed on Havoc, crushing him. Through the water, Wawa felt the dog's bones breaking. She swung around to fire as a tentacle batted her in the face. The monster bolted and went after another officer.

A small hand grabbed her by the scruff of the neck and pulled her to her feet. It was Grace. With her other hand, the human fired her pistol with the barrel leveled sideways. *Bap-bap-bap.* A few of the officers retreated to the Chief of Tranquility's office, only to find themselves cornered. Wawa was sure she hit one of the creatures square in the shell, but the bullets must have skidded off the armor.

The windows at the other side of the room burst open, with two more fish-heads leaping through. With their claws and tentacles fully spread out, the creatures were twice as big as the emaciated cadaver in the morgue.

Wawa shouted for the others to follow her upstairs. Her voice died out in the noise. Four of the monsters mowed through her officers as they took cover behind their desks. The human Nell Becker crouched in a corner and fired, but a creature charged through the bullets and gripped her by the neck with its claws. Her arm flailed and she continued shooting, forcing Wawa to dive to the ground as the bullets skimmed by her.

"Come on!" Grace shouted.

Wawa aimed at the monster as it dropped Becker's body. She emptied the magazine. The creature fell, then rose again, its wet eyes focusing on her.

It was time to run.

Grace covered her as Wawa retreated to the staircase. Daiyu Fang followed, with Carl Jackson limping behind her. Peering over the railing, Wawa caught a glimpse of the floodwater, now painted red. They left bloody footprints on the stairs.

The group retreated to Wawa's former office. Fang and Jackson propped a bookshelf against the door.

"Can we get to the roof from here?" Grace whispered as she reloaded.

"There's a ledge. We can climb."

"The communion's about a mile away," Grace said. She pointed to an area of the city that had gone completely dark, like some black hole blotting out the stars. "If they're going for Michael, we need to get there."

Wawa tried to hold it together. Grissom and the dispatchers were surely dead. If anyone had made it out of the main room, they were getting butchered in the streets as they tried to swim to safety. And how many officers in the city drowned in the initial wave? How many survived only to find some nameless abomination lunging for them?

Wawa opened the window and immediately heard a scream, many blocks away. It died out. Once again, the humans did not seem to hear it. A fetid breeze laced with ammonia brushed across Wawa's face. She took her first step onto the ledge.

# CHAPTER 16

## FACE TO FACE

'ARC CLUNG TO a tilted light pole, several feet above the rushing water. She couldn't hear anything in her clogged left ear. In her right, she heard the river churning, along with a few screams for help, cries of agony. The striped body of a cat floated underneath her, tail up, the fur plastered to the skin. The corpse bumped against the pole, twirled around, and continued south with the current. At the nearest intersection, three cars had been stacked on top of one another by the force of the water. A few animals paddled over to the roof of a bus. D'Arc counted a dog and two rats, with others swimming closer. More people floated near the entrance of the Prophet's residence, while the humans on the roof shouted down to them, asking who needed help.

Somehow, a single candle, still lit, lay horizontally on the brick wall in front of the Prophet's residence.

D'Arc called Falkirk's name. When he didn't answer, she scanned the street for him. Only then did she realize that the wave had carried her well over a block from where she once stood. Above her, the streetlamp flickered out. Several others remained lit, giving the water the appearance of some gelatinous oil. Or blood.

Gunfire popped from the roof of the Prophet's house, like snare drums. D'Arc hugged the pole tighter until her heart throbbed against it. The humans aimed into the water, and the bullets hit the surface in neat vertical splashes. As the muzzles flashed, the survivors below blinked in and out, in different poses each time. Some tried to move away, while others pounded on the door of the building, demanding to be let in.

Then she heard it—a series of gasping sounds, almost like a cough. People screamed and splashed as they tried to escape. Strange shapes broke the surface of the water. D'Arc made out heads, claws, tentacles. The appendages reached into the crowd, wrapping around the hapless animals. One tentacle lifted a squirrel out of the water by its neck and then dunked him, holding him under until a few bubbles broke at the surface.

The monsters rammed the front door of the Prophet's residence. More gunfire spat from the windows and the rooftop. A few of the people fell, struck by ricochets and flopping into a cloud of their own blood. The door buckled.

Panicked animals made their way past D'Arc. Some tried to swim, while a few stubbornly tried to run. Two of the fish-heads were in pursuit. Under the water, their tentacles flowed behind them, squirming like snakes.

D'Arc searched for the nearest high ground. Behind her, another bus was pinned against the wall of an office building. The vehicle's windows were caved in, with only the top of the steering wheel above water. D'Arc slid down the lightpole, gritting her teeth as she dunked herself. The river was as high as her chest here. Floating, she kicked off the pole and swam for the bus.

She heard the coughing sound, closer this time.

D'Arc made it to the front grill of the bus and planted her foot on the bumper. Gripping the rearview mirror, she pulled herself to the roof.

Something crashed into the vehicle, making the frame squeal. D'Arc unsheathed her sword. A single tentacle flopped next to her foot, its suckers dilating and contracting as it searched for a grip. D'Arc swung the sword. The blade slashed through the limb, severing it, cutting clean through the metal rooftop. The tentacle retracted, followed by another gagging cough. Two claws clamped onto the roof, and the creature pulled itself up. The eyes—black, with no irises—homed in on D'Arc. The mouth and gills burst open simultaneously, making the strange gasping sound.

With the creature halfway over the roof, D'Arc lunged, aiming the tip of her sword at the base of the neck. Before the blade could find its mark, the three remaining tentacles swirled and caught it. The fourth one—the stump—batted against the side windows. D'Arc yanked and twisted the sword free, spraying cold, thick blood onto the roof. She fell backward and rolled, getting to her feet quickly. Having seen enough, she ran to the rear, launched herself from the vehicle, and splashed into the river. More people streamed by. A terrified cat nearly crashed into her. Before D'Arc could do anything else, the creature leapt from the bus. It landed on the cat, wrapping its tentacles around its victim. Spitting out water, D'Arc hacked at the beast's shell two, three times, leaving small gashes in the armor. Ignoring her, the fish-head twisted its flexible body until D'Arc felt the crunch of the cat's spine. The tentacles loosened, and the corpse dropped away. The creature's head swiveled as it searched for its next target.

D'Arc spun around and collided with something furry. Someone grabbed her by the shoulders and shook her.

"Come with me! Now!"

It was Falkirk, alive again. She felt the intense urge to smell him, to lick the nape of his neck and ears, to show that she was a member of his pack. D'Arc looked over her shoulder to see the three-tentacled fish-head attacking another victim, no longer concerned with her. Swimming beside Falkirk, D'Arc held onto his belt with her free hand. They made it to the next block, where an overturned SUV sat wheels-up, tilted on the curb. Falkirk pointed at it before plunging under the surface. D'Arc pulled in a lungful of air and dove in. The water muffled the screams and the gunfire. Falkirk squeezed into the sunroof of the vehicle. His tail slipped in last. D'Arc put her head through the opening and found, to her amazement, that she broke the surface once again. Inside the tiny space, Falkirk shook off the excess water, spraying the cabin with droplets.

"Air pocket," he said. His voice reverberated in the small compartment.

"We should keep going," D'Arc said.

"No. There are more of them that way. A lot more."

He held out his hand, and she realized that he was not issuing an order as her superior. He was begging her to stay. She took his hand and shimmied her way into the vehicle. They sat on the ceiling, while the seats hung suspended above them. The water stopped rising at ankle level, but the moisture brought out the smell of plastic, leather, and cloth. It was like being inside a mouth.

Something swam by in the murky water. She yelped and drew closer to Falkirk. She felt his breath on her coat.

"Quiet," he whispered.

D'Arc held the sword over the sunroof. "Are we safe here?" she asked.

"No. But maybe we will be once the water level goes down."

The windows fogged. A completely irrelevant memory flashed in her mind. She recalled her time on the boat, the *Ronin*, right after she had transformed. While Mort(e) drove, she pressed her snout to the window of the main cabin and exhaled. When she bumped her nose into the glass, it left an imprint in the condensation. *That is me*, she had thought. But then, each time, the shape dissolved, no matter how hard she pressed her snout into it. It was her moment of self-awareness, when she finally woke up from the dream. She would pass into this world and then blink out of it. The imprint vanished so quickly, without a sound.

D'ARC'S HANDS ACHED from holding the blade over the sunroof. She suggested going outside, to try to help people. Falkirk said no. He had unloaded all of his bullets into one of the monsters only to see it stagger and rise again. If they left the vehicle, the most they could hope to accomplish was to flee with the others.

D'Arc could no longer hear the panicked voices and desperate splashing. The water grew turgid from the debris. Several times, something brushed against the windows. D'Arc resisted the urge to scream, even when a tentacle attached its suckers to the glass before sliding away with a little squeak.

"Won't they smell us?" she asked.

"I thought about that."

"And?"

He hesitated. "Maybe there's too much blood in the water for them to detect us."

"Sorry I asked."

More water leaked in. They would soon have to abandon their shrinking air pocket. Until then, they would wait in the dark.

"What do they want?" she whispered.

"What did the spider want?"

With the tip of the sword resting on the floor, D'Arc leaned her head on the hilt and tried to imagine the ranch, the Alphas, the Old Man. Was Mort(e) perched on his roof picking off these fish-heads with his rifle? Or was he fleeing west, away from the sea and the rivers that fed it?

"I have another reason to be angry with the fish-heads," Falkirk said.

"What's that?"

"They interrupted me. I had some news about the expedition."

They had not discussed the *al-Rihla* in some time, not since she applied. When she handed in her paperwork a few weeks earlier, a woman asked her about her eyesight, her military status, and whether she had ever been treated for worms. When the woman dismissed her, D'Arc assumed she had been rejected outright.

"I guess the expedition is called off," D'Arc said. "We'll never meet that jaguar who speaks Brazilian."

"Brazilian's not a language." They grudgingly laughed.

Falkirk took a long breath. "They accepted your application," he said.

Only a few hours earlier these words would have made her swoon. They rang hollow in the stale air. "When did you find out?"

"A few days ago. I have a friend in Tranquility who knows about these things."

When she asked him why he waited so long to tell her, he lowered his head.

"Because there's more," he said. "After I helped you apply— after hearing you talk about it so much—I decided to put in a request of my own."

"You're going? That's great! We could—"

She stopped talking when he looked at her. "I'm not going. They rejected me."

"But you're more qualified than I am."

"That's the problem. They need me here. And that was *before* all this."

"But that doesn't explain why they picked *me*."

"You're an expert on Alphas, as well as the other mutations we've encountered. And you definitely had the best recommendation letters."

"Did you write one?"

"Of course. So did the chief. She thinks you'd be safer out there anyway."

The vehicle rocked a little in the current.

"I was waiting for the right time to tell you," he said. "I had this crazy idea that I would take you to communion, and you'd see how wonderful and peaceful it was, and then you'd be ready to hear what I had to say."

His hands wrapped around hers at the base of the hilt. She did not realize how cold she was until the warmth from his palms loosened her knuckles.

"There was a prophecy about you," Falkirk said. "And we didn't have to wait forever for it to be fulfilled. You, and Michael, and Mort(e)—you proved that it was all true."

"I'm not sure about that."

"I know. I'm not trying to convert you. I just want to say that the prophecy isn't the end of the story. It doesn't have to be."

He squeezed her hands.

"I've told you about some of the mistakes I've made. I abandoned one family. Couldn't save another. Got kicked off the *Vesuvius*. I've been lost. And the question I've been asking is, how will I know when this penance is over, and I can go on with my life?

"You're the answer to that question," he said.

"Why are you pinning this on me?"

"I'm not. I'm not asking you to do anything. I know you were with Mort(e)—"

"I was never *with* Mort(e). Not like that."

Falkirk shifted in his seat. "You've never . . ."

One of the walls she had built inside her began to crack, and the cold fluids it held at bay seeped into her heart, into her gut. She turned away from him and let the feeling of helplessness wash over her. "We tried," she finally said. "I mean, *he* tried. For me. But it's not like that. It *can't* be like that. Do you understand?"

"I think so."

"The bond we have is . . . more than that. And less. It's not his fault. But it doesn't really matter whose fault it is."

She remembered that one time, during a hike near the beaver city, when Mort(e) told her that he imagined them growing old together. He would most likely die first, and she would stand at his side as he expired. She would read to him from one of her books about the sea, or one of her favorite adventure stories, so he could hear her voice as he left. Then she would spread his ashes in the Alpha pen, in the forest, and in the river. She did not ask him who would spread her ashes.

"Let me start over," Falkirk said. "I thought about asking you to stay here. I *want* you to stay. But I know who you are now. Who you really are. You should go. Don't let anyone else hold you back. Not even me. Go before it's too late."

He pulled his hands free. A chill closed in around her. She inched toward Falkirk, placing a numb hand on his shoulder and easing it along his collarbone. Her other arm, still holding the sword, slinked around his waist, the wet fur mingling, trapping what little warmth remained. Falkirk pulled her into his chest, so that their cheeks rested against one another. Their breath sounded like the ocean waves in her dreams. Under the water, their cramped legs intertwined, and the pads of their feet pressed together. Her shivering eased.

"I want to stay," she said, her voice shaking.

"I won't let you."

"But what about you? I thought you said your penance would be over someday."

"Maybe it's not supposed to end."

The silence returned. She sank deeper into his fur until his heartbeat thumped in her skull. Despite the water paralyzing her, she felt the heat from his body soothing her muscles, unclenching her jaw. She rose to her feet suddenly. A few drops trickled from her fur. Falkirk stood so quickly that his head bumped the ceiling. With a grunt he dug his claws into her hips and turned her around. He brushed her tail aside, pressed against her back, and then suddenly all the warmth in this tiny space, all the warmth in the world, bloomed inside of her, spreading outward so rapidly that she thought she would see it leaving her as her jaw dropped open. The hilt of the sword, still firm in her grip, tapped against the armrest with each movement. The husky bit into her neck. D'Arc's face brushed the seat hanging next to her. She caught the seat belt in her teeth. Falkirk finished suddenly, his fangs grinding together so hard she thought they would crack. The two bodies sank into the water, the chill bringing a relief this time. She spun around once more and embraced him, settling into the same position they were in before, like nothing happened.

D'ARC RESTED, UNSURE if she was asleep or awake. The hours crept by. Falkirk mumbled in his dreams.

The sound of his heartbeat became stronger and faster until it started puttering in her ear. She sat up and realized that the vibration continued. The water level had reached her chest. The rumbling passed near the vehicle, startling Falkirk.

"It's a boat!" she said.

He nodded yes.

Stiffly, she grabbed the sword, took two deep breaths, and plunged into the water, with Falkirk right behind her. At the surface, she squinted at the sunrise. Two motorboats approached, each with the word TRANQUILITY stenciled in black paint. "We got two here!" someone said. D'Arc suddenly noticed how thirsty she was, and almost dipped her mouth into the water to drink. The memory of her master swatting her away from the toilet made her reconsider. She giggled deliriously at the thought.

"Oh, God," Falkirk said.

The front door of the Prophet's house had collapsed, with

pieces of wood floating about. Dozens of bodies gathered at the entrance, almost indistinguishable from the wreckage. The walls and trees were riddled with bullet holes, and a charred section suggested that a bomb had detonated in the courtyard. One of the fish-heads bobbed in the wake from the motorboats. The creature floated on its armored spine, jaw yawning open, its tentacles spread out so that it resembled some hideous lily pad.

A boat pulled up next to her. A human hand lowered from the side. She reached out to grasp it.

# PART IV
# DESOLATION

# CHAPTER 17

## THE CHILD OR THE DEMON

HE SARCOPS RETREATED to the mouth of the river, where they could taste a hint of salt from the ocean. The wounded lay prone on the rocky floor with blood streaming from bullet holes, gashes, and severed limbs. Taalik sustained a direct hit in the attack when a projectile punctured a segment in his armor. He tore it out with his claw, leaving a frayed wound that bled for hours. The Queen had made the Sarcops difficult to kill, which would only prolong the suffering of the mortally wounded.

Taalik hated this place. The endless maritime traffic during the human age had polluted the delta, leaving a coat of oil on the riverbed and random garbage submerged in the mud. Metal and plastic would sit here long after his death. Taalik counted three automobiles so far. Masterpieces of engineering, and the humans simply discarded them.

Amid the waste and decay, a mound of fresh eggs pulsed in the water, perfectly smooth. Zirsk had performed her duty by depositing them the night before the attack. Behind the transparent membrane, a new crop of tiny soldiers danced and twirled, unaware of the hopeless situation that awaited them.

Taalik had failed. He could no longer deny it. They came all this way to find the secret of the sun and free their people. Did he misunderstand the Queen's message? Was he unworthy? He could not keep these questions to himself any longer. He needed to know who still believed. And so, when he finished brooding, he asked his people—all twenty-three of them at this point—to gather round.

*You have suffered with me*, Taalik said. He thought of Orak's severed tentacle, the way she brandished it when issuing orders to the others. He thought of Asha, ambushed by the rodents in the north and lost forever. He thought of the Queen's silence.

*We came here to find the human who could free our people*, he said. *But we are too late.*

*It is another test*, Orak said. A few of the Juggernauts clicked in approval.

*Test or not, there is nothing for us here.*

*Our enemy is here*, Riyya said, her claw covering a wound in her torso.

Another piped up: *Give the word and we attack. We finish them off.*

Then another: *We came all this way.*

A few of the Juggernauts swam in circles, signaling aggression and danger. Taalik steadied himself against the current.

*The Queen led us here for a reason*, Riyya said. Taalik had never heard his people try to interpret the Queen's revelations. That burden was for him alone.

*Perhaps the Queen wanted to show us this human city*, Orak said. *So we could see how these surface animals betrayed her. We will not fail her in the same way.*

*That is another reason to attack!*

*Wait*, Taalik said. He waved at the Juggernauts to get them to stay still. *The Queen is not some book we can consult. She is not waiting nearby to tell us to go left instead of right. Up instead of down. She sacrificed herself so we could learn how to move forward on our own.*

*What are your orders then?* Orak asked.

*We must rest first. I will decide when the light returns.*

He suspected that even those hungry for war felt some relief upon hearing this. The multiple wounds, along with the difficulty in breathing the thin air, left all of them exhausted.

*But will the Queen speak to you?* Riyya asked.

Taalik almost lashed out at her for not listening. But then he remembered what Orak once told him. *You gave us meaning and hope. But you cannot take it away. You cannot tell us what to do with it now.*

*The Queen may speak to us,* he said.

He gave Orak a final glance before retreating to his chosen spot in the muck. Surrounded by the wreckage of the human civilization, he drew in his claws and wrapped his tentacles around himself. With the water flowing in his ear holes, he faced south, where the delta gradually opened into the vast kingdom that was rightfully his.

THAT NIGHT, ORAK visited him. When she swam into view, she uncoiled her tentacles, including the injured one. The wound had closed, and the limb would grow again. If they abandoned this place, she would be completely healed by the time they reached the ice.

*Did you mean what you said about the Queen?* she asked. *You never told us before that she gave us this . . . freedom. To decide for ourselves.*

*Which do you prefer?*

She pulled her tentacle from his grasp. *You do not answer my question.*

*Sometimes, we must listen,* he said. *Other times we are on our own.*

*But how can we know the difference?*

*She trusts us.*

Orak swam away from him. *How long before the others ask these same questions?* she asked.

Suddenly, he felt the Queen's echo leave him, like oxygen escaping a lung. The sophisticated creature he had become suddenly vanished, leaving the frightened monster of the deep, unable to think or feel, reacting only to changes in the environment, to threats, to sounds. Taalik darted toward Orak and clamped his pincers around her throat. He lifted his other claw and aimed the sharp point at her eye. Orak let him do it. Her tentacles drifted, and her claws hung harmlessly at her side.

*You threaten me?* he said.

*I warn you.*

*And I warn you. Know your place. Who gave you the intelligence to question the Queen's orders? Who found you in the dark? Who gave you a family? A home?*

*My Egg, I do not follow her. I follow you. But I cannot speak for the others. Do you think their devotion to you will overcome their doubts, as mine has?*

Taalik let her go. As he began to sink, she embraced him, keeping him afloat.

*I die at your side*, she said. *I kill at your side. No one else's. No one.*

The other Juggernauts approached, frantic. Taalik heard their clicking sound, an alarm signal.

*First of Us*, Riyya said. *You must come. Now.*

On the other side of a mound of earth, the Sarcops clustered around a wounded Juggernaut. Her blood entered Taalik's nose, and he recognized it right away. The soldiers gave him space to enter the circle. There, Asha, alive after all, lay sprawled out in the mud. Her gills opened like separate mouths, gulping in the oxygen. *First of Us*, she said. *Taalik.*

*I am here*, he said.

*They tell me that we attacked the humans.*

*Yes.*

*And you still need someone who can control the sun.*

*That is true.*

*It is no human we seek*, she said. *The Queen has spoken to the surface animals. They possess her knowledge, even if they do not realize it. I saw one of them.*

*Who?*

Someone brought her a bundle of seaweed. Asha stuffed it into her mouth and chewed. Her tongue slid out to collect the scraps before they could float away.

*The night creature you told us about. With fur. And—*

She held her claws over her head to indicate ears. *And teeth*, she said. *Sharp like ours. And a tail.* She indicated this by waving a tentacle behind her. The others got out of the way to give her room to move.

*There are many creatures like that on the dry dirt*, Taalik said.

*This is the one who murdered the Queen. You saw this in your visions. You warned us.*

Asha told him that she had been wounded so badly on the river that she slipped into a premature hibernation. When she awoke, the land animals stood over her, debating what to do next. And she recognized the killer. She even heard his name before she escaped.

*How can you be certain it was him?* Taalik asked.

*The Queen showed me. The same way she showed you.*

Only Taalik possessed this ability, and yet there was no reason why the Queen would not communicate with any of them. Perhaps this was the sign he'd been expecting.

*She speaks to you?* Riyya sneered. *Why does she not speak to the rest of us?*

*The Queen speaks through those she has chosen*, Taalik said. *Those who can hear.*

*This creature I saw*, Asha said. *He is a demon. He killed one of us already. The land-crab. He . . . butchered her children. He ordered the other animals to break open the eggs and extract the young ones.*

Taalik remembered his vision of the creature's final moments. The land dwellers swarmed around her, destroyed her nest. Like humans.

*If the child cannot help you*, Asha said, *perhaps the demon can.*

This cat was not worthy. And yet, if he could access the Colony's knowledge, then he would be their only hope. Even if Taalik had to force him to do it.

*We are too weak*, Orak said, quietly. *We cannot attack again.*

*There are other ways*, Taalik said.

Before Orak could respond, the other mates pulled in closer until they formed a swirling mass of scales and fins.

*The Queen speaks,* Taalik said. *We will find this demon. We will save our people.*

The Juggernauts swam around him, forming a whirlpool that made his limbs lift from his sides. For a moment, the movement of the water banished the rotten smell of this desolate place. The Juggernauts tightened the vortex, with Taalik at the eye of the storm. Through their swiftly moving bodies, he saw Orak swimming away into the deep.

# CHAPTER 18

## THE REMNANTS

HE TEMPLE BECAME the focal point for the search and rescue operation. Chief Wawa converted the open-air lobby into a command post, from which the surviving Tranquility officers divvied up tasks, distributed supplies, and delivered updates. Above, the *Upheaval* circled the city, completing one orbit every twenty-eight minutes—D'Arc timed it. The *Vesuvius* remained in its dock at one of the skyscrapers. Though no one said it out loud, the reason became obvious—her captain had perished in the flood. In fact, so many humans had died that the chief hastily promoted the survivors. Daiyu Fang became head of Special Operations, or what was left of it. Carl Jackson was put in charge of the patrol units.

On that first morning after the attack, D'Arc and Falkirk stood in the plaza with dozens of others, all shivering and glass-eyed, while Wawa issued a grim report. The Archon was missing and presumed dead. Two refugee camps had been swept away, the bodies en route to the Atlantic. The rupturing of the dam fractured the concrete levees that kept the river from entering the streets. A construction team would need to build a temporary barrier and bail out the water by hand, like the crew of a doomed ship.

The good news: the Sons of Adam repulsed an attack on the Prophet's residence. The fish-heads made it as far as the inner chamber of the building, only to retreat. Rumor had it that Michael himself fired a few shots. Though Wawa could not confirm that, she did say that a few of the monsters had been left behind, and the scientists were studying the bodies. The strators would present their findings later in the week.

For the time being, Tranquility was left with the immediate response. Jackson set up a system for locating the survivors, having lived through a similar flood in his native New Orleans many years earlier. From the plaza, rowboats spread out to search the area. All homes and apartment doors would be marked with an X. In the left quadrant, the search team would add their initials. Going clockwise from there, they would write the date, list any dangers like broken glass or unstable walls, and count the bodies. A second wave of boats would collect the biohazards. D'Arc and Falkirk volunteered to go with the first shift, preferring to deal with the living rather than the dead.

Together, they paddled into the same neighborhood where they had set up the stakeout a few days earlier, a time that seemed separated from the present by a great boundary. It made her wonder if the murderer they sought had drowned, or still awaited rescue on some rooftop. They started with an apartment building, where the water level reached as high as their chests. Everyone on the first floor was dead. Two cats had expired in their beds. An elderly dog couple floated together in their living room, holding hands like otters. D'Arc watched them spinning, two lovers who tried to hold on, only to become another piece of debris. On the floors above, people called for help, including a pig in a studio apartment, and a family of squirrels next door. The boat could hold only a few passengers at a time, and it took three trips to evacuate everyone.

By dusk the smell became unbearable. With no cloud cover,

the spring sun heated the water, allowing all kinds of microscopic colonies to bloom. D'Arc figured that torching the city and starting over might be the only way to get rid of the stench.

Searching well into the night, D'Arc became dizzy from the lack of sleep. At one point, Falkirk had to take the paddles from her when she began rowing with her eyes closed, her head rolling on her shoulders. An exhausted silence set in, making her wonder if she had hallucinated what happened the night before. If she kept her eyes on the water, and blocked out the buildings and the streetlamps, the river became the ocean, and the rowboat became the *al-Rihla*. But she felt nothing when she imagined it. It was merely another path she could take that would splinter everything around her, like walking on a frozen lake.

WHEN FALKIRK JOSTLED her awake the next morning, D'Arc did not recall lying down to sleep. Despite the commotion nearby, she must have passed out for at least five hours on a grassy patch at the edge of the plaza. A few feet away, on a plastic tarp, a human male stitched a wound on the leg of a baby raccoon. The child's mother held the young one's hand.

"Come on," Falkirk said. "We're going to headquarters."

Falkirk moved into professional mode so quickly that D'Arc began to wonder if he had somehow forgotten what happened during the flood. Since that night, he had kept her close, but said little, as if he were a mere observer of their pack of two. He would not stroke her fur while she retched over the side of the boat. He would ask if she was okay only if it meant offering some food or a few minutes of rest. They were partners again, for as long as this ordeal would last. She heard from Razz and the others that this was how some dogs were. Perhaps she should be grateful for his aloofness. It helped her focus, even when the memory of biting the seat belt popped into her mind, to briefly take her away from this place.

With Wawa in the lead, a convoy of rowboats made its way to headquarters. Falkirk and D'Arc each paddled an oar to keep up. D'Arc made an awkward joke about Falkirk becoming the captain of a ship again. In typical fashion, Falkirk did not seem to get it. "Not much of a ship," he said. Once they arrived, they found Tranquility in a far worse state than she had imagined. The water lapped at the concrete steps leading to the entrance. Inside, a layer of mud the texture of melted chocolate covered the floor, emitting a horrible stench. Unidentifiable footprints traversed the room. Droplets of rusted blood speckled the desks. A great swath of brownish-red fluid stuck to the wall.

Wawa led the agents to the staircase that went to the dispatch room in the basement, now flooded with rancid water. A section of the wall had collapsed onto the stairwell, sealing off the entrance.

"Who was the one who heard it?" the chief asked.

A young man stepped forward. He scampered over the rubble, shifting the smaller chunks of mortar until he uncovered a steel pipe poking through the wreckage like a periscope. "Here it is," he said in a squeaky voice.

Wawa put her nose to the metal tube and recoiled in surprise. The chief pulled out her knife and tapped the pipe three times. She waited. Then something hit the pipe from beneath the rubble. *Klink-klink-klink.*

"Dig," she said. "Now."

It took most of the morning to move the concrete from one pile to another. The water rose to their ankles, their waists, their chests. Falkirk dunked his head under and said he saw someone using the pipe like a snorkel. It required their collective strength to remove a slab of concrete wedged into the entrance. As soon as it tumbled away, a cat swam through their legs and burst from the surface, gasping. Wawa splashed over to him.

"Grissom!" she said, her arms tightening around his neck. "You stubborn little bastard."

When she finally let go, the cat held out his paw and opened it. Wawa peeled away a soggy brown object from his palm. It took a few seconds before D'Arc realized it was a tea bag.

"Nobody fucks with the chief's tea," someone said.

"Damn right," Wawa replied.

TWO DAYS LATER, the Tranquility agents returned to headquarters. By then, the waters had subsided enough for D'Arc and Falkirk to walk to the station. Dirt caked the streets, drying in the sun. On every wall, an ashy horizontal line indicated the high water mark.

On the way there, they made sure to pass by the *al-Rihla*. The night before, D'Arc overheard a human claiming that the boat ran aground. But the *al-Rihla* remained intact, bobbing in its dock, windmills spinning. Falkirk bowed his head and whispered a prayer of thanks when he saw it. Amid all the ruin, something remained for the future.

Inside headquarters, workers scrubbed the floor clean, and a fog of bleach and detergent hung in the air. It did not mask the odor completely, but it was a start. A crew was already draining the basement.

Wawa told the agents to salvage as many of their case files as they could. They had twenty minutes before the maintenance team threw the moldy furniture into a bonfire.

While D'Arc riffled through her waterlogged manila folders, Falkirk helped a human officer remove items from a desk that no longer had an occupant. The husky pulled out a watch, a family photo, and a burgundy baseball cap with the letter *P* knitted in white thread. The human—a man in his forties—burst into tears. A few people stopped to look at them before returning to their work. Falkirk hugged the man and let him cry for a few minutes. Maybe something good could come out of this, D'Arc thought.

The Old Man may have been right to warn her about this place, but he could not have predicted how the citizens of Hosanna would have handled the last few days. Maybe Mort(e) needed to see this. Or maybe seeing it still would not have convinced him. D'Arc imagined him rolling his eyes, making a snide remark, reciting some bitter anecdote from the war to prove how bad the humans were. She didn't need any of that. There was too much work to do.

AT 1100 HOURS, the Sons of Adam arrived at Tranquility to give a briefing on the fish-heads. In the cavernous, nearly empty main hall, the officers stood at attention as the strators filed in. D'Arc and Falkirk watched from the second row. Grace Braga entered first. She exchanged glances with the chief as she sauntered by. Harold Pham waddled closely behind her. Clad in his military fatigues, Pham was one of those short humans who swung his arms wide with each step to give the illusion of size. Behind him, a taller strator entered whom D'Arc did not recognize, a man with orange hair cut into a Mohawk and a necklace made of bones and teeth from various species. "Duncan Huxley," Falkirk whispered. Then came Dr. Marquez, the scientist with the sunken eye sockets and graying hair.

The officers prepared to stand at ease when a final guest entered the hall. An orange cat with a white face and belly, a utility belt . . . and a rifle . . . slung over his shoulder . . .

"No," D'Arc whispered. In the first row, a dog looked around, anxious for someone to acknowledge what he saw. Wawa noticed the commotion and walked over to him. The dog stood at attention and pretended that Sebastian the Warrior had not just entered the room.

D'Arc's heart pounded so hard that her vision blurred. Her ears grew hot, her tail flicked about. Her thoughts came in fragments. *Old Man. Here? How did he . . .*

"Let's get started," Braga said. The chief ordered the officers to gather in the corner of the hall, in front of a laptop that sat on a table, connected to a projector. Pham dimmed the lights. The projection switched on, showing a blank screen on the bare wall. As the crowd tightened, Falkirk gave her a look that asked, *are you all right?* She nodded.

Braga gave the Blessing of Michael by tapping her fingers on her temple and her chest, and then extending her palm. Everyone in the room mimicked her, except for D'Arc and the Old Man. "Before we get started," Braga said, "I want to thank you for everything you've done for this city. I know that we don't always get along, and that's often my fault. I hope this crisis can bring us closer together. Better late than never."

She pointed to Pham to start the slideshow. A black and white image of the ocean appeared, with three scaly humps surfacing amid the waves.

"As you know, Tranquility and the Sons of Adam have been tracking anomalies associated with the Change," she said. "For years, we have recorded sightings of creatures, the most recent being the Gulaga incident at Lodge City."

Another slide showed the corpse of the spider washed up on a riverbank, with a woman standing beside it for scale.

"These are not random mutations. These creatures are connected. Some of them have very advanced brains. The Queen must have known that the hormones would pass from our waste into the water system, producing sentient beings in the ocean."

A dog raised his hand. "No questions yet," Braga said. The hand lowered.

The next slide showed several creatures lying on slabs—a fish, a monster with tentacles, a crablike thing with a severed claw.

"They are called the Sarcops. And they adapt. They adapt very well." She pointed out the fish with its elongated body and serrated jaw. Then she traced the outline of the crab's gills, which she said could operate on land. She explained that the monster with tentacles had a full set of lungs, and its skin could go from permeable to rock solid depending on its environment. Like a chameleon that could mimic both color and texture.

"What we have here are three classes," she said. "Class one Sarcops are highly intelligent fish. Class two are amphibious creatures like this crab-spider . . . Thing."

The slide switched to a photo of the Prophet's residence, its front doors ripped off their hinges, huge chunks of the wall torn out. Claw marks reached as high as the rooftop.

"A group of class three Sarcops attacked us earlier this week."

On the screen, a fish-head lay stiff on a stretcher.

"These creatures make up the command structure for the entire species. And we think this one is their leader."

A black and white still of a massive Sarcops, stepping over a shattered door, taken from a security camera at the Prophet's home.

"We call him Big Boy. He's the only male in the group. He can speak. We don't know what exactly he was saying, but he was definitely giving orders to the others."

In another still, a smaller creature lurked behind Big Boy.

"What's more, they take on the attributes of other animals. You've already seen the claws, the tentacles, the shell. And they have a very fast reproductive cycle."

The slide switched to a pile of translucent eggs sitting on a beach.

"But their physical attributes may be the least of our worries."

Marquez took it from there. "Thank you, Strator Braga. I'll try not to get too complicated. Short version: we found a familiar organ in the Sarcops brain, the same thing found in Alpha soldiers. It can detect and process the Colony's chemical signals. When the Sarcops come into contact with these chemicals, it triggers a reaction in the brain."

To illustrate his point, he held his hand next to his temple and shook it hard. "The Sarcops may even experience the presence of the Queen. As if they are using a translator."

This time, D'Arc couldn't stop herself from staring at Mort(e). He had spoken only briefly about his experience with the translator. He saw things that made no sense, things that pointed to the past and to a series of possible futures. Each time he woke, she would ask what was wrong. He said that in his dreams he became trapped in the world of the Colony. In visions that seemed to last for months, Mort(e) lived and killed and died as an ant, a subject of the Queen.

Despite all of that, the Old Man stood stoically at the mention of the device. He must have known that she was watching.

"This mutation might be a fail-safe that the Queen initiated before she died," Braga added. "Or she planned it all along—another phase in the war." She gave the idea some time to take root in the audience. D'Arc smelled a bloom of sweat on some of the humans.

"If we're right," Braga said, "then they regard this city as a threat. Hosanna should not exist. By targeting Michael, the Sarcops wanted to break our spirit before they wiped us out.

"Now. Let's talk about how we kill them."

She waved Mort(e) over. As the cat approached, Braga explained that the *Upheaval* had spotted a firefight upriver a few days earlier. When the Sons of Adam arrived at the scene, they found the cat, a bat, and a dead Sarcops. "I believe you know who this is," she said. "Captain Mort(e), formerly of the Colonial Army."

The Old Man whispered something in Braga's ear.

"Sorry, Red Sphinx," she said.

D'Arc saw the hate in his eyes. He had not slept, had barely eaten. He had traveled all this way, fought off a monster, and collaborated with his sworn enemies, all so he could stand before her once again, mere days after she mated with someone else. She was afraid of him then—still angry and shocked as well, but mostly frightened of what he could do, of what he wanted. For years, he was the only person she knew. Now, she wondered if she ever knew him at all.

"I recognize a few of you from Golgotha," Mort(e) said. "That time, we won because we had a secret weapon. This time, no such luck."

He told the story of how the beavers from Lodge City brought him a seemingly dead fish-head, only to watch the creature spring to life and escape into the forest. He followed her downstream. On the day after the dam broke, Mort(e) identified another class-three female swimming in the river. Though he tried to keep his distance and maneuver around her, the creature emerged from the water and attacked. Mort(e) retreated to high ground, and opened fire with his elephant rifle. The beast collapsed, and a malformed egg dropped from her abdomen. Mort(e) speculated that she must have been protecting a clutch of younglings.

A new slide showed a crude diagram of a Sarcops soldier. Mort(e) noted the armor on the chest and spine. A few of the creatures had spiked tails and tentacles. "These things regenerate," he said. "Even when they seem dead, they may be hibernating. Severed limbs can regrow. Hearts can start beating again."

"Then how do you know you killed this one?" someone asked.

Mort(e) smiled when he recognized the speaker: Chief Wawa. "Chopped her head off," Mort(e) said. "If she wakes up after that, she's not gonna be happy."

The officers laughed. Even Braga smiled.

"What scares me more than their bodies is their minds," Mort(e) said. "They're learning. And they have a purpose. They serve the Queen. Or they think they do."

"How do you know all this?" Wawa asked.

"Because what's happening to them happened to me," Mort(e) said. "They can both receive signals and send them. And I can . . ." He stammered a bit before lifting his head and facing D'Arc. "I can hear them."

D'Arc heard a collective intake of air. The strators again performed the reverential gesture to the Prophet.

"I've had dreams and visions, ever since the fish-heads made landfall. In this last encounter, I heard the word Sarcops." Mort(e) asked Marquez what the word meant.

"It is the name of a genus," Marquez said.

"Right. Anyway, I know that some translator users have been murdered. Maybe the fish-heads think that we pose a threat."

"Are they coming back?" Wawa asked.

"Yes."

Braga told the officers that Tranquility would reassign a dozen people to the Prophet's residence. Everyone would be issued a nerve gas canister, leftovers from the war, powerful enough to kill an Alpha. In the meantime, reinforcements would arrive from some of the outer districts. Before the chatter could begin, Wawa told everyone to shut up and listen.

"We've got a lot of work to do," she said. "No one is coming to the rescue. We built this city together. We have to save it together. Everybody got that?"

The officers responded with a resounding, "Yes, Chief!"

Someone flicked the lights on. The crowd dispersed noisily, with footsteps and voices pinging off the walls. Officers returned to their posts. D'Arc and Falkirk had been assigned to the new watchtower guarding the river delta. Amid the movement in the room, D'Arc zeroed in on the Old Man, standing proud with his rifle, pretending not to notice the commotion he spent years trying to escape. In her peripheral vision, she saw Falkirk about to ask her if she was coming with him. Following an awkward pause, he gave up and let her go to her friend. When Mort(e) spotted her, he licked his wrists and ran them along his head to straighten out the fur.

Several officers—both human and animal—hovered nearby, hoping to get Mort(e)'s attention. They jumped at the sound of Wawa shouting. "Did I say stand around, or did I say get to work?"

D'Arc would have to make this quick. This was not the place for a tearful reunion, yet she felt the urge to wrap her arms around his neck. She lifted her hands to him.

Mort(e) stopped her with his paw and stared at her. "Calm yourself, cadet."

He wouldn't even wink at her to let her know it would be all right. She had no choice but to lower her hands to her side, clear her throat, and speak in a voice even colder than his.

"I'm glad to see you," she said. "I'm glad you're alive."

"It's good to see you."

"What are you going to do now that you're here?"

"I came to visit an old friend. Someone I haven't seen in a long time."

D'Arc covered her face with her hands. *Does he know? Does he know what I did?* "I'm so sorry, Mort(e). I wish I were better at explaining all of this. There's so much—"

"I wasn't talking about you, D'Arc."

She took her hands away. Mort(e) flicked his chin in the direction of the strators. "I'm off to see the Prophet. The Wonderful Prophet of Hosanna."

The Old Man performed the Blessing of Michael. He let his filthy palm dangle in front of her, as if begging for something he knew she would never give.

"Captain," Braga said. "We're leaving."

"I'll be there in a minute."

Mort(e) stood waiting for D'Arc to end the conversation. She knew then that she could never go back to the ranch. And the person she had been there—a stupid, silly dog named Sheba—would never leave.

"Well, good luck, Captain."

"Good luck, cadet. Stay safe."

The Old Man checked his belt to make sure he did not forget anything. Then he left.

D'Arc's feet almost gave out from under her. She noticed two dogs in conversation, both staring at her. They turned away, pretending to focus on a piece of paper one of them held.

Another dog approached. D'Arc had become so blinkered she didn't realize at first that it was Falkirk. "Are you okay?" he asked.

"I'm fine. Let's go to the watchtower."

"We don't have to leave right this minute. You can go to the barracks if you need to."

"No. The watchtower. Let's go."

In no mood to answer questions, D'Arc walked swiftly to keep Falkirk behind her. Passing through the doors, she stepped into the bright sun and caught a whiff of the stench rising from the stagnant floodwaters. The Old Man had made her tough for exactly this kind of situation. She would take that and use it. She would be grateful. She would not look back.

# CHAPTER 19

## PILGRIMAGE

ORT(E) SAT IN the in the rear of a pickup, behind the driver, as the vehicle bounced along the potholed streets. Duncan Huxley sat across from him. The man's ginger Mohawk gleamed in the afternoon sun, rising so high off his head that it shadowed his face. His freckles gave the only hint of his youth. Everything else about him—from his faded ring tattoos to his calloused hands—suggested that he survived the worst of the war. On his necklace hung several battle trophies. Mort(e) recognized a wolf's fang, a bear's nail, a knuckle bone. With a small handheld drill, the human punched a hole into a new trophy: a tooth extracted from a dead Sarcops.

In the front seat, Harold Pham drove while Grace Braga spoke to Mort(e) through the rear window. Like a tour guide, she described the various neighborhoods and the ongoing rebuilding projects. She noted the garment district, a haven for raccoons. A nest of rats reinforced the subway lines under City Hall. Braga knew the history of the area well—including the story of the disastrous evacuation at the sports complex along the river. During the war, thousands of human refugees waited for rescue boats that never arrived. Rather than speaking with bitterness about the carnage, Braga described the events with a hint of admiration, from one warrior to another.

Mort(e) asked if she had lived in the area. No, she said. She came from Florida. "We don't have all this construction where I'm from," she said. "After the war, everything got swallowed up by the swamp. I'm part Seminole, so I think that my ancestors would have wanted it that way." Huxley laughed as he continued to twist the drill into the tooth.

Mort(e) did not know what to make of these humans. When they found him in the woods, with the dead Sarcops lying before him, he was in no shape to object to their presence. His confrontation with the fish-head left him dazed. The beast had launched herself out of the water like a missile shot from a submarine. Gaunt swooped in to distract her, but one of the tentacles swung and smashed the bat in the face, sending him crashing in a heap of fur and skin. As Mort(e) opened fire, he heard something else, a rapid clicking that bypassed his ears and scraped the inside of his skull. It was worse than the battle with Gulaga. This fish-head could somehow drill into his mind. Disoriented, he kept shooting to drown out her voice. And even after the beast slumped over in the dirt, Mort(e) could still hear it. He drew his knife and stood over her, the blade raised.

That was when he heard a single word whispered in Michael's voice, slicing through him. *Sebastian*. A taunting word, meaning, *We see you. We know who you are.*

Mort(e) hacked at the tough flesh on the creature's neck again and again until the head rolled away from the shoulders. Trembling and covered with a yellowish blood, Mort(e) sat beside the creature and rested his head on the shell. Twenty feet away, Gaunt watched him, a trickle of blood oozing from a cut below his left goggle.

Had he not killed a fish-head almost single-handedly, the human scout team would have refused to believe that he was the legendary

Mort(e). But once he convinced them, the strators radioed head-quarters for a transport. When the Humvee arrived, the soldiers strapped the creature's body to the hood and mounted the head on the gun turret. Gaunt refused to get inside, choosing instead to fly the rest of the way. Mort(e) endured a bumpy ride in a car stinking of humans, all asking ridiculous questions about Sheba. He hated hearing her name on their sleazy tongues, but at least they didn't know where she was.

The humans detained Mort(e) at a base in the northern end of the city. Marquez needed to interview him about his encounter. The doctor asked if Mort(e) heard anything familiar in all the static he picked up from the beast. Mort(e) reluctantly told him about hearing his slave name in the Prophet's voice. "Maybe I was panicking," he said. But Marquez had been expecting something like this. "You are connected," he said. "Like one of the Queen's daughters." *Wonderful*, Mort(e) thought.

In between these conversations, Mort(e) managed to get his hands on a casualty list taped to a cinderblock wall. He saw neither a D'Arc nor a Sheba, but this did not bring him any relief. The last few weeks had whittled him down to a sharp point. The exhaustion, the time spent alone in the woods, and the fight with the Sarcops made him question what he was doing here at all. What would finding D'Arc even mean? He couldn't get to Hosanna in time to save her from the flood. He doubted that he could talk her into returning to the ranch. Perhaps now the best thing to do was to simply say goodbye.

Sitting in the pickup, Mort(e) wondered if his encounter with D'Arc at headquarters would be his last. Mort(e) replayed the conversation in his head, mouthing the words. Brushing her off the way he had brought neither closure nor a satisfying sense of revenge. But he would keep reliving it until something clicked, or broke. Then he would find some gray area between happiness and sadness, and none of these things—the doomed city, the babbling humans, the friend who left him—would ever hurt him again.

Braga talked about finding her daughter alive in the rubble of a municipal building. She claimed that the Prophet led her to the right spot. The Prophet saw everything. "Tell me," she said, "what is it you seek from Michael?"

Huxley's head lifted. His little drill stopped twisting.

"I told you already," Mort(e) said. "Haven't seen him in a long time."

"There must be something more concrete," she said.

She told him about her first meeting with Michael. When she bowed before him, the child looked into her eyes and knew exactly how to set her mind at ease after years of bloodshed.

"He said, 'Be still.' And he touched my hand." At this, Braga lifted her right arm, and placed her left palm over the knuckles. "And I knew he meant all the things in my life. All the bad thoughts in my mind. Be still. You want to keep fighting a war? No, be still. You want to settle old scores? No, be still."

No one tried harder to be still than Mort(e), and it merely brought him here. And no one had known Michael longer. Mort(e) remembered the boy as a happy, curious child. Michael laughed, whined when he didn't get his way, broke things and blamed it on his sister, watched the same garishly colored cartoons on an endless loop. *This* child was the visionary who spoke in profound riddles? *This* boy was the glue that held the city together? These humans would believe anything.

At the Prophet's residence, the vehicle passed through two checkpoints, one at the intersection, the other at the front driveway. Armed guards paced along the roof. When Mort(e) hopped out, he realized that he had not seen this many humans since his time on the *Vesuvius*.

"I hope the Prophet tells you to stay," Huxley said. "We could use someone who can kill a fish-head." He tied on the completed

necklace. The Sarcops tooth gleamed alongside the other trophies. Braga stepped out of the pickup and told the others to
check on a guard tower near the navy yard. Huxley gave her the
Blessing and got into the passenger seat. Pham wheeled the truck
through the inner gates.

A wall of sandbags barricaded the enormous hole in the front
of the building. Behind it, a row of human heads poked over
the top. Someone hastily set down a footstool just in time for
Braga to step over the barricade. The underlings saluted her as
she passed. Mort(e) went next. Inside, a crew of workers—all
human—sawed and hammered the exposed beams of a newly
constructed wall. In the wide hallway, more guards waited
behind sandbags. If the fish-heads returned, they would have to
make it through a gauntlet of machine gun nests.

On the second floor, the stench of the flood yielded to a harsh
disinfectant. White linoleum and aqua ceramic tiles shimmered
under the fluorescent lights. The noise from downstairs died out,
save for the hammering that vibrated throughout the foundation. At the end of the hall, three strators guarded a set of double
doors. It was there that the Sons of Adam had mounted their last
defense, repelling the Sarcops in the nick of time.

"I need to tell you something before we do this," Braga said.
"The Prophet has not been well as of late. We may not have
much time with him."

"I only need a minute."

"There's more. You're the only animal to see him this close in
a while. If you were anyone else, I don't think even I could have
gotten you this far."

"I'm not interested in your politics," he said. "I just want to
see him and go."

The guards parted for them. Braga inserted a keycard into a
sensor. The light changed from red to green, and a bolt slid out
of the doorjamb. Braga opened it, releasing a whoosh of cold

air. Mort(e) noticed the temperature drop as they crossed the threshold into a spacious, sunlit room. Located in the corner of the building, the Prophet's quarters had windows overlooking the street. Standing near the other wall, a woman in a lab coat flipped through a stapled printout. She wore her hair in a thick braid, along with a ring tattoo on her neck. The nurse acknowledged them by glancing up from her report.

In a bed in the center of the room, obscured by wires and tubes, lay the Prophet Michael. His heartbeat pinged on the EKG meter. A ventilator pumped air into his lungs through a plastic face mask. An IV drip pierced his bony arm. This close, the antiseptic smell could not mask the scent of death and decay on the boy.

"Please keep it short today, strator," the nurse said.

"What happened to the other nurse?" Mort(e) asked. "The one with the shaved head."

The two women looked at each other. "Adele passed away over a year ago," Braga said.

Michael's eyes stared at the ceiling. When he blinked, the lids drooped before peeling open again, first the left one, then the right. Though the oxygen mask obscured his face, it was clear that the boy had aged since Mort(e) saw him last. He should have been entering puberty by now, seeking a mate and playing sports and planning for a future. Instead, they locked him in here, a living testament to the war with no name.

"Does he still speak to you?" Mort(e) asked.

"In his own way," Braga said. "We have to learn how to listen."

Mort(e) leaned over the bed to put his face in the boy's line of sight. The Prophet saw straight through him.

"Ask him what you need to ask him," Braga said. "You don't even have to speak it."

Mort(e) remembered the voice he had heard in Lodge City. *Help me. Save me.* He held Michael's hand and considered the possibility that this child could see into his mind, the way the

Sarcops could. He would tell Mort(e) what all of this meant. The prospect made Mort(e)'s stomach flutter. What if the humans spoke the truth? What if Mort(e) had walled off his heart to this revelation? He suddenly wanted this boy to tell him he was forgiven for all the pain he had caused. It was that easy, wasn't it? One word from this boy would fix everything. That's what this entire city believed, while Mort(e) hid in the forest refusing to listen.

Michael began to cough violently. The heart monitor spiked. His hand fell away. When the coughing subsided, drops of spittle stuck to the inside of his mask.

"Please, give it some time," Braga said. "He speaks as God wills it."

"God wills him to be silent then." Mort(e) recalled the echo again. *Help me.*

Braga turned to the nurse. "Can you boost the adrenaline?"

"No," Mort(e) said. "He gave me a message already. A long time ago."

"What was it?"

"You wouldn't like it." Mort(e) headed for the door.

"Perhaps he'll speak to D'Arc," Braga said.

Mort(e) stopped and stared at her.

"We know who she is," Braga said. "We know she's here, and she's conflicted about staying, especially with that husky manipulating her. She is at great risk right now. Even I can't protect her."

"Are you threatening my friend?"

"I'm not threatening her. I'm warning *you*. There are people in this city who want to use her. And until she hears the Prophet's voice, until she believes in him, she'll be a danger to herself. And to others. If they find out who she is."

This strator wanted him to believe that she saw everything, like the Queen. She had studied his weaknesses, and knew exactly what to say to him.

"There is one thing I needed to ask the Prophet," Mort(e) said.

Pleased to hear this, Braga walked with him to the bed. Mort(e) took the boy's hand again and leaned in. Like a four-legged cat from before the Change, he ran the side of his neck against Michael's face. The boy did not react. But the voice echoed in Mort(e)'s mind again, like a rock tossed into an alley. *Help me.* Gently, Mort(e) slid both of his hands around Michael's cheeks. In one quick movement, he jerked Michael's face violently to the left. The neck snapped, sending a crunching vibration all the way to Mort(e)'s elbows. The heart monitor stuttered before flatlining. Michael's mask fell off, revealing the prematurely wizened face. The eyes rolled into the lids as if he were about to doze off into a peaceful dream.

Mort(e) let go. The two women gaped at the sight of the Messiah standing over the murdered Prophet.

"He's not yours anymore," he said.

The screaming began. The two women raced to the bed. They shook Michael, saying *no* over and over. The doors burst open as the guards flooded the room. The sound of boots and angry voices mingled with the shouting. When they seized him, Mort(e)'s laughter cut through all the noise. He couldn't remember the last time he had laughed so loud.

They dragged him into the hallway and beat him on the cold floor. He let them do it. Doctors and guards rushed into the Prophet's room. As the rifle butts and boot heels rained down on him, a dark haze spilled over the world until he felt himself sinking underwater.

MORT(E) AWOKE ON a stretcher. Wheeled down a hallway. Cinderblock walls whizzing by. Painted lime green. Reflecting the light of overhead bulbs.

He couldn't move. Tied down. Arms crossed over his chest. Ankles cuffed.

Voices. Human voices. Arguing.

He blinked a few times. Then he blacked out.

MORT(E) LAY IN a room. Still tied down. No window. Three brick walls and a metal gate. Cream-colored bars. A big lock—a metal box with an enormous keyhole.

He opened his mouth, dry as sand. The saliva crackled.

It was the only noise. And it echoed.

SOME TIME LATER, he stared at the ceiling, where copper-colored flakes fell from rusty pipes. Tired and dazed, Mort(e) stayed still for a long time before he realized he could sit up. Someone had untied him.

With only a hanging overhead lamp, he could not determine how much time had passed, if it was day or night. His ribs screamed as he rose from the stretcher, gingerly. Once he felt steady, he limped to the metal gate. His hip joint burned, the socket grinding like sandpaper. At the bars, he saw a long, dank corridor that extended beyond his field of vision in both directions.

His bladder was full. In the corner was a plastic bucket filled with kitty litter. Stiffly, he squatted and relieved himself.

A few hours later, a cow walking on all fours delivered a metal plate filled with a pasty gruel. Mort(e) asked her who was in charge, but she left without answering. Her hoofs clopped away on the concrete floor.

With each bite, he tasted blood from the beating he took. He tried shouting into the corridor, but no one answered. Eventually he gave up and fell asleep again.

A DOOR CREAKING on rusted hinges woke him. Judging from the footsteps, the people approaching did not wear shoes—this was good. He was not in a human prison.

Mort(e) threaded his arms through the bars and folded his

hands. Wawa arrived first, with D'Arc behind her. D'Arc now, not Sheba, wearing a Tranquility-issued vest along with her trusty sword. She was safe. Maybe it was all worth it.

The two dogs waited for him to say something. In the distance, a leaky pipe dripped, sending an echo through the hallway.

"Did they bring you some food and water?" Wawa asked.

"Yes."

Another awkward silence. "You broke your promise," she said.

"What promise?"

"That I'd never see you again. Actually, this is the second time you've broken it."

"I've been told that I'm a liar." He refused to acknowledge D'Arc when he said it.

"Captain, you have left a swathe of destruction I cannot even begin to describe. Lodge City burned to the ground. The matriarch handed over to the bats like currency. And now this."

"Right. How long am I going to be here?"

"It's your fault we couldn't process you sooner. The Sons of Adam blamed Tranquility for what you did. So they attacked headquarters. And the temple. You've been here for forty-eight hours, and you've already triggered a civil war."

"Sounds like I did you a favor. You can run the city on your own now. You're the only honest person around here. Might as well be you."

Wawa gritted her teeth. "You think that's what I wanted? I was trying to save this city."

"You wanted to be a loyal dog, protecting her pack."

"Yes, and I don't apologize for it!" She stopped for a second to allow the echo to cease. "I try to work with others. To build something. To become something more. You could have tried that, but no. You went and hid in the forest and hoped the world would never find you."

"I don't apologize either."

"I know you think that what you did was an act of mercy. But the clerics and the other humans are calling it murder. We have to follow through on the charges. Especially now. We can't let people think we're falling apart."

Wawa told him that there would be a hearing in a few days. Until then, they would keep him here, away from the main holding cell, for his own protection. When Mort(e) rolled his eyes at that, Wawa explained that the prisoners in general population had placed a bounty on his head. Meanwhile, Tranquility agents arrested his accomplice, Gaunt of Thicktree. They netted him while he slept dangling from an overpass. He would be released within a few days. Mort(e), on the other hand, would stay.

"So it might be goodbye for real this time," she said.

"Goodbye then."

"You were always welcome here, Captain. Could have used you. Before all this."

Wawa stomped away. "Two minutes," she said to D'Arc. Seconds later, a distant metal door opened and then slammed shut.

D'Arc folded her arms. "Don't think you're gonna talk to me like that."

"No," he said, suddenly exhausted in her presence, after acting like the tough one for so long.

She reached out and clutched his hands. He managed to hold it together while she wept. He wanted so badly to run his cheek along hers, but he could not fit his head through the bars.

"Old Man," she said.

He pulled away and got a better look at her. "So what are you now? A member of Tranquility?"

"Unofficially," she said. "Mort(e), do you know about the expedition? The one that's sailing into the Atlantic?"

Something hard and heavy and warm sank into his stomach.

"Yes," he finally said. Marquez had mentioned it to him during their sessions together. But he never thought—

"I'm going." D'Arc said. "They chose me."

For a few seconds, he listened to her breathing. And then he couldn't help himself. "Are you going on the expedition to be with *him*?"

She let go of his hands. "Falkirk isn't going. I'm doing this by myself."

He leaned his forehead on the bars.

"I'll get you out of here first, Old Man. I won't leave until you're safe."

"You don't have to do anything. I don't want to stand in the way anymore."

"I'm trying anyway. Like you would for me."

Someone knocked on the steel door three times.

"I have to go," she said.

She gave him two licks on the crown of his head before running off. Once she was gone, and the place fell silent again, the warm patch left behind by her tongue evaporated. He felt nothing at all, and wondered if he had imagined the whole thing.

# CHAPTER 20

## THE SUMMIT

'ARC RETURNED TO the barracks on foot as the broken city shut down for the day. Nearly a week of digging, rowing, and bailing forced her to walk with a stooped gait. Along the way, she heard singing coming from an abandoned building—a human, belting out some mournful gospel song in the waning light. Several blocks later, D'Arc passed a fire flickering in an alley, around which people shared stories of rescues and hardship. At this hour, the flames provided most of the light in the city.

Candles and oil lamps lit the windows of the barracks when she arrived. D'Arc brushed past the cadets who loitered in the main courtyard. There were fewer of them now. At least ten deserted after the Prophet died. With classes canceled indefinitely, they had nothing to do but wait for Tranquility to assign them to different work crews or guard posts. The cadets in the courtyard were filthy, with a layer of grime on their vests, most likely from the construction site near the river.

In the living quarters, Razz rested her head on her desk. The pug's nose twitched when D'Arc walked by. She looked up with enormous bloodshot eyes.

"You smell too good to be in here," Razz said.

"I used the hose at headquarters. My reward for helping to carry in the new equipment."

"I helped put out the fire on 11th Street."

D'Arc knew what she meant. The strators had set a series of blazes during the melee that followed the Prophet's death. The latest was at a nearby apartment building. "No survivors," Razz said. "And no shower afterward."

Razz asked if the husky would be coming for her in the morning, in the same tone she always used. The pug had already grilled her about mating with Falkirk, something D'Arc denied even after Razz swore she could smell it on her. "You better jump on that soon," Razz told her. "These wolf dogs can't help themselves. He'll be humping some poodle if you don't act fast." To illustrate the point, Razz thrusted her pelvis and stuck out her tongue.

This time, D'Arc cut her off before she got going. She had not seen Falkirk since the Prophet died. On the day after, D'Arc waited for him in her usual spot in front of the barracks. He never arrived, so she went to headquarters without him. It took some asking around before she learned that Falkirk was involved in the skirmish near the dam, which drove most of the strators out of Hosanna. No one would tell her anything else.

"Do you want to complain about it?" Razz asked. "I made a new concoction and I need a test subject." She lifted a canteen from her desk, removed the cap, and held it under D'Arc's snout. It smelled like cleaning fluid and cherries.

"I don't think so," D'Arc said.

"Come on, just a little this time. I call it Razzamatazz."

"I thought that's what you called the last one."

"No, that was Razzle-Dazzle. We'll drink it on the roof. No one will see us."

The last time D'Arc did this, she woke up with a swollen tongue and a headache that pressed against her eyeballs. Still, she relented.

From the rooftop, D'Arc could see that the flooding had spared most of the area. Several of the apartment buildings remained occupied. Farther away, the lights faded, save for the enormous trash fires. From the relative quiet and stillness, D'Arc got the sense that the city had worked itself into a state of exhaustion.

D'Arc leaned on the concrete wall separating the roof from the ledge. Beside her, Razz poured her latest experiment into two cups. "To the Prophet," she said, raising her drink. D'Arc took a sip. The fluid scorched its way to her belly. She exhaled a fruity scent through her nose.

"What do you think?" Razz said.

"It's terrible. You're getting better."

Laughing, Razz drank some more and wiped her mouth with her paw. "You know, I saw some humans toasting the Prophet by pouring wine onto the ground."

"Should *we* do that?"

"No!"

Razz lifted her cup to her lips. She paused. "See how my arm shakes? Three days of manual labor. I wasn't meant for this."

"You weren't meant to have arms at all."

Razz asked if D'Arc had tried alcohol before the Change. D'Arc didn't remember. "I think I may have," Razz said. "I know my master kept the house well stocked."

Her master was an old woman, a widow named Lois. She refused to leave her home during the evacuation of Baltimore, choosing instead to sit in her parlor and drink herself to death. When Razz entered the room, fully transformed and walking upright, Lois calmly invited her to sit at her table. "If you're going to kill me, then let's at least have a drink first," the woman said. But this human was a good master, kind and fair even as the Colony invaded. Razz could not say that out loud during the war. It was bad enough that she had been someone's pet—a pug could never claim to have been a stray. So she played along with everyone else, and even made up a story about killing Lois. She assumed that almost everyone told a variation of the same lie until they started to actually believe it.

"What happened to her?" D'Arc asked.

"I helped her commit suicide," Razz said, her eyes reflecting the distant bonfires. "She had been planning to do it for a while. So I wasn't totally lying when I bragged about killing her."

Without going into any detail, D'Arc said that she ran away from home the same day she changed. Her master was long dead by the time she even considered searching for him. When Razz asked about her slave name, D'Arc said she didn't remember it.

"I'm not telling you mine, either," Razz said. "A pug has enough problems."

A chill crept across the rooftop. D'Arc felt impervious to it. The drink warmed her gut and numbed her skin. She held out her cup for a refill. "Not too much," she said.

They toasted again. Razz's arm still trembled. "I think God's trying to tell us something," she said. "He brings the Messiah here, takes the Prophet away. Maybe he's telling us that we need to sort this out on our own, without his messengers to tell us what to do."

"I wish everyone saw it that way."

D'Arc wondered where Falkirk was. She imagined him warming his hands by a fire, wondering who would hear his prayers now that Michael was gone. If he really did mate with some poodle like Razz said, perhaps he thought of D'Arc. Or he did it to forget her.

Hiccupping, Razz said she was done for the night. D'Arc said she would go downstairs later. After the pug left, D'Arc stayed in the same position, thinking of what she would say to Falkirk and Mort(e) the next time she saw them. When she caught herself nodding off, she sat down and curled into a ball, letting the wall protect her from the wind. She soon fell asleep under the clouds with the artificial cherry flavor coating the inside of her mouth.

THE CADETS AWOKE at the usual hour, when the first hints of sunlight crept above the skyline. The alcohol from the night before left D'Arc groggy, though not as hungover as the last time. Without speaking to anyone, she gathered her things and walked past the sleeping area. Razz huddled against a pillar, snoring softly while the other students bustled around her.

D'Arc made it two whole blocks before she started thinking about the Old Man again. While she strolled at her own pace under an open sky, the cat who rescued her wallowed in a jail cell because he had put a dying boy out of his misery. D'Arc imagined sneaking into the prison and helping him escape. When that fantasy ran its course, she settled on being angry at Mort(e) for following her here, and for breaking everything he touched.

A dump truck overloaded with debris rumbled alongside her. Behind it, a motorcycle beeped its horn and tried to squeeze past the truck, only to stop abruptly. The driver—a dog—swung around in his seat and waved at her.

"D'Arc!" he said.

It was Falkirk. She ran to him.

"Get on. Something's happening at the pier."

She slid onto the seat behind him. "What is it?"

"They're back."

D'Arc wrapped her arms around his waist as the bike accelerated. He was leaner than before, having spent days on the prowl trying to root out the last of the strators. His muscles felt taut and sinewy, but they emanated the same warmth that she remembered.

"Are the strators all gone?" she asked.

"I think so. We followed them to the other side of the river. But they broke camp before we got there. They must be halfway to the Poconos by now."

He cranked the accelerator, enough for the front wheel to levitate for a second. They overtook the trash truck. D'Arc closed her eyes to keep out the dust.

"Are you doing okay?" she asked. "I mean . . . with all of this."

"I'm fine. I will be."

They hit a traffic jam on the street that ran parallel to the river. Tranquility officers tried to redirect the vehicles around a roadblock, using flares and bright orange flags. On the other side, a narrow pier stretched into the river. With a brick walkway and a row of trees, the pier had once been a pedestrian oasis in the middle of a noisy city. But on this day, a row of sandbags sealed the entrance. Wawa and several other agents hid behind the barricade. D'Arc recognized the human Daiyu Fang next to the chief, wearing olive cargo pants and a flak jacket. Her shiny black hair was greased so that it lay stiffly behind her ears. Fang pointed at something in the river, and the officers nodded.

Falkirk parked the motorcycle at the roadblock, where a bearded man asked for ID. Falkirk showed it and asked for an update.

"Two fish-heads have been circling the pier," the man said. "They have a hostage."

Falkirk turned to D'Arc. "You'll have to fall in with the others. I'm going to talk to the chief."

They split up. D'Arc drew her pistol and took cover behind one of the squad cars. A dog held a shotgun across the hood while D'Arc propped herself on the trunk.

With Falkirk beside her, Wawa ordered the officers to take a position along the railing. D'Arc and the others scurried to the edge of the river. She caught a glimpse of tentacles undulating and then disappearing into the murky water. Another creature surfaced, covered in sopping wet fur. It was a female raccoon, belly up, her pink teats exposed, a tentacle wrapped around her torso. The raccoon gasped for air before the Sarcops pulled her under again.

The soldiers aimed their rifles at the dark shadows under the surface. In response, the intruders moved away from the river's edge.

Someone shouted. "They're out of the water!"

At the end of the pier, a tentacle lifted the raccoon over the railing and dropped her on the other side, her wet body slapping the concrete. She shook off the excess and jogged to the barricade.

"Don't shoot!" she said. "Don't shoot!" The raccoon stopped when she realized that the soldiers were not about to lower their weapons.

The chief aimed her pistol at the raccoon's head. "Who are you?"

"I'm Dice," the raccoon said, shivering. "From Kensington."

The word sent murmurs through the crowd. Kensington was a refugee camp washed away in the flood.

"How did you get here?" Wawa asked.

"I was stranded on a tree branch. Way downriver. The fish-heads rescued me."

"*Res*cued?"

Falkirk pointed at the edge of the pier. "Chief!"

One of the monsters climbed the railing and slid over the top, like a sheath of wet leather. The other one followed. They stretched out their claws and tentacles and marched toward the barricade, with the larger of the two in the lead. The creatures made the same odd choking sound that D'Arc remembered, the eyes blinking each time.

Dice held out her hands. "They wanna talk! That's all!"

Still dripping, the fish-heads put their full arsenal on display. A breastplate made of solid bone covered their torsos. Their claw-like feet gripped the cement as they moved.

D'Arc recognized the larger one. It was Big Boy, the leader.

Dice held her ground. "They told me that they would speak to you at the end of the pier."

Wawa laughed. "Choke that."

"Please. The guns make them nervous."

"That's the idea."

The Sarcops came closer, bringing with them the stench of ammonia. Wawa growled. D'Arc could tell that she wanted a sim-ple fight, not this peace offering. The chief snapped her fingers and pointed at Dice. Two soldiers hauled the raccoon away.

"They saved my life!" Dice said. "Please, just talk to them!"

The Sarcops came to a halt about thirty feet from the barri-cade. A minute went by. Wawa ordered everyone to lower their weapons. Nothing. "Speak!" she said. Still nothing. Finally, she jumped over the barricade, gun drawn.

The officers closed ranks at the foot of the pier. D'Arc posi-tioned herself directly behind Falkirk. Fang whispered something in his ear. He nodded in agreement, and then the two of them mounted the sandbags. D'Arc took their place at the barricade and rested her gun on it.

"This is a bad idea," someone said. A dog grunted in agree-ment.

The smaller fish-head pointed her tentacle right at D'Arc. The tentacle had been severed, a mere stump, with a fresh wound that still needed time to heal.

Big Boy made a choking sound. "You did," he said to D'Arc. With all the officers watching her, D'Arc descended into full puppy dog mode, with sinking head and sad eyes.

"Yes," she said.

The smaller fish-head said something to her companion. It came out in a series of clicks and moans. "She says you come,"

Big Boy said. D'Arc hesitated. "Yes!" the creature insisted. D'Arc climbed the barricade. Nervously, she glanced at the bewildered officers. Several of them shook their heads in disbelief.

With Wawa in the lead, the officers followed the fish-heads as they backed their way to the end of the pier. The Sarcops stopped at the edge, ready to jump over the barrier at the first sign of trouble. "That's close enough," Wawa said. With that, the human and the three dogs formed a line, facing the Sarcops—the first summit of its kind in Hosanna.

Big Boy lifted his claw. "Taalik. The First of Us. Of Cold Trench." He pointed to the other one. "Orak. My Prime."

Wawa gave her name. "Chief of Tranquility," she added. "I help to protect this city." She introduced the others. Then she asked what the Sarcops wanted.

"Peace," Taalik said. "And help."

"Peace and help? You attacked us. Unprovoked. Many of our people are dead."

"*You* attack. Before."

No one knew what Taalik meant. Orak began to click and chirp. Taalik responded in their alien language, in a tone suggesting that she keep quiet and let him handle this.

"You kill us," Taalik said. "In the high grounds."

"I don't understand."

"One of us. Walks on land. Builds a nest. I hear her crying."

"He might mean the class two," Fang said. "The arachnid."

"Up the river?" Wawa said to Taalik. "In the mountains?" She moved her arms like a spider crawling.

"Yes!" Taalik said.

"She killed our people. We had no choice."

"You *steal* our people. Place them in . . . Tubes. In cages. On the floating island."

"Floating island?" Fang didn't know what this meant. Falkirk shrugged. Before they could start arguing, Wawa waved her hands to silence them. "We have attacked each other, it's true," she said. "We do not wish to attack again. We do not wish to be attacked. What is it that you want?"

"We come from the ice. At the top. My people trapped. Surrounded. Hunted. Dying."

Taalik made the choking sound. Orak clicked something that he seemed to ignore.

"The Queen, she speaks," he said. "She shows me . . . light. She shows me the sun, coming down. Breaking the ice. Setting my people free."

"Your people are trapped up north," Wawa said. "In the ice. In a . . . glacier."

"Yes!"

"But the sun can come down—"

"And free them! Yes!"

Wawa shook her head. "I don't know what he means."

"You have the sun!" Taalik said. "You push it up. You pull it down."

"We do not control the sun. It comes up and goes down on its own."

"You must bring it down. Break through the ice."

Orak started in with her chirping again. Taalik argued with her.

"Chief," Falkirk said.

"Quiet."

Taalik moved closer, his claws extended, pleading for her to understand. Everyone lifted their guns higher, aiming right between his glassy eyes. "You know," he said. "Speak to me true. Or we will return with a thousand more."

They looked to Wawa. The pit bull grinded her teeth. "We have a device," she said.

"Yes."

"The Rama satellite, in the sky. It can reflect the sunlight. It can *aim* it."

"Yes!" Taalik said. "Break through the ice. Set the people free."

"Break through the ice," Wawa repeated.

"Wait," Fang said. "How large of an area are we talking?"

"Here," Taalik said. Then he gestured to the skyscrapers, half a mile away. "To there."

"The satellite wasn't meant to be used like that—"

"You must try! Or my people, dead."

"It doesn't matter," Wawa said. "We can't operate the satellite. No one knows how."

"The Queen knows," Taalik said. "People who speak to her, they know."

"People who speak to her . . ."

"People who used the translator," D'Arc said. In a satisfying moment, they all turned their heads to her. They knew she was right.

"Is that why you went after Michael?" Wawa said. "The boy? You thought he knew how to operate the satellite?"

"The Queen remembers his voice," Taalik said. "We found him silent. He cannot help."

"People who have used the translator have been turning up dead lately," Wawa said. "You want me to hand them over to you? How do I know you're not hunting them?"

"No hunt. We need."

Falkirk growled. "So you have nothing to do with people being murdered?"

Orak hissed at him.

"No," Taalik said. "We will not kill again. But you must help."

"You don't understand," Wawa said. "The people who spoke to the Queen—they don't always remember what she said. Their minds can't hold all of that information. They . . . They . . ."

"They forget," Fang said.

"Exactly."

"No," Taalik said. "The Queen's voice stays. It sleeps. In here."

He reached out to Wawa and clicked the pincers. "I take. I take the voice. Yes?"

Wawa did not seem to understand, and so the creature repeated the motion of plucking the memory from her mind and placing it into his own.

"There is a place," Taalik said. "The humans dug a cave. There, they move the sun. I make the listener remember."

"What if we don't have any users left?"

"I know he is here," Taalik said. "He speaks. I hear him. I speak. He hears me. All of us, connected." The creature made this point by wrapping his tentacles into a cord.

"I'm not handing anyone over to you. You forfeited that kind of trust. There must be another way."

"No. We take the user to the cave. There, he will remember."

Wawa looked at the ground as she contemplated her next move. Everyone knew who the user would have to be.

"Chief," Falkirk said. "You're not going through with this, are you?"

She ignored him. Her lips parted in a smile that revealed her fangs, stretching the pink scar along her jaw. "What if we brought him there? Would that be acceptable?"

Taalik said yes. Orak clicked twice in what sounded like an agreement.

"So we bring the user to the bunker. And you make him remember so you can use the satellite to free your people. Then what?"

"We make peace. We go away from you."

"And what if we say no?"

"Then we make war. We go where you go."

Falkirk looked ready to interrupt again. But the chief's grin told him to keep quiet.

"After the darkness passes three times, we go to the cave," Taalik said. "Three days. We wait for you there."

"What if we try and it doesn't work?"

"Try so that it does work."

He edged toward the railing. But Orak stayed, her eyes fixed on the hilt of D'Arc's sword. The two Sarcops clicked at each other again.

"She wants to see," Taalik said.

D'Arc unsheathed the sword and held it at arm's length. Orak's three good tentacles closed in on it and hovered. Each took a turn tapping the point. When she finished, Orak returned the weapon and slipped over the railing, her entire body shifting from solid to liquid.

"Three days," Taalik said. Then he was gone.

The officers of Tranquility stood quietly for a while. One at a time, they each turned to D'Arc.

"D'Arc," Wawa said. "I think we have to—"

"I know," D'Arc said. "I know."

They gave her a few seconds to calm down. She picked out a spot in the river, far downstream, and tried to focus on it until her heart stopped pounding.

AT HEADQUARTERS, WAWA assembled what remained of her senior staff. This included Fang as well as Falkirk and Carl Jackson, head of the patrol units. Jackson wore dreadlocks and a graying goatee. He insisted on growing and chewing his own tobacco. During the meeting, he spat brown fluid into a steel cup. When the silent cat Grissom arrived to pour the tea, he took one look at Jackson and moved on to the next person at the table, unfazed.

The officers let D'Arc attend the meeting. She knew why. At some point, the chief would ask her nicely to persuade Mort(e) to get himself killed.

Wawa leaned forward on her elbows. "I know you think this is crazy. Under normal circumstances, I would have consulted all of you. These circumstances were not normal."

"We're making a mistake going along with this," Falkirk said.

"I agree," Jackson said, wiping the spittle from his beard. "They said they needed a translator user. And someone's killing the users. Something's not right here."

"They're negotiating from a position of weakness," Wawa said. "They could have attacked again, but they asked for help instead."

"Okay, maybe. But it's dangerous to give them control of the satellite. We don't even know what that thing can do."

Wawa turned to Fang. "Tell him."

"The Rama project is a failure," Fang said. "It's true that we could not establish contact. But we also found all the old files. And we know this: the device is defective. Maybe at full strength it could crack the ice, but it would probably burn out before it even got to that point."

"The Sarcops don't seem to know that," Wawa said. "Which gives us the advantage."

"You never told anyone about the satellite," Falkirk said.

"Yes, we did. The strators didn't believe us. And besides, it was more convenient for them to blame Tranquility. God forbid the humans ever got something wrong during their golden age."

Jackson stroked his beard. "What happens when the Sarcops figure this out?"

Wawa smiled, pinched the St. Jude medal on her chest. "It'll be too late."

She laid it out for them, speaking in a cold voice, like a human. An elite unit would escort the user to the bunker. They would wear full body armor, with gas masks. And at the right moment—presumably when the fish-heads entered the chamber—the soldiers would fire canisters of nerve gas at the enemy, the same kind used on the ants in the war.

"I couldn't risk trying to kill them on the pier," she said. "I've seen them survive a bullet wound. This way, we can be sure. Take out their leaders, and maybe the rest run away."

"This isn't like you," Jackson said. "It's a huge risk."

"Not really. If it doesn't work, we're back to where we started. Nothing changes."

Jackson and Falkirk did not seem convinced.

"Look," she said, "this is something I learned in the Red Sphinx. It's the art of war. The Sarcops just told us when and where they'll be. When the enemy hands you an opportunity to wipe him out, you take it."

Grissom brought in a map of the area and unrolled it on the chief's desk. As he smoothed it out, Wawa waited for the husky and the human to object. But their silence amounted to consent. And no one was about to suggest that perhaps the Sarcops were telling the truth. A heavy weight sank into the pit of D'Arc's stomach. The chief was a different person now, hardened by this long war, and D'Arc knew then that she would not be able to stop this madness.

"Let's continue," Wawa said. "The bunker that the humans built is . . ." Grissom, standing behind her, pointed to a location on the map. "It's here, right. A little over a hundred miles away."

Fang slumped in her chair. "That's wolf country. The last envoy barely made it out of there alive. And *he* was a wolf."

"I know, I know. But we can take motorboats as far north as Bushkill. It's a short hike from there."

"No, no, no. That's crazy."

"No way," Jackson said.

They talked over one another. Wawa reminded them that Tranquility had infiltrated wolf territory before. Jackson and Fang called it suicide. Even Grissom seemed dubious.

"Why don't we fly in?" Falkirk said.

"We need the *Upheaval* for reconnaissance," Jackson said. "Hell, for all we know, this whole thing could be a ploy to get the warship out of here. So the fish-heads can attack again without warning." Jackson turned to Wawa to plead his case. Taking away the *Upheaval* would leave the city defenseless. The chief agreed.

"I'm talking about *Vesuvius*," Falkirk said.

"The captain and most of his officers are dead," Fang said. "We don't have anyone who's qualified to command an airship."

"Yes we do."

Wawa reminded him that the communications network was still inoperable, ever since the strators disabled the tower. The *Vesuvius* would be out of range as soon as it entered the wilderness. Besides, flying a ship over wolf territory would only cause more problems with the tribes, maybe trigger another attack.

"The wolves already hate us, Chief. Are you sure that's your reason?"

Wawa folded her hands. "You haven't flown in a long time, Lieutenant."

"You just gave us that art of war speech. When the enemy hands you an opportunity to wipe him out, you take it, right?"

Wawa squinted at him.

"I can do it," he said.

D'Arc detected a slight growl in his voice. His lips could barely contain his fangs.

"Inspect the crew," Wawa said. "But if they're not ready, we go with my plan."

Falkirk exhaled. D'Arc could not tell if he was relieved or disappointed.

"But first, we need to get Mort(e) on board," Wawa said. She swiveled her chair toward D'Arc, who squirmed in her seat. The Old Man said that something like this would happen. Hosanna would lure them in only to tear them apart. He never predicted that it might be her fault. But he must have known.

"If you're going to kill the Sarcops, then why bring Mort(e)?" D'Arc said.

"Because they're connected. Psychically. Mort(e) said so himself."

"So you're going to use him as bait."

"That's the plan."

One by one, the other people in the room lowered their heads.

"What if I can't get him to do it?" D'Arc asked.

"You can tell him we'll pardon him if he goes."

Everyone shifted in their seats.

"We'll say the Sons of Adam killed Michael," Wawa added.

"Chief, we cannot do that," Fang said.

"Why not? It's true, isn't it? That boy died ages ago. They just forgot to bury him."

"He might still say no," D'Arc said. "Will you force him to do it?"

"You might be the only one who can convince him."

"That doesn't answer my question."

"Fine. The answer is yes."

D'Arc's throat clutched. A rage at her own weakness boiled in her stomach.

"I'm loyal to Mort(e), same as you," Wawa said. "Despite all the things he's done. But none of that matters. We have to protect this city."

"Even if it means sacrificing someone."

"At this point, yes. Besides, Mort(e) sacrificed the Prophet, didn't he?"

D'Arc bared her teeth at that.

"He's the only user left," Wawa said. "Would you rather he goes with us, or do you want the Sarcops to find him a few months from now?"

D'Arc rose from her seat, scraping the feet of the chair. The sound of it made Grissom cover his ears.

"I'll take care of it," she said.

Before anyone else could speak, D'Arc exited the stuffy office and stepped into the main hall. Falkirk got out of his seat, but a quick glance from D'Arc made him stay.

Even with fewer officers, Tranquility almost seemed normal again. But she noticed a lull in the noise as people stopped their conversations. She marched between the new desks with her sword rattling in its scabbard, daring anyone to whisper a single word about her.

# CHAPTER 21

## SKYDOG

HE ELEVATOR ASCENDED through the innards of the ruined skyscraper. Under a flickering lightbulb, Falkirk buttoned his ill-fitting jacket. Originally designed for a human, the jacket had the sleeves cut off so that Falkirk's arms could breathe. The epaulets on the shoulders and captain's star on the right breast indicated his new rank, gaudy reminders of the promotion that he did not exactly deserve.

The doors opened to reveal the thirty-third floor, where the building had been cut in two by missile strikes. Only part of the ceiling remained. Near the elevator shaft, a booth with a large window housed the control tower. Three humans sat inside, speaking into headsets, their faces illuminated by computer screens. The rest of the floor had been converted into a flight deck, with a new concrete surface. Near the edge, the *Vesuvius* hovered with its port side facing the deck. The reflective surface created a fun-house image of the tower. Mooring lines tethered the ship to the floor, and a portable staircase led to an open door on the gondola. The officers stood in a neat row, all wearing their aquamarine jumpsuits with gold piping on the sleeves and pants. Falkirk counted three humans, a wolflike dog with black and golden fur, and an odd creature with bright reddish hair. As he got closer he recognized the animal as an orangutan, a species he had never encountered before. The primate must have escaped from a zoo. Or a lab.

"Attention on deck," one of the humans shouted. The officers waited for him. While the animals were of indeterminate ages, the humans were astonishingly young. The barrel-chested man who saluted Falkirk must have been in elementary school when the war started.

"Sir, Lieutenant Ryan Ruiz," the man said. "Acting commander of the *Vesuvius* while she is in airdock."

In the name of the Prophet, a *lieutenant* in charge of all this? Then again, Falkirk was merely a lieutenant as well. No one wanted to say out loud that the people most qualified to save Hosanna lay at the bottom of the river.

"I relieve you, sir," Falkirk said.

"I stand relieved." His hand dropped to his side. "Sir, may I introduce the bridge crew?"

"Please."

The officers went through the motions, stating their names, ranks, and responsibilities. Ruiz would serve as Executive Officer for the trip. Falkirk hesitated to ask him how many flight hours he had logged. Lieutenant Charlotte O'Neill served as operations officer, in charge of the navigation and propulsion systems. She had pink skin, with freckles and auburn hair tied in a bun, like some doll for human children. Next to her, the pilot, Ensign Thomas Unoka, towered over all of them, so thin he appeared ready to topple over. While O'Neill and Ruiz wore American flag patches on their sleeves, Unoka wore one that Falkirk did not recognize. Maybe a country in Africa, judging from his name. Considering the bloodbath that had taken place across the sea, Falkirk decided not to ask.

The German shepherd introduced himself as Church, the security officer. When the time came, his team would try to kill Taalik

and his mates. A gun with an enormous barrel hung from his belt,
far too heavy for a typical human to wield. Falkirk detected in his
yellow eyes a hint of the trigger-happy fury that his brother Wendigo possessed. He was surprised this dog hadn't named himself
Stab or Gash or something. The orangutan introduced herself as
Bulan, the communications specialist. Her face sagged, weighing
down the sockets on her enormous brown eyes. She handed him
a palm-sized walkie-talkie, which he clipped to his jacket.

"Let's start the inspection," Falkirk said.

The officers escorted him on board. A crew member greeted
him in the airlock by blowing a whistle. "*Vesuvius* arriving,"
the man said. They entered the enormous oval-shaped promenade, the common area where the floor, walls, and ceiling
gleamed a blinding white. A crescent-shaped amphitheater
stood empty at the far end of the room. One of Falkirk's class-
mates at flight school described the ship as a cheesy version of
the future, like a giant walk-in smart phone. At the center of it
all, a fountain bubbled in a small patch of perfectly manicured
grass.

Ruiz led the tour through engineering, a cramped, noisy room
in the stern. The three crew members stood at attention while
Ruiz rattled off the enhancements made to the monitoring system. To demonstrate his familiarity with this section of the ship,
Falkirk asked when the last time the kill switches for the engines
had been inspected. To his surprise—and relief—Ruiz said that
he changed them himself the week before.

They proceeded to the lower decks. While the chapel
remained unchanged, most of the living quarters for the humans
had been converted into storage areas and science labs. At the
end of the long corridor, near the bow, stood a metal door with
a wheel attached to the front. "The prisoner goes here," Church
said, a growl in his voice. "If anyone tampers with the door, the
computer will seal the entire bulkhead. Only the captain's order

can reopen it." The dog rapped his knuckles on the metal to demonstrate its thickness.

On the bridge, a horseshoe-shaped window provided a 180-degree view of the city and the wilderness beyond. Cold steel railings, molded plastic chairs, and see-through floor grates gave the room a functional yet sterile feel, more like a cellblock than a command center. The bridge had a two-tier design. Ensign Unoka and his copilot sat in the lower level, facing the front window of the gondola. The command crew operated their workstations on the level above and slightly behind them. The stations formed a half-circle—navigation, communication, a direct link to engineering, a tactical display, radar. A captain's chair sat in the middle, with a digital tablet fastened to the armrest and a podium bolted to the floor beside it.

When the security team had removed him from this same bridge—when they pried his fingers from the railing—Falkirk was confused and broken. He returned this time a true follower of Michael, who had pulled him from the abyss. And because of all that, he careened from total astonishment to smug acceptance and back again.

"Captain," Ruiz said. "The change of command protocol mandates that you declare the inspection over. Unless, of course, you had some concerns?"

"Everything is fine," Falkirk said. "The inspection is complete. Good job, everyone." The crew seemed genuinely relieved to hear the news. O'Neill released a long breath that puffed out her cheeks. The orangutan smiled with enormous yellow teeth.

"Look," Falkirk said. "We don't know each other. And I realize you've been given a difficult task here. If anyone feels uncomfortable with me coming aboard, you can leave. No questions asked. I'll list it in my report as a request for transfer to the *Upheaval*, nothing more."

They lowered their heads. And then, one by one, they turned

to Ruiz. "Sir, we've already discussed this," he said. "Two people deserted. But we're staying. No matter what." Beside him, the orangutan nodded and grinned.

"I promise you I'm going to keep us safe," Falkirk said. "We all have people waiting for us. Now, what's the scheduled departure time?"

"0700, sir."

Too little time to prepare, not enough time to kill. Falkirk couldn't resist hoping that Mort(e) would say no, canceling the mission altogether.

"All right," he said. "I need a full report on the efficiency of the solar batteries. My guess is they haven't been checked in a while."

"Aye aye, sir."

"Bulan, we won't be able to communicate with Hosanna once we're out of range. I want you to see if you can detect any signals from the wolf territories. They might have a tower."

"The wolf territories?"

"We're just going to listen. But we might have to call on them for help. Or to warn them."

He gave each of them some mundane report to process, simply to show that he knew his way around the ship. They went off to their workstations.

While the officers and crew prepped for takeoff, Falkirk had little to do beyond strolling through the decks and surprising people. Kitchen workers in the galley, custodians polishing the pews in the chapel, machinists testing the airlocks—all of them stumbled over themselves to salute him. And then there were a few crew members whom he recognized from his last time on board, including a beady-eyed man with a neck tattoo, and another man with thick glasses. They knew who he was. He could tell. Word would spread throughout the entire crew, assuming they didn't know already.

To get his mind off things, Falkirk killed another twenty minutes talking to Unoka about the helm controls, to see if there were any problems with the old equipment. Unoka told him that the replacement parts were working just fine. "Anything else I can do for you, Captain?" the ensign asked, eyebrows raised.

Falkirk's walkie-talkie came to life, startling him. "Captain, this is Church. Come in."

"Go ahead."

"Sir, Tranquility is here to deliver the prisoner. Please meet us on the flight deck."

"On my way."

On deck, Church and four human guards stood in a row, casting long shadows in the late-afternoon sun. Standing apart from their neat little formation, D'Arc waited with her hands folded behind her back. The sight of her almost made Falkirk stop in his tracks, but he pressed on, pretending he expected to see her. At the elevator, another troop of guards formed a wall around Mort(e). Metal cuffs bound the cat's ankles and wrists. Church signaled for the prisoner to come forward. Mort(e) could take only small steps in his chains. The guards matched his pace.

D'Arc stood beside Falkirk. "That didn't take long," he whispered.

"Mort(e) said yes right away."

"He didn't try to haggle?"

"He had one request."

She opened a pouch on her belt, pulled out a folded piece of paper, and handed it to him. Falkirk opened it and read the first line: "Subject: Transfer of Officer." He skipped to the bottom to find the chief's signature and paw print.

"He asked that I come along," D'Arc said. "He wants me to see him do the right thing." There was a bitterness in her voice, something he had never before detected. Mort(e) had outmaneuvered her, to maximize whatever guilt he thought she should feel for leaving him.

"So . . . permission to come aboard?" she said.

"Yes, permission granted. We'll get your quarters ready as soon as possible."

Mort(e) and his jailers arrived at the base of the stairs. D'Arc moved aside to give them room. After the German shepherd searched Mort(e) by hand, his guards surrounded the prisoner, ready to march him to his cell.

"Wait," Falkirk said. He stepped between the guards and stood face-to-face with the monster who killed the Prophet. Mort(e) seemed smaller in his cuffs, but no less dangerous.

"I'm grateful you're doing this," Falkirk began. "We all are."

"Yes." A gust of wind blew Mort(e)'s ears back.

"I need you to know something," Falkirk said. "We're going along with the Sarcops. But we don't trust them. We don't trust you, either. The chief has given me full discretion to fire on your position at the first hint of trouble."

The cat did not respond. He didn't even blink.

"In other words, if you do anything to jeopardize the safety of my crew, I swear I'll kill you."

Mort(e) tilted his head toward Falkirk. "You swear to the Prophet?"

A searing heat exploded in Falkirk's gut. He clamped down on it, controlled it. He would save it for later. "I swear to the pack that raised me. I swear it on the graves of my children and my mate. I swear it on the life of the person you and I both love."

The cat pondered this. He then turned to D'Arc. "I *like* him!" he said, laughing. She would not join in. "Now take me to my cell."

The guards escorted Mort(e) through the corridors and into the promenade, the same compartment where Mort(e) was once greeted as a savior. Falkirk asked D'Arc to wait by the fountain while they brought the prisoner the rest of the way. She did not object. Mort(e) stayed focused on the corridor ahead. At the end of the hall, two sentries guarded at the cell. Mort(e) shuffled inside, and the heavy door locked behind him.

Falkirk returned to the common area. Standing on the grass, D'Arc craned her neck as she examined the architecture of the room—the fountain, the amphitheater, the windows, the track lights on the floor and the curved ceiling. "Are you all right?" he asked.

She shook her head yes. Then no. A painful silence followed. And then, overcome, D'Arc wrapped her arms around Falkirk's neck and buried her face into his chest, right on his captain's star.

"I thought I was strong and I'm not," she said, her voice muffled.

"You're strong."

She pulled away from him and tried to compose herself. "He's not even doing this for me. He doesn't care anymore. He *wants* to get himself killed."

"That's not your fault."

A strong wind shook the airship, causing the floor to tilt before leveling off again.

"Is there anything I can do on this ship?" she asked. "I want to be useful. Even if it's cooking in the galley."

"Well, we don't serve Alpha meat."

As always, she failed to get his joke. Which, strangely, made him feel better.

"Church could use you on the security team," he said.

She nodded.

"Come on," he said. "I'll show you the armory. That ought to cheer you up."

They walked through the promenade, though at a wider distance than Falkirk wanted. Despite that, he imagined that they looked normal together, like longtime friends. To fill the silence, he daydreamed about ordering Unoka to steer the *Vesuvius* east, toward the ocean. They wouldn't need the *al-Rihla*. Let Hosanna sink into the sea behind them. They would keep flying over the blue water and never mention this place again. He let the idea pass through him, like a warm wave. By the time they reached the corridor, he had returned to his senses, determined to die for everyone on this ship if he had to.

FALKIRK ARRIVED AT the bridge the next morning at 0630. The sun hid behind the horizon, and the overhead lights were still in night mode, coloring the room red. Among the frantic crew members, he caught Bulan yawning, her mouth opening so wide that it exposed her pink throat. The moment she saw him, she snapped her jaw shut and fixed her headset.

"Attention on deck," Ruiz said.

"Carry on," Falkirk said. The daytime lights switched on. Falkirk walked past O'Neill as she directed three crew members to their posts. Unoka and his copilot took a break from checking the controls to glance at the new captain.

Falkirk approached Ruiz. "Are we on schedule?"

"Yes, sir. The coordinates are logged into your tablet. Winds out of the southeast, but they won't affect the launch. Should have good visibility through the entire trip."

Falkirk tapped the screen and scrolled through the inventories and the engine reports. With all the commotion on the bridge, he needed to appear busy. So far, the crew seemed up to the task, despite the trauma of the last couple of weeks. The night before, Falkirk attended a dinner with the officers in the wardroom. The meal consisted of bean soup with salted tofu and a spinach salad. The cooks provided bread and cheese, which only the humans ate. Ruiz explained that they might as well eat the food before it spoiled. The lieutenant's awkwardness made Falkirk realize that only humans had served on the senior staff before the flood. It required a catastrophe to get two dogs and an orangutan promoted this high.

Falkirk asked about their backgrounds. O'Neill and Ruiz were civilians before the war, and only in Hosanna did they have a chance to work their way through the ranks. O'Neill had served on the *Upheaval* before getting transferred a few months earlier. Ruiz took part in the failed pacification of the wolf territories. He kept his description of it simple, but everyone knew that he must have seen some terrible things.

Unoka flew planes loaded with relief supplies for the United Nations. When the North African front collapsed, he took a plane full of refugees to Cape Verde, where they hid for most of the war.

As Falkirk expected, Bulan had escaped from a zoo. With a mouth full of the leafy salad, she said that she tried to free the other animals, but only the lions left with her. The rest insisted on waiting for the zookeepers to deliver the next meal.

Church related a more subdued story. His owner was a retired police officer who rescued German shepherds who failed to qualify for the K-9 unit. Had it not been for his master's intervention, Church would have been put to sleep because he wasn't mean enough.

"*You* weren't mean enough?" O'Neill asked.

"Don't tell anyone," Church said. Everyone laughed. The moment of levity drew out more stories, more banter, until finally Bulan addressed Falkirk.

"This is the first time we have done this, sir," she said. "We have not gathered together to talk like this. I see we needed to." Everyone agreed.

The dinner would be the only opportunity to bond before setting out. And with the sun finally cracking open the sky, Falkirk suddenly remembered that he had refrained from sharing his own story. And even if he told them, he would have left out the only parts that mattered. During the war, his commanding officer often said, "You are the master over someone who has told you his story." It was a miserable, cynical proverb that the Colony helped to spread. Nevertheless, it made sense here.

Ruiz gave the signal that the ship was ready. Falkirk nodded. "Com?"

"Liberty One Tower says we are cleared for takeoff," Bulan said.

"Release the mooring cables. Helm, take us to three hundred."

"Aye aye, captain."

The tethers broke free one at a time. The air thundered through the propellers. As the ship lifted, a gust of wind rocked it slightly. Falkirk pretended not to notice his podium wobble. The ship rotated, shifting the rising sun to the starboard window.

"Three hundred feet, sir," Unoka said. "We have cleared the tower."

"Course laid in," O'Neill said, tapping away at a keyboard.

The city dropped out of view, leaving only the purple, cloudless sky like an ocean flipped upside down. Falkirk stared into it and wondered if all he had seen, and what he had become, would be enough to get him through this.

"Take us to wolf country," he said.

The ship accelerated. Falkirk clutched the podium to keep from falling over.

# PART V
# COLLISION

# CHAPTER 22

## TRIANGULATION

HE INTERROGATION ROOM sat at the end of a quiet hallway in Tranquility headquarters, tucked behind a storage closet that no one used. Grissom led the way, carrying manila folders under his arm. Wawa and Daiyu Fang walked behind him. A canine guard waited for them at the door. With a gloved hand, the dog knocked once before opening it.

A musty smell greeted Wawa as she entered, like mildewed wood and cracked leather. The room had no windows, only a checkered linoleum floor with a metal table bolted to it. Carl Jackson leaned against a wall, spit cup in hand. A human soldier stood in the far corner wearing sunglasses and holding a rifle.

At the table, an opossum sat in a wooden chair, dressed in faded blue overalls, his wrists handcuffed. A nasty scar drew a line from his cheekbone to his neck, so thick that the fur would never grow over it again. He watched them file in, almost relieved at the diversion. But the relief drained away once the door slammed shut, and Wawa stood before him with her arms folded.

"You go by the name Teyu?" Wawa asked.

"Yes."

"Do you know who I am?"

"You are the Director of Tranquility."

"That's right. This is my assistant Grissom. And this is Daiyu Fang, head of Special Operations. You've met Major Jackson. So if we're all here, this must be important. Right?"

"Yes."

Wawa motioned for the files. Grissom handed them over. She opened the first folder to find a report on Teyu's arrest earlier that day, at the sanitation truck depot where he worked.

"My understanding is that a few weeks ago, two of our agents paid you a visit," Wawa said. "They were looking for your brother Yatsi. He is now presumed killed in the flood. I'm very sorry."

The opossum rested his chin on his chest.

"Grissom has been going through all the pending cases since the attack," she said. "Most of them can't be salvaged. But on a hunch, he cross-referenced the agents' report with your medical history. You were in the hospital because of an infection in your mouth, correct?"

"Yes."

"And how did your mouth get infected?"

"I do not know."

"We do."

Jackson spit a fragrant rope of tobacco juice into his cup.

"You had a fake tooth put in," Wawa said. She placed both manila folders on the table and opened them. One showed the medical records for Teyu. The other for Yatsi. Each had an illustration of the jaw in the upper right corner, with every tooth numbered.

"Where did you get that scar?" she asked.

"At work."

"And you lost some fingers in the war."

"Yes."

"Yes. But it says here you made it through with all your teeth. Your brother Yatsi is the one who lost that incisor. The very same one you tried to replace. On the cheap, I'm guessing."

The opossum said nothing. Which was perfect.

"Here's what I think," Wawa said. "Yatsi, for some reason, needed to become Teyu. Probably wanted to hide the fact that he used the translator. So he cut his face, and even sliced off a few of his fingers. The last part was fixing the tooth, and he almost got away with it. But Grissom just couldn't help himself. He kept digging. Very stubborn, that one."

Grissom nodded.

The opossum seemed more annoyed than scared. He stretched forward as far as he could and examined the two reports. His nub of a nose sniffed the paper, causing the ugly scar to wrinkle and then stretch taut again. The uneven teeth grinded in his jaw.

"I request a trial," he said. "I can do that. It says so in the Hosanna Charter."

He phrased it almost like a question. Wawa suppressed a laugh. She glanced at the guard standing like a statue in the corner. "You. Get out."

Jackson and Fang moved out of the way as the man exited the room. Wawa could sense the fear building in the prisoner as the door clicked shut.

"The Hosanna Charter," Wawa said. She swore an oath on the original copy, which washed away in the flood.

"Yes. I have rights. They say, 'The Charter gives rights.'"

Wawa rested her palms on the table and leaned in until she could make out the contents of his breath, rancid with partially digested garbage. A yellowish stain tinged the fur around the opossum's obscene mouth.

Her whole life, Wawa tried to do the right thing, which for her meant serving some master in the best way she could. First her human owner, then Culdesac and the Queen, then the Prophet and the city he blessed. All of them had slipped out of this world. She was the only one who remained. There were no masters anymore. Only her and God. And he decided long ago to dump her in this city and leave her to guess at right and wrong.

"Do you know what's going on here?" Wawa asked. "The creatures who attacked us were looking for people who have used the translator. And those same people have been dying. And I'm going to find out why. I'm going to find out if the two are connected. And you're not going to stop me."

Teyu gazed out a window that wasn't there.

"Look around," she said. "No one knows you're here. No one knows I'm here. This is as far as you go. This might be the end of your life. You might die in this little box. And you sit there telling me that you have rights according to the laws of Hosanna?"

Wawa got close enough so that her snout brushed his ear. "I'm Hosanna," she whispered.

It felt good to talk like this. She regretted waiting so long to try it.

"Did the creatures . . . find someone?" he asked.

Wawa walked around the table so the opossum would face her. "What if they did?"

Teyu's eyes widened into large black marbles. "Tell me what happened."

"Tell me what you did first."

The opossum looked at the two humans. Neither of them budged. Frustrated, he slouched in his chair, weighing his options. And then, as if possessed by some spirit, he lifted his head and stared at Wawa. And she knew then that Teyu was gone. Someone else watched her with those shiny obsidian eyes.

"You win, Chief Wawa," he said in a deeper tone. "I congratulate you and your intrepid team. I am in fact Yatsi of the Quiet River Nest."

Jackson halted mid-spit. Fang began to smile, then pursed her lips to hide it. Grissom, as usual, remained expressionless.

"I will confess to everything," Yatsi said. "I will put it all in writing. But you need to tell me right now. Do the Sarcops have a user?"

"Not yet. He's on his way to meet them."

"To do what?"

"To operate the Rama satellite. The user has the knowledge. The Sarcops believe they can extract it from him somehow."

"And you let him go?"

"It's a peace offering. The Sarcops tell us they have people trapped in the ice near the North Pole. They think the satellite can break open a section so they can escape. But they're wrong. The Rama doesn't even work. And we have a little surprise waiting for them."

Yatsi pondered this for a moment. He began to rock nervously in his chair.

"What is it?" Wawa asked.

"I know what those fish-heads are going through. Because I can still hear her. I still hear the Queen, like they can. She speaks to me in my mother's voice, from before the Change. It's not even words. It's all squeaks and whistles, but I under*stand* it."

He kept rambling about how he could smell the Queen, about how he closed his eyes and appeared in the Colony as one of her handmaids, licking debris from her abdomen, speaking in their chemical language. His arms pulled taut against the handcuffs. Wawa could hear the tendons straining, the bolts twisting. Fang and Jackson backed away, unsure if this animal possessed the strength to break the chains and come bounding over the table.

"What are you trying to tell us?" Wawa asked.

"This knowledge that we were given. It's everything. It's all that she ever learned. We're not just talking about how to build a plane or drive a car. We're talking nuclear launch codes. Locations of old weapons depots. Dangerous things."

"That's why you killed them."

"No one can be trusted with that power. Even if they don't know they have it."

"But the satellite isn't a weapon."

"It is if they use it to melt the entire ice cap. That would be a lot worse than the dam breaking, don't you think?"

Wawa pictured it—the glaciers collapsing and crumbling into a black sea. Her throat suddenly went dry.

"Chief," Fang said. "We have been over this. Even if the Rama worked, it cannot generate that kind of power."

"Not by itself," Yatsi said. "But there are other satellites that can reflect the sunlight. Correct?"

Fang swallowed. "The Chinese built two prototypes. But they are inactive. Their orbits have decayed."

Yatsi laughed. "You thought you could outwit an omniscient being. If the Sarcops can triangulate the devices, it would generate enough heat to melt the ice cap and flood the planet."

"The people who designed the Rama would have known that this was a danger," Wawa said. "They would have . . ." She imagined herself in the fighting pit with Cyrus, her master at her side, and hordes of angry human faces, their teeth flashing under the fluorescent lights.

"Oh, they knew exactly what it could do," Yatsi said. "They were humans after all."

*Oh, God*, Wawa thought. *It's my fault.* The air in the room grew thick. When she glanced at Fang, the woman meekly nodded her head.

"Carl, can we reach the *Vesuvius*?" Wawa said.

"No, Chief. She's out of range."

"What about the *Upheaval*? Can she tell Falkirk to abort?"

"*Upheaval* is patrolling the mouth of the river. In the opposite direction. Even if we ordered her to pursue, it might be too late."

The opossum laughed bitterly.

"What's so funny?" Wawa asked.

"I'm watching you try to plot out your next move. Weighing your options. Pros and cons. So inadequate. For the Queen, there is no cause and effect. There is no past and present. Like drops of rain falling into a river—it all flows in one direction."

"You talk about her like she's still alive."

"She is. As a matter of fact, she can never die."

Perhaps later, Wawa would have the time to sit by the window and think about what she did wrong. But that would have to wait. She needed to figure out how to contact the *Vesuvius*. Getting to the bunker by land was out of the question, given the distance. And bird patrols were notoriously unreliable.

"Chief Wawa," Yatsi said. "Promise you'll kill me. After you come to your senses."

Wawa answered by turning away from him and pounding on the door until the guard opened it. Wawa motioned for Grissom, Fang, and Jackson to follow her outside.

"Chief!" Yatsi said. "You have to kill me! You have to kill all the users!"

As he screamed, Wawa hurried down the hallway, with the others trailing behind. "Daiyu, I need someone to do a quick analysis of those satellites. See if he's telling the truth."

"Yes, Chief."

Behind her, the guard told the opossum to keep quiet. It did not work.

"The Queen told me all about you, Chief! I know who you are!"

"Carl, send word to *Upheaval*—"

"You're Jenna the house slave!" Yatsi continued. Hearing her true name from the mouth of this lunatic made Wawa stop. Grissom almost crashed into her.

"You killed for your human master," Yatsi said. "Jenna the house slave! You killed your own people for sport! *You* should be in this cage, not me!"

The guard slammed the metal door and slid the rusty bolt into place. The echo of it brushed past Wawa's ears. For a moment that lasted far too long, Grissom, Jackson, and Fang looked at her, possibly imagining her as some kind of attack animal.

*Let them believe it*, she thought. She continued walking. It took a few seconds for the others to catch up with her.

# CHAPTER 23

## WOLF COUNTRY

Y MIDDAY, THE sky became a polished blue slate in the window of the bridge, with the verdant forest rolling underneath. Falkirk sat in the captain's chair, his hands folded in his lap. Somewhere in the room, a computer made a pinging sound. The gondola shuddered amid some turbulence, producing a noise like an old man clearing his throat. Behind him, O'Neill mumbled something about coordinates, either to herself or to one of the crew members. To appear busy, Falkirk tapped the screen on his tablet for what must have been the tenth time in the past five minutes. The display came alive, showing the time in the lower right corner, 10:53 A.M. Over fifty-six minutes since the *Vesuvius* had left communication range.

Falkirk tapped a dropdown menu and selected "Crew." He cycled through the personnel files until he found Church's security team. At the bottom of the list appeared the name "UNKNOWN" with the species marked as "CANINE." The computer yielded no further information about what D'Arc was doing at that moment. Falkirk tried to think of some reason to bring her to the bridge. Maybe he could request a security detail. There was no guarantee that Church would pick her for the job. Unless Falkirk asked him to.

"Captain," Bulan called out. "We're receiving a signal from the *Upheaval*."

Falkirk swiveled his chair to face her. "*Upheaval*?" That wasn't right. The sister ship should not have been anywhere near the *Vesuvius*. Falkirk went over to Bulan's station. Her monitor displayed a message, repeated over and over in green text: SU 002. "*Upheaval*'s call sign," Bulan said.

Ruiz stood behind Falkirk. "Is that a distress call?"

"Maybe. It's the default signal when regular communications go silent."

"Have they responded to us?" Falkirk said.

"No, sir."

"O'Neill, can you give me their itinerary?"

"Opening it up right now. *Upheaval* was ordered to patrol an area south of Hosanna. She is . . . approximately . . . fifty-three miles off course. And counting."

"Ruiz, is this normal?"

"Orders change. But we can't be sure without an update from Liberty One."

"Right. O'Neill, what's their heading?"

"North, fourteen degrees. They are running almost parallel with us. Not a direct intercept course. But at their current speed, they'll be within visual range about eighteen miles southwest of our destination."

"Is it possible something happened to the crew?" Falkirk asked.

"If their speed and heading doesn't change, maybe it means they're on autopilot."

Falkirk imagined the ship dropping too low, low enough for the fish-heads to leap from the water and grab hold of the gondola. Perhaps the ship would arrive with some creature in the cockpit working the controls with its tentacles.

"We could head back to communication range and ask

Tranquility what's going on," he said. One by one, his officers stopped what they were doing and watched him, waiting to see if he would follow through on this suggestion.

"Under normal circumstances, we would do that," Ruiz said. "But if we go back, we may not complete the mission on time."

Falkirk waited for him to say something else. If only one of them quoted some obscure rule requiring them to return to base, he would have shoved Unoka out of the pilot's chair and steered the ship himself. "Monitor the *Upheaval*'s progress," he said at last. "I want to know the moment anything changes."

"Aye aye, sir," O'Neill said.

"Bulan, keep trying to reach them."

"Yes, sir."

As the crew went about their work, Falkirk pulled Ruiz aside. "I want you to inform Church of the situation. Quietly. Ask him to have a plan ready in case we need his people."

"What are you expecting exactly?"

"I don't know."

The lieutenant gave a nervous laugh before exiting the bridge. Falkirk returned to his chair only to spring from it immediately. He couldn't sit still, and didn't want anyone to see him fidget. He rested one arm on the podium and stared out the window.

IN THE ARMORY, D'Arc shoved bullets into a magazine until her thumb became stiff. When she finished, she placed the magazine on a stack of five, then slid the stack over to the corner of the table. Across from her, a teenage private named Josh Lasky tried to match her pace, but fell far behind. The boy had skin so white it was almost translucent, with blue veins, and his baggy fatigues barely hung onto his thin shoulders. A sad little mole pocked his cheek, while another showed through his freshly buzzed hair.

Lasky insisted on playing his music on a small stereo. It was some heavy metal band, with fast drums and a singer barking like a dog. Despite the racket, the familiar routine of loading the ammunition put D'Arc's mind at ease, as did the oily smell of the guns. When Falkirk assigned her to Church's team, the German shepherd listed a few tasks that needed to get done before the *Vesuvius* reached the bunker. She jumped at the chance to sequester herself here. To hide.

The Old Man had introduced her to all of these weapons as they scavenged them from abandoned houses, police stations, and sporting-goods stores. He showed her the quirks of each one—how they malfunctioned, how to maintain them. This armory offered even more options for dismembering an enemy, including claymores, a flamethrower, and three enormous canisters that reached from floor to ceiling. "Loaded those yesterday," Lasky told her. "Bunker busters. Russian made. Fifteen hundred pounds each. If the fish-heads try any funny business, they'll regret it." Mort(e) often complimented the engineering skill that went into building the tools of war. "What if the humans put that know-how to better use?" he would ask. D'Arc wondered how there could still be so many of these weapons lying around. So many other achievements of the human age had crumbled away in a mere decade, and yet their killing devices lived on.

The song on the stereo ended, followed by another that sounded identical. Lasky bobbed his head while mouthing the lyrics. D'Arc picked out the words "death," "bitch," and "fucker." The human loaded the magazines only one bullet at a time. D'Arc considered showing him a trick for inserting two rounds at once, but decided against it. No point in going faster when she was here to pass the hours.

"Did you see the new captain?" he asked.

She didn't like his tone. "I did."

"There was a dog commander not too long ago. He had a breakdown on the bridge, and they had to shoot him with a tranquilizer dart and carry him off."

D'Arc finished another magazine, slapped it onto the table, and slid it toward the pile. "I've heard that."

"Well, I heard that this is the same dog. And he's the only one qualified to fly Big Vee."

He dropped a few rounds, but scooped them in his palm before they rolled off the edge. D'Arc continued loading without saying a word.

"Nothing against dogs," Lasky added.

"Of course."

"It's just, you know. It makes you wonder."

"Right."

Some turbulence tilted the airship for a moment. D'Arc's sword, resting on a stack of boxes, fell over. It made Lasky nervous. His hands shook as he loaded the bullets. He asked if she had ever seen a wolf. "I've only smelled them," she said. "Out near Lodge City."

"What brings you to Hosanna?"

"The *al-Rihla*."

He stopped loading and stared at her. "You're going on the *al-Rihla*?" Lasky said that he had applied, but they rejected him on account of his age. Hosanna needed young men like him to replenish the human population. "I told them they need to find me a girlfriend first," he said. D'Arc imagined little weak-chinned babies squirming in tiny blankets.

She couldn't say it out loud, but more than ever D'Arc wanted to get on that boat and stare out into the water while the land melted behind her, leaving nothing but blue in every direction. Even now, she dreaded the day—far in the future—when the *al-Rihla* returned to Hosanna. Perhaps, after the exploring was done, the crew would find that the city no longer existed, another settlement that failed on this accursed river. And then they would simply keep going. If she had to, D'Arc would start over again and again and again.

The intercom crackled to life. D'Arc and Lasky stopped what they were doing and waited for the announcement.

"Security personnel to the commons," a woman's voice said. She repeated it several times. Outside the door, footsteps stomped and people shouted. Some human barked, "Move it, move it, move it!" In response, the traffic became more frantic.

"We're not there yet, are we?" she asked.

"No. Must be a drill. Though they said there wouldn't be any drills on this trip."

"Who said that?"

"The people who run the drills."

Lasky would stay at his post. D'Arc jammed the last two bullets into a magazine and left it on the table. As she strapped on her sword, she tried to recall the image of the sea again, but saw only the stagnant water left over from the flood.

RUIZ CLIMBED THE steps to the upper tier of the bridge. He handed a pair of binoculars to Falkirk. "Sir, we have visual contact."

On the port side of the bridge, Falkirk peered through the lenses until he located the *Upheaval*. The ship flickered. He rubbed his eyes and tried again.

"It's not your eyes, sir," Ruiz said. "Their stealth mode is switching on and off."

Falkirk could see it. The hull sparkled like a fuzzy television screen. It blinked out altogether only to reappear seconds later. With the *Upheaval* running silent, he imagined the entire crew lying dead with the autopilot engaged. In theory, the ship could travel indefinitely so long as it stayed above the clouds to collect sunlight. But a storm could knock it off course. Then the ship would begin a steady descent before crashing in some mountain range, or a desert.

"Altitude?" Falkirk asked.

"Cruising altitude of nine thousand. Same as us."

"What's the status of her weapons?"

"Their tactical display appears to be offline," O'Neill said.

Falkirk no longer needed the binoculars. Soon the crew could see the *Upheaval* looming in the window, flickering like some giant broken toy.

"Captain, we have a new message from the *Upheaval*," Bulan said.

"I'll keep an eye on her," Ruiz said.

At Bulan's station, Falkirk scanned the text on the monitor until he came across the words: STAND BY—INCOMING MESSAGE.

Bulan fiddled with her headset. "I'm getting Morse code," she said. She pressed a button on her control panel and the sound crackled through a small speaker. "It's the call sign again." The signal repeated several more times and then stopped. Static fizzed in the speaker. A voice broke through the noise, saying something in gibberish at first, and then coming through clearly.

"*Vesuvius*, this is *Upheaval*, do you read me?" a man said.

"*Upheaval*, we read you," Bulan said. She gestured at Falkirk so that he could respond.

"*Upheaval*, this is Falkirk, acting captain of the *Vesuvius*. To whom am I speaking?"

More static. Falkirk thought he heard two voices arguing. "This is Lieutenant Commander Jeffrey Trestman, first officer."

"Lieutenant, it's good to hear your voice. Where is Captain Demir?"

A pause. "Captain Demir is dead."

The bridge froze as everyone waited for Falkirk to respond. "What is your situation?"

"Sabotage in engineering." A wave of static drowned out his next sentence. Falkirk made out something about a coolant pipe bursting. When the interference cleared, Trestman continued. "Caused a chain reaction that disabled the ship. We have casualties. Heavy damage to the onboard systems."

"We have to help them," O'Neill said.

Falkirk put up his hand for silence. "Who sabotaged you?"

"It was a fish-head. A stowaway. Killed five crew members before it was all over."

"Jesus," Ruiz whispered.

Falkirk remembered the inspection from the day before. He thought of all the hiding spots he may have missed. "Lieutenant, were you able to contact Liberty One?"

"Negative. Out of range. But I can tell you that Tranquility ordered us to follow you right before we were attacked. They want both ships back in Hosanna."

"What about navigation and propulsion?"

"Barely operable. We need to . . . reboot the system. We're down one engine."

Falkirk turned to O'Neill. "How far are they?"

"One mile and closing."

"And how far are we from our destination?"

She read the number, but did not speak.

"How far, O'Neill?"

"Seventeen miles. Captain."

"Sir, they say that Tranquility wants us to go back," Ruiz said.

"I heard what they said. But we can only abort on direct orders from Liberty One."

"But given the circumstances—"

Falkirk ignored him. "Lieutenant Trestman, can you hear me?"

"Yes, Captain. Go ahead."

"We are under strict orders to proceed to our destination. If you have regained control of propulsion, you need to turn around and request help as soon as you can reach Liberty One."

The speaker whistled with feedback. Falkirk covered his ears. "Uh, negative *Vesuvius*," Trestman said. "You've been ordered back. And we require assistance. We have casualties."

Falkirk called Ruiz over. Outside, the *Upheaval* grew larger, its blinking surface casting odd shadows on the bridge.

"Has this crew ever attempted a docking procedure?" Falkirk whispered.

"No, sir. I'm sorry. There was no time—"

Falkirk made a throat-slashing gesture to cut him off. Docking in midair would take too long, even with an experienced crew. Anchoring the ships and transferring the wounded over the ground would take even longer, and would run the risk of provoking the local wolf tribes. The wolves would love to capture the first canine airship commander, put his head on a spike.

"Is there anything we can do for these people?" Falkirk asked. "Anything short of stopping the entire mission?"

Ruiz searched for an answer, but the expression on his face said enough.

"Captain," Bulan said. "*Upheaval* is requesting a flyby so we can examine their hull damage from here."

"Yes, of course. Unoka, slow to one quarter. Let *Upheaval* pass us."

"Aye aye, Captain. One quarter."

*Upheaval* veered to the north, expanding from a perfect circle into a horizontal oval that filled the entire port window.

"Everyone on the bridge," Falkirk said. "If you see anything, call it out."

"We're within fifteen hundred feet, sir," O'Neill said.

"Gondola looks fine," Ruiz said. "They're not venting. Other than the stealth malfunction, I don't see anything wrong with the hull."

Falkirk went to the com station. "Bulan, see if you can get them to transmit a full damage report. Maybe then we can know what to look for."

"Aye, sir. It looks like—"

A Klaxon sounded. A row of red lightbulbs flashed on the ceiling.

"Sir, *Upheaval* is listing toward us," O'Neill said. "Twelve hundred feet."

Voices erupted in shouts and technical babble. Unoka yelled something that Falkirk could not make out. Bulan screamed into her headset. "*Upheaval*, change your course! Change your course, *Upheaval!* Left . . . Thirty degrees!" Trestman shouted something about a malfunction. Outside, a trail of smoke twisted from the ship's starboard engine. It would sideswipe *Vesuvius* in a matter of seconds.

"Nine hundred feet!"

"The wind is pushing them."

". . . *Upheaval*, break left! *Upheaval* . . ."

"Captain, they're right on top of us . . ."

"Seven hundred feet!"

And for a second, the sound drained from the room until Falkirk could hear his lungs expanding and releasing. He felt his legs moving. His feet fell on soft earth. He was running away from his family's house again on the day of the quarantine. The day he lost control of his life and became a stone kicked along a dirt trail. *The white takes you*, his mother's voice said.

"Helm," he shouted, "port engines, full reverse. Starboard engines, full speed."

Unoka and the copilot looked at one another.

"Five hundred feet!" O'Neill said.

Falkirk bolted down the steps and stood behind Unoka. "We can't turn away," he said. "We have to rotate the ship so we miss them completely."

If they could slow the ship enough and angle it, the bow of *Vesuvius* would slide right past *Upheaval*'s starboard side. Unoka spun the wheel hard to the left. Falkirk ordered him to lower the altitude—maybe they could slip under. On the control panel, the dials whirred and the digital readouts flashed.

"It will be close, sir," Unoka said.

"I know."

"Three hundred feet!"

The crew held onto their workstations as the *Vesuvius* pitched hard to port. Falkirk gripped Unoka's chair. The Klaxon sounded at a higher pitch. Bulan kept screaming into her microphone, hearing nothing but static from the other end.

"Captain, they're slowing to match our speed!" O'Neill said.

"What?"

"They're *trying* to hit us!" Ruiz said.

*Upheaval* loomed in the window. Her crew knew exactly the maneuver Falkirk would use in this scenario. There was nothing he could do.

"One hundred feet! Collision is imminent!"

"Everyone hang on to something!"

There was no time to buckle into the captain's seat. Falkirk gripped the top of Unoka's chair. The *Upheaval* blotted out the sky. A shadow crept over the room. No one spoke. Only the Klaxon made a sound that Falkirk could recognize.

The hulls collided. Like two enormous drums. *Bwooom.* Falkirk slammed face-first into a control panel. A body fell on top of him. He smelled blood, then tasted it dripping into his throat. Dazed, Falkirk reached for anything that would help him get to his feet. When his hand found purchase on the edge of the panel, he reminded himself that he was not dead, that he needed to live. *Get up*, he thought. *Get. Up.*

D'ARC LAY FLAT on the white plastic floor of the common area. Her rifle was wedged underneath her, the stock jammed into her ribs. The other members of the security team, who only moments before stood in perfect columns, struggled to their feet beside her. Church was going over their assignments when the force of the collision tossed them all like dolls, leaving the lieutenant curled underneath the window. A grinding sound reverberated through the ship as the two vessels scraped against each other.

Church clutched his elbow and stretched out his arm to make sure it wasn't broken. "Is anyone hurt?" he asked.

Along with the others, D'Arc checked herself for any cuts or bruises. She felt a tenderness in her side where she landed on her rifle, but was otherwise unharmed. The other soldiers gathered at the window, some walking, some crawling. The tail end of the *Upheaval* swung into view. The *Vesuvius* had jackknifed the other ship near the bow. Now the stern came yawing at them.

"They're going to hit us again," Church said. "Grab something."

D'Arc pressed against the wall, with two humans on either side of her. She faced the promenade, where the fountain gurgled in its calm green oasis. After hearing the stories from the Old Man, she spent years imagining this incredible machine. Never once did she picture it crashing. But with the sirens ringing, the guards around her whimpering, and Church's panicked voice, she thought that the *Vesuvius* had begun a nosedive into the mountains, where it would explode in a massive cloud that would vaporize everything.

The *Upheaval*'s stern slammed into *Vesuvius*. D'Arc's intestines went weightless for a moment. Her teeth clacked and her rifle fell to the floor. Then the vibrations faded out. Feeling nauseous, D'Arc rested her head between her knees and took in long, slow breaths.

A new sound cut through the chatter of the guards—a whistling noise repeated three or four times. D'Arc tried to listen. It almost sounded like a whip. *Whoot-tissshh, whoot-tisssh.*

"What is that?" someone said.

Everyone looked to the ceiling. The sound continued.

"Cables," Church muttered. "They're cables. They're trying to board us."

In the window, the *Upheaval*'s gondola was a mere thirty feet away, looking as innocuous as a next-door neighbor's house.

"Look!" Church said. D'Arc was squeezed among several guards, all struggling to see what was going on. On *Upheaval*'s starboard side, a tube extended from the gondola like a retractable telescope. Wide enough to fit a person inside.

Church unhooked the walkie-talkie from his belt. "Bridge, this is Security, come in."

"Security, we read you." Despite the static, D'Arc recognized Falkirk's voice.

"*Upheaval* is attempting to dock with us. Are you seeing this?"

"Affirmative. Get your team to the airlock. There may be Sarcops on board."

"Copy that."

The docking module made contact with the *Vesuvius*. The metal screeched, echoing through the chamber. The *Upheaval* became a giant mosquito piercing the *Vesuvius* with its hypodermic tongue.

"You heard the captain," Church said. "They're trying to pull some *Star Wars* shit on us. I need a team in the airlock, and another in the hall."

"Sir, who's doing this?" someone asked.

"Fish-heads. We're gonna kill 'em."

The soldiers marched two-by-two, with Church in the lead. Their boots created a strange music, a percussion of rubber on metal. The overhead lights passed above like flying saucers. Beside D'Arc, a human's oversized helmet bounced on his skinny head, the visor sometimes falling over his eyes. They reached a metal door with a wheel attached to the front. One of the guards spun the wheel until it clicked and the door hissed open. Fifteen of the soldiers poured into the airlock. Inside was another sealed hatch. On the other side of it, the tube from the *Upheaval* fastened to the hull, making a sound like screws tightening.

*They're here for the Old Man*, D'Arc thought.

The guards stood in a semicircle around the hatch. D'Arc took a position at the entrance, her shoulder pressed to the doorframe as she aimed her rifle. The others formed a gauntlet in the corridor.

Church pulled his pistol from its holster and peered out the window, into the dark mouth of the docking device. He flicked on his walkie-talkie. "Bridge, this is Security. The docking procedure is complete."

"Copy that," Falkirk replied. "What is your status?"

"We're in position. No one's getting through."

"Keep me informed. We're working on a way to get us detached."

Inside the tube, a string of lightbulbs switched on. Church raised his pistol.

"Everybody stay calm."

In front of D'Arc, a woman asked the cat to her right if they could dislodge the docking device. The cat told her that he never knew the ships could dock in the first place.

Somewhere behind them, a light patter of footsteps whispered across the common area. Only the animals heard it. One by one, their heads turned, starting with D'Arc. Church stepped out of the airlock, still holding the walkie-talkie by his ear.

At the end of the corridor, a slender figure appeared. A teenage girl with frizzy hair, no older than fourteen. She walked barefoot, wearing only a tank top and black spandex shorts. Grease and grime covered almost every inch of her skin, making the whites of her eyes stand out like two incandescent rings.

In her taut little arms, she aimed a grenade launcher right at the airlock.

D'Arc shielded her ears as the grenade released with an innocent sounding *plunk*. Barely missing Church, the object struck the wall and exploded before the soldiers in the airlock could even scream. It was just a concussion bomb, but the force of it knocked D'Arc off her feet. The blast whistled in her left ear, so loud she could barely hear the gunfire.

With the spent grenade launcher smoking at her feet, the girl fired a machine gun. It was impossibly loud in this cramped space, like a fist punching D'Arc in the chest. A soldier crawling on the deck crumpled instantly. Another dropped to the floor like a marionette with the strings cut. Sparks burst along the walls and the ceiling, knocking out one of the track lights. Disoriented, D'Arc tried to aim, only to have another man step in front of her. A bullet clipped the side of his head, bursting it apart in a red cloud. To avoid getting trapped, D'Arc moved forward to the next intersection in the hallway, firing as she advanced. Two soldiers frantically brushed past her. The girl hit one of them in the spine, dropping him flat on his nose.

When D'Arc's trigger clicked, she retreated deeper into the corridor. Just then, the little girl ran past the intersection, firing blindly but missing. Behind D'Arc, the remaining soldiers shouted and argued. The gunpowder hung in the air, so thick she wanted to spit it out. In the middle of reloading her weapon, she felt a hand on her arm. It was Lasky.

"Is she in the airlock?" he said.

"Yes."

Out of breath and shaking, the boy gripped a wound on his shoulder. Blood seeped through his knuckles. Lasky opened a pocket on his jacket and pulled out a gauze bandage. The cloth turned red when he pressed it to his arm.

"What happened?" D'Arc said. "Where did that girl come from?"

"The armory. She was hiding inside one of the bunker busters. She popped out of the fuckin' thing and slashed me with a knife."

The other soldiers were gone. D'Arc and Lasky crawled to the intersection. When she poked her head around the corner, she saw the girl swinging open the main door of the airlock. A woman entered from the docking tube, aiming a machine gun as she stepped over the dead bodies. She wore a black T-shirt and khaki cargo pants, with a bandolier slung over the shoulder.

"What do you see?" Lasky whispered. "Is it the fish-heads?"

"Worse. It's Strator Braga. That girl must be her daughter Maddie."

One of the wounded guards moaned near the entrance of the airlock. Through the ringing in her ears, D'Arc could hear a dog whimpering. It had to be Church.

"Do you know how many humans I killed in the war?" he said, letting out a wet cough. "I counted. It was twenty-sev—"

A gunshot silenced him.

More strators entered through the hatch. Duncan Huxley. Harold Pham. A woman with a black baseball cap whom D'Arc did not recognize.

"There's more coming," D'Arc said.

"We need to warn the bridge."

She helped him to stand. His pimpled forehead glistened with sweat, and his entire body shivered when he twisted his shoulder the wrong way.

"First we have to go to the cellblock," she said.

"What for?"

"I think they're here for the prisoner."

Lasky snorted. "They can have him." Gingerly, he lifted the gauze from his wound. Under the torn fabric, a bead of thick blood emerged from the cut. He covered it again.

"Look at me, human," D'Arc said.

He did as he was told.

"That prisoner down there is Sebastian. The Warrior. I am Sheba, the Mother. Foretold in the Book. Do you understand?"

It registered in his blue eyes. His mouth dropped open.

"They're not taking him," she said.

Lasky bit his lip. She could tell that he had many questions. "Lead the way," he said.

ON THE BRIDGE, the Klaxon kept ringing. The noise matched the throbbing in Falkirk's head. He wiped his bloody nose on his arm, leaving a crimson streak in the fur. In the window, the horizon scrolled from right to left as the two conjoined ships spun in a circle.

Transmissions from the *Upheaval* fell silent. Bulan tried to reach Lieutenant Church, but received no response. Ruiz took over one of the consoles and tried to access the security cameras. A wounded crew member sat in the captain's chair while O'Neill reset his broken arm. The injured human handled it well, grunting only slightly. A few others applied bandages to their cuts and gashes. Falkirk thought that they were lucky before correcting himself—true luck would have allowed them to avoid the *Upheaval* altogether.

"Captain," Ruiz said. His computer screen was split into sections, each showing the view from a different camera. The upper left corner displayed the airlock. Falkirk saw a grainy black-and-white image of humans marching over dead bodies. Another camera feed showed two soldiers sprawled out in the hallway. Yet another showed the surviving security guards regrouping in the common area. Two of them appeared to be wounded.

The invaders filed through the airlock, using the standard room-clearing procedures. Like they were running a drill. Suddenly Duncan Huxley's face blocked the view. The man smiled, ran his hand through his Mohawk, and then lifted a can of spray paint. He waved goodbye as he blinded the camera. The last thing Falkirk saw was Huxley's jangling necklace.

"Put everything on lockdown," Falkirk said. "Seal the compartments."

"Aye, sir. Already done." Ruiz opened a window on the screen that displayed a three-dimensional view of the gondola. "Engineering, weapons, infirmary, living quarters. They're all shut down."

Another camera angle showed three humans at the door to engineering. One of the strators tapped the keypad to gain entry, but the door would not open. Another knelt with a laptop computer and connected a wire to the keypad. The calmness with which they operated unnerved Falkirk. They resembled technicians checking the efficiency of a solar panel.

Two women stepped into view. Falkirk recognized Braga right away, along with her daughter. The girl was covered in oil that glistened black onscreen. She confidently stood upright next to her mother, a strator in training. Braga must have spent years preparing the girl for a day like this, when they would finally reclaim what the animals had taken.

"What are our options if they take engineering?" Falkirk asked.

"We won't have many. They could control all the power from there. Unlock most of the doors. But they still have to get to the bridge to navigate."

"So, they can shut off power to the bridge, and then force their way in."

"Exactly."

Falkirk pictured it—the Sons of Adam controlling both airships, ruling the skies over the city that God promised them. At that very moment, the strators in Hosanna may have been storming Tranquility with their loyal pilgrims cheering them on.

"What if we tried to break free of the docking device?" Falkirk asked.

"I wouldn't recommend it. Even if we released the cables, we'd risk tearing the gondola apart. Probably lose an engine. Or breach the balloon."

The Klaxon stopped, leaving the room chillingly quiet.

"What if we—" Falkirk leaned in and lowered his voice. "What if we opened fire?"

"We're too close. An explosion at this range would destroy both ships."

Falkirk knew that. But at this point, scuttling the ships might be the best option.

"Get a message to engineering. Let them know we're sending help."

The speaker on Bulan's desk let out a muffled sound. Someone on the other end was fiddling with the buttons. "Bridge," a voice said. "Bridge, come in."

Bulan pointed at Falkirk to let him know he could speak. "This is the bridge. Go ahead."

"This is Sergeant Vance. We need assistance."

"I know. We're sending it. What is the situation?"

"A stowaway took us by surprise. Church is dead. The rest of us got split up."

"It's the Sons of Adam. Some of them are headed your way. I want you to send as many people as you can spare to engineering. Use the staircase near the bow side. Do you understand?"

"Yes, sir."

"Captain, they're inside," Ruiz said. On his monitor, the humans streamed into the hatch leading to the engine room. Another camera showed the crew members kneeling on the deck with their hands behind their heads. Though the image provided no sound, Falkirk could hear the shouting in his mind—the gentle human voices that could bark like dogs when they needed to.

Falkirk turned to Ruiz. "Pick four people from the bridge. People with combat experience. Gather the rest of the guards and get to engineering."

"Yes, sir."

*I just ordered a man to his death*, Falkirk thought. *I asked him to choose his pallbearers.*

The Klaxon sounded again, like a child demanding a toy.

"Turn that off!" Falkirk said. "We can see the *Upheaval* is right there!"

"It's not the *Upheaval*, sir," O'Neill said. "There's another aircraft coming in."

"What?"

O'Neill's monitor displayed a map of the area, with a line rotating from the center. With each revolution, the line blinked on a small dot, closing in from the south.

"Is it a bird?" Falkirk asked.

"Too big."

The line continued to spin, and yet the dot made virtually no progress.

"Too slow to be a plane," Falkirk said.

"It's coming in at three o'clock. We should be able to get a visual."

Ruiz was already at the window with his binoculars.

"Well?" Falkirk said. "What do you see?"

Ruiz lowered his binoculars. "I think it's one of ours."

"One of our *what*?" Falkirk hurried to the window. Before Ruiz could offer him the binoculars, Falkirk spotted the vessel bouncing along the horizon, black as pitch, wings flapping madly. "There's an escape hatch," Falkirk said. "Under the stairs. Open it."

He pointed to the first two crew members he saw. They jumped up from their consoles and hurried to a red hatch beneath the steps. This exit led to the tiny airlock from which the crew could escape by parachute if necessary. The men flipped the latches that released the outer door, letting the air rush out. The mechanism lowered a set of metal stairs from the bottom of the ship. Falkirk felt the machinery rumble through the deck plates.

At the window, Ruiz waved at the incoming flyer. "He sees us!"

One of the crew members pressed his face against the glass portal on the hatch. Falkirk heard a thud on the gondola, followed by a scraping sound.

"Contact," the man said. "Closing the outer seal."

The two men pulled the latches into place. The mechanism retracted the staircase and sealed the outer door.

"Open it," Falkirk said.

As soon as the hatch lifted, a leathery claw reached from the tunnel and gripped the floor. Then a furry head emerged, with goggles covering most of the face. A few people rose from their consoles to see this creature, a great mass of skin and hair. Despite the goggles and an oxygen mask, there was no mistaking Gaunt of Thicktree, the proudest family of the Great Cloud and Protectors of the Sacred Forest. Exhausted, the bat flopped onto the floor, spreading out like a rug, his hairy back rising and falling like a bellows.

Gaunt's passenger emerged from the airlock, a brown pit bull wearing wraparound sunglasses and an oxygen mask. The tank of compressed air clanged on the deck. Tearing the mask away to reveal her scarred face, the dog looked around the room until she found Falkirk.

"Captain," she said.

"Chief."

Wawa took a moment to look around. "Yes, I'm here," she said. "You can close your mouths now." There was a smattering of nervous laughter at this. Wawa's stubbornness was legendary, but she topped herself with this one.

"Your mission is aborted," she said. "The Sarcops have no intention of honoring their peace agreement. But I see we have other problems at the moment."

"Sons of Adam," Falkirk said. "They've got the engine room. Ruiz is taking a team to stop them right now."

"Good. I'll go with them."

"Chief, you're the ranking officer here. If you want, I'll go with Ruiz."

"No. You know how to fly the ship. I just kill things."

He watched her for some sign of a guilt trip, or some hidden plea to have sympathy for her. But her eyes betrayed nothing. She merely stated a fact, with no remorse.

"Chief?" Ruiz said.

"What is it?"

The human seemed embarrassed to ask. "Should I save Braga for you?"

Wawa eyed him, noting the rank on his epaulet. Then she smiled. "Thank you, Lieutenant. But if you have the chance to kill her, who am I to object?"

As Wawa left with Ruiz and the others, Falkirk knew that this would be their last conversation. One or both of them would be dead. Only now, with the choices so clear, he no longer felt like a feather tossed around in the wind. He would choose how to die, after all these years of failing to live.

# CHAPTER 24

## GLADIATORS

'ARC MADE IT to the cellblock first. Lasky limped behind her with one hand gripping the wound on his shoulder. At the end of the corridor, a steel door sealed the Old Man inside. D'Arc tried to spin the wheel mounted on the front, but it wouldn't move.

"Let me try," Lasky said. He took a swipe card from his front pocket and inserted it into the slot beside the door. Nothing happened. He tapped a code into the keypad. Still nothing.

Lasky shook his head. "It's the security protocol. Everything's locked."

D'Arc rapped on the door with her knuckles. "Mort(e)! Can you hear me?"

She heard footsteps approaching. "D'Arc?" Through the door, Mort(e)'s voice sounded like a salvaged radio.

"It's me, Old Man."

"Old Man?" Lasky said.

"Mort(e), where are the guards?"

"They left. What's happening?"

"We've been boarded. It's the strators. They—"

Somewhere in the distance, humans were closing in on their

position. Their boots slammed on the deck plates. She counted three runners.

"Someone's coming," Lasky said.

"Mort(e), stay where you are," D'Arc said.

"Sure. I'll try."

D'Arc and Lasky took cover on opposite ends of an intersection. She took the left, he the right. The corridor curved up ahead, with another intersection about thirty feet away. The footsteps closed in. Three people emerged—a tall man, followed by Duncan Huxley and the girl Maddie. The man in front wore yellow goggles, and sported a thin goatee that appeared drawn onto his chin with a fine pencil. A perfect target. D'Arc pulled the trigger. A hole ruptured on the man's neck, spraying blood onto the wall. Lasky hit the man in the chest, while another bullet went over his head and blew out one of the lights on the ceiling. D'Arc kept firing as the other humans retreated to the next intersection. Maddie fired from the left side of the corridor. She hung her machine gun around the corner and sprayed the room. Bullets whined and ricocheted from the metal surface, imprinting tiny craters on the door to Mort(e)'s cell.

Through the noise, D'Arc made out Grace Braga's voice buzzing in Maddie's walkie-talkie. "Fall back! Wait for us! Fall back, Maddie!"

D'Arc emptied her rifle and dropped it on the deck. She pulled out her sidearm and squeezed off a few shots. Maddie responded with another wild barrage. D'Arc listened for the sound of someone reloading. She placed her hand on the hilt of her sword and glanced at Lasky. He shook his head no. She nodded yes.

Then she heard it, the hollow sound of an empty magazine. It was Maddie.

D'Arc sprang to her feet and charged at Huxley, the pistol blazing in her left hand. She jumped over the dead man. Lasky fired, drowning out D'Arc's howling. While Maddie reloaded,

Huxley ducked behind the corner. Her pistol emptied, D'Arc tossed it into the air. It threw off Huxley's aim. He lifted his rifle as he pulled the trigger. A bullet whizzed by D'Arc's cheek. In one clean movement, she unsheathed the sword and slashed him. The blade entered at the man's collarbone and carved a red line across his ribs. His necklace dropped, the trophy bones spilling on the floor. A bullet from Lasky exploded in Huxley's chest. D'Arc spun around to find Maddie aiming, her gun now loaded. With the tip of the sword, D'Arc knocked the weapon from the child's hands, then smashed Maddie in the face with the pommel. Another swing grazed the child's arm. Maddie yelped, but she wasn't finished. She reached for the pistol on her belt.

D'Arc raised her sword. "Don't," she said.

D'Arc saw no fear, only disgust, a raw anger corked in the body of this skinny child, ready to burst. The cut on Maddie's arm dripped blood onto her shoes.

More footsteps approached. Lasky shouted D'Arc's name. Sensing an opportunity, Maddie yanked the gun from its holster. The blade swung in a flash. D'Arc didn't even feel herself do it. The gun clunked to the ground. Maddie clutched her neck. Two jets of blood burst from between her fingers. Her eyes blinking, the girl fell to one knee, then flopped onto the deck.

D'Arc felt the silence closing in around her. She waited for her victims to move, to stand up and put themselves together again. But they lay stiffly in place. The girl's hair covered her face as the blood pumped out. Underneath her, the walkie-talkie continued to speak. Grace's voice told Maddie to stay where she was until help arrived. Nearby, Huxley clenched his teeth, the muscles unable to relax in death. D'Arc spent years imagining her pups in the moments before their murderer tossed their bodies away, still warm to the touch. She pictured them in grotesque poses, their tails stiff beside them. They appeared to be asleep until she noticed their faces stiff with fear.

Lasky stood behind her. "I didn't know the Mother could do all that."

A single drop of blood fell from D'Arc's sword and splattered on the deck.

"We need to go," he said.

"No. We need to get the Old Man."

"There's no time. They're coming."

Once more, the sword moved on its own. D'Arc brought the blade to her shoulder, ready to strike. She could kill again. It didn't matter anymore—one person, two, a hundred. She needed Mort(e) to see what she had done. What she had become. What he had made her.

"We need to get to the bridge," Lasky said. "We can open the cell from there."

His words cut through the haze. "Yes," she said. She repeated it a few more times until it stuck.

While Lasky gathered the weapons from the dead, D'Arc sheathed her sword and returned to the Old Man's cell. She called his name.

"Still here," he said.

"We'll come back for you. We have to go to the bridge to let you out."

If the strators took him, this would be their last conversation, delivered through a steel barrier. "Then what are you waiting for?" the Old Man said.

D'Arc followed Lasky around the corner, toward the bow of the ship. They made it fifty paces before she heard a piercing scream, the sound of Grace Braga discovering the body of her daughter, the child promised to her, the one she had spent the entire war protecting. The screeching seemed to grow louder even as it got farther away, pursuing D'Arc like a ghost.

• • •

FALKIRK WATCHED ON the monitor as Ruiz, Wawa, and the other guards tried to breach the strators' defenses at the engine room. Three times, the soldiers made it as far as the nearest compartment, where they took shelter while trying to return fire. After each failed attempt, they dragged one of their wounded comrades to safety, leaving a shiny streak of blood on the deck. Smoke glazed the camera lenses. Shell casings littered the floor. Three dead bodies lay in twisted positions, with a single bloody footprint on the deck nearby. The strators advanced to the nearest intersection in the hallway, from which they could target intruders approaching from any direction. Wawa and Ruiz retreated to the common area.

On another screen, in the top right corner, two strators tried to break into Mort(e)'s cell, using a laptop connected to the keypad. Falkirk could not find D'Arc on any of the security cameras. It was better than finding her lying on the ground.

Falkirk clicked on his walkie-talkie. "Ruiz, come in."

"Yes, Captain?" Ruiz twirled around until he faced the nearest security camera. In the stark black-and-white image, the young lieutenant aged suddenly, with harsh lines on his forehead and around his mouth.

"You have to abort," Falkirk said. "This is going nowhere."

"Sir, if they take the engine room—"

"They've *taken* the engine room. We have to find another way."

Onscreen, Wawa placed her hand on the human's arm. Ruiz switched off the walkie-talkie as she spoke. He reluctantly nodded. On another screen, the strators spray-painted the lens of the camera near the engine room.

"What are your orders?" Ruiz said.

"Fall back to the bridge. If you can slow them down, you might buy us enough time."

"Time to do what?"

Falkirk was glad that Ruiz could not see him at that moment. "We're working on it."

He walked away from the console. The bridge got quiet. Everyone knew what was happening. Everyone knew that Falkirk was helpless, issuing orders that no one could execute. In the captain's chair, Gaunt sat slumped over, chugging water from a canteen, his goggles covering most of his face. He emitted an odor, like ripe fruit and guano. Falkirk could not blame Gaunt if he jumped out of the escape hatch and flew to safety, away from these troublesome land animals and their flying machines.

Bulan frantically tapped away on her keyboard, trying to access the *Upheaval*'s mainframe. Falkirk hovered over her shoulder. "Any progress?" he asked.

"They knew we would try to get into *Upheaval*'s system. It's locked."

"What about triggering a drill, a malfunction, something like that?"

"I tried all of that. Nothing works."

The lights went dark. Then the images on the monitors collapsed into microscopic dots before fading out. The emergency lights flicked on, bathing everything in a red haze. When the screens switched on again, they showed an ominous white field. The crew members tried tapping the keys, hitting ESCAPE. Nothing happened.

"Sir," O'Neill said. "This is bad."

"What's going on?"

"They're trying to reboot the system."

"Can they control the ship from the engine room?"

"Not yet."

"The bridge has a manual switch. We can restart the computer and add a new password."

"We can do that, but it'll take at least ten minutes to get everything back online."

Falkirk tried to think. Maybe the strators wanted them to switch off the computers. It could allow them easier access to the bridge. He tried to remember the countless manuals detailing each of the ship's functions. He had scored the highest on the schematic tests, and now all of the diagrams were like bowls of spaghetti to him, twisting about with no design or purpose. It was all slipping away. Soon the strators would be the ones dragging him from the bridge. They might even make a joke or two about his nickname before they shot him.

Falkirk would crash the ship. It was the only way. They could take out the Sons of Adam, along with these war machines that hovered over the city. What more could he have expected from this life but a noble death? It was more than most people got.

He called over Lieutenant Unoka. The pilot hopped up from his chair.

"Remind me what you can control from the cockpit," Falkirk said.

"We can steer. But steering is useless without the engines."

"Can you control the air pressure in the balloons?"

Unoka glanced at Bulan and O'Neill before answering. "We can. Why?"

"I need you to do some math in your head. Now, we're at nine thousand feet. Let's say we . . . vented the gas in the balloon."

"We need the computers to do that."

"Not if we trip the fire alarm. Both balloons will evacuate if a fire is detected inside."

Unoka thought about this. "Yes, that is true."

"Right. So we vent the balloons. And we start to descend." Falkirk demonstrated by holding out his hand and letting it sink to his waist. "If the crew of the *Upheaval* is smart, they'll cut us loose. So let's say we drag them about fifteen hundred feet before they disengage. That gives you over seven thousand feet to activate the emergency tanks and re-pressurize the balloons. Can you do that?"

"The emergency tanks are meant to keep the ship afloat if something punctures the hull. They were not meant to be used in free fall."

"I know."

Unoka did not want to answer. "I . . . we would still need the computers."

Falkirk turned to O'Neill. "You said ten minutes."

"Yes," she said, almost like a question.

"I can do it," Unoka said. "I think I can do it."

Falkirk told them to get started. Throughout the bridge, his orders spread to the crew in desperate whispers and sudden movements. With nothing to do but wait, he returned to the captain's chair to find the bat still sitting in it. Gaunt did not seem interested in the controlled panic settling in all around him.

"Do you think we can do it?" Falkirk asked.

The bat let out a single chirp that could have meant yes or no.

WAWA TOOK THE legs of the wounded man, while Ruiz carried him under his armpits. A raspy moan gurgled in the man's throat. Blood pooled in the two bullet holes in his jacket. Three soldiers led the way, while two others guarded the rear, keeping an eye out for any strators that may have followed them. They were all humans—all children, more or less, with freckles and peach fuzz. And they were all that remained of the security force on board the *Vesuvius*. Despite the failed raid on the engine room, Wawa wanted to believe that they had slowed the strators down. Then the lights went out, and the generator kicked in. The red bulbs cast an eerie glow with no shadows, turning the blood on the dying man's chest into black syrup.

"Stop," Ruiz said. "Just stop."

They eased the man onto the deck. His head rolled onto his

collar. A final breath exited through his nose. Wawa did not know this man, though she likely shook his hand at an initiation ceremony for new recruits. He probably told himself he would give his life for Hosanna without having the slightest idea of what that meant, and how dying was never noble nor dignified. A wet stain glistened on the front of his pants. His lips curled into a grin. In a matter of minutes, Wawa would be able to smell the rot from the shell of a body he left behind. A total waste.

"Someone's coming," one of the soldiers said.

A young man emerged from around the bend, holding his rifle in both hands over his head. A dog followed close behind, the one the humans called D'Arc.

"Lasky," Ruiz said. "Where were you?"

"The cellblock. The strators have it."

The boy spotted Wawa. His head tilted as he wondered how in the world the Chief of Tranquility stood in front of him.

"We're falling back to the bridge," Ruiz said. They would form a perimeter outside the door. If the strators wanted to take control of the ship, they would have to walk single file through a hail of gunfire.

As they began to move, Wawa waited for D'Arc. The dog was in some kind of shock. A sticky red handprint wrapped around the hilt of her sword, while droplets of blood dotted her fur from her chest to her ears. Someone had expired in gruesome fashion right in front of her, and D'Arc did not even bother to wipe off the remains.

"How did you get here?" D'Arc asked.

"The bat flew me in. And now Hosanna owes the Great Cloud a new nature preserve."

D'Arc shook her head. The bats' penchant for haggling was legendary. "What else?"

"The reservoir. And a mine shaft near Lancaster."

D'Arc seemed grateful for the small talk, even if she couldn't laugh or smile. Despite everything she had been through, Wawa wanted to tell this dog that the strators would never get their hands on her friend. She wanted to shield D'Arc somehow, because there was no telling what would happen to a person when the world collapsed on top of her. Wawa's life as a fighter wore her down until she was like a smooth stone on a beach. But so many people cracked after that first wave, leaving them bristling with sharp edges. D'Arc could go either way.

The common area was empty. *Upheaval* still blocked out the sky on the portside window. Ruiz led the team at a full sprint up the seats of the amphitheater, to the corridor that led to the bridge. As they passed through, Wawa realized that the amphitheater would serve as the perfect cover. The strators would be able to hide behind the steps as if peering over the top of a trench. Still, the corridor—a metal tube about twelve feet wide—acted as a bottleneck, giving the defenders a slight advantage.

Ruiz and the other humans unscrewed the steel panels from the walls and used them to create a barricade. Within minutes, four metal plates sealed off the corridor from the common area. The soldiers aimed their rifles over the top. Ruiz asked for an ammo count. Wawa had only one magazine left before she would have to use her sidearm. The humans admitted to having only a few shots as well. D'Arc was down to her pistol. "And this," she said, tapping her sword.

While Ruiz hailed the bridge, Wawa thought about how she would die. She was not afraid. It felt like contemplating what to eat or what clothes to wear. When the lethal wound struck her down, would she lie there and go to sleep, or would she flail her claws at the strators until she collapsed? Would she think of Cyrus in those last moments? Or Culdesac? She had nothing left to say to God. They would have plenty of time to talk later. How she chose to die would be her final prayer, maybe the only one that ever mattered.

"Here they come," one of the humans said. On the other side of the room, the strators forced the door open and scrambled in, little insects blotting out the pristine white surface. Wawa stopped counting at ten. They were too far away to waste ammunition. Instead of speaking, the invaders communicated with hand signals, operating like a team of Alphas scouting new territory. Pham took the lead, his squat little body pressing against the walls. Two dark stains shaded the pits of his olive-colored T-shirt. The humans gathered in the slight depression of the amphitheater, out of sight. Then, the first head popped over the top step, about forty feet away. Then another.

"Ruiz, come in," Falkirk said over the walkie-talkie.

"Stand by, bridge. They're here. They're right in front of us."

In the amphitheater, the humans whispered to each other about what to do next. Wawa figured that they were mere seconds away from rising over the top and rushing this pathetic little machine-gun nest.

"Ruiz," Falkirk said. "Even if you can't answer, just listen. We need you to buy us some time. Ten minutes. We're going to vent the balloons, force the *Upheaval* to break off."

"Copy," Ruiz whispered.

"Ten minutes. Sing them a song if you have to."

The strators lifted their rifles over their trench. Pham's fat bald head made him resemble a toad. Wawa aimed at the silver earpiece he wore.

"Chief Wawa, is that you?" Pham said.

"Happy to see me?"

"Of course. I was hoping you could talk some sense into your friends and get them to surrender. No one has to die here. We just want the ship. And the prisoner."

Wawa heard a hitch in his voice, perhaps a clue that he was bluffing. Humans spent so much time talking that they forgot how much they gave away.

"We have the advantage," Wawa said. "Win or lose, a lot of your people get killed."

"We'll win. And we're ready to die. You know that."

"You want to risk puncturing the balloon? This isn't the airlock. A firefight in here might get us all killed."

"Don't worry about that, Chief. We have very good aim."

She was running out of ways to keep him talking.

Grace Braga entered the room, not even bothering to take cover. A patch of blood stained her shirt. She wore a dead look on her face that dared Wawa to try to shoot her.

"Why aren't we attacking?" Grace said. Pham left his spot at the front of the trench.

Wawa listened as the man whispered. "We need to find another way into the bridge," Pham said.

"No! We attack now. I'm gonna cut those dogs open myself." Grace began to laugh, a gasping sound that quickly devolved into an uncontrolled cackling. With Ruiz's walkie-talkie switched on, the bridge crew could hear it, like some witch from the dark ages of humanity, channeling demons and speaking in tongues.

"Sheba!" Grace howled. "Sheba the Mother! You'll tell me what my daughter said to you. I will take it back. I'll cut it from your throat!"

Wawa turned to D'Arc and mouthed the words, *what did you do?*

"I killed Maddie."

Grace yelled more threats. "Did she die like your children did? Or did she die like a human?"

Wawa put a hand on D'Arc's shoulder. There would be no negotiation, no more stalling.

"Strators," Wawa said. "Did Grace tell you about the time she killed a dog with her bare hands?"

A murmur rippled through the room.

"She loves to tell that story," Wawa said. "But I don't buy it."

"You will, Chief."

"In that case, I have a proposal for you. You and I settle our differences. No weapons, just claws and teeth. If I win, your people return to your ship. If you win, we surrender."

More mumbling and whispering followed. The humans liked this idea.

"You can't get through us without sustaining heavy casualties," Wawa said. "This is the best option you have."

When Grace failed to answer, Wawa slid a knife from her belt and tossed it over the barrier. It clinked against the deck. "If you're afraid, I'll let you fight me with a knife."

The strators egged Grace on. Someone shouted, "Kill her!"

"Do it, Strator!"

"Cut her open!"

They weren't challenging Grace to fight simply to save their own skins. They truly wanted her to carve up one of these animals and walk away with the pelt.

"God favors one of us, Grace. Don't you want to find out who it is?"

Grace lifted her hand. The shouting ceased. A satisfying silence followed as the invaders waited for their leader to decide. "We're lowering our weapons. You lower yours."

The strators shouted and stomped their feet and bashed their rifle butts on the deck.

"Are you going through with this?" Ruiz asked.

"I'm not trying to win, Lieutenant. I'm buying us some time."

It was a lie. She wanted to twist Grace's head off and toss it into the crowd.

Her opponent climbed the last few steps of the amphitheater, like a demon rising from hell, while the other devils cheered her on. A single strand of hair hung loose over her face. Her eyes drained of tears, Grace retrieved the knife, spun it in her palm, and held it blade down.

"Chief," D'Arc said. "Please don't do this."

"It's okay. If something happens to me, you and Falkirk can watch over the pack."

Wawa hopped over the barricade to deafening shouts.

Staring at Braga, Wawa lifted the St. Jude medal from her chest and kissed it. It felt cold on her lips, as if the magic had run out. By entering the arena, Wawa ventured into the unknown, where not even the Patron Saint of Lost Causes could protect her.

The voices lifted, the way human voices tended to do in the midst of combat. Wawa recognized it from the fighting pits, a primal chant full of rage. The humans evolved this way. They embraced the hunt and the blood that came with it because it kept them alive. But long after they stopped needing it, they still loved it, even the most peaceful among them.

The two fighters circled one another, closing the space between them. Wawa smelled sweat on Grace, along with Maddie's blood. While the strators whooped and hollered for their warrior, Wawa's companions waited behind the barricade, aghast at what unfolded before them.

"Did I ever tell you what I did before the war?" Wawa asked Grace.

"You were probably someone's pet."

Wawa grinned. "That's right. Just a pet. A house slave."

Grace lunged at her, slashing the blade from above. Wawa blocked her with her forearm, but the metal made contact. She retreated. A hot ribbon formed on her arm, oozing blood. Grace attacked again, this time thrusting the knife, barely missing her. Wawa grabbed Grace's other arm. The human gave her a vicious head-butt to the snout. Wawa slashed blindly, her nails catching Grace in the chest. Three red cuts dripped from the bottom of the human's neck. Fluid filled Wawa's left nostril, a viscous combination of blood and snot. She licked at it as it leaked from her nose. Grace flashed the blade again. Wawa spun away.

"Put her in a body bag!" someone shouted, followed by roaring laughter.

Like a pit bull, Grace moved in a jerky, unpredictable fashion. Her shoulders rose and fell. Sour sweat popped from her forehead and neck. Grace faked with the knife one way to make Wawa flinch. Then she thrusted, nicking Wawa across the ribs. Wawa batted her arm away, leaving claw marks on the woman's wrists. The spectators cheered again.

A siren rang out. Above, the balloons hissed as the gas evacuated. The *Vesuvius* lurched and tilted toward the starboard side. The tethering cables shuddered.

Still in a fighting stance, Grace tried to process what was happening. Her black irises rolled upward. Her knife lowered, but only a little.

"Listen to me, Grace," Wawa said. "That sound you hear is the balloon deflating. We're going down, and we're dragging *Upheaval* with us. We'll crash both ships if we have to."

The deck tilted again as the *Vesuvius* sank. The metal from the docking clamp moaned under the strain, like a whale with a harpoon in its side.

"Strator!" Pham shouted. He pressed his index finger to his earpiece. "We're getting called back to the ship. They're going to release the docking device."

"No! We're taking the bridge!"

Ruiz, D'Arc, and the other guards propped their rifles on the barricade.

Pham tried to make out the orders coming through his earpiece. "We have to get back to *Upheaval*. They're cutting us loose."

"No one leaves!"

The ship lurched again, tilted at an even steeper angle. A weightless sensation swelled in Wawa's gut as the *Vesuvius* descended.

"Don't follow this woman to your death," Wawa said. "Go back to your ship and live."

"Maddie's dead," Grace said.

"A lot of people are dead."

"Grace, please!" Pham said. "We have to go."

Grace ignored him. One by one—and then in small groups—the humans retreated to the airlock. Soon, only six or seven remained. Grace refused to watch, even when Pham ran away. The wager still stood.

Suddenly, the *Upheaval* accelerated. The motion jerked the ships forward, knocking the humans over. Wawa and Grace tumbled onto the stairs of the amphitheater. Each step dug into a different part of Wawa's body—her spine, her ribs, her hip. She landed on her tail and felt the cartilage crunch under her weight.

Grace got to her feet before anyone else. Wawa rolled onto her stomach to see the human bounding up the stairs. She was rushing the bridge while she still had the chance.

Wawa got up and chased after her. She jumped over Lasky, who came to rest on the second level of the amphitheater. Ruiz, D'Arc, and the other guards were spilled about, still dazed. Grace charged into the corridor. If she burst through the door with her sidearm, she could take out most of the bridge crew before anyone could even draw a weapon.

Sprinting at full speed, Wawa turned the corner to find Grace standing there, waiting for her, her black eyes filled with hate. Something slipped into Wawa's gut, ice cold at first, then eerily warm. It didn't hurt until the human slid the blade toward Wawa's heart. Wawa grabbed Grace's sticky hands and halted the knife's progress through her torso. The blood that flowed was so dark it was almost black.

As the ship tilted once again, Grace pressed Wawa to the wall, using her weight to plunge the knife deeper. Wawa blinked and felt herself fading. In the common area, people shouted. Boots stomped on the deck. Perhaps her friends had arrived to help her, but she could no longer tell. She was standing in the fighting pit again, rising on her hind legs for the first time and facing her master while the ugly human spectators gazed in horror.

Wawa let her tongue flop out of her mouth. It went dry instantly. Only a few inches from the human's face, she leaned forward and licked Grace on her brow, the way she used to whenever her master gave her a treat. With clenched teeth, Grace smiled.

As the smile faded, Wawa used her last ounce of strength to open her jaws and snap them around Grace's head. The human grunted in surprise. Wawa dug her fangs into Grace's temple, her cheekbone, her eye socket. Grace tried to wriggle free, only to have the teeth sink deeper into the flesh. Her grip on the knife loosened. Wawa worked the blade out of her stomach. The pain burned all the way to her ears, and she fought through it by biting harder until she felt the human's skull crack. When the knife came loose, Wawa twisted it, breaking Grace's wrist and then ramming the blade into her neck. A warm fountain blossomed there, dribbling over them and pooling at their feet. The two warriors toppled over.

The world grew dim. Footsteps stamped the floor around her. Voices shouted her name, the name she chose for herself, but she was already so far away. Wawa was standing in the arena again. Only this time, Cyrus stood beside her. They did not speak. They ran into the forest, free from the chains and the cages. They followed the trail under the stars. They were a pack.

ON THE BRIDGE, the green horizon sliced through the front window at a forty-five-degree angle. Loose objects rolled to the starboard side of the room—documents, pens, a pair of glasses, a plastic Jesus statue, a fire extinguisher. Unoka and the copilot tilted in their seats to stay level. Falkirk held onto the railing while Gaunt clung to the deck like it was the ceiling of his cave.

"Computers are back online," Bulan said.

The monitors kicked on, all with blue screens that flicked over to black and white.

"We're at seventy-eight hundred feet," O'Neill said.

"I have control again," Unoka said. "Balloons are at thirty percent capacity. Ready to inflate the tanks."

"Not yet," Falkirk said. "We have to wait for them to let go of us first."

"Seventy-two hundred, sir."

The ship tilted further. More objects dropped from desktops, rolling and tumbling into the growing pile. Falkirk watched the *Upheaval* through the port window. On the other ship's bridge, the humans pressed against the glass and watched him. Falkirk stood taller. He wanted them to see the first dog captain, calm and collected on his bridge.

"Sixty-five hundred," O'Neill called out.

Unoka swung around in his seat, desperate for Falkirk to give the order.

*Come on*, Falkirk thought. *Let us go.*

"Six thousand," O'Neill said, more anxious this time.

Finally, the deck shuddered.

"*Upheaval* is disengaging," O'Neill said.

The docking device released with a hollow *ker-chunk*. Falkirk felt weightless for a moment. Through the window, he watched as the retractable clamp snapped backward like a rubber band pulled too far. The tube corkscrewed into the engines of the *Upheaval*, colliding with one of the propellers.

"Unoka, fire up those tanks!"

"Aye, sir!"

Outside, the deflated balloons rippled in the wind like tarps in a windstorm. The resulting turbulence shook the bridge violently. The *Vesuvius* pitched forward. The forest below lifted into view.

"Five thousand! Picking up speed."

"Captain, *Upheaval* is out of control," Bulan said. "She's dropping right on top of us."

The port tank ejected its gas first, followed by the starboard. Falkirk hoped that the tanks would inflate the canvas in a great burst, but the material continued to flap helplessly.

"Unoka, can you steer us away from *Upheaval*?"

"We need to level off first. We're at . . . Thirty degrees. Balloons are at fifty percent."

"Put it in reverse until we straighten out."

"Four thousand feet!"

A sparkling creek flowed between the trees. The shadow of *Vesuvius* expanded into a black hole that engulfed the forest. Beside it, *Upheaval*'s oblong shadow spun clockwise.

"Balloons are at sixty percent," Unoka said. "Engines are topped out at full reverse."

"Thirty-five hundred!"

The nose of the Vesuvius began to tilt upward. If they crashed, they might at least land on the belly of the ship, rather than striking the earth like a missile. The descent slowed as the balloons inflated. Gravity sealed Falkirk's feet to the floor.

"Three thousand!" O'Neill made it sound like they'd won a prize.

A new Klaxon switched on, this one signaling the approaching ground with an obnoxious coughing sound. *Err-err-err-err-err.*

"Twenty-five hundred!"

At this altitude, the forest had texture, with the pine trees resembling the fur of some unkempt animal. The hills dipped like a funnel into the stream, which emptied into a river.

Gaunt rose to his hind legs. With his spindly finger, he pointed at the river and screeched. When Falkirk failed to respond right away, the bat flapped his wings frantically.

Falkirk understood. "Unoka, take us into the valley."

"Way ahead of you, sir."

"Fifteen hundred!"

"Take us out of reverse," Falkirk said. "We'll fly through the valley."

"Aye, sir."

The engines recalibrated, whistling and wheezing before shoving the ship forward. The *Vesuvius* leveled off, but the forest continued to rise, the tops of the evergreens reaching for the hull.

"Balloons are at seventy percent," Unoka said.

"One thousand feet!"

"Helm, can you pull us up in time?" Falkirk asked.

"Nine hundred!"

"Helm!"

Unoka glanced at the copilot. "No, sir."

"Eight hundred!"

In the window, the river widened, unaware of the behemoth bearing down on it. Falkirk wished that D'Arc were there, if she still lived. And his mother. And Wendigo. He wanted to tell them that it almost worked.

"Five hundred feet!"

"Aim for the water," Falkirk said. He sat in the captain's chair. Gaunt took Ruiz's seat beside him and strapped in.

The treetops brushed against the hull, gently at first. Then the limbs and trunks groaned and cracked. The ship, still dropping but moving forward, pitched over the last row of trees and into the valley. The earth opened, like a great set of jaws ready to slam shut. The gondola skimmed along the river, rocking the bridge so hard that Falkirk's head bounced forward. Skipping like a stone, the ship made contact again, this time sending a great wave against the front window. Two of the engines cut out. The *Vesuvius* listed to starboard and spun toward the muddy shoreline. A wall of trees waited to break the ship's momentum. With water streaming from the windows, the trees collided against the ship with loud thunks until one of them shattered the glass. Unoka maintained the controls even as pine needles and shards rained on him. The trees snapped at their base, dozens at once, then slowing to a few at a time until *Vesuvius* at last skidded to a halt. The ship rested on the canopy, teetering, the treetops blocking the windows on all sides.

The altitude Klaxon continued to cough. *Err-err-err-err.* Falkirk could not accept that he was alive until O'Neill blurted out, "Fourteen feet." A few people laughed. Beside him, Gaunt unbuckled his belt, seemingly ashamed to have worn it in the first place. Unoka brushed off the debris from his jacket.

Falkirk stood and walked to his podium. In a few more seconds, he would have to issue new orders, demand a damage report, check on the wounded. Until then, he could stand amid the wreckage and whisper. "The white. The white takes you." The bat heard him, and squeaked something in response. He may have been asking if Falkirk was going crazy.

Falkirk didn't care. *You can punish me all you want*, he thought. *You can keep cursing me, keep taking people away. I'm still here.*

That was all it took. The weight of it slid off of him, an unburdening so abrupt he expected to hear a steel anvil hit the floor.

He had to find D'Arc.

# CHAPTER 25

## THE LAST PRAYER TO ST. JUDE

'ARC KNELT OVER Wawa, pressing both hands into the shredded wound in the pit bull's stomach. All around her, the soldiers shouted orders. Lasky demanded that they get the adrenalin and bandages from the infirmary. Ruiz and his comrades pointed guns at the remaining strators, who lay on the deck, hands clasped behind their necks. The prisoners whimpered prayers, begging for mercy. A soldier stepped over Braga's corpse and pounded on the door to the bridge. With the ship tilted, the chamber became a bizarre alternate universe, a reflection in a broken mirror. Wawa lifted her hands away from the wound, letting the blood go where it may. The scent of it left the taste of iron in D'Arc's throat. Wawa pawed at her chest until she grabbed hold of the medallion. Her tongue rolled out of the side of her jaw, almost touching the floor.

D'Arc could do nothing but kneel in the sticky pool of blood and watch the chief die.

Wawa lifted the necklace from her chest until the chain pulled tight. She offered it to D'Arc.

"No," D'Arc said.

The pit bull coughed. A drop of blood rolled along her chin.

D'Arc caught herself wheezing, the same noise she made the

first time one of the Alphas died. All those years ago, she thought she knew death well enough to stare it in the face. The chief needed her to be strong in these last moments, and D'Arc was failing her.

"The pack," Wawa sputtered. "The pack. The pack." She convulsed in a fit of coughing. Then her muscles softened. The eyelids drooped. A gust of air escaped the mouth and nose. Life slipped away from the tired body.

D'Arc rolled on top of Wawa and wrapped her arms around her neck, like cradling one of her Alpha sisters in their final moments. Like two dogs spooning in a forest, their bodies gave off a low heat that was already beginning to fade.

D'Arc let go and sat on her heels for a while. Then she unclasped the necklace and slipped the chain off. Grasping the medal between her thumb and index finger, she rubbed away the red dot covering St. Jude's face. Lasky asked if she was all right. She said yes.

She took a few steps away from the body, the heap of mangled flesh that used to be a person. The smell of gunpowder wafted in from the corridors. She sensed the people in the room trembling. They needed time to accept that they survived all of this while others had not, and there was no sense to any of it. Mort(e) spent years trying to teach her this. Going out into the world meant witnessing terrible things and shoving them deep into your gut and fooling yourself into thinking that everything was okay, the good outweighed the bad. Somehow that would keep you moving forward, because moving forward was the only thing that really mattered.

D'Arc took a moment to inspect herself. She didn't recognize what she saw. Blood from Wawa, Grace, and Maddie mingled in her fur, drying out and becoming brittle. A red patch covered the handle of her sword. She patted her limbs, ribs, and hips, searching for injuries she could no longer feel. Satisfied, she wiped her hands on her sides, leaving sticky imprints. She would have to soak in a long bath to get it out, and the water would be pink when she finished.

Something slammed into the gondola from the outside, rocking the entire ship like an earthquake. D'Arc thought that the *Vesuvius* had begun to slip from its perch. But then she heard the sound of metal squealing as some ungodly force twisted it out of shape.

It came from the lower decks. From the detention area.

D'Arc raced through the winding corridor, passing flickering lights, hurdling dead bodies. At the cellblock, the bodies of Huxley and Maddie lay twisted in their permanent sleep. Near the door to the Old Man's cell, someone had left a laptop crumpled in a pile, its screen broken off at the hinge. A set of wires extended from a jack in the computer to the keypad. D'Arc tried the door, but could not get it open. She called Mort(e)'s name. The Old Man would not answer.

Lasky arrived, out of breath, stinking of sweat. "Tell them to open it!" she said. He returned the way he came, heading for the bridge. D'Arc sat by the door and waited, with the three people she murdered on the ground nearby, and the person she left behind trapped in a cage.

"Can you hear me, Old Man?" D'Arc said. No response. "I'm sorry." She was not sure what to be sorry about. She was sorry they had met, sorry she took the pill, sorry she became the person she was and not someone else. It didn't matter. The words left her mouth and disappeared, so meaningless.

After a while, a green light on the keypad switched on. A latch clicked. D'Arc opened the door. At the far end of the cell, a massive hole pierced the wall, framing an image of the forest floor below. The wind howled through the opening.

She heard Lasky again. "Oh, good, you got it open," he said. "We had to—"

He stopped at the threshold. The jagged edges of the hole

resembled metal teeth, bent inward. Something had punched the hull from the outside, a giant hand that snatched the Old Man away. D'Arc approached the hole cautiously. She placed her paw on the frayed metal, sniffing at it until she caught the scent she expected—ammonia. She peeked through the opening and saw a tree trunk nearby.

"Wait, you're not gonna—"

She jumped from the gondola before Lasky could finish. Her claws latched on to the bark, allowing her to slide a few feet before jumping again. The *Vesuvius* blotted out the sky. The flexible surface of the balloons dimpled and curved to accommodate the shape of the treetops. Everything reflected off of the silvery hull, flipping the entire forest so that it stacked on top of itself.

Above, Lasky stuck his head out of the opening. "Get back here! This is wolf country!"

D'Arc followed the scent, dropping to her knees and rubbing her nose into the dirt. She drew her sword and broke into a run until she felt the ammonia all around her, making her eyes wet. She passed underneath the engines of the ship, tangled with branches from the pine trees. Beyond the *Vesuvius*, the sun reflected on the surface of the river. The current carried the scent away, mocking her. In only a few minutes, the ammonia dispersed. D'Arc bent her knee, planted the sword in the dirt, and rested her head on the hilt. When the roar of the water became unbearable, she sheathed the blade and hurried back to the *Vesuvius*.

IN THE ARMORY, D'Arc exchanged her machine gun for a Barrett M99, the strongest sniper rifle on board. She palmed a nerve gas canister and hooked it to her belt. In the hallway, the guards marched the prisoners to the cellblock. Someone from the bridge spoke over the PA system, though the voice was garbled. "We are still under attack. Be on alert, we are still under attack. There may be intruders on the ship."

Lasky appeared in the doorway, nervously checking to make sure no one saw him. He handed her a small electronic device that would allow the *Vesuvius* to locate her. About the size of a cell phone, the device clipped right next to the canister. "I got the map, too," Lasky said. He unrolled it for her and pointed at the hastily drawn red X that indicated the bunker.

D'Arc tucked it into her vest pocket. "What's the word on the ship?"

"Engines are out. Balloons need to be repaired and fully inflated. And we have to untangle ourselves from the trees. We're stuck here until at least tomorrow."

She continued chambering rounds into the rifle. Lasky hovered nearby, watching her.

"What is it?" she asked.

"I still can't believe it," he said. "You really are her."

"Yes." The boy may have been in shock. D'Arc could not help him. They were alive—that would have to suffice.

"I didn't think you were real," he said. "Some people said you were a myth."

D'Arc holstered her handgun. "They were right."

She checked the rations and water bottles that she took from the galley. On foot, she could make it to the bunker by morning, assuming she did not run into any locals.

"Those things that attacked the ship," he said. "Why do they want the Warrior?"

"Same reason you did, I suppose."

"Well, I heard—" Lasky spotted someone approaching. He hopped into the corridor, squared his feet, and stood at attention. "Sir!"

Falkirk brushed the boy aside and stepped into the compartment. His sleeveless jacket was torn from the lapel to the breast. When he saw what she was doing, his pointy ears dropped. But with Lasky nearby, he could not let his guard down, even with

D'Arc standing before him spattered with blood, wearing the chief's sacred medallion.

"Did you see them?" he said.

"No. I could only smell them. They headed for the river."

She mounted the rifle onto her back, pretending that it wasn't too heavy. She hung the sword over it while Falkirk watched her, waiting for his chance to suggest that he tag along. Maybe he thought he could order her to stay, as if the captain of a downed airship at the end of the world could control anything.

"We could send someone with you," he said.

"Can the bat fly me there?"

"He's too exhausted. I wouldn't risk it."

"I could go, sir," Lasky said.

"That would slow me down," D'Arc said. "I've tracked Alphas before. Remember? I can hunt these things. They smell even worse."

Falkirk reached out and tapped the nerve gas canister with his fingernail. "Where's your gas mask?"

"Too heavy. I already have enough equipment."

"This stuff is dangerous—"

"I know that. But if things go bad, it won't matter, will it?"

Falkirk followed her to the cellblock. Lasky wished her good luck, a strange thing to say in this mess. On the way, Falkirk reminded her to stay on high ground as much as she could. If she needed sleep, she should find a tree and rest there for the night. The wolves would be less likely to catch her scent, and they were afraid to climb trees anyway—so the story went. The *Upheaval* crashed north of their position, and she would need to maneuver around it. With the smoke trail giving away the location, any wolf pack entering the area would start there. Falkirk did not mention the rumors about how the wolves dealt with "traitors"—the canines who worked with the humans. He probably didn't want to hear the words coming out of his mouth.

Amid the steady stream of instructions—the most she had heard him speak in days—she heard Falkirk's voice cracking and straining as he realized that this might be goodbye. She couldn't feel anything yet, so soon after the crash, the battle, the blood. Some primitive defense mechanism kept her focused on survival. Later—perhaps in the terrifying seconds before her own death—she would remember this and wonder what could have been with this husky. All that would have to wait for her to return. She would let him hold her then. They would weep together. But for now, she needed to find the Old Man. It would pay him back for all he had done. And it would set her free.

When they arrived at Mort(e)'s cell, Falkirk told her to wait, and to listen. "The ship should be operational in another twenty-four hours, maybe sooner."

"I heard."

"Once we can get airborne, I won't be able to keep us here."

"I'm not asking you to."

"And we'll have to destroy the bunker. No matter who's inside. Those were the orders."

"I know."

Defeated, Falkirk looked at the floor. D'Arc put her hand on his shoulder.

"You have a crew to protect," she said. "The chief trusted you."

"Yeah. It's just that . . . I never got the chance to say I'm sorry. For what happened."

"Nothing to be sorry about. We took care of each other. Dogs do that."

He did not seem convinced.

"Hey, look at me," she said, jostling him. "You did good, Falkirk. We're still alive. And I'm coming back."

A few dead leaves blew into the hole and landed at their feet.

"Now I know how Mort(e) felt," Falkirk said. "When you set out on your own. He couldn't stop you."

D'Arc hugged him quickly, so that he would not have time to return it. She then stepped her foot through the hole, resting it on a bent tree trunk. With her claws digging into the bark, she inched her way to the forest floor. Above her, Falkirk stood stoically, with the hull expanding all around him. As D'Arc moved away from the gondola, she saw her reflection, a mere dot rolling along the surface.

"Wait," Falkirk said. "They say that the fish-heads can get inside people's minds. Like the Queen. What if they trick Mort(e) into helping them?"

"Then I'll kill him." She wasn't sure if she meant it. And yet the words escaped her lips so easily.

"Good luck, Captain," she said. "Tell them to hold the *al-Rihla* for me."

Falkirk gazed at the forest. "You need to find that panda who speaks Mandarin," he said.

"Or a Canada goose. That speaks Canadian."

"Canadian's not a language."

At the exact moment he smiled, she ran away. That was how she wanted to remember him.

# CHAPTER 26

## THE LABYRINTH

AALIK CARRIED THE demon on his shell as he swam upriver. With two tentacles, he fastened the prisoner to his body, while his other limbs propelled him against the current. More than once, the monster struggled and squirmed, forcing Taalik to constrict him until he became still again. About a mile from the wrecked air vessel, the cat slipped his arm free and slammed his knuckles into Taalik's bony skull. Taalik dove, submerging them both. He waited for air bubbles to escape from the prisoner's mouth before rising to the surface. The cat sputtered and gasped, coughing water from his lungs. He behaved himself after that.

Taalik did not hate the cat. They were brothers in a way—children of the Queen. Earlier that day, Taalik could sense the cat's presence as the ship lifted away from the human city. He tracked the aircraft from the river until it sailed so far away that it became a silvery dot in the sky. Then the Queen gave him a sign, a vision of two great ships colliding, descending to the ground, bloated angels burning and smoking. When he approached the wreckage, the sound of the cat's thoughts penetrated the hull of the ship, a steady thumping. With his claws, Taalik tore open the wall to find the prisoner cowering inside. Ignoring the noise coming from the cat's mind, Taalik plucked him from the cell and dragged him to the water. This animal had served the Colony once by destroying the Queen's body, freeing her from the confines of space and time. In a few hours, he would fulfill her plan for this world. The oceans would rise and the planet would become a perfectly blue sphere, marbled with white clouds. The humans who declared him to be a messiah would wonder, in their final moments, how they had gotten it all so wrong.

The mountains cast long shadows across the river. Every few miles, campfire smoke trailed into the darkening sky, lit by the mammals who controlled this territory. Though sworn enemies of the humans, these wolves would have to die as well. They indulged in their baser instincts, and showed nothing but ingratitude for their uplifted status. Many wished to return to their prewar state, living in squalor and dying of starvation or war. They knew nothing but conflict and suffering, and rebelled when the Queen offered them a new path.

It was well past dark when Taalik picked up the scent of his people. He dipped his head under the waves to see if he could spot any of them waiting on the riverbed. Nothing moved, save for some billowing weeds and a fish fleeing in terror.

He saw an egg lying by itself. Then another, this one ripped open. When he left this place a day earlier, stacks of eggs formed rows along the floor of the river. On this night, the pods were scattered and smashed, oozing their thick yolk downstream.

Taalik heard three quick chirps. It was Orak, summoning the Juggernauts to battle. She hovered above the wrecked nursery, holding her wounded tentacle close to her body. Taalik saw new injuries on her body. A cut on her mouth. A bite mark on her torso. A broken pincer from someone's claw was lodged in her bony chest plate, with ligaments trailing from it.

It had finally happened, he realized. Something the Queen could not show him. The harem had turned against his Prime. They turned against *him*.

Taalik dragged the cat to the shoreline. The prisoner shook off the excess water, shivering. Orak emerged from the waves, bloodied and limping. Taalik wrapped a tentacle around the cat's ankle to keep him from bolting into the woods. Above, the stars twinkled in the blackness, and a sliver of moon hooked around a mountaintop to the west.

*It was Asha*, Orak said. *She told everyone that the Queen gave her a vision. She saw the Sarcops following the river into the sea.*

*What about our people in the north?*

*Asha said she saw them as well. They were all dead. Their blood filled the shallows. The sharks left nothing.*

*A dream*, Taalik said.

*Yes. But Asha said that your visions might also be dreams. How can we be sure?*

Taalik imagined how he would have reacted if challenged in this way. He would have killed Asha in front of everyone. And what would that accomplish? Another false prophet would rise, leading another rebellious faction. It would never end.

*They cut open the eggs*, Orak said. *They let the strong hatchlings join them. Ate the rest. I tried to stop them.*

He coiled his tentacle around hers. *When we finish this, they will understand.*

*What if Asha was telling the truth about our people?*

*It cannot be true. The Queen did not lead us this far to abandon us.*

He did not have the energy to discuss it further. They were so close now. Despite all that had come before, everything pointed in one direction. He would follow the current to his destiny.

THEY LEFT THE riverside and hacked their way into the forest. Orak took the lead, swinging her claws to knock down branches. Taalik trailed behind in the path she created. He kept one tentacle fastened around the cat's neck. To give the prisoner some strength for the journey, Taalik fed him a raw fish. The cat lifted the food to his mouth and tore it apart until only the spine and the rear fin remained. When he finished, he licked his paws and rubbed them on his face, the way he must have done before the Queen liberated him.

"Can you understand me?" the cat asked. "Can you speak my language?"

Taalik responded by tightening his grip until the cat stopped talking.

The trail connected to a highway, colored blue-gray under the moon and stars. Thick cracks split the street open, allowing the grass to sprout forth. Farther down the road, the highway split off, curving into an abandoned town. Wooden poles strung together by cables rested on their sides, split at the base. Taalik recognized some of the buildings, including a row of stores facing a large patch of asphalt. A gas station stood on the other side of the street, with one of the pumps connected to a military vehicle, its door hanging open. Beyond that, a sign directed traffic into a sprawling office complex, protected by an iron gate. Orak turned to Taalik so he could translate.

*Rama Corporation*, he said.

They passed through the empty security checkpoint. The building was shaped like a bent arm, made almost entirely of glass and steel beams. In Taalik's dreams, humans moved about inside, like blood cells pumping through an artery. A dormant fountain sat in the courtyard. On the other side of the building, a wooded area occupied the rest of the property, a poor attempt to mask the doomsday experiments that took place there.

Taalik dragged the cat to a concrete walkway, which terminated at a domelike bunker made of concrete. A sliding metal door sealed the building shut. Next to it, the humans had installed a smooth, flat surface. A touchscreen. Taalik tapped it with his claw, and the screen came alive. The surprising brightness forced him to squint. The screen displayed the ten digits of the human numerical system. Taalik needed to tap the numbers in sequence for the door to open. With Orak's help, perhaps he could over-power the door, tear it from its hinges. But this would surely trip the humans' defense mechanisms, assuming they still worked. Breaching the wall could disable the entire bunker. He needed to probe this cat's mind for the access code. He would go step by step, no matter how painful it became, no matter how long it took.

Taalik released his grip on the demon's neck. The prisoner massaged the fur, his face lit by the screen. Then Taalik lifted his claws to the sides of the cat's head.

"I'll fight you," the demon said.

"Yes," Taalik replied.

He pressed his claws to the cat's temples. Above them, the stars twinkled, then glowed like thousands of suns until the entire landscape was ablaze. The ground dropped away, and the light engulfed everything in a white flash.

TAALIK COULD NOT see, even when he opened his eyes. He stood in some darkened room, inside a human dwelling. His blindness made the noises louder. Rain pounded the walls, collecting in puddles outside. A flicker of lightning flashed through a window, imprinting a white square on the floor. A moment passed, and then the thunder rolled in, sounding like a glacier crumbling.

A human entered—a man holding a candle with a tiny flame dancing on top, bright enough to throw eerie shadows on the wall. A terrified boy clutched the man's pant leg. The man said soothing things, but the child would not stop crying.

A woman arrived, holding a sleeping infant. Another bolt of lightning painted everything white for an instant. The thunder woke the baby, who squirmed and whimpered. The woman tried to rock her to sleep again. To show he was not afraid, the man walked over to the window and beckoned the boy to come to him. The child shook his head, his face wet with tears.

Taalik could not decipher the words exchanged. From what he gathered, this was a family—they all shared the same stink—and the house was in some kind of danger. Darkness descended, while a storm shook the home. The man seemed disappointed in his son for being afraid. When the woman told him to stop, the man giggled at her and kept at it. Another explosion outside made the entire family jump.

Standing in the doorway, a cat with orange fur and a white belly inched its way into the room. Taalik understood now. He was trapped in the cat's memories. The little demon must have retreated to this place. If he wanted to retrieve the information he needed, Taalik would have to become a part of this broken world, locked inside a feeble mind.

Taalik realized that he was not simply a pair of eyes floating about, like in so many of his visions. He was here, standing among these humans. And yet they could not see him. The couple argued, making the children cry louder. Taalik walked between them. They kept shouting, oblivious to this creature passing by.

The cat hissed as Taalik approached, a warning to his human masters. The little creature wished to protect them, and actually believed that he could. Taalik could feel it—anger boiling inside the cat's guts, fear tickling his spine. When Taalik got closer, the cat fled, like a fish knifing through the water. Taalik chased him to a staircase leading to the lower level of the house. In the blackness, the cat's pupils reflected the scant light, and his fear became like a chilly current.

Taalik focused on the two glowing orbs until they were all he could see, until they were the only source of light in the entire universe. The rain and the voices faded. Taalik knew then why the cat sought refuge here. This place was the cat's Cold Trench.

He met his companion here—the dog, the one who cut Orak with her blade. But the memories of her were all jumbled, out of order. Taalik saw all of it at once—their first meeting, their time spent hiding in this basement, their life on the farm. The cat's unbound emotions surged through Taalik, a mixture of warm joy and sharp rage, like a claw sinking into his flesh forever, the wound never healing—but never killing him, either.

The walls blacked out, leaving Taalik floating in a soundless void. The eyes pulled him along as if he were some celestial body caught in their orbit. They flew into space to join with the stars, forming a galaxy so thick it resembled a cloud. All around him the universe spun, with his body as its axis. The stars zipped past, each constellation representing a person who joined with the Queen. They became gods like her. And here, they obeyed her only true successor.

He needed to find the right star, the one that would allow him to operate the human device—the weapon that masqueraded as an instrument of peace, as they all did.

The galaxy came to a halt. One star stood out from the rest, pulsing, humming, growing brighter. Taalik lifted his claws. For a moment, he held the star aloft. The warmth traveled through his limbs into his gut, along his spine. He was not afraid. He controlled this place. The barriers in this maze could not hold him off forever. Taalik would endure. He would survive.

MY EGG, A voice said. *First of Us.*

Taalik lay on his side, his mouth hanging open with a trickle of water leaking from it. All the euphoria from the dream world melted away. His gills fanned out to collect more air, but it was not enough to stave off the disorientation. The earth swayed like the floating island. He looked to the stars for some relief. Here, the points of light stayed fixed in place, as they were supposed to.

Orak knelt beside him. *What did you see?*

*The link. I saw the link between all the Queen's children. I could touch it. I was there.*

Nearby, the cat convulsed and vomited, choking for air.

*Their minds can hold many things, many worlds*, Taalik said. *But they cannot control it.*

Orak lifted him to his hind legs. Holding onto her for support, he shambled over to the keypad. He did not know exactly what to do next. He could only replay the memory of the star approaching from the constellation. Then blinding whiteness. Then he saw a human hand, with hairy knuckles and a white sleeve at the wrist. The index finger typed a sequence of numbers on the keypad.

Taalik closed his eyes and mimicked the movement. The numbers disappeared from the screen, replaced by a simple phrase: "Welcome, Dr. Mehta." Two logos appeared underneath, one for the Rama Corporation, the other for the United States Air Force.

The doors grinded open. Bits of rust fell away from the threshold. A string of overhead lights switched on, extending all the way into a long tunnel that sloped deeper underground.

*You know how it works*, Orak said.

*No. Not yet. I have to go back.*

Taalik told her to bring the cat to him. Sensing her approaching, the prisoner growled. Orak lifted him by the scruff of the neck and dropped him at Taalik's feet.

*Wait here*, he said. *His companions are on their way. Do not let them in.*

*You must rest.*

*No. We keep going.*

She lifted a claw to touch him, then hesitated. *If you die, I die*, she said.

*I do not die.*

He steadied himself. The ground stayed still this time. He

grabbed the cat's arm and pulled him to his feet. "You will fight me," Taalik said in English.

The cat spit out the last of his bile. "Yes."

With his claw on the cat's neck, Taalik marched the prisoner into the tunnel. Halfway in, he glanced at the entrance, where Orak stood watching him. After all this time, he would finally show her that this had been worth it. She suffered for a greater good. When the water swept over this place, drowning the wicked and shielding the righteous—perhaps then, at last, she would hear the Queen's song.

"Afraid she won't be there when you come out?" the cat asked.

Taalik squeezed his claw.

"I know what you're thinking," the cat gasped. "You saw my thoughts. I saw yours."

The tunnel ended at another set of doors, halfway open. Inside, three long tables stood in horizontal rows. Each had five computers, connected to headsets and telephones. The screens switched on, displaying the Rama logo. Behind the tables stood a command station—a terminal with a computer, a micro-phone, and a stack of manuals. At the front of the room, a large screen glowed with a greenish-blue image of the earth. Three red dots floated in orbit, one over the American hemisphere, and the other two drifting above the North Pacific. Smaller panels blinked with numbers indicating angles, locations, and weather patterns.

Tiny fans inside the machines clicked on to keep them cool. The humming felt familiar. Taalik could recall humans working at the stations, pointing to the screens, speaking into their head-sets—an image not so much remembered as imprinted. But he would need more.

Taalik pulled the cat toward the command center. The image of the globe appeared on screen, along with a window where the cat could enter instructions. This control room was engineered so the human commander could bypass the technicians and operate the system manually. Taalik would have to disable the workstations, establish control of the satellites, and then move them into position. This was no mere password, but a set of instructions that he needed to string together and execute.

"You're afraid," the cat said.

"So are you."

These land animals spoke too much. Taalik shoved the cat toward the computer, pressing his face close to the screen.

"Look," Taalik said. "Look and remember."

"I know what you're trying to do," the cat said. "You're going to slaughter everyone because the Queen told you to."

Taalik spun him around. The cat's eyelids hung low and listless. He would not give Taalik the honor of seeing him angry, and would rather die with this smug expression on his face, the only dignity his people were designed to have.

"You can say no," the cat said. "You can look her right in the eye and tell her, 'No.'"

"I cannot."

"*I* did."

The cat turned from him and rested one hand on the control panel. On-screen, the globe rotated as the satellites circled above, like flies over a carcass.

"Take what you need from me, if you can," the cat said. "But don't tell me you have to obey. Don't tell me you can't say no."

Not even Orak could speak to him like this. She could never know how deep this creature had reached into his mind. Taalik would have to kill him quickly and make sure the floodwaters carried him away, washing everything clean.

Standing behind the cat, Taalik placed his claws on the sides of the creature's head. Nothing happened at first. Then the globe spun faster until it became a green blur. The shape extended beyond the monitor and engulfed the entire room.

Taalik smelled fresh water, reeking with algae. He smelled pine trees. He smelled a storm coming.

TAALIK STOOD IN a forest at dusk. The dying sunlight pierced the trees, creating the illusion of distant fires. He recognized this place—the land-crab lived here, as did the cat and his dog companion. The cat thought that he could hide in the forest. He built a labyrinth in his mind, hoping that the leaves and the dirt would mask his scent.

"I will find you," Taalik said. The branches rustled in response. By running away, the cat was only making this worse. His mind could collapse. Taalik needed to find him quickly, before they both became lost here.

He emerged from the trees into a clearing, where several moss-stained boulders sat at various positions. On top of one of them, the cat reclined like a fat human in a soft chair, watching the setting sun burn a hole in the horizon. The dog with the floppy ears sat beside him, holding his hand. More animals appeared. A trio of cats occupied a nearby boulder. Four others gathered around a campfire, exchanging jokes and laughing. A bobcat with ears the color of ink stood near the edge of the mountain slope, staring out with a pair of binoculars. Beside him was a smaller black cat with white fur on his feet and hands. All of them wore backpacks and rifles strapped to their shoulders. Some kind of military unit, relaxing after a long march. These were the cat's comrades when he fought for the Queen. The cat once named Sebastian. Mort(e). Taalik choked it down. He did not want to think of the demon as having a name, but it was too late.

Still more animals gathered. The mud-colored pit bull—the one from the riverbank—polished the barrel of a rifle. A pig sat with a raccoon and two cats. They played some game in the dirt, using their military pins as baubles that they moved around in a square.

The pig won this round, and celebrated by snorting and clicking his hooves together.

When Taalik extended his tentacles and opened his pincers, Mort(e) laughed. "You're welcome here," the cat said. He gestured to someone behind Taalik. Four humans emerged from the forest, the same family from the darkened room. Only here, they were older. The husband and wife had gray hair, and their children had grown into teenagers. Taalik recognized the boy, the one the humans called the Prophet. Instead of rotting away in a stretcher, here the boy grew strong, living a life denied to him in the real world.

Taalik noticed more people. Near the dog named D'Arc, three pups playfully fought over her sword until she took it away, scolding them but smiling at their mischief nevertheless. They were her children, Taalik realized. And they did not belong in the world either. All the timelines of Mort(e)'s life intersected on this mountaintop, giving the dead a second chance.

Taalik approached the boulder where Mort(e) sat with D'Arc. The dog's children hid behind her, giggling and pointing at him. Mort(e) was serene, his face bathed in the orange light of the sunset.

One of the pups tapped Mort(e) on his shoulder. "Papa. Who is that?"

"A friend," the cat said.

The pup did not seem convinced. D'Arc, meanwhile, stared at Taalik, her hand resting on the hilt of her sword. A strange warmth emanated from the cat, a wave of peace and contentment that Taalik had never known. This cat could conjure it and mold it, constructing entire worlds where he would be safe.

"You cannot fight me," Taalik said. In this joyful atmosphere, he felt obligated to whisper it.

"No one's fighting," Mort(e) said. "The fighting's done."

"Here it comes!" the bobcat shouted. Next to him, the

black-and-white cat snatched away the binoculars to get a better view.

At the horizon, a row of snowcapped mountains lifted from the earth, cutting the sun in half. But they were no mountains. A tidal wave approached, the great hand of Hymenoptera Unus sweeping across the land, purifying everything.

"Papa, I see it!" one of the pups said. No one seemed afraid. Even Sheba let go of the sword and held Mort(e)'s hand.

The earth rumbled. Patches of clouds darkened the sky. Seasons changed in mere seconds, the leaves turning orange and brown and then bursting from the trees in a gust of wind. A thunderstorm brewed in the south. To the north, a sudden snow flurry painted the trees white. The cat struggled to hold the illusion together. It was the only way he could undo all he had lost, all that had been taken from him. As the wave drowned them all, he would cling to this fake memory, these unlived lives. His hatred gave him the strength to hold on to all this love.

The aching overwhelmed Taalik. He stumbled and fell, bracing himself with his claws. Like some hatchling, he searched for others like him. He needed Orak to wrap her tentacles around his. These strangers did not even acknowledge his distress. They kept their gaze fixed on the wall of water approaching as if it would bring salvation, the answers to everything.

It was happening—he was lost in this cat's polluted mind. Taalik spoke in his own language, begging the Queen to save him. She did not answer. *Please*, he said. *Please*.

With the last of his strength, he sprang to his feet and grabbed the cat by the shoulders. No one, not even the dog beside him, seemed to care. Taalik would fulfill the Queen's wishes. He would take what he needed from this mammal before the cat slumped over dead. All of the emotions swirled inside them both.

Anger, grief, love, joy. Their memories intertwined until they saw through each other's eyes.

"Who will join *you* at this place?" the cat said. And yet his mouth did not move. He no longer needed to speak for Taalik to hear.

The wave crested the hill in a great explosion, sending a geyser into the sky before crashing down on them, shutting out the last of the dying light.

# CHAPTER 27

## THE DESTROYER OF WORLDS

'ARC FOLLOWED THE river upstream until her pace slowed to a limp, and her legs felt ready to give out. The rifle strap dug a welt into her chest, and her tongue flapped about as she panted. In the dead of night, she checked the map and pinpointed her location at a bend in the river, south of the bunker. Realizing that she would have to swim across, she regretted not bringing some kind of waterproof case for the firearms. On the bright side, if the wolves were tracking her, they would lose her scent once she entered the water.

D'Arc put the rifle on her shoulder and held the handgun in her mouth. She could not bring herself to simply jump in, and thus suffered the agony of stepping into the frigid stream, one foot at a time. She bit so hard on the barrel that her teeth moved slightly in their sockets. D'Arc thought of the Old Man hammering shingles on the roof. She thought of the long walks with the herd. She thought of Falkirk. She thought of days to come, on a ship bound for new worlds. None of it made her any warmer, but it kept her from breaking her teeth on the gun.

On the other side, D'Arc pulled herself ashore and ran faster, mainly to get her blood flowing again. On three separate occasions, she thought she smelled animals approaching. She took cover behind a tree and scanned the area with her nightscope. Each time, she waited until she could count to ten without hearing anything, only the crickets.

D'Arc made it to the highway ramp shortly before sunrise. Her legs shook. She dry heaved a few times before sipping some water. According to the map, the concrete road cutting through the forest led to an abandoned human settlement, where the Rama Corporation sat at the edge of a forest.

D'Arc took the main road into the town. Hiding behind the rusted hulk of a truck, she scoped out the front of the building. Nothing moved in the courtyard, and the interior appeared empty. D'Arc considered charging through the open area, past the fountain and toward the bunker. But this would leave her exposed, so she decided to use the forest for cover.

As she crept through the woods, the wet leaves and branches chilled her bare toes. She hopped over a tiny trickle of a creek, which formed a divot along the forest floor. For the last few feet before entering the property, D'Arc crawled on her belly, rifle in hand, until she could see the grassy lawn, the office building, and the concrete dome of the bunker.

A few dead leaves skittered along the cement plaza. Through the sniper scope, she focused on the dome and caught something moving. She blinked, thinking her vision needed to adjust. But then she saw it again, like an imperfection on a photograph. On top of the bunker, she caught the outline of a Sarcops, crouching on its claws, its tentacles slithering. The creature faded out as its skin matched the color of the purple clouds behind it. Another fish-head appeared in front of the bunker before its skin mimicked the gray concrete. Still another slithered in the grass and turned green, leaving a depression on the lawn where it stood.

They were on the lookout. D'Arc's heart pounded against the dirt. Trying to make as little noise as possible, she glanced around to see if any of the camouflaged monsters roamed the forest. Nothing stirred. She peered through the scope again to try to get a headcount. Taking out multiple targets from this distance was difficult enough. But these targets could move fast and change color.

D'Arc detected a pattern in how the creatures revealed themselves. One appeared in the grass, one on top of the bunker, one beside it, one in front. The fish-head guarding the entrance materialized suddenly, and then, before it vanished, it stood on its hind legs and walked off. D'Arc figured it out—there were only two or three of them. Eventually, she determined that there was only one, changing positions in order to give the illusion of strength. She could tell from the severed tentacle who it was. Orak. The one who admired her sword.

D'Arc took aim, but could not get a solid lock on the target. Getting closer would leave her out in the open. And if she missed, Orak could charge at her across the grass, invisible until it was too late. D'Arc would have to draw this creature out to get a better shot.

Luckily, she had experience with this kind of hunt. And though these Sarcops were smarter than a wayward Alpha, D'Arc was willing to bet that they would give chase if the bait were tempting enough.

AMONG THE LONG shadows draped across the lawn, D'Arc emerged from the forest, holding her pistol at her hip. Orak remained still, leaving a faint outline against the bunker.

D'Arc lifted the gun and fired. The report echoed off the glass building. A bullet sparked. Orak screeched. One of the rounds may have hit her, but D'Arc could not say for sure.

Orak charged across the grass, kicking up clumps of sod. Her camouflage transitioned from gray to bright green. D'Arc spun on her heels and sprinted through the woods. Behind her, the creature plowed through the trees, ripping off chunks of bark. D'Arc dropped into the creek and followed the tiny valley as it curved to the right.

She arrived at a small nest of branches and leaves, where her rifle sat mounted and ready to fire. D'Arc knelt in position as Orak rounded the bend. The fish-head's camouflage adapted quickly, blending with the dirt. It would not save her—the trench was too narrow for D'Arc to miss. When Orak saw the barrel pointed at her, her eyelids blinked, first the inner transparent membrane, then the outer lid.

D'Arc pulled the trigger. A fireball bloomed from the muzzle, sending out a shock wave that levitated the flowing water for a split second. The round pierced Orak's chest plate and exploded from her shell, taking muscle and bone with it. The force of it lifted her from her feet and dropped her in the stream. The creek flowed green with her blood.

D'Arc unsheathed her sword. Gripping it with both hands, she approached the wounded creature. A thin column of smoke rose from the bullet hole in Orak's chest, giving off the charred stink of burnt skin. The gills flapped as she coughed up the blood-tinged water.

D'Arc pressed the point of the blade under Orak's chin.

"How many of you are in that bunker?" D'Arc asked.

Orak let out a high-pitched squeal. Definitely a *fuck you*.

D'Arc swung the blade at the wounded tentacle, the one she cut during the flood. A pink gash split open, about a foot from the stump, nearly severing the limb entirely. Orak tried to lift it, only to find that the rest of the tentacle remained on the ground, attached by a few strands of flesh. D'Arc pressed the blade to Orak's throat.

"How many?"

D'Arc considered the possibility that the fish-head simply could not understand her. But Orak's eyes gave it away. She hissed at D'Arc, probably cursing the day the first mammals scurried about on the jungle floor, plucking scraps from the bodies of dead dinosaurs. For Orak, D'Arc was the monster, the abomination.

D'Arc raised the sword and slashed the creature again and again, grunting each time. The blade chopped off another tentacle, along with chunks of armor and raw flesh. Orak let out a series of guttural clicks and groans, like Morse code in reverse. The sword grew heavy, and D'Arc's fatigued muscles locked when she tried to lift it once more. By then, another severed tentacle spasmed on the ground, while Orak's body leaked from multiple slash wounds. Her right claw hung by a few tendons at the joint.

"I don't want to kill you," D'Arc said. "I just want to get my friend out of there."

Orak stopped clicking. "One," she said.

"One?"

"First of Us. All . . . That is left."

D'Arc sheathed the sword and lifted the rifle from its nest. "I know you're hurt. But you're coming with me to the bunker."

Orak rolled painfully to one side. Once she stood erect, cradling her wounded arm, she stared at the debris lying about. Tentacles, patches of blood, chunks of carved flesh.

"You make a noise, if you give them a signal, I'll make you bleed," D'Arc said. "And if anything happens on the inside, I use this." She patted the nerve-gas canister on her belt.

They marched through the woods to the unkempt lawn. Orak limped a few feet ahead, leaving a trail of smeared blood in the long stalks of grass.

A musty odor wafted from the entrance of the bunker, where a long hallway sloped underground. When Orak hesitated, D'Arc poked her with the muzzle of the rifle, still hot from the bullet. They marched into the unnatural fluorescent light, the overheads reflected on Orak's shiny skin. At the end of the tunnel stood an open door, where D'Arc could hear computers humming, and a steady pinging noise. D'Arc pinned Orak to the wall, keeping the barrel trained on her head. She peeked inside. Dozens of computer monitors gave off a strange aura. On the giant screen mounted to the front wall, numbers endlessly scrolled upward. D'Arc's nose followed the ammonia vapors until she saw Taalik standing behind Mort(e) at the main computer terminal. Both of them were lost in some kind of trance. Mort(e) seemed to dangle from the monster's claw fastened to his neck. Even the Warrior could be subdued, defeated, left gasping and shivering. Even he could become old and weak. Everything D'Arc believed in could fall apart if given enough time.

From this angle, D'Arc could not get a clear shot without hitting the Old Man. Then again, the bullet would go right through him and hit Taalik. She heard the chief's whisper in her ear. *Might be worth it.*

The numbers on the screen came to a halt. Below them, an ellipsis blinked, one dot at a time, waiting for a new page to load. Or for a new command.

D'Arc pulled her head away from the entrance and leaned on the wall. Across from her, Orak clutched the wound on her elbow joint.

"Now," D'Arc whispered, "whether we live or die depends entirely on you. Do what I say, and both you and your mate can walk out of here."

Orak blinked.

With a nudge from D'Arc, the fish-head lumbered inside. D'Arc followed a few feet behind. The large screen went blank, darkening the room for a moment before lighting up again with an enormous image of the globe. Upon sensing the intruders, Taalik woke from his dream state. His tentacles tightened around Mort(e) and raised him from the floor.

On the main screen, a rectangular box appeared, dividing the globe in half. The word INITIATE appeared inside.

"Stop what you're doing, or I kill everyone in this room," D'Arc said. "Starting with her." She jabbed Orak with her rifle. The fish-head sank to the ground, propping herself on her good claw. Her lone tentacle hung lifeless at her side.

Taalik hissed. Mort(e) hissed along with him.

"If I have to kill my friend, I'll do it," she said. "Then I kill her. Then I kill you. I have enough bullets."

The INITIATE box disappeared. Three red dots hovered around the globe. Beside each one, a set of numbers tracked their movement. The pinging sound increased its frequency, showing that the satellites had come to life. D'Arc considered opening fire on all the computers in the room, but figured it would take more bullets than she had. She needed to save them in case these fish-heads tried to attack. Or if they sent a brainwashed Mort(e) after her to see if she really had the guts to shoot him.

Taalik chirped in his strange language. Mort(e) mimicked him like a ventriloquist's doll.

D'Arc tapped her foot on Orak's armor. "Talk to him." When Orak responded with clicks of her own, D'Arc aimed the rifle at the computers and pulled the trigger. One of the monitors exploded, sending debris to the ceiling.

"No!" D'Arc said. "Talk to him in my language."

Kneeling, Orak reached out her claw to Taalik. "Asha," she said. "Asha speaks truth."

Taalik did not respond.

"Asha sees our people in the ice," Orak said. "She sees them die. All of them. Yes?"

"The Queen speaks to *me*," Taalik and Mort(e) said.

"Asha sees. Asha speaks truth! You *know*! The Queen knows!"

Though Taalik remained silent, Mort(e) bared his fangs.

"If you die, I die," Orak said. "If I die, you die."

Taalik shuddered. And then something happened that D'Arc thought she would never live to see. Mort(e) covered his face with his hands and wept, his shoulders rising and falling with each breath. D'Arc did not recognize it at first, and mistook it for laughter—something she saw almost as rarely.

"The Queen," Taalik began.

"The Queen . . . not here!" Orak said. She pounded her claw on her chest. "*I* here! *I* am here!"

On the big screen, three red lines connected the satellites, forming an acute triangle above the North Pole. One by one, the monitors displayed the same image. Another box appeared, this time with the word HALO and a clock counting down from five minutes. Below that, a message scrolled out: AWAITING CONFIRMATION. A cursor flashed beside it.

"She's right in front of you," D'Arc said. "Time's up. You have to decide."

Taalik growled. Mort(e) tried to squirm free of the tentacles, but they coiled around his throat. The Old Man was fighting to break the connection. Mort(e) struggled to turn his head so he could face Taalik.

"Who will join you at this place?" the Old Man asked.

Taalik looked at him. The creature's face relaxed. The fangs slipped behind his lips. The tentacles uncoiled. Mort(e) fell to his knees, exhausted. Taalik shuffled toward Orak, still prone on the floor. The leader of the Sarcops knelt beside her. Her one tentacle lifted and intertwined with his. A clicking noise began in her throat. Maybe she told him the story of what happened to her, or perhaps it was a more primal message, a sign of recognition. *I know you. Where have you been?* Taalik clicked in response. His tail swished on the floor.

Mort(e) walked over to the main computer. Uninterested in the reunion of two sea creatures, he began tapping on the keyboard like some office secretary. D'Arc stepped around the Sarcops to get closer to him. On the big screen, a new box materialized with the word COORDINATES inside. Beside it, a new series of numbers scrolled across as Mort(e) typed them out.

"Mort(e), what are you doing? We need to leave."

He continued pecking away at the keyboard.

"The *Vesuvius* is on its way," she said. "They're going to destroy this place."

Mort(e) remained fixated on the screen. "Are you still going on the expedition?"

Her blood went cold. She wasn't talking to the Old Man anymore. She was talking to some artificial version of him, a piece of software with bad coding.

With the coordinates logged in, the screen returned to the image of the globe with the triangle floating above it. The HALO countdown dropped below two minutes. Beneath it, a simple prompt appeared: COMMIT? Y/N.

"I asked you a question," Mort(e) said.

"Mort(e), please. Let's go."

He stared at her.

"Mort(e), when you linked with the Sarcops, he must have infected your mind."

"No. I've infected his. Look."

D'Arc turned to Taalik. But the Sarcops were gone. A greasy puddle expanded in the middle of the floor, with a wet streak leading to the exit.

"Now answer me," Mort(e) said. "Are you joining the expedition?"

His paw hovered over the keyboard. Still aiming at the ceiling, D'Arc felt her finger curl around the trigger. The countdown reached one minute.

She swallowed. "Yes. I'm sorry." The muscles in her arms tightened, ready to swing the rifle and fire.

His eyes still locked on hers, Mort(e) pressed the button.

D'Arc flinched, but kept the barrel pointed in the air. She let him do it. He knew she would.

One of the three red blips winked out, its numbers freezing in place. Two of the lines connecting the halo vanished. A second satellite disappeared as well, breaking the halo. A single, lonely dot hovered over the pole, dead and cold in space.

A box appeared with two words in all capital letters. SYSTEM FAILURE.

The rifle became so heavy that D'Arc almost dropped it. The Old Man backed away from the computer. As he walked past her, he glanced at her trigger finger. The computers in the room switched off, several at a time. The main screen was the last to shut down. D'Arc listened as the Old Man padded up the sloped hallway. Soon he was gone, and only the hum of the overhead lights remained.

D'Arc hoped that by the time she made it outside, she would find the words to say to Mort(e). Not *sorry*, but perhaps something about how she would miss him, how she would return, how grateful she was that he had rescued her from the dirt and helped her to become this new person. She could not make him understand, but she could say the words and hope they would take root.

As she approached the door, she saw Mort(e) standing stiffly, his face washed in the late morning sun. His ears pointed straight to the sky. D'Arc stepped through the doorway. "What's wrong?"

Before she could finish her sentence, she smelled horse manure. And dog hair. And steel and leather. Her finger instinctively caught the trigger of the rifle, but it would make no difference. Standing in a row in the plaza were at least ten mounted riders. Wolves on horseback. They each carried hand-crafted swords that curved like scimitars, along with leather armor fashioned from some unnameable beast—maybe some of their own. A few of them wore headdresses made of feathers and claws. Their horses could have stood upright, if they chose to. But as slaves of the Lupine Confederacy, they wore bridles around their heads, with thin bones fixed in their mouths. They kept their gaze squarely on the ground. Glyphs were branded on the horses' sides, indicating them as property of the tribes.

The ringleader tugged on the reins. As the horse clopped toward them, D'Arc noticed the red and orange war paint spattered on the wolf's face, dribbling onto his neck and chest. The handle of a sawed-off shotgun hung over his right shoulder. Among the trinkets and war trophies that festooned his armor, D'Arc noticed a grayish white object dangling from a necklace: a tiny human skull, its jaw removed, the little teeth plucked out. This wolf resembled a demonic Falkirk.

The rider stood over them for a while. The horse's wet nostrils expanded with a snort, making D'Arc flinch. The rider did not notice. He seemed interested only in Mort(e), who watched the wolf with red-rimmed eyes.

The wolf lifted his sword and pressed the hilt to his chest. D'Arc readied her rifle.

"Mort(e) of the Red Sphinx," he said. "Welcome to wolf country."

"Of *course*," D'Arc whispered, lowering the rifle.

"Hello, Grieve," Mort(e) said.

A wolf named Grieve. Falkirk once told her that the Confederates preferred one-syllable verbs, like Hack or Gnash. Perhaps this name referred to what people did after they crossed the wolf's path.

"I must ask what you're doing here," Grieve said.

"This bunker is dangerous. The computers inside control a human weapon, from before the war. We disabled it."

"The humans were interested in this place during the occupation."

"They won't be anymore. Neither will the fish-heads."

"You saw fish-heads?"

Mort(e) explained that both species wanted to use the weapon. But it was all over, and now an airship was on its way to destroy the entire compound.

"Yes, I figured," the wolf said. "You'll be happy to know that they lifted off before we could welcome them. Is it true that they have a dog for a captain?"

"A husky, yes."

The wolf smiled, using his blade to pick at a chunk of dirt under his fingernail. "So you saved us," Grieve said. "Is that it?"

"That would be two that you owe me. Not that I'm counting."

Grieve wheeled the horse around so that he could face D'Arc. "You know this cat has a thing for canines, right? I guess he found another dog who likes a little catnip." The wolf tilted his head as he ogled her. A line of spit dangled from one of his yellow fangs.

"I'm the only one," D'Arc said.

Grieve looked at Mort(e). "Wait. Is this . . . ?"

"I'm Sheba."

The Old Man nodded to confirm it. Even so, the wolf needed some time to believe it.

"Well, this just warms my heart," Grieve said. "I mean, I heard the rumors, but I thought it was a story the humans made up."

He gestured for D'Arc to come closer. It was pointless—the Old Man could still hear them—but she supposed that the wolf needed to look important.

"You're lucky to have this cat," Grieve said, leaning forward. "That's a special thing you two have, in this crazy world of ours."

Rather than grabbing the wolf by his baby-skull necklace and telling him to shut his mouth, D'Arc said yes, they did have something special.

Grieve placed his sword into its scabbard. "I wish I could say you're welcome here," he said. "But all I can offer is safe passage."

"That's all we ask," Mort(e) said.

The wolf pulled on the reins and led his horse to the row of cavalry riders. They exchanged some words. A younger wolf objected to letting them go. Grieve told him to shut his mouth, and then said something about the wolf being too young to remember the war. Another one made a joke about interspecies lovers that made his comrades laugh. When they finished, Grieve turned to the intruders and waved them on.

"I'll tell my mates about you two," he said. "Maybe it will inspire them for once!"

As the wolves laughed, Mort(e) started to walk through the courtyard. D'Arc trailed behind him, still brandishing her rifle. Even after they reached the highway ramp, he would not face her. She did not want him to. Not yet. Not until she was ready to say whatever it was she needed to say. Until then, she would have to be content with reaching out her hand, the one she was never meant to have, and placing it on his arm. He patted her knuckles with his palm, but would not take his attention from the road ahead. They walked like that for a while until she let go and allowed him to take the lead, exhausted but still moving forward, the only thing that mattered.

# CHAPTER 28

## THE WATER FLOWS

ORT(E) AND D'ARC leaned on the concrete barrier of the highway ramp and watched as the *Vesuvius* arrived. The great ship slowed to a hover above the Rama Corporation, its hull bisected by the reflection of the landscape. A puff of smoke burst from the gondola, and a rocket streaked through the air, leaving a comet trail. The missile hit the front of the building. The windows shattered and fell away. A few seconds later, the boom popped in Mort(e)'s ears. More rockets ejected from the ship, striking the building and bursting into columns of flame and smoke, lifting metal and glass into the sky. Another relic of the human age left in ruin.

As he came down from the union with Taalik, the voices in his head grew quiet, but the echoes remained. His mind felt hollow without this burden, his body spent. He imagined himself as Sebastian again, with Sheba at his side, both hypnotized by the fiery spectacle. Two animals—two children, really—finally coming to accept the true beauty and terror of the world, and how small it rendered them. No matter how much they expanded their horizons, no matter how many lands they conquered, the world would always remind them of who they were, where they came from, how easily it could all be taken away.

As the fire burned, D'Arc tried to talk to him, to ask if he was all right. Mort(e) noticed something shiny twinkling on her chest. He recognized the St. Jude medal, the one he dropped in Wawa's hand years earlier. D'Arc caught him looking at it.

"The chief sacrificed her life to save us," she said.

Mort(e) dropped to his knees and rested his head on the concrete wall. D'Arc brushed her hand through his fur. It was going to be all right, she said. They made it. She repeated it again and again. Sometimes it registered in the voice of Janet, the woman who had owned him as a pet. Sometimes he heard the voice of Tiberius, or a series of clicks from the Sarcops. But as the dizziness finally passed, he could hear D'Arc once again, summoning him from the deep.

Having completed its bombing run, the *Vesuvius* rotated on an axis until its nose pointed straight at them. In a matter of minutes, the zeppelin would arrive to take them to Hosanna, the place that had defeated Mort(e) in so many ways. On this occasion, he would let it win, and he would move on. He was done fighting.

"Can I see you off?" he asked her. "When you leave on the expedition?"

"Of course. I need you to."

The ship drew closer. Behind it, the smoke spiraled from the ashes.

MORT(E) SPENT MOST of the trip in his quarters at the front of the *Vesuvius*, the same place where he stayed on the night before the Battle of Golgotha. The green forest splashed across the window, covering over the deserted human towns. Still woozy from his encounter with Taalik, Mort(e) stared at the landscape for hours, his forehead on the cool glass. Over each hill, he expected to see his beloved ranch, with the Alphas marching in formation, and the shingled roof still in need of repair. But the forest kept sprawling out, big enough to hide in, and forget, and be forgotten.

When D'Arc checked on him later that evening, he told her that he needed to rest. It was mostly true. He had tender bruises on his limbs and ribs, and his head still sloshed with the sounds of the ocean floor. A few times, he stuck his finger in his ear to root out the water that clogged it, only to remember that he merely imagined the sensation. Whenever he felt like dozing off, a phantom tentacle jostled him awake. He could feel it growing from his torso and stretching out until it felt ready to break off and drop to the floor.

But even without all of that, Mort(e) was grateful for the time alone. He did not need to see the husky talking with D'Arc, nor did he need to exchange small talk with the same guards who held him captive only hours earlier. Though he was afraid to fall asleep because of the dreams he might have, the exhaustion soon overcame him. He let it happen, like being submerged in warm water. A chorus of Sarcops warriors sang their hymns from some far-off trench, calling him to abandon the skies and the earth and return to the sea where he belonged.

He woke in the morning as the battered *Vesuvius* entered Hosanna airspace. From here, he saw the devastation below— the swollen river, the broken bones of the dam, the charred buildings, the lines of people waiting for food. This civilization was so fragile, and yet it had the capacity to rebuild. The believers were stubborn, if nothing else.

D'Arc arrived at his quarters as the ship was docking. She took his hand and escorted him to the queue of wounded soldiers as they marched off the ship. On the deck of the Liberty One tower, a crew of medics and doctors waited to take them to the nearest hospital. Other people were there mainly to cheer for the returning heroes. When the noise became too loud for Mort(e), he pressed closer to D'Arc.

Among the people waiting on deck was Marquez, the human who examined him when he first arrived at Hosanna. Beside him, a charcoal-colored cat stood with his arms folded. The doctor waved to Mort(e) as he and the cat worked their way through the crowd. Marquez's eyes were bloodshot, his face thinner and in need of a shave. As one of the few physicians who had survived the flood, he must have worked for days on end with no break.

"They tell me you speak with the fish-heads," Marquez said.

Mort(e) tried to bull-rush his way past him, dragging D'Arc along with him.

"Please, Captain," Marquez said, clasping his hands in prayer. "I work with patients who have used the translator. Let me examine you."

"It's okay, Mort(e)," D'Arc said.

Her sad eyes were enough to get him to agree. Besides, once he returned to the wilderness, he might never see another doctor again. Might as well get a checkup before he disappeared.

D'Arc told him that she needed to stay, and would meet with him later. He knew what she meant—she needed a few more moments with Falkirk. She repeated it several times before he released her hand. Marquez said that he had reserved a suite at the hospital for him, hidden away from the pilgrims and the hero-worshipers. "If I could have a few days with you, it would help so many others," the doctor added.

While Mort(e) contemplated this, the charcoal cat stepped in front of D'Arc. He plucked the St. Jude medal from her chest and examined it. Mort(e) flinched, but D'Arc put up her hand to let him know it was okay. "This is Grissom from Tranquility," she said. "Wawa's assistant."

Without acknowledging Mort(e), the cat let go of the medal.

"I'm sure you've heard the news," she said. "I'm very sorry."

The cat nodded.

"She gave it to me before she died." D'Arc lifted the necklace

to her chin. "Maybe you should have it." The cat stopped her by
raising his hand, shaking his head. Without a word, Grissom let
her know that the medal had found its rightful owner. "Thank
you," D'Arc said.

All around them, the crowd cheered as Falkirk emerged from
the portal, along with his senior officers. Ignoring the shouts,
Falkirk continued issuing orders to his staff. The dog pointed at
the wounded soldiers and said something to the doctors, like a
worried mother making sure her young ones were safe.

It was the perfect time to slip away, though Mort(e) was not
entirely ready to do so. He squeezed through the mob, managing
one last glance at D'Arc before she disappeared among the faceless animals and humans. At the elevator, Marquez flashed his ID
badge to the guards stationed there. The doors slid shut, sealing
off the racket.

To avoid the crowd in the lobby, Marquez led them through
the building's parking garage. They hopped into a jeep, with
Grissom driving and Marquez on the passenger side.

Moments later, the vehicle puttered through the nearly empty
streets. In the early morning light, the broken city was slow to
awaken. The tall buildings, casting shadows from one end of
the street to the other, became like the walls of a canyon. For a
brief flash, Mort(e) imagined them as the sides of the trench in
which the Sarcops lived, with the sky rolling like the surface of
the water. When the moment passed, he saw something moving
among the clouds. He blinked a few times, thinking at first that it
was a bird. It was Gaunt of Thicktree. He must have jumped off
the side of the building and begun his long flight home. Mort(e)
regretted not saying goodbye—not that the bats had much interest in sentimentality. But having learned some Chiropteran,
Mort(e) thought it would have been nice to share war stories
with the bat one more time.

Gaunt veered to the right and disappeared behind the

buildings. Once Mort(e) got his bearings, he realized that the bat flew to the east, toward the river, rather than west to the mountains, to his homeland. At each intersection, Mort(e) caught a glimpse of the bat heading northeast, along the river.

"Where's he going?" Mort(e) asked.

"Where's who going?" Marquez said.

"Wait. Stop the car."

He had to say it a few more times before the grumpy, silent cat applied the brakes and glared at him. "Do you hear that?" Mort(e) asked.

"No," Marquez replied. *Of course you don't*, Mort(e) thought. But there it was, a deep humming sound that throbbed in his head. When the sound changed pitch, Grissom was able to hear it as well. The cat rolled his eyes, spun the wheel to the right, and headed for the riverfront.

As they made a left onto Columbus Boulevard, Mort(e) caught sight of the bat again. Gaunt circled over the wreckage of the dam. The river gushed through the gap in the jagged concrete. On the side of the road, a pack of furry animals stood in a circle, some of them singing, some of them humming. One of them stood in the middle of the formation with his hand placed on a wooden altar.

Grissom parked the jeep. Mort(e) hopped out just in time to hear the lyrics.

> *We will meet again*
> *In the darkness*
> *Where you and I*
> *Will be the only light.*

> *And by our light*
> *We call everyone home*
> *Where the water flows*
> *And the dirt knows your name.*

One by one, the beavers stopped singing and turned to face Mort(e). Castor, who stood at the altar, was the last. The others moved aside as the beaver waddled over.

"My friend!" Castor said. "You are welcome!" Mort(e) bent over slightly to let the diminutive beaver give him a sloppy hug. "How is your queen?"

"She's well," Mort(e) said. "What are you doing here?"

Castor laughed. "The water flows. So here we are."

The beavers had staked out a construction site, with logs ferried along the river and then stacked in neat little pyramids. Hosanna needed experts to rebuild the dam, and who else to ask but the cleverest engineers in the entire Union? Wawa herself had made the request.

Gaunt landed on the concrete. He folded his wings and crawled over to them. When he said hello in his bat language, Mort(e) replied with a simple greeting, a few basic screeches that meant *good morning, brother*. Or so he hoped.

"Mort(e), we could use someone like you," Castor said. "Have you ever built something this big? It's the greatest adventure there is!"

"I'm no engineer." Mort(e) thought about saying that he had blown up bridges this size, but the beaver was too damned earnest to hear something like that.

"Come on," Castor said. "Don't go back to your ranch. There'll be plenty of time to rest later. There's so much work to do."

Mort(e) held in a laugh. The day before, a warlord saluted him as Mort(e) of the Red Sphinx. It was absurd to picture himself humming along with these rodents. Culdesac would have spit out his coffee if he ever witnessed such a thing.

"I'll have to pass," Mort(e) said. "But I'm glad to see this is in good hands."

He started for the jeep, but Castor got in his way. "You helped us," the beaver said. "We can help you."

"How?"

"Maybe you were meant to find us again. Maybe the Three Goddesses brought you here to discover your true destiny."

For a second, while the beaver's eyes pleaded with him to reconsider, it all sounded so perfect. If he considered all of the events of the past few months from just the right angle, everything fell into place to bring him here.

He came to his senses with a chuckle. "Good luck, my friend." Mort(e) tried to say goodbye in Chiropteran. Gaunt replied with something too complicated to understand, but he made out the words *brother*, *safe journey*, and *peace*. It must have meant something good.

Mort(e) hopped into the jeep and told them he was ready to go. As the vehicle rolled away, the humming started again.

TO MORT(E)'S SURPRISE, the suite at the hospital comprised the entire top floor, complete with a stocked kitchen, a lounge with a billiards table, and a private bathroom. Over the next few days, Marquez ran a series of tests on him, one every few hours. He gauged Mort(e)'s reflexes, his senses. He shined a penlight into Mort(e)'s eyes until it left purple blotches in his vision. He took samples of hair, nails, stool, urine. Mort(e) asked him why he was so interested in the well-being of animals. Marquez gave him the standard answer, about how he wanted to use his skills for good after so many years of war. But then he pinched the bridge of his nose as he tried to say something more honest.

"I know this is not, uh, politically correct," he said. "But I often think of my pet dog, from before the war. I saw him right after he changed. He watched as I drove away from the house. He wanted to be brave, but all I could see was fear in his eyes. I wanted to help him, but I knew I could not."

Culdesac would have ripped the man's throat out for saying something so condescending. Then he would have asked, *who looks scared now?* But Mort(e) believed him. He was in good hands here.

Thanks to the solitude, the quiet, and the pampering, Mort(e) felt like a resident at some rest home, doddering about in a robe, feeling drowsy from the drugs and the food, getting chilly even in the sunlight. It was a future that drew closer. If he could not stop it, then he might as well get some practice. To complete the effect, D'Arc visited him each day, during the hour or so that Marquez would allow for guests. She brought him snacks, along with a jar of honey that she swore was almost as good as the stuff he produced on the ranch. She seemed so different now, a new person forged from the madness of the last few weeks. While the other animals were altered in a mere day, D'Arc endured a longer transformation, one that she chose for herself.

It took three visits before he asked about the expedition. She spoke cautiously, sticking to the details about the preparations, the food stores, the itinerary. The crew members attended an orientation one morning. D'Arc met the captain, an Indian woman who claimed to have been chosen for a mission to Mars before the war. Another human recognized D'Arc's medal and said that it would bring good luck. Mort(e) conceded that it might.

He asked about Falkirk. The husky would stay in Hosanna, she said. The *Vesuvius* would have a new captain. Falkirk had discovered his true calling. Or it discovered him. Again.

Mort(e) remembered the husky posturing with him when he boarded the *Vesuvius*. "But what about . . . I mean, did anything happen between the two of you?"

"No," D'Arc said. "Nothing happened. He's a friend who I trust. And he gets to start over. Like we do."

In between D'Arc's visits, Marquez evaluated Mort(e)'s cognitive functions. Every morning began with a memorization game, a set of cards with random images that Marquez would flip over. Mort(e) felt great relief when he got them correct. Before he went to bed at night, Marquez would repeat the procedure. In the afternoons, after a lunch of seaweed and insect fritters, Mort(e) reclined on a couch, sipping tea, while the doctor asked him questions about what he saw in Taalik's mind, what he heard, what he could smell and taste. Mort(e) told the same story again and again. But one time, the process of describing the memories took Mort(e) straight into Cold Trench. The Sarcops swam around him, protecting their eggs, watching out for predators. Marquez's soothing voice became like an echo ricocheting through a tunnel. As Mort(e) sank deeper into the dream, he heard Marquez shouting for him, begging for him to wake up, to swim to the light. It was only when he heard D'Arc calling out to him—barking for him—that he managed to extract himself from the illusion. He awoke on the floor, with the doctor towering over him.

"How long was I gone?" Mort(e) asked, his throat raw, as if he had screamed for hours.

"Long enough to make me worry. We will not do this anymore. I have seen enough."

Marquez told him about some of his other patients, including the opossum who confessed to killing the last translator users. Many of them had deteriorated to the point where they could no longer distinguish the past, the present, and the future. Mort(e) was one of the lucky ones.

"In fact," Marquez added, "I think this Sarcops showed mercy."

"Why would he do that?"

"You tell me."

Mort(e) smiled as he imagined the fish-head on the couch next to him, his tentacle wrapped around a mug of coffee. He would have to keep digging to find out what Taalik was thinking when he let him go. But perhaps he did not need to know for sure. A few echoes and whispers here and there were enough to show that the Sarcops had changed as well. They would have to learn to live with who they were. Or they would keep running away.

That night, unable to sleep, Mort(e) sat by the open window and watched the windmills spinning, the lights switching on, the vehicles rolling along the highway. Crimson clouds tumbled across the sky. Though he could not see the river from here, he knew that the *al-Rihla* was docked a few blocks away. D'Arc may have been on board at that very moment, preparing her quarters for the journey, taking inventory. The odor of salt water wafted into the room. Mort(e) rose from his chair, panicked and shaking. Like in his dream, a great wave washed over the horizon, consuming everything. The crest of the wave carried with it debris, overturned vehicles, corpses. As the streets became like rivers, Mort(e) squinched his eyes shut.

"No," he said.

When he opened his eyes, the wave was gone. The city was safe, going quiet for the evening.

"No," he repeated. He sank into his chair, tired but at peace.

ON THE MORNING of the launch, a mob descended on the pier, eager to catch a glimpse of the explorers. Onlookers, well-wishers, friends, and relatives crowded the dock, many of them walking right across the highway. The resulting traffic jam created a bottleneck for over a mile. Tranquility officers tried to divert vehicles around the mess. An interspecies choir from the temple claimed a space along the railing. Their voices provided some harmony to the murmuring and the occasional crying. Behind them, the *al-Rihla* sat anchored in the water. Two gangplanks extended from the hull to the pier. Crew members dressed in olive jumpsuits formed a line to pass the last few crates on board. With all the movement, the ship bobbed and jostled, creating waves that smacked the barrier.

Mort(e) watched it all from a bench at the end of the pier. No one seemed to recognize him in his straw fedora hat, windbreaker, and aviator sunglasses. He resembled any other old cat in the city. Maybe he would have to pose as some homeless stray in order to get by in a place like this. That sounded nice. Once in a while, he would tell people at a bar or at the park that he was in fact Sebastian the Warrior, and they would laugh and say, "Good one!"

His heartbeat spiked when D'Arc emerged from the crowd. With a duffel bag over her shoulder, D'Arc pulled an identification card from her belt and showed it to the guards waiting at the gangplank. An eager crewman arrived to take her bag. She handed him her sword as well, and said something that Mort(e) interpreted as a warning to keep it safe. The young human nodded and ran off. D'Arc looked around until she spotted Mort(e), sitting where he told her he would. She put her hands on her hips and tilted her head to show that she did not approve of his disguise. She said something to the crew members and then ran over to him.

They embraced. Mort(e) did not realize how cold he had become sitting there in the breeze until he held her close. "Thank you for coming," she said.

"Of course. Is there anything else you need to do before you go?"

"No. Just needed to sit with you."

They parked themselves on the bench. She slipped her hand in his and squeezed it before resting her head on his shoulder. He placed his chin on her forehead and listened to her breathing. More crew members boarded the ship—humans, canines, cats, a raccoon, a pig. The choir continued to sing.

The *al-Rihla* blasted its horn. The engines growled, churning the water. The crowd became more animated. Sailors stood on the deck and waved. On the pier, hundreds of arms waved in response. D'Arc wrapped her arms completely around Mort(e), the way she had when they were still pets, when he was just a small thing in her paws.

"I have to go, Old Man."

"I know."

Another blast from the horn. They stood up, still embracing, taking in deep breaths of the other before letting go. She left him there and went to the gangplank, where the crowd let her pass through. She crossed over and stepped inside the ship. Mort(e) swallowed.

The *al-Riḥla* retracted its catwalks. Crew members untied the ropes and pulled them onto the deck. The enormous chain lifted the anchor from the riverbed while the engines switched into a higher gear. With a shudder, the ship began to move.

D'Arc appeared on the top deck, sword in hand. When she saw Mort(e), she unsheathed the blade, which frightened the short woman next to her. D'Arc held the sword aloft, a defiant pose in the face of the unknown. Mort(e) heard himself laughing.

The ship puttered out into the middle of the river and pointed south, toward the sea, to the delta through which Mort(e) first brought Sheba. Once the *al-Riḥla* disappeared around a bend, its horn let out a final report.

The crowd dispersed around him. Mort(e) felt a chill as the wind penetrated his jacket. He wandered to the foot of the pier. In the street, the traffic jam slowly untangled itself to allow the vehicles to get through. The city would go about its day. So much noise, too many smells. But so much life.

Mort(e) glanced at the river once more, watching it slide from the past and empty into the future. To the north, a light fog cast a haze over the ruined dam. For a moment, he thought he heard the beavers humming while they worked, the sound of it bouncing across the water.

And before he knew it, he was running toward the dam, no longer cold and hunched over. He would find Castor. He would stay and help. And when the beaver asked him why, what changed his mind, Mort(e) would smile and say, *The water flows.*

# CHAPTER 29

## THE STORY OF D'ARC

'ARC LEANED ON the gunwale as a sharp wind carried the scent of the approaching ocean. The land on either side opened and gave way to the great expanse, a gray sea under a white sky, much like the day she had first entered this body of water. The day she became the person she was never meant to be, the person she had nevertheless come to accept. The same delta birthed her again, only this time she chose her own path. She reached out and took this life. She would hold onto it with her claws and her teeth if she had to.

But before she could stand in defiance of the approaching fog, the endless sea, D'Arc needed to weep for the life that she was shedding. The tears formed salty trails in her fur before dropping into the water. The home she left, the people she lost, would remain with her. Her children, the Old Man, the brave husky— they would appear before her when she needed them to give her strength. And sometimes, at her weakest, they would cry out to her. They would ask her what she was doing, who she thought she was. She would beg them to stop and they wouldn't.

The other passengers moved about the deck, some taking photos with old cameras. A man stood near the bow and waved at the pilot, a canine stationed in the front of the tower. D'Arc had met the man the day before. He was a former college professor named Harlan who had once taught agricultural science. He was chosen to oversee the garden on deck, as well as identify edible plants wherever the ship made landfall. Though she could not make it out at first, Harlan seemed to be demanding that the ship go faster.

"Come on!" he said.

The engine revved under D'Arc's feet. She gripped the railing to keep from tumbling over. Harlan wanted more speed. "Let's see what she can do!" Soon others joined in. The engine jumped to a higher gear, with a different pitch. The boat began to bounce on each wave, its bow lifting and dropping. D'Arc could hear the windmills spinning, barely able to keep up. The wind dried her tears into tiny specks of salt.

The humans howled like wolves. Harlan's cap flew off his head, revealing a pink bald spot. The animals pounded their palms on the gunwale like a giant war drum. They chanted the name of the boat in three deep syllables. *AL-RIH-LA! AL-RIH-LA!* D'Arc had never laughed so hard in her life, but she could not even hear herself. So she let out a scream that faded into a long howl.

The engine slowed to its regular speed. The captain had seen enough. The crew booed the pilot before applauding and breaking into another fist-pumping chant.

D'Arc looked beyond the people on deck to the land they left behind. She saw nothing but the white sky on the horizon. She turned again to get the complete view. The ocean grew calmer here, stretching in all directions. The *al-Rihla* was a mere toy bobbing on the water.

"It's gone," she whispered. All of it pitched over the edge of the world. The terror and the regret and the sadness built up one last time and then lifted away, releasing her, letting her fill her lungs again.

D'Arc propped her elbows on the railing and tilted her head over the side. In the overcast light, she saw only a dull reflection on the choppy water, something closer to a shadow, a person no one had ever seen before.

# ACKNOWLEDGMENTS

**AS ALWAYS, THERE** are too many people to thank. I start of course with my tireless agent Jennifer Weltz and her team, who have been guiding me for nearly five years now. I hope this is merely the latest of many accomplishments we share.

I will never be able to thank Bronwen Hruska and Soho Press enough for supporting my work, even as it threatened to grow from a quirky one-off to an unwieldy series. My editor, Mark Doten, has turned this novel from a weird fever dream into a coherent story, and his optimism and advice kept me writing even when I was not entirely sure where things were headed. Given how much they did to improve and promote the books, I have to name names: Abby Koski, Meredith Barnes, Paul Oliver, Rudy Martinez, Juliet Grames, Dan Ehrenhaft, Rachel Kowal, and Amara Hoshijo. And Kapo Amos Ng has once again produced an amazing cover.

My friends in the Emerson Diaspora have been listening to me talk about The War with No Name for a while now, and somehow they still hang out with me. Ashley Wells endured months of pretentious griping about my writing process, for which I am eternally grateful. Brian Hurley and Jane Berentson have been the most enthusiastic champions of my work. I look up to all of them both for their own writing and for their love of life. And though a great distance separates us, I have to thank Mike Hennessey, who encouraged me to keep writing even after I asked him to read some of my shitty poems back in 2000. I'm with you in Rockland.

A literary community is vital to the success of any book. There are so many people who have helped spread the word about this series, either by sharing with their friends and colleagues, organizing an event, or saying some kind words. They include Eric Smith, Katelyn Phillips, Brad Andrews, Ryan Britt, Corey Redekop, Annalee Newitz, Charlie Jane Anders, Jane Satterfield, Clea Simon, Kelly Caldwell, Alex Steele, Bridget McGovern, Katharine Duckett, David Hahn, Maria Haskins, Matthew Gallaway, James Scott, Paul D. Filippo, Cat Rambo, Ismet Prcic, Alex Norcia, Steve Perry, Pat Murphy, Nelson Appell, Rick Kleffel, Sam Sattin, Shane Jones, Mac Rogers, Ronald Koltnow, Michael Kindness, Daniel H. Wilson, Josh Christie, Kelly Justice, Anmiryam Budner, Cathy Stiebel Fiebach Steve Himmer, and Jenn Northington.

A special note of thanks goes to Dan Fitzpatrick, who offered advice on the military jargon I used throughout the book. I hope I did it justice. And also, I have to admit that I kind of borrowed the story of Yeager and Amelia ("Will we die?") from Jennifer and Vincent DiPillo. Thank you!

Finally, to my parents and my brother, Nick: I love you, I miss you, I'm proud to be one of you, and I'm grateful every day for all you've done for me. See you soon.